A hundred yards downstream the creek tumbled over a ten-foot drop. The woman scrambled out of the water and picked her way down the slope, holding on to trees and rocks along the bank.

Maneuvering around a pile of boulders, she detected a movement out of the corner of her eye. Her heart lurched, and she gasped and ducked down out of sight.

She stayed low, and prayed. Her heart pounded so loud she was certain the sound echoed through the forest like a tom-tom beat. After a moment she eased up just far enough to peer between two boulders. Through the trees, about a quarter mile away, she spotted her pursuer.

Ducking back down, she pressed herself tight against the rocks and covered her mouth with her hand. Dear Lord. She had not expected him to be so close.

She eased up again for another peek. The man walked parallel to her, but in the opposite direction, studying the trail ahead of him. The trail she'd left. He held his hunting rifle at the ready with both hands. Then, without warning, he stopped and raised his head. A predator scenting the air for his prey. He turned slowly, and seemed to look directly at her for several seconds.

GINNA GRAY

Fatal Flaw

MIRA®

MIRA

ISBN 0-7783-2165-7

FATAL FLAW

Copyright © 2005 by Virginia Gray.

MIRA and the Star Colophon are trademarks used under license and registered in Australia, New Zealand, Philippines, United States Patent and Trademark Office and in other countries.

www.MIRABooks.com

Printed in U.S.A.

Fatal Flaw

One

He was coming for her.

She could feel him getting nearer. Closing in for the kill.

The woman plunged through the forest undergrowth. Sharp branches and briars snatched at her clothing and snagged her hair, but she barely noticed.

She ran flat out, leaping over downed logs, tearing through brush, arms and legs pumping, every muscle straining. Every few steps she cast a fearful glance over her shoulder. The breath rasping in and out of her lungs made a raw, scraping sound. Her heart clubbed against her ribs.

Terror clawed at her, threatening to send her headlong into mindless panic.

No. No, she couldn't let that happen, she cautioned herself, slapping aside a thorny branch. She had to keep her wits about her. She *had* to.

Otherwise she was dead. Like those other poor women. The murders had been the main topic on the evening news for months. Their killer and the man tracking her had to be one and the same.

The sicko liked to make a sport of his killing, she thought bitterly, ducking under a low-hanging branch without slowing down. Tantalizing his victims with the chance of escape, slim as it was. Vicious damned pervert.

The bastard would rue the day he'd targeted her, she swore, doing her best to whip up her courage. This time he'd picked on the wrong woman. She was no fluttery little weakling to go down without a fight.

She ground her teeth and leaped a dry creek bed, ignoring the jab of pain that shot through her ankle. Thought he could give her a minute's head start then hunt her down like an animal, did he? Well, she had a surprise for him. She'd been hunting with her father and brothers in the forest that surrounded Mears all of her life. She knew these woods as well as the killer did. Maybe better.

The other women had run, willy-nilly, with no idea of where they were going or how to evade him, but not her. She had a plan.

Of course, that didn't stop her from being scared spitless. But she was also mad as hell. Her only chance was to make both work for her. She had to. Dear, God, she *had* to.

She ran in an almost straight line up the mountain slope into the depths of the forest. It was tough-going. In places the grade was gentle, but in others the slope was so steep she had to grab hold of branches to haul herself up, but fear and adrenaline kept her moving. When she calculated that she'd covered about a half mile, she veered off to the left in an irregular wide arc. After a while she found what she was looking for. Leaping into the shallow mountain stream, she turned left again and splashed back down the slope in the center of the rocky stream bed.

She wasn't foolish enough to think the tactic would fool the man for long. But if she was lucky it would take him a few minutes to pick up her trail again. He might even assume that she was running aimlessly like the others, and wouldn't catch on that she had doubled back.

At least not until she'd had time to get back to the forest service road. She'd be out in the open there and few vehicles traveled these back roads, especially at this early hour of the morning, but at least she could make good time.

Lying in the back of her captor's van, she had counted the switchbacks as he had driven up the gravel road, and she knew they were only three loops above town, possibly not even out of the city limits.

When he'd pulled over to the side of the road and hauled her out, she'd caught a glimpse through the trees below them of the Ebenezer Baptist Church spire and the golden dome on top of the First National Bank Building, glistening with frost in the early morning light. Both were on the eastern edge of Mears. So was a police station.

It was downhill all the way into town. If she stayed close to the inner side of the switchbacks, she'd be out of sight of anyone above her most of the time. And if she was really lucky, some four-wheelers or a forest ranger would come along and give her a lift. If not, she'd run like hell all the way into town.

A hundred yards downstream, the creek tumbled over a ten-foot drop. The woman scrambled out of the water and picked her way down the slope, holding on to trees and rocks along the bank.

Maneuvering around a pile of boulders, she detected a movement out of the corner of her eye. Her heart lurched, and she gasped and ducked down out of sight.

She stayed low, and prayed. Her heart pounded so loud she was certain the sound echoed through the forest like a tom-tom beat. After a moment she eased up just far enough to peer between two boulders. Through the trees, about a quarter mile away, she spotted her pursuer.

Ducking back down, she pressed herself tight against the boulder and covered her mouth with her hand. Dear Lord. She had not expected him to be so close. She must have misjudged the distance she had gone after turning away from her original course. What was she going to do?

She eased up again for another peek. The man walked parallel to her, but in the opposite direction, studying the trail ahead of him. The trail she'd left. He held his hunting rifle at the ready with both hands. ·

Without warning, he stopped and raised his head. A predator scenting the air for his prey. He turned slowly, and seemed to look directly at her for several seconds.

The woman held her breath. She didn't dare move. Or even blink. Experience had taught her that in the still of the forest, the least hint of motion attracted attention.

A magpie in a nearby tree squawked at her. Somewhere in the distance chickadees chattered, and a small animal rustled through the underbrush. The woman remained motionless. After what seemed like forever, the man returned his gaze to the ground and continued to follow her trail.

She waited as long as she dared, as long as her nerves would let her. But when he disappeared into the forest undergrowth she exploded into action.

Before, though she'd run full tilt, she had tried to make as little noise as possible and stay out of sight. But seeing the killer so close had unnerved her, and the control she'd fought so hard to maintain shattered like brittle glass.

Seized by hysteria and a terror she could no longer fend off, she abandoned all attempts at stealth or caution and bolted.

She flew, skittering down the slope in a dangerous sidestepping lope that was little more than a controlled fall, setting off minislides that sent rocks and tree limbs and other forest debris tumbling before her. The crashing sounds echoed through the woods, but she didn't hear them.

Her lungs and throat burned. Her clothes were ripped, and bloody scratches covered every inch of exposed flesh. Gasping for breath, she barreled headlong down the mountainside, every fiber of her being intent on one thing, and one thing only: escape.

She burst out of the forest, and her heart leaped. Thank God. Luck was with her. From the left, a pickup truck rumbled down the road in her direction. She slogged through the icy creek that churned along beside the road, almost losing her balance several times in the knee-deep, fast-flowing water. Frantic the truck would pass by without the driver seeing her, she scrambled up the bank, desperate little noises rasping from her throat. The vehicle was almost upon her by the time she gained the verge. Darting out into the middle of the dirt road, she planted herself directly into the truck's path, waving both arms.

The driver slammed on the brakes and served to avoid her, missing her by mere inches. Before he'd fully stopped the woman hurried around to the passenger side.

"Dammit, woman! What the hell do you think you're doing, running into the road like that? I coulda killed you."

"Pl-please help m-me," she gasped. "You've got to ge-get me out of here. There's a ma-madman trying to k-kill me!"

"Damn!" The driver cast a wary look around, then leaned over and threw open the door. "Climb in."

She put one foot on the running board and grabbed the door frame to hoist herself up, and the first bullet struck her back dead center.

"Holy shit!" the Good Samaritan yelped.

The force of the shot slammed her forward and sent a spray of blood and tissue across the lower part of the dashboard and the floor mats, and a thumb-size hole appeared in the floorboard just inches from the man's right foot.

For a second her stunned gaze locked with that of the horrified man. Then the second bullet struck her. She jerked, and her eyes widened. Slowly, they dimmed and rolled back in her head. She went limp and slid down the side of the seat and onto the ground.

Cursing nonstop, the driver stomped on the gas. Tires spun and gravel and dust flew. Gaining traction, the pickup peeled out like a bat out of hell and fishtailed its way around the next switchback, the open passenger door flapping and banging.

The woman lay crumpled on the road, past caring.

Two

"What've we got, Novak?"

Pulling on latex gloves, Detective Casey O'Toole ducked under the crime-scene tape and approached the body. Taking care not to contaminate the crime scene, she stepped carefully, scanning the surrounding ground for foot or tire prints as she went. Already several patrol cars, an ambulance and the CSI van had gathered, but as lead detective, Casey was in charge and got first look.

"Female DOA. Gunshot victim," the uniformed officer replied.

Oh, great, Casey thought. Another woman murdered. At least Novak'd had the good sense to stay off the police radio. The veteran patrolman had called in the case on his cell phone to keep the news media from descending on the crime scene and turning it into a circus.

They'd get wind of the murder soon, of course. The vultures always seemed to sniff out trouble. For the past couple of months they'd been giving Sheriff Crawford hell over the other killings. So much so, that, as little respect as she had for the man, she almost felt sorry for him.

Casey grimaced. When the reporters got wind that there'd been a third woman killed they'd go into a feeding frenzy.

"It happened just a few minutes ago, a little after dawn," Officer Novak explained. He nodded toward a man sitting on the tailgate of a pickup truck parked on the other side of the police crime-scene tape. "We were nearing the end of our shift, so me 'n my partner were cruising along Pinion Avenue heading for the station house, when all of a sudden that guy over there came rocketing down this road like the devil himself was after him."

Casey walked around the body, taking pictures from every angle. Later the crime-scene people would photograph the victim and surrounding area, but she liked to take her own shots.

When done, she hitched up her slacks and squatted down on her haunches beside the victim. The woman was attractive. Early thirties. Trim, well-toned figure. Nice skin, if you ignored the bloody scratches. Long red hair. A dye job, but well done.

Her clothes were unusual, Casey noted. Skin-tight, low-slung black spandex leggings and a matching cropped black top that fit like a sports bra. Something you'd wear to the gym or aerobics class. The small diamond studs in her earlobes were her only jewelry. On the exposed flesh of her midriff was a tiny rose tattoo.

Her athletic shoes and the legs of her tights were wet up to her knees. Red ligature marks circled her wrists and ankles, but her body bore no other obvious signs of violence or struggle that Casey could see.

The woman lay slumped on her side with her knees bent at a sharp angle, as though she'd fallen to her knees and toppled over. Her arms were somewhat raised.

Death had been so recent that blood still oozed from her wounds, matting the ends of her hair and forming a dark circle in the dirt beside her back.

"The guy's name is Alfred Denner. He must've been going seventy when he hit town," Officer Novak continued. "I was gonna pull him over, but before I could turn on the siren he spotted the squad car and damned near ran us over trying to get to us. He was so shook up he was babbling. When me 'n Henderson finally got him calmed down enough to make sense, he said a woman had just been killed right before his eyes."

Casey looked up. "He witnessed the shooting?"

"Yeah. He's got blood splatter on his right pant leg and the inside of his truck is a mess. He said she'd been about to climb into his truck when the bullets struck her. Poor guy, he's still pretty shaken up."

"Make sure he doesn't go anywhere. I want to talk to him when I'm finished here. And don't let anyone near that truck."

"You got it, Detective." Officer Novak headed for the witness.

The crunch of gravel signaled the approach of another vehicle climbing the road. A few seconds later a plain gray sedan came around the switchback. Announcing his arrival with a chirp of the siren, Dennis Shannon, Casey's partner, eased the unmarked police car to a stop on the other side of the crime-scene tape and climbed out of the vehicle.

He ducked under the tape and hurried toward her with his usual lumbering, bearlike gait. A former linebacker for the Denver Broncos, Dennis was big, burly and intimidating. His size alone was enough to scare most collars into submission. On the rare occasion when his visual impact failed to put the fear of God into a suspect, he leveled the guy with the same feral expression he'd used to face down his opponents on the football field. Among the squad, Dennis's nickname was the Hulk.

But his ferocious-beast persona was all an act. Casey had long ago learned that beneath that rugged exterior, Dennis was an amiable old softie. Especially when it came to his wife and two-year-old son, Roger.

"Hey, Tiger. How's it going?" he called.

Casey sent him a narrow-eyed look, curled her lip and snarled, "I got the call from the boss in the middle of my morning run. I'm starting my day with a sense-less murder. And to top it all off I haven't had my coffee yet. What do you think?"

"Uh-oh. Hold on a sec." Dennis stopped and cupped his hands around his mouth and hollered, "Red alert! Casey hasn't had her coffee! Anybody got any?"

A collective groan went up, and uniformed officers and detectives alike began to scramble. Within seconds a young rookie scurried over with a thermos and handed it to Dennis. "This is from the urn at the station house. It's strong enough to float an iron wedge and there's no telling how old it is, but it's caffeine."

"That's all that matters. Thanks. You're a lifesaver."

"Hey, I'm just protecting my own hide," the young cop said, rolling his eyes.

Tales of Casey's addiction to coffee and the adverse effect on her disposition when deprived of the drink was of urban legend proportion among the MPD, espe-cially at the Second Precinct. She was well liked and re-spected by all her fellow cops, treated as one of the guys by the other detectives on the squad, and since her husband's death the year before, everyone on the force felt a certain degree of protectiveness toward her. But when the caffeine content of Casey's bloodstream dropped below a certain level, even the toughest cops ran for cover.

"Here you go, Tiger. Take a swig of this," her partner said, handing her the thermos cup.

She accepted the drink like a drowning man grabbing a lifeline and downed the brew in three swallows. If she noticed the strong flavor or scalding temperature, it didn't show.

"Jeez, the inside of your mouth must be lined with asbestos," her partner grumbled, wincing.

"What?" Casey said, giving him a bewildered look. "It's just coffee."

"Are you kidding? That stuff would take the hide off a rhinoceros. I wouldn't put it in my mouth."

"Yeah, well, better an old-fashioned cup of java than that herbal tea Mary Kate has you drinking."

"You've got a point. Sorry I'm late, by the way," Dennis said, recapping the thermos. "My day got off to a rough start, too."

"What's the matter? Did Mary Kate have another hormonal surge?"

"Oh, yeah. All I did was open the bedroom drapes and say it looked like it was going to be a beautiful day, and she burst into tears. Man, I thought those first four months of morning sickness were bad." Dennis removed latex gloves from the inside pocket of his suit coat and began to pull them on. "Every time she puked she gave me one of those 'you did this to me' looks. But these mood swings she's been having ever since the sickness stopped are even tougher to deal with. At this rate I'm not sure I can make it through these last two months. I love that woman to distraction, but she's driving me crazy."

"Poor baby." Casey looked up at her partner and grinned. "You'll get no sympathy from me, boyo. Three kids in three years of marriage is enough to make any woman a little nutty."

"Hey, how was I to know she'd have twins the second time? Anyway, you're my partner. You're suppose to be on my side."

"Too bad. Mary Kate's been my cousin and best friend a lot longer than you've been my partner, partner."

He rolled his eyes and muttered to no one in particular. "Women. They stick together like glue. Even Aunt Maureen. When I left for work this morning she was clucking over Mary Kate like a mother hen."

"Good," Casey pronounced without an ounce of sympathy. "Mary Kate deserves a little extra pampering right now. And my mother is in heaven, having someone to fuss over."

Her cousin was having a difficult time carrying the twins to term, and in the middle of her fifth month of pregnancy her obstetrician had ordered complete bed rest—an impossible situation for a mother of a supercharged two-year-old boy, unless you had help from your family.

That, fortunately, Mary Kate had in abundance. On hearing of the doctor's orders, Maureen Collins, with the help of her best friend and next-door neighbor, who happened to be Casey's mother-in-law, Francis O'Toole, had swooped down on the Shannons' apartment like a SWAT team. The two women had loaded up the young family's belongings and moved them into the cottage located on the five-hundred-acre property on which Patrick Collins and Joe O'Toole had built their own family homes more than thirty-five years ago.

Casey's father and Joe had built the cottage as a wedding present for her and Tim when they'd married ten years ago, but the place had been empty for almost a year now, ever since Casey had moved into a town house in Mears.

Now, every morning before leaving for work, Dennis transferred his pregnant wife and their son from the cottage to her aunt and uncle's home and left them in the care of Casey's mother.

The arrangement worked well for all concerned. Mary Kate got the care she needed, her mother and mother-in-law enjoyed babysitting little Roger, and Dennis could go to work secure in the knowledge that his wife and son were in good hands.

Dennis stepped to Casey's side and bent over for a closer look at the body. "Aw, jeez. Not another murdered woman."

"Afraid so." Using the eraser end of her pencil, Casey lifted the victim's hair to get a clear view of her wounds. "She took two shots to the back."

"Hmm. Just like Sheriff Crawford's two cases."

The previous two victims had been found in the woods by hikers. Both had been shot and both had ligature marks on their wrists and ankles. Since Casey did her best to avoid Sheriff Crawford whenever possible, she didn't have direct knowledge of the cases, but according to what she'd heard, what few clues they'd found had led the sheriff to believe that after sexually assaulting the women, the killer had turned them loose in the woods and hunted them down like animals.

"Looks like it," Casey agreed. "Except those victims

had each been shot only once. It appears that this one, instead of hysterically flailing through the woods and getting herself lost, was sharp enough to double back. I'd say she was looking for help on the road or hoping to make it to town. Smart move. Just a few more seconds and she might have succeeded.

"Unfortunately for us, by making it this far she put herself into our jurisdiction. Barely." Casey pointed to the side of the road. "The city limits runs along that verge. Fifteen feet that way, on the other side of that stream, and this case would have landed in the sheriff's lap like the other ones."

Dennis made a disgusted sound. "Instead, she's ours. Which means we're probably going to be assigned to work with that arrogant blowhard."

"Please. I don't want to even think about that," Casey protested. "I've only had one cup of coffee, remember."

"Three women murdered in two months." Dennis shook his head. "That's got to be a record for this area."

A population of just over ninety thousand made Mears one of the largest towns on Colorado's western slope, and it was growing steadily, thanks to an influx of retirees and big-city dwellers trying to escape big-city crime and crowding.

The usual cluster of office buildings and shops made up the downtown area. There were ritzy neighborhoods, slums, a restored historic district and modern middle- to upper-class subdivisions sprawling to the north and south of the town.

Nestled in a high, narrow valley between two long spines of mountains, Mears, Colorado, was called the picturesque paradise of the Rocky Mountains by the Chamber of Commerce. Casey and her fellow officers had a more realistic view of the place they called home.

Like any fair-size town, Mears had its share of burglaries, barroom brawls, rapes and drugs dealings. Once in a while they even had a bank robbery, but the yearly murder rate in the entire county usually averaged about eighteen to twenty a year. This year, however, the count had already hit fourteen, and it was only June 1.

The murders they did have were mostly crimes of passion, the result of a domestic dispute or an ex in a jealous rage or a drunken brawl that got out of hand. As far as Casey knew, they'd never dealt with a psychopathic killer before.

She stood up and moved to the other side of the body. "From the size of the exit wounds, I'd say the killer used a high-powered hunting rifle. Shooting her twice seems like overkill to me. The first shot was probably fatal."

"Yeah," Dennis agreed. "Either he really had it in for her, or he wanted to make sure she was dead. If I had to guess, I'd say he was shooting a .300 Winchester Mag. There are five or six popular hunting rifles that fire that cartridge. I've got a couple myself."

"Uh-huh. So do my dad and brothers," Casey said.

"A load that hefty can drop an elk at four hundred yards."

"Hmm. The exit wounds are several inches lower than the entrance wounds," Casey noted. She stood up again and stared at the slope above them. "The shots had to have come from up there. Look, you can still see her footprints in the frost on the other side of the creek where she came running out of the woods."

"Then the kill was recent."

"Less than a half hour ago, according to our witness."

Surprise widened Dennis's eyes. "We've got a witness? Hey, that's a lucky break."

"I hope so. Depends on how much he actually saw." Casey's gaze scanned the mountainside. "The killer could still be up there, watching us."

Dennis frowned. "Or sighting in his next victim." Casually, he shifted his stance, putting himself between Casey and the mountain.

Subtle as it was, the move did not escape her. "What're you doing?" she demanded, giving his arm a cuff. "You're my partner, not my protector. I thought we'd gotten that straight years ago."

"Yeah, well, that psycho is targeting women, not men. Anyway, you know Mary Kate would kill me if something happened to you."

"Oh, I see," she drawled, giving him a dry look. "It's yourself you're really concerned about, is it? Well, don't worry. I think you're safe. Even if he's still up there I doubt that he'd try anything with this many people around. If this is the same guy who did the first two killings, he gets his kicks out of assaulting his victims, then terrorizing them by hunting them down."

"Poor things. Helluva way to spend your last few moments on earth."

"Yeah," Casey agreed somberly.

She'd been trying not to think about what the victims had gone through—the degradation, the mind-numbing, heart-pounding fright of being the prey in a deadly game. The murders horrified her. Sorrow and compassion for the unfortunate women weighed heavy on her heart, and she simmered with anger on their behalf, but her job was to find the killer and stop him before more women lost their lives. To do that, she had to focus all her attention and energy on working the case.

"I want some men to backtrack the victim's trail. C'mon. Let's get them started."

A cluster of uniformed officers and a few plain-clothes detectives milled around just outside the cor-doned-off area. Usually they would be busy canvassing for possible witnesses or working crowd and traffic con-trol, but the remote location and early hour made that unnecessary. A couple of guys had stationed themselves about a hundred yards down the road to stop any vehi-cles that might come along, but so far the forest road was deserted. Most of the officers were waiting for orders from her.

"Is that Keith?" Casey asked as they approached the group, nodding toward the man clad in jeans and a leather jacket who stood with his back to them, talking to two other detectives.

"Yeah, I think so. He's the only one on the squad with hair that color."

"Keith, what are you doing here?"

The blond man turned and flashed his flirtatious smile. "Hey, Casey. Martin here was just telling me that you caught the case. Helluva way to start a beautiful morning."

"Tell me about it. But lucky me, I was first up on the duty roster. What's your excuse? I thought this was your day off?"

"It is." He gave her a sheepish look. "But you know how it is. I was heading out to do a little fishing when I saw the CSI van and a string of black-and-whites head-ing up here, so I tagged along."

"Since you're here, mind if I put you to work?"

"'Course not. You know I'd do anything for you, doll."

Ignoring the endearment, she pointed to the visible

swath in the frosty grass. "You're a big deer and elk hunter. I need your tracking skills. The vic left a trail. Take a few men with you and backtrack to where the shooter let her go. When you find the spot, give me a holler. Go slow, and look for anything that might help us. And don't let that bunch of clod-footed cops tromp through any evidence."

Keith laughed. "You got it. Just let me get my gun out of my truck. Hey, Bennetti. Adams. Come with me," he called, heading for his pickup.

"And be careful," Casey called after him. "The shooter may still be up there."

"Will do. Actually, I hope he is. I'd like to bring the bastard down."

"I'm sure you would," Dennis muttered under his breath.

"What?"

"Nothing. Just mumbling to myself."

Casey cocked her head to one side and studied her partner with a shrewd expression. "You don't like Keith much, do you?"

Dennis shrugged. "He gets under my skin, is all. He's fussy as an old-maid aunt about everything. If it weren't for his womanizing I'd think he was gay."

Casey laughed. "Oh, c'mon, Keith isn't that bad."

"Are you kidding? Haven't you ever noticed his desk? It's so neat it looks as though everything on it was aligned with a ruler—and God help you if you move anything or open one of his drawers. The guy's paperwork is always letter-perfect, and he never has a hair out of place. His shirts are always precisely folded at the side seams and tucked in tight, his pants are always creased. He keeps a complete extra suit of clothes in his locker—shoes, socks and underwear included—just in case he gets dirty or mussed up making an arrest. I don't know why he worries. He's the only guy I know of who can tromp through a Dumpster looking for evidence and come out fresh as a daisy."

By the time Dennis finished his tirade, Casey was openly laughing. "C'mon, now, be fair," she playfully scolded. "I know Keith can be a bit of a neat freak, but that's hardly reason to dislike him. You have to admit, he's a hardworking cop and a good detective."

It was all true, though privately Casey knew that it was that very by-the-book, almost compulsive adherence to the rules and orderliness that would prevent Keith from advancing much higher in the department than he was right now. He lacked flexibility and vision. Truly good detectives went with their gut feelings and sometimes bent the rules—not seriously, but just a little—to solve a case. Casey doubted that Keith had ever had a hunch in his life.

"Oh, yeah? You can't prove it by me," Dennis groused.

Casey tipped her head to one side again. "There's more that you're not saying, isn't there. C'mon, Dennis. I know you. You're too fair a person to dislike someone just because he has a neat fetish. So what is it?"

Dennis clenched his jaw, reluctant to answer, but he knew her, too, knew that she would not stop until she got the truth out of him. "If you must know, it's because the guy's a glory hound. You just mark my words. When we do catch this killer, ole Keith will somehow manage to take credit for the collar.

"Ever since he got his picture in the paper last year you'd think he was some kind of celebrity. And it doesn't help that everyone in the station house treats him like a hero."

A look of pain flashed in Casey's eyes, but she blinked it back and turned away to head for the witness. Dennis fell in step beside her. "Give him a break, why don't you," she said, her voice no longer steady. "After all, he did take down Juan Santos."

"Damn. I'm sorry, Casey. Hell, I knew I shouldn't have told you. I didn't want to bring up painful memories. I know how grateful you are to Keith for taking out your husband's killer. It's just that…"

"That what?"

"Oh, never mind. I need to learn to keep my big mouth shut."

"No. C'mon, spit it out."

"Well…I can't help but feel that Keith would've been more of a hero if he'd've shot Santos *before* the guy pumped four shots into Tim."

"He explained what happened."

"Yeah, I know. I know." Dennis slung his arm around her shoulders and gave her a brotherly hug and a rueful smile. "Forget I said anything, okay? I'm probably just jealous of the guy's good looks, that's all."

She glanced up at her partner with a wan smile, her tension easing. She doubted that. Dennis was the most down-to-earth person she knew, content with life and his place in it. Besides, Mary Kate adored her big bear of a husband just the way he was, and Casey knew that he wouldn't change that for the world.

There were, however, plenty of Mears cops who did envy the man who had been her late husband's partner. Detective Second Grade Keith Watson had the boyish blond looks and build of a California surfer, a toothpaste-ad perfect smile, sexy blue eyes and the reputation around the Second Precinct as a ladies' man.

From all accounts, he enjoyed the single life to the fullest. Women were always calling the station house and leaving messages for Keith. Tim had once told her that he dated a whole string of women, but never the same one for long.

"Mr. Denner?" Casey said, approaching the man sitting on the tailgate of his truck.

Officer Novak, who had been keeping an eye on the witness and his truck, stepped forward. "This is Detective O'Toole, and her partner, Detective Shannon, Mr. Denner. Detective O'Toole is in charge of the case. She needs to ask you a few questions." He looked at Casey. "You want me to turn the CSI guys loose now?"

"They can start with the body, but hold off on the truck until I've had a look at it." Turning back to the witness, she gave him a quick once-over, automatically taking mental note of his physical description. He was so tall and skinny, his trousers seemed to hang from his hipbones by sheer willpower, and his joints—knuckles, wrists and elbows—struck out like knobs. He had thinning brown hair, deep-set hazel eyes and the leathery skin of an out-of-doors type. At present he was shaking so hard his bones were practically rattling.

"What's your full name, sir?" Casey asked pleasantly.

"Alfred Picket Denner." A lit cigarette smoldered between the yellowed first two fingers of the man's right hand. He raised the smoke to take a drag, but his hand shook so badly he had difficulty getting his lips around the end of the filter tip. He inhaled deeply, then blew out a stream of smoke and flicked ash onto the ground.

"Nasty habit," he said with a rueful shake of his head.

"I quit four months ago, but after what happened I had to have something to calm me down. I bummed a few cigs off one of your officers. I hope you don't mind me smoking."

Casey shrugged. "They're your lungs." She pulled a small pad and pencil from the inside pocket of her blazer. "Now then, I'd like you to tell me what happened. Take your time, Mr. Denner, and try to remember every detail, no matter how small. Okay?"

"Right." In an unsteady voice, he relayed how the woman had come running out of the woods, flagged him down and asked for a ride, claiming a madman was trying to kill her.

"I told her to climb in, but she'd barely got one foot on the running board when someone shot her in the back. It was awful. The bullet went clean through her and through my floorboard, too. Blood went everywhere.

"She just looked at me, all shocked and glassy-eyed. Then a second shot hit her, and she slithered to the ground. That's when I took off.

"I couldn't do anything for her, you understand," he added in a rush. "If I'd stuck around I'd of just gotten myself killed, too."

"I understand, Mr. Denner. You did the right thing," Casey assured him. "From the look of her wounds she was probably dead before she hit the ground."

"That's right. She was," he agreed, anxious to absolve himself from the guilt he was obviously experiencing. "I'll never forget the look on her face as long as I live." He raised his trembling hand and took another drag on his cigarette. "Helluva thing."

Casey turned to Dennis. "Go tell the CSI people to look for a couple of bullets in the ground near the victim."

"Will do." Dennis lumbered off in that direction.

"Did you know the victim, Mr. Denner?"

"Nope. Never saw her before."

"I see. What were you doing up here at such an early hour?"

"I was— Hey! Wait just a doggone minute here!" He slid off the tailgate of his truck, bristling. "What're you asking that for? Do you suspect *me?* I just told you what happened. Look at my clothes, all splattered with blood. Check out my truck. You'll find the bullet holes in the floorboard, just like I said."

"Take it easy, Mr. Denner. No one is accusing you of anything. These are just routine questions. The D.A.'s office will need to know what you were doing up here in order for you to make a credible witness if we catch who did this and go to trial."

Actually, at this point, Casey wasn't ruling out anyone or taking anyone's word as fact. If Alfred Denner was telling the truth, his story was easy enough to check out, but until then she reserved judgment.

"Oh, I see. Sorry," he said, relaxing his stance. "I'm still a bit shook up. I'm a forest ranger. We've been having a problem with vagrants setting up permanent camps in the National Forest around Echo Basin. We ran them out a few days ago, but to make sure they hadn't come back I drove up there before dawn to check. They hadn't, so I was on my way back to town to grab a bite of breakfast."

"I see. Did you happen to see any other vehicles on the road?"

"Just a light-colored van—tan, I think, or maybe a dirty white. It was parked just up the road around that next bend. I thought about stopping to see if it was a poacher. This time of year varmint hunting is about the only legal hunting there is. But I was anxious for a cup of coffee, and since nine times out of ten the driver of a parked vehicle is just someone relieving himself in the woods, I drove on."

"Did you notice the make? The model?"

"A Plymouth, I think. One of those commercial-type vans with no back side windows. I didn't pay attention to the year or model. It did have Colorado license plates, though. I didn't get the number. Sorry."

"Was there anything unusual about the van? Any identifying markings? Dents? Logo? Anything like that?"

"I don't think so, but I can't say for sure. You think the driver was the killer? Jesus!" Alfred Denner turned pale and swallowed hard, his prominent Adam's apple bobbing. "Man, am I glad I didn't track him into the woods and confront him. I coulda been killed."

"Is there anything else you can tell us? Anything at all."

"That's it. That's all I know."

"All right. Thank you for your help, Mr. Denner. Here's my card. If you happen to think of anything else later, just give me a call. For now, though, if you'll go wait by that car over there, I'll drive you to the station house as soon as I'm done and take your formal statement. Then you'll be free to go."

"What about my truck? I can't just leave it here. That's government property."

"I'm afraid I'm going to have to impound your truck. Once it has been thoroughly processed and photographed by our crime-scene investigators, it will be returned to you."

"Oh, great. My boss isn't going to like this. He's

going to ream me out good for relinquishing possession of government property."

"When we get to the station house I'll give him a call and explain the situation if you'd like."

"Thanks," he grumbled, ambling away toward Casey's car. "It probably won't do any good, but thanks, anyway. Boy, this sure is starting off to be one helluva day."

Casey opened the passenger door of the pickup and, without touching anything, scanned the interior of the cab. Just as Ranger Denner had said, two thumb-size bullet holes pierced the floorboard near the accelerator, about four inches apart, and blood and tissue splattered the seat, dashboard and floor. Along the outside of the passenger seat and running board a long smear of blood marked the victim's downward slide to the ground. All of which bore out the witness's account.

"Hey, Casey."

She closed the truck door and turned to see Keith jogging toward her. Behind him, the small posse of trackers waited at the edge of the woods. "That was quick."

"That's because I lost the trail." He pointed to the small stream that tumbled down the mountainside and emptied into the creek flowing alongside the road. "She must have jumped into the water somewhere upstream. There's no telling where."

"Can't you follow the stream up the mountain until you pick up her trail again?"

"I can, but there's no guarantee I'll find it or how long it'll take."

"I see. Well, I guess I'd better get Oscar Tuttle and his dogs up here."

Keith groaned. "Aw, hell, I can't stand that old geezer. He smells worse than those hounds of his. I'd lay odds he hasn't taken a bath in years. Look, before you call him in, let me take another shot."

"Okay, but I can't wait too long or the trail will go cold."

"Right." Keith turned and jogged back to the group of men, and within seconds they all disappeared into the woods again.

"We got the bullets, bagged and tagged," Dennis called to her with a triumphant grin, holding up two paper evidence bags.

"Great. Be right there," Casey replied, heading toward the team working around the body.

She looked again at the spot where the victim had emerged from the forest. The sun would clear the mountains to the east soon, and when it did the frost would evaporate in moments, along with all but the most subtle signs of the trail.

Holding up the paper bags for her inspection, Dennis grinned as she drew near him. "Finding these could break this case wide open."

Casey gave her partner a wry look. As crime scenes went, so far this one had yielded little, but, as usual, that had no effect on Dennis's optimism. He was like a big, gentle bear. Nothing got him down for long, not even his wife's current mood swings.

"Oh, definitely," Casey drawled. "Now all we have to do is find the one hunting rifle out of the thousands in this county that fired them."

"Hey. Right now it may not be much, but it's the first solid physical evidence anybody's got against this guy." He grinned again, this time with a devilish twinkle in his eyes. "It's a heck of a lot more than the sheriff has."

Casey shook her head, a reluctant grin tugging at her lips. A long tendril of curly, bright red hair escaped the twisted knot on top of her head and fluttered in the air, catching the early morning light like a ribbon of fire as Casey approached the head technician on the CSI team. "Mark the spot where she fell carefully, Rob. I want a trajectory on those bullets."

"You got it, Detective."

From beyond the next bend in the road a shout sounded, and Casey turned in that direction, absently tucking the errant strand behind her ear. "That must be Keith. C'mon," she said to Dennis, and took off at a jog.

Around the next bend, a hundred yards or so down the road, they found Keith and the other cops. Keith and Tony Bennetti, another detective on the squad, were down on their haunches, examining the ground. The other two cops wandered around nearby, scanning the surrounding area and staying well clear of the suspect area.

"Find something?" Casey asked, coming to a halt beside Keith.

"Yeah. This is where the bastard let her go." He pointed to two sets of footprints and some tire marks in the soft dirt along the side of the road. "Looks like he pulled her out of the back of his vehicle here. Probably the trunk of a car or the back of a van. I don't think he'd transport her in the bed of an open pickup. Too big a risk of someone seeing her."

"I agree," Casey said.

"See how her first footprints are pointed away from the back of the vehicle? His prints come around from the driver's side to the back. There was a bit of shuffling here," he said, pointing to a trampled spot. "Then her prints take off in that direction. See how deep they're dug in? That means she was running. I figured he gave her just a bit of a head start, then went after her."

"How do you know that? Maybe she made a break for it and he took off after her."

"I don't think so. See how his prints parallel hers? If he had been chasing her, he wouldn't have been so careful not to step on her prints. No, he was definitely tracking."

A chill rippled through Casey. What kind of man would track down another human being as if she were a trophy animal?

"The trail is a wide, upside-down U-shape. Our girl was crafty. She ran straight into the forest for a half mile or so, then veered off that way until she found the stream and doubled back. The hunter must have spotted her, though, because his trail only follows hers partway in, then angles across. Looks like he ran down the mountain and stopped over there, where he had a clear view of the kill sight."

"Did you find anything there we could use? Cartridge casings? Anything dropped?"

"No, nothing. But I marked the spot, if you want to take a look around."

"Thanks, I do, but first I need to call the house and check in with the boss." She turned to her partner and said, "While I do that I want you to get CSI down here. Tell them I want photos from every possible angle and a cast made of both sets of shoe prints and the tire print."

"I'm on it," Dennis replied, and headed back down the road.

Casey pulled her cell phone out of the pocket of her blazer and punched the automatic dial. Her boss answered on the first ring.

"Second Precinct. Lieutenant Bradshaw."

"It's Casey, boss."

"It's about time. What've we got?"

"Enough to know we're after the same man who committed the murders in Sheriff Crawford's cases."

"Ah, shit." A silence followed. Casey could almost see her boss pacing his office, raking his hand through his shock of silver hair in that characteristic way he had when he wrestled with a difficult situation.

"You're sure?"

"I'm sure." She paused, then added in a grim voice, "We've got ourselves a serial killer running loose."

Three

"That's it? A couple of slugs, a witness to the murder who didn't see the shooter?" Lieutenant Bradshaw frowned at Casey over the top of his desk.

"Plus shoe and tire prints," she calmly reminded him, unperturbed by her boss's gruffness.

Lieutenant Arthur Bradshaw was a seasoned police officer with thirty-one years on the job, the first nineteen of which had been spent working the street, as both a uniformed officer and a detective. He was crusty as a barnacle and as tough as an old boot. Blunt and often irascible, he didn't suffer fools or slackers, period. But he was also a straight arrow—honest, fairminded and sharp. Above all, he stood up for his detectives. If you did your job and were straight with him, you could count on him to back you in any dispute, whether with the D.A.'s office, Internal Affairs, the brass or politicians. In short, Lieutenant Bradshaw was a cop's cop.

With Bradshaw, you never had to worry about him having a hidden agenda. What you saw was pretty much what you got—a hard-charging, demanding veteran cop who lived and breathed police work.

There was comfort in knowing where you stood, Casey often thought. She much preferred having a no-nonsense, grumpy old warrior for a boss than an over-ambitious ladder-climber whose primary motivation for clearing cases was to advance his own career.

According to some, it was Lieutenant Bradshaw's very loyalty to his people that had prevented him from being promoted to captain years ago—and what endeared him to every man and woman on his squad.

"We'll have to wait for the medical examiner's report to know for certain if the guy sexually assaulted our vic," Casey continued. "But cause of death was definitely the gunshot wounds to the back, just like the county's cases."

"Our witness did see a light-colored van parked by the side of the road before the woman ran out of the woods," Dennis put in. "But he didn't take down the license number."

"Great," Lieutenant Bradshaw snapped. "Helluva lot of good that's going to do us. There must be thousands of light-colored vans in this county alone, assuming the killer is from around here."

"CSI is still processing the scene." Propping her elbows on the arms of her chair, Casey steepled her fingers together and pursed her lips. "I doubt they'll find much more, though. This guy is no dummy. He left zip in the first two cases. The only reason we got anything on this one is the vic kept her head and darn near managed to elude the murderous SOB.

"That was a break for us in two ways. With a witness hightailing it for town, the killer didn't have time to erase the tire tracks and footprints. He knew we'd be there within minutes and he had to get out of there. And we were able to recover the slugs that killed our vic because she was killed on the road instead of in the forest."

"Yeah," her partner agreed. "There's been so much hunting in those woods over the years that even if the sheriff's men had recovered bullets, they wouldn't have much chance of proving they were the ones that killed those two women."

"Ballistics will document the markings on the slugs and the lab will go over the witness's clothing and the truck, plus the dead girl's clothing. I'm also sending the tire molds to an expert to try to pin down the brand and type and document any individual marking, but until we find the truck or the weapon or have a suspect, nothing we have so far will be of much use to us."

"Do we know the vic's name?" the lieutenant asked.

"So far she's a Jane Doe. She had no identification of any kind on her. Her spandex leggings and bra top had no pockets and there hasn't been a purse or wallet located as yet."

"That also jibes with the sheriff's cases. Damn," Dennis spat. "This means we're going to have to contact Crawford and try to get him to cooperate."

Glass formed the upper half of the two interior walls of the lieutenant's corner office. Dennis leaned with his hips braced against the sill, his back to the squad room. With his legs stretched out in front of him, his beefy arms crossed over his massive chest, he was the picture of dejection at the thought of having anything to do with Sheriff Crawford.

"I'll take care of that. I want you two to get busy finding out who this woman is," Lieutenant Bradshaw ordered. "No one should die without her family knowing about it."

"Right, boss." Casey stood up, and she and Dennis headed toward the door. "I'll check with Missing Persons. If that doesn't turn up anything, Dennis and I will canvas the gyms and dance studios."

"Good. Keep me posted."

Fifteen minutes later Casey was still on the telephone with Missing Persons when an older man dressed in jeans, a western shirt, cowboy boots and a Stetson entered the room. He was tall and whipcord-lean, with leathery, sun-baked skin, the very image of a broken-down old cowboy. Two younger men, similarly built and attired and wearing the same worried expression, flanked the old man. They also had the same weathered look.

The trio stopped by the desk of their civilian assistant, Monica Hudson, and all three men politely removed their hats before addressing her.

"Pardon me, miss. My name is Henry Belcamp. I want to report my daughter missing," the older man said, turning the battered Stetson around and around in his huge, callused hands.

Casey quickly ended her phone conversation and stood up.

"I'm sorry, sir, but Missing Persons is up on the fourth floor. This is—"

"That's okay, Monica. I'll talk to Mr. Belcamp," Casey interrupted. Stepping forward, she extended her hand to the old man. "Hello, sir. I'm Detective O'Toole, and this is my partner, Detective Shannon."

"Henry Belcamp. These here are my sons, John Henry and Rafe."

After she and Dennis had shaken hands with the

three men, Casey said, "Let's talk in the coffee room, shall we?"

When they were settled around the long table, she asked, "What is your daughter's name, Mr. Belcamp, and how long has she been missing?"

"Her name is Becky. Becky Sue Belcamp. Best we can tell, she hasn't been seen by anyone we know since around six last night. That's when the other two instructors who work for her got off work. Becky keeps the studio open until nine for members who work out after they leave their jobs, but she takes that shift.

"We have a ranch about twenty miles north of town. Me 'n my boys get up before first light, so we're always asleep by the time Becky gets home. We didn't know she was missing until this morning when she didn't show up for breakfast."

"Your daughter lives with you?"

"Yes. She just opened her aerobics studio about four months ago, and money is tight."

"Becky has always lived at home," Rafe said. "She's been saving up to open her own studio ever since she was about twenty."

"And how old is she now?"

"Twenty-eight."

"She saved up a tidy sum," her father said with pride. "And I loaned her the rest of the money she needed. Anyways, this morning I sent John Henry to wake her up and he discovered that her bed hadn't been slept in."

"Has your daughter ever stayed out all night before?"

"No! Of course not," the old man barked. "What kinda question is that? My Becky's a good girl."

"Please, sir. Don't get upset. There are certain routine questions that I have to ask. Is it possible that your daughter spent the night at her studio? Or with a friend?"

"Not without calling home to let us know. We called the studio soon as we realized she wasn't home. Called her cell phone, too, but got no answer on either one. Then, somewhere around six-thirty, one of her instructors telephoned us and said the place was locked up tighter'n a drum and she couldn't get inside or get anyone to come to the door. Becky is always there by then.

"Me 'n my boys drove into town to find out what was goin' on. We found Becky's car still in the parking lot. From the looks of it, it'd been there all night. It was still covered with frost when we got there. I used my key and opened the studio." The old man raked his fingers through his steel-gray hair. "I tell you, I was scared to death of what we'd find inside, but it turned out the place was empty."

"Any sign of a disturbance? Or items missing?"

"No. Becky always leaves the place neat and clean. There wasn't anything out of place."

"I see. Could you describe your daughter for us, Mr. Belcamp?"

"Sure. She's about five-seven, brown eyes, long hair. It's red now, but next week it may be blond or black. With Becky you never know."

"She's slender, in good physical condition, with sort of a muscular build," her brother John Henry supplied. "And she always wears our mother's diamond stud earrings."

"And she's got a tiny red rose tattooed on her midriff," Rafe added.

The elder Belcamp snorted and muttered, "Damned foolishness if you ask me, marking up your body thataway. Me 'n Becky, we had a big row about that. She said it made her look 'hip,' and that was important in her business."

"Did you and your daughter argue often?"

"What're you driving at? If you think my father—"

Casey fixed John Henry with a steady look. "As I said before, these are merely routine questions. I would be derelict in my duty if I didn't ask them."

"Sometimes you ask unpleasant questions in order to rule out someone as a suspect," Dennis inserted.

"Calm down, boy. Detective O'Toole knows what she's doing," the old man said. "Other than that tattoo, about the only thing me 'n my daughter ever got cross-ways over was the way she always complained about her looks. She was always doing crazy stuff to improve her appearance. I told her it was a waste of time and money. She's beautiful, just the way God made her."

A smile tugged at Casey's mouth. The statement reeked of a father's love and pride and sounded like something her own father would say.

Casey and Dennis exchanged a look, and she knew he had the same sinking feeling in the pit of his stomach that she had in hers. Identifying the victim was essential to solving the case, but she did not want to tell this family that their beloved daughter and sister was dead.

"Normally, we don't initiate a search for an adult until they've been missing forty-eight hours. However, I have reason to believe that we might have information on your daughter." Reaching across the table, Casey put her hand over the old man's clenched fist. "Mr. Belcamp, would you be agreeable to looking at some photos?"

"What kind of photos?"

Concern and pity glistened in Casey's eyes. "Photos of a dead woman."

"*Dead!* You think it's my Becky?"

"I don't know. The woman in the pictures was murdered early this morning on Forest Service Road 18," she said as gently as possible. "But she fits the general description of your daughter."

"Oh, God." Stark fear slackened Henry Belcamp's weathered face and his eyes filled with tears.

"How was she murdered?" Rafe demanded.

"She was shot in the back with a high-powered hunting rifle."

"You mean like those other two women?"

"I'm afraid so."

The old man moaned.

"I'll look at the pictures," John Henry volunteered, visibly bracing to take over the unpleasant task for his father. He put his hand on Henry's arm. Sitting on the other side of their father, Rafe scooted closer and put his arm around the old man's shoulders.

"No, I'll do it," Henry said. "She's my child." He sniffed and wiped his eyes with the back of his hand, then straightened his shoulders and nodded. "Go ahead."

Wordlessly, Casey pulled the photos from her pocket and spread them out on the table in front of the three men.

One of the younger men gasped, and all the color drained from Henry's face an instant before it crumpled. "No. No, no, not my little girl. Not my baby. Oh God, oh God, oh God," the old man wailed, burying his face in his hands.

Fighting back their own tears, the two younger men did their best to comfort their father, huddling close to the old man, who seemed to shrink before Casey's eyes.

"I'm sorry for your loss," she murmured. "My partner and I will step out for a few minutes and give you some privacy."

"Damn it to hell," Dennis snarled when the door closed behind them. "Why do horrible things happen to nice people? This is the worst part of this job, telling decent folks like that their loved one has been killed."

"I don't know why," Casey murmured, shaking her head. She'd asked herself that question at least a thousand times during the past year. God knew, if being a decent human being made you immune to tragedy, then her husband Tim would not have been murdered by a drug dealer.

Leaving the grieving family alone, she and Dennis reported to the lieutenant that they had a positive ID on the victim. They then returned to their desks and shuffled through some paperwork and made a few telephone calls. When sufficient time had passed, they returned to the coffee room. The Belcamp men had their emotions under control, but the pall in the room was thick enough to cut with a knife.

"We apologize for intruding on your grief. I know you're feeling raw right now, but my partner and I need to talk to you some more about your daughter," Casey said, sitting down at the table across from Henry Belcamp. "We'd like your permission to search the aerobics studio and your home and Becky's car."

"What for?" John Henry demanded in a belligerent voice. "Isn't it bad enough our sister was murdered by some maniac? You want to pry into her business and her personal life, too?"

"We're not trying to rake up dirt on your sister. We're just doing our jobs, trying to find who did this and bring him to justice. You never know what you will find in a search. Sometimes the tiniest of things can turn up a connection between the victim and the killer or lead us to important information."

"Our sister had no connection with this murdering bastard," John Henry insisted. "These were random killings, just like the newspaper said."

"They may be, but until we know for sure we have to explore every possibility. We can do this the easy way, with your permission, or I can get a search warrant. It's up to you."

"Go ahead. Search whatever you need to," the old man said in a dispirited voice.

"But, Dad—"

"Settle down, son. We can't do anything for Becky now, except help in any way we can to catch her killer. If I'm any judge of character—and I think I am—Detective O'Toole, here, is a good person to put your trust in. I get the feeling that she knows what she's doing, and I think she'll do her best to get the man who did this." He looked Casey right in the eye, and she felt the full weight of his faith and trust settle over her shoulders. "I'm depending on you, little lady."

Normally Casey would have taken offense at the term, but Mr. Belcamp was from a different era when men idolized and protected the "fairer sex," and she knew that he meant no insult.

She drew a deep breath and gave the old man's gnarled hand a squeeze. "I'll do my best, sir. I wish I could guarantee that I'll find your daughter's killer, but I can't. However, I can promise you one thing. I'll never stop trying."

After a quiet lunch, Casey and Dennis spent most of the afternoon conducting a thorough search of the Belcamp ranch house, which was located eighteen miles northeast of Mears in a pleasant, if rather isolated, valley.

The Belcamps, Casey learned, had been ranching the Rocking B for four generations, ever since Henry's grandfather had homesteaded the place in the 1870s. The ranch house was old and had that lived-in look, the furnishings comfy, if a bit on the shabby side, but the whole place was orderly and spotlessly clean, especially Becky's room.

They found little of interest, certainly nothing obvious that linked her to a psychopathic killer. The only items of possible use that Casey and Dennis took from the house were Becky's address book and diary.

They had only slightly better luck at the Body Beautiful Aerobic Studio, located in the new Tundra Mall on the north side of town. Her car was still in the parking lot, cordoned off with crime-scene tape while the CSI team conducted preliminary testing prior to towing the vehicle into the lab.

Like her home, Becky's studio and office were clean and organized. The desk in her office was immaculate—pens and pencils were put away, the papers in the "in" and "out" boxes neatly stacked, her stapler, electric pencil sharpener, desk mat and calculator precisely aligned.

"Becky was a neat freak," Casey commented as she and Dennis methodically combed through every square inch of the office.

"I'll say. But at least her books should be easy to go through."

There were a few notations on the desk calendar, but the one that caught Casey's eye was written under yesterday's date, the day their victim had disappeared.

"Take a look at this," Casey said to her partner.

Abandoning the file drawer he was rifling through, Dennis peered over her shoulder at the notation. It read, "Dr. Adams—4:30."

"Hmm. She must've returned here after the appointment," he mused. "According to the other two instructors, Becky was here when they left around six."

"True. Still…it wouldn't hurt to pay the doc a visit." She located the doctor's address in Becky's Rolodex and jotted it down in her notepad. "His offices aren't too far from the station house. We'll stop by on the way in."

That the search yielded no solid leads came as no surprise to Casey. If the case was connected to the first two in the sheriff's jurisdiction, the victims had probably been chosen randomly—up to a point.

Serial killers rarely knew their prey. However, Casey had no doubt that there was something that connected the women, at least in the perpetrator's mind. Studies had shown that most serial killers targeted their victims for a specific reason. They might resemble one another physically, or share the same profession. What had put them all at risk could be something as innocuous as having brown eyes or freckles. It wasn't necessarily logical or reasonable, but in the killer's twisted mind, it made sense.

If she could pinpoint that commonality it might help solve the case. That, however, would require access to Sheriff Crawford's case files.

City, county and state agencies operated as separate entities. Lieutenant Bradshaw could request the sheriff's cooperation, but they were all aware that unless his bosses, the county commissioners, ordered it, he wasn't likely to be of help.

Casey and Dennis confiscated the aerobic studio's

books, customer records and the victim's Rolodex and
day planner, then boxed up everything to take back to
the station house and study. After that, they headed for
Jim Bridger Boulevard and the Powers Building, which
housed Dr. Mark Adams's offices.

"I hope he's still here," Dennis said as they entered
the lobby a short time later. "The afternoon is almost
gone. Some docs knock off early to make hospital
rounds."

"Well, well," Casey murmured, checking the direc-
tory. "Looks like the doc is a plastic surgeon."

"Now, why would a young woman like Becky Belcamp see a plastic surgeon? She looked fine to me."

Casey rolled her eyes, then reached up and gave her
partner's cheek a pat. "Men. You're so naive sometimes.
Ever heard of eye lifts, nose jobs, tummy tucks, butt
lifts, silicone implants, chin implants, cheek implants—"

"Stop! Stop! Jeeeez. Thanks a lot, Tiger. Now, every
time I see a good-looking woman, I'm going to wonder
how much of her is real and how much is store-bought.
Thank God my Mary Kate never went in for that kind
of stuff." No sooner had the statement left his mouth
than a frown creased his brow. "She didn't, did she?"

"Relax, boyo." They stepped into the elevator and
Casey punched the button for the fourth floor. "Trust
me. Everything about your wife is genuine. You are
married to one of God's finest creations. One of the last
of the true red-hot mamas."

"Yeah," Dennis agreed with a sappy, self-satisfied
smile.

The moment they stepped into Dr. Adams's waiting
room he gave a low whistle. "Wow."

"I'll say," Casey agreed, fully understanding his awe. The room was so serene and sumptuous it almost had a dreamlike atmosphere.

Dr. Adams had obviously employed the psychology of sensual response to put his patients at ease and calm any jitters they might have over having cosmetic surgery. Decorated in shades of teal and cream with accents of muted apricot, the space exuded a soft elegance that you experienced almost on a visceral level, your body responding instinctively to the tranquil ambience. "I'll bet everyone's blood pressure goes down automatically as soon as they step into this place," she whispered.

No typical bought-in-bulk waiting-room furnishings here. Plush carpeting cushioned the floor, tone-on-tone cream-striped wallpaper covered the walls, and elegant silk-brocade Queen Anne chairs and sofas, scattered with velvet throw pillows, provided comfy places to sit. Teal velvet draperies flanked the wide expanse of windows, which were covered with cream-colored silk sheers to soften and filter the light that flooded the room. Misty watercolor landscapes in ornate frames dotted the walls.

The china lamps, the floating rose-scented candles, small cloisonné boxes and crystal dishes filled with butter mints, scattered around on the coffee table and end tables, the vases filled with fresh cream-and-apricot roses—every item had been chosen with care. Symphonic music flowed softly from hidden speakers and, in the corner, in a large, four-foot-tall cylindrical aquarium, colorful fish swam through swaying aquatic plants with mesmerizing grace.

"Yeah," Dennis agreed. "The doc must be a clever guy. I defy anyone to have the jitters in a place like this."

Certainly none of the three attractive women seated around the room appeared anxious, Casey thought.

As they approached the reception desk, a nurse opened an inner door and called a name, and a statuesque blonde rose and followed her inside.

"May I help you?" the woman behind the counter asked.

"We need to speak to Dr. Adams, please."

"I'm sorry, but without an appointment that's impossible. He's booked solid today." The woman checked her wristwatch and nodded toward the waiting women. "These are his last two appointments."

"He'll see us." Casey pulled out her badge and showed it to the woman. "I'm Detective O'Toole. This is Detective Shannon. We're here on police business."

Shock flickered over the receptionist's face. "I—I see. Very well. If you'll come with me, you can wait in the doctor's office while I let him know that you're here."

Furnished like an English library, with two walls of books, oversize leather furniture and a dark mahogany desk, Dr. Adams's office was warm and masculine, but no less soothing than the reception room.

"If you'll have a seat, I'll go get the doctor," his nervous receptionist said on her way out.

"Wow." Dennis gave the globe in the walnut stand a spin before sitting in the leather wing chair beside Casey. He looked around the room. "Plastic surgery must pay better than I thought. This place even smells like money."

Casey made a sound somewhere between a snort and a chuckle. "It's called the high cost of beauty."

"Huh. I should've forgotten about playing in the pros and police work and gone straight to medical school. I'm obviously in the wrong profession."

A grin curved Casey's mouth. "I can see it now. Dr. Hulk."

The door opened behind them. "Good afternoon. I'm Dr. Adams. I understand from Jolie that you want to talk to me."

Casey glanced over her shoulder and experienced a dart of surprise. In her mind she had pictured Dr. Mark Adams as middle-aged and on the geeky side, perhaps with thinning hair and a paunch. After seeing his waiting room, she would not have been surprised to find that he was effeminate. Nothing could be further from reality.

The man who entered the office was in his midthirties and a drop-dead, gorgeous hunk. Tall, broad-shouldered and leanly muscled, he had black hair, sexy pale gray eyes surrounded by ridiculously long black lashes and elegantly chiseled features.

There was more to his appeal than just good looks, though, Casey realized, studying him as they introduced themselves. He shook her and Dennis's hands and took his seat behind the massive walnut desk. The man had that intangible something, a sort of quiet animal magnetism that did not require bluster or overt aggressiveness. One look and you sensed that beneath that starched white lab coat and expensive tailored shirt and silk tie was a virile, thoroughly masculine male.

That quality manifested itself in everything he did—his body language, the confident way he walked and talked, the masculine grace of his hand gestures. Dr. Adams was a confident, secure man who was totally at ease with himself.

The direct way he looked at you was a bit disconcerting, Casey thought, shifting uneasily in her chair under his intent scrutiny, but at least you knew you had his attention.

No wonder the women in the waiting room had looked so eager.

The doctor looked at her partner. "You look familiar. Shannon, Shannon. Say, you wouldn't happen to be the Dennis Shannon who played for the Denver Broncos a few years back, would you?"

"Yeah, that was me. You a football fan, Doc?"

"You bet. Especially the Broncos. I have season tickets. I try never to miss a home game. That's not always possible, with my practice, of course, but I try."

"Actually, I'm surprised you remember me, Doc. I played only three years before a knee injury cut my career short."

"Yeah, but you were a great player."

"Thanks."

The doctor leaned back in his chair. "How may I help you, Detectives?"

Add a wicked grin to his list of manly attributes, Casey thought. Glancing down at her notepad to avoid his mesmerizing gaze, she asked, "Do you have a patient named Becky Belcamp?"

"Yes, I do. Why do you ask?"

"When was the last time you saw her?"

"Yesterday afternoon. She was my last patient of the day."

"I see. And when she left, did you accompany her?"

"Pardon me?"

"After her appointment, did you and Ms. Belcamp, say…go out for a drink? Or have dinner together maybe?"

"No-oo," the doctor replied, drawing the word out. "As I just told you, Becky is a patient of mine. Social interaction with someone you are treating is against medical ethics. Besides, I have a hard, fast rule. I don't get romantically involved with patients. That *is* what you were asking, isn't it, Detective O'Toole?"

He stared at her intently, as though he found her fascinating. *Like some alien life form,* Casey thought wryly. *He's probably making a mental list of everything that needs correcting.* As though he'd read her thoughts, a teasing smile flirted with his beautifully chiseled mouth and his pale eyes twinkled at her.

For the first time since the death of her husband, Casey experienced an instant of acute physical awareness—a sudden tightening of her chest, accompanied by that fluttery sensation that made breathing difficult, as though a swarm of butterflies were beating their wings against her ribs.

It was a shocking and unwelcome feeling. *For Pete's sake, Casey, get a grip, will you. Now is neither the time nor the place for your sleeping libido to wake up. The man's a potential suspect, for God's sake. Anyway, since when have you had a thing for pretty boys?*

She tipped her chin up a notch and met the doctor's gaze squarely. "My partner and I are trying to ascertain Ms. Belcamp's movements yesterday afternoon."

"Again, I have to ask. Why? Is she in some sort of trouble?"

Casey waited a beat, studying the man. "Becky Belcamp is dead."

"What?" His relaxed demeanor vanished. He sat forward, a look of stunned surprise on his face. "Dead? How did she die? She was a young, vigorous woman in the prime of life."

"She was murdered this morning around dawn. Shot to death by, we believe, the same person who murdered the two women who were killed last month."

"Dear, God." The doctor looked at her as though he couldn't believe what he was hearing. "That's terrible. That poor girl. Her family must be devastated. Look, I'm sorry if I was flippant before, Detective. Please, tell me how I can be of help."

"You can start by telling us why Becky came to see you."

He shook his head, and this time his smile was regretful. "I'm sorry, Detective O'Toole, but you know I can't tell you that."

"Why not? As I'm sure you know, doctor-patient privilege does not extend beyond death."

Dr. Adams rose and came around to the front of the desk and hitched one leg over the edge. He was so close that his outstretched leg nearly touched Casey's. She swallowed hard and resisted the urge to scoot her chair back.

Folding his hands together, he rested them on his thigh and smiled down at her. "That may be. But, personally, I'm not comfortable with handing over patient information without a court order, or at least the permission of the deceased's next of kin. Besides, what does her medical history have to do with her murder?"

"Perhaps nothing," Dennis inserted. "We won't know until we have a look at her file."

Dr. Adams spread his hands. "Sorry. As I said…"

"Fine." Casey gestured toward the telephone on his desk. "Call Ms. Belcamp's father. I'm sure he's listed in her file as the person to notify in case of an emergency. I'm confident that he will give his permission. He's been very cooperative and willing to do whatever is necessary to help us solve his daughter's murder."

Dr. Adams hesitated, studying Casey's determined expression. "Very well." He reached around behind him and punched a button on the intercom. "Jolie, get me Becky Belcamp's father on the phone, please. Thanks."

Within seconds the call came through. Without budging from his perch on the corner of the desk, Dr. Adams again reached around and plucked up the receiver on the first ring. "Hello, Mr. Belcamp. This is Dr. Adams. First of all, let me say how sorry I am. I just heard what happened to Becky. Which is why I'm calling. There are two detectives here in my office...."

The conversation was short. When the doctor hung up he looked at Casey and smiled. "Looks like you were right. Mr. Belcamp authorized the release of his daughter's file to you. He said he has complete faith in you. That's saying something.

"I met the man. He and his sons accompanied Becky on the morning of her surgery, and they stuck right by her side until she was released. I've never seen such a devoted family. From what I observed, her father is as crusty as they come and not easily won over, but he's a shrewd judge of character."

Never comfortable with compliments from anyone, especially not from this handsome doctor, Casey quickly looked down at her notepad. "Can you tell us what time it was when Ms. Belcamp left here yesterday?"

As though he knew exactly how uneasy he was making her, he smiled before answering. "Let's see, my last appointment is at four-thirty. So my guess would be between five and five-thirty. You can check with my receptionist, though. She might be able to pinpoint the time a bit better."

"And where were you this morning around dawn?"

"Me?" Dr. Adams gave a startled laugh. "Am I a suspect, Detective?"

"Until I know otherwise, everyone's a suspect."

"I see. Well, this morning, between four-thirty and ten I was performing emergency surgery. I was doing my best to put back together the face of a little boy who was involved in a car accident earlier this morning. You can check with St. Mary's Hospital. There were at least a dozen people on duty there last night who can verify that."

"Good. We'll do that." Casey closed her notepad, slipped it into her blazer pocket. As casually as possible, she scooted her chair back and stood up but still found herself too close to the man for comfort. She could actually feel the heat from his body, and she caught a whiff of antiseptic and soap...and male.

She had expected him to stand and get out of her way, or at least shift sideways to give her room, but he didn't budge. "Thanks for your help, Doctor. Here is my card. If you think of anything else that might be of help, call me."

He took the card and glanced at it. "Your first name is Casey. I like that. It suits you."

"Thank you." Casey's gaze was drawn to his hands, the long, slender fingers that held the card. His fingernails were clean and short, well manicured, she noticed. Though his hands were big, they were beautifully shaped and graceful, in an utterly masculine way. Between the first and second knuckles and across the backs were sprinklings of short, silky black hairs. For some inexplicable reason, just looking at those hands sent a tingle down Casey's spine and made her chest tighten.

For Pete's sake, get a grip, she silently scolded herself, but it did no good. Though it didn't make any sense, those big, capable hands were the sexiest things she'd ever seen.

"I'll buzz Jolie and tell her to make a copy of Ms.

Belcamp's file," the doctor said. "You can pick it up on your way out."

"Thank you."

He held her gaze and smiled as she sidestepped around him. "If I can be of further help, just call. I hope to see you again, Detective."

On the way out of the office neither Casey or Dennis spoke, but the instant the elevator doors closed behind them she collapsed back against the rear wall and fanned her face with her hand. "Whewee! Is that man ever a hottie."

Dennis chuckled. "Yeah, even I noticed that. And he seemed to think the same thing about you."

"*What?* Oh, pul-leeze!" Casey shot her partner a disdainful look. "Don't be ridiculous."

"I'm not. Didn't you notice how the guy was flirting with you? I sure did."

"He wasn't flirting with me. That's preposterous. Why in God's name would a man that gorgeous look twice at me?"

On a good day Casey considered herself, at best, sort of cute. She had a long mane of wildly curly, bright red hair, and though her skin was creamy, she had exactly nine freckles across the bridge of her nose that no amount of astringent or potions would make disappear. If that weren't bad enough, she had delicate features and absurdly big blue eyes fringed with long lashes that gave her a perpetual look of wide-eyed innocence, even though she was pushing thirty.

Thinking about her looks, Casey sighed. She knew that she tended to be hard on herself, but it was difficult not to be. Growing up with four rough-and-tumble older brothers and enduring their affectionate teasing had turned her into a scrappy, independent female, but had done little to develop her perception of herself as a desirable woman.

Not only had she shot up to her adult five feet nine inches before puberty, she'd also been a late bloomer, not developing breasts or womanly curves until she was eighteen. As though to make up for shortchanging her earlier, Mother Nature had endowed the adult Casey with a full C cup, long legs and a waist that most men could span with their hands.

Of course, if any of them dared to try such a thing she'd knock them on their keister in a New York second.

By the time that Casey had bloomed, Will, Brian, Ian and Aiden had all joined the Mears police force and left home, and in typical brotherly fashion, none of them noticed any change in their baby sister. To this day they all fondly called her by their favorite teenage nickname: Stretch.

Given a choice, she would rather be called by her own name. But since everyone seemed determined to pin a nickname on her, she preferred Tiger, the name bestowed on her by her partner and the other detectives at the precinct. However, she loved her brothers too much to complain.

Stepping out of the elevator, Casey strode across the lobby and pushed open the plate-glass door before Dennis could open it for her. "Besides," she declared as they headed for the squad car. "Didn't you see those lovelies waiting to see the doc? They were all practically salivating."

"Don't sell yourself short, Tiger." Dennis ambled along beside her with his hands in his pockets and a Cheshire cat grin on his face. "Trust me. A guy knows when another guy is interested in a woman, and the doc is definitely interested in you."

Casey wrinkled her nose and blew him a raspberry.

Four

Lugging the boxes of items from Becky Belcamp's home and business, Casey and Dennis entered the station house and found a pack of clamoring reporters crowded around the front desk.

Sergeant Bartowski, the officer on duty, was red in the face and obviously at his wit's end. The media people jostled and pushed one another for position, everyone shouting questions at once.

"Was the latest victim raped and shot like the others, Sergeant?"

"Do you have a line on any suspects?"

"Will the FBI be called in, now that there have been three victims?"

The sergeant held up his hands for quiet. "Will you people shut the hell up!" he bellowed to make himself heard over the din. "I told you. I don't have any answers for you. You'll have to wait until the press conference at five. Now, pipe down! All of you!"

Recognizing a female reporter from one of the network affiliates in Denver, Casey groaned. She'd hoped to have some breathing room before news of the third murder made it as far as the front range.

"C'mon, let's get out of here before someone spots us," she muttered to Dennis. Ducking her head, she made tracks for the stairs. Doing the same, Dennis followed close on her heels. "Damned bunch of vultures," he snarled.

In the squad room the first thing that caught Casey's eye was the crowd of people in Lieutenant Bradshaw's office. Among them was Sheriff Crawford.

"Uh-oh. This doesn't look good," her partner muttered.

Stopping by Monica's desk, Casey braced the box against the top and nodded toward the glassed-in office. "What's going on in there?"

"I don't know," the assistant replied, looking peeved. "They got here about a half hour ago. That Sheriff Crawford stormed right by my desk as if he owned the place. I tried to stop him, but he ignored me and barged right into the lieutenant's office unannounced. I might as well have been invisible."

"Typical. But don't worry, it wasn't personal. He treats everyone that way.

"Asshole," Dennis spat.

"Lieutenant Bradshaw stuck his head out a while ago and said that as soon as you and Detective Shannon got here, I was to send you both in."

"Oh, great."

Wondering if they stood a chance of backing out of the squad room without being seen, Casey cast another glance toward her boss's office, but luck was not on their side. He'd already spotted them and was waving for her and Dennis to come in.

Resigned, they deposited the boxes on their desks and entered the lion's den.

"You wanted to see us, sir?"

"Yes. Meet Mayor Guthrie, Police Chief Peterson, County Commissioners Albright, Swanson and Attee. Gentlemen, Ms. Albright, this is Detective Casey O'Toole and her partner, Dennis Shannon. Sheriff Crawford you already know."

Everyone in the county knew the sheriff, at least by sight. He'd seen to that. A big, blustery man with a beer belly and a surfeit of "good ole boy" charm when he chose to exert it, he had wowed the voters during the last election with a blitzkrieg campaign of glad-handing, tough talk, false accusations and empty promises to win the office of sheriff.

Never mind that he was a relative newcomer to the area, had virtually no experience in law enforcement or that he'd tap-danced around the important issues. He talked, walked and looked like everyone's image of a western sheriff, with his cowboy boots and big Stetson hat and his authoritative manner. In the closest election in the county's history, he'd edged out longtime sheriff, Dwight Henman, a quiet, mild-mannered man who'd forgotten more about law enforcement than Charlie Crawford would ever know if he lived to be a hundred.

"Wait just a damned minute!" the sheriff boomed. "*This* is the detective you want to head up our task force? The one you want me to turn my case files over to? Why's she's nothing but a girl. A green-behind-the-ears kid, at that."

"Uh-oh," Dennis murmured. "Now he's done it."

"Now, Sheriff," the mayor began in a placating tone. "Let's keep things civil, shall we."

Lieutenant Bradshaw opened his mouth to steer the conversation back to safe ground, but he wasn't quick enough. Casey already had her back up.

Straightening to her full five feet nine inches, she squared her shoulders and fixed Sheriff Crawford with a look that any man in the precinct would have had the good sense to heed.

In general, Casey was good natured and easygoing, but when she got her Irish up her temper was an awesome thing to behold. Feisty, determined and absolutely fearless, she kept her firearms and martial arts skills honed to razor sharpness with three-a-week workouts at the MPD training center and her slender body firm and fit with daily runs.

She also possessed her ancestors' nimble command of the language. When riled, Casey was capable of wiping up the floor—both verbally and physically—with anyone foolish enough to take her on. She didn't have bright red hair for nothing.

"Sheriff Crawford," she began in a deceptively soft voice, taking a step toward the florid-faced man.

Easing back a step, her partner shook his head and murmured to no one in particular, "Look out. It's going to hit the fan now."

"Don't let my freckles fool you. I am *not* a girl. I am a twenty-nine-year-old woman. I've been with the Mears Police Department for almost nine years, and I'll stack my record against anyone's. During my career as a law enforcement officer I've cleared more cases than you've ever even heard of."

She took a step closer, her eyes narrowing, the timbre of her voice growing harsher and more clipped with each word, in direct proportion with her rising ire. "You, of all people, have a helluva nerve, questioning *my* experience and capability." She thumbed her chest. "I *earned* my rank. I didn't finagle my way to Detective First Grade by seducing unsuspecting voters with big talk, twisted half truths and evasions."

The color of his face went from florid red to apoplectic purple.

"Now, see here—"

"O'Toole!" the lieutenant barked. "That's enough. You are talking to a senior law enforcement officer."

Casey clamped her mouth shut, gritting her teeth. Simmering with the need to tear a strip off the man, she shot a smoldering look between him and her lieutenant. Deep inside she knew that her boss was right. No matter the provocation, she was out of line speaking to the sheriff that way. Like it or not, he was duly elected by the people of the county, and as such was entitled to respect. But, oh, that was a bitter pill to swallow.

The best she could muster was a curt nod. "Sorry. The office, at least, does command respect, I suppose."

Sheriff Crawford did not miss her emphasis on the word *office,* nor the contempt in her eyes.

"Dammit! I will not tolerate this kind of insubor—"

"That's enough, Sheriff," Police Chief Peterson intervened. "This bickering is pointless. The decision has been made. We are forming a task force to work these murders, and it will be headed by Detective O'Toole. She has the experience and, as she pointed out, the track record."

It had been that phenomenal record for clearing cases that had put Casey on the fast track for promotion years ago. She had earned her gold shield within three years of joining the force, becoming the youngest person to make detective in the history of the department. After that she had risen quickly from Detective Third Grade, to Second and then First.

Her reputation as a crack investigator was well known among the men and women of the MPD. Casey chalked her success up to hard work and dogged determination, combined with old-fashioned woman's intuition. Some, however, claimed that she had to be psychic.

Again, Sheriff Crawford started to protest, but this time the mayor stopped him.

"Police Chief Peterson is right. And I'm sure the county commissioners agree." He glanced at the three for confirmation, and they all hurriedly bobbed their heads. "The public is already edgy over the first two killings. The media got wind of today's murder when the body was brought into the coroner's office. There's a whole pack of reporters downstairs right now, clamoring for details. When they break this story there's going to be panic. This case calls for experience and a quick resolution. Mind you, we're not disparaging your abilities, Sheriff, but this is a special situation."

"We have a press conference scheduled for five o'clock. That's just a half hour from now," Lieutenant Bradshaw interjected. "We'll announce that we're forming a task force and introduce you to the press, O'Toole. You'll be expected to say a few words. Do what you can to reassure the public that we're on top of things."

Casey had been so caught up in her anger that only now was the full import of the discussion registering with her. She looked around, blinking. "Whoa. Wait a second. You're forming a task force and putting me in charge? Aren't you jumping the gun? Dennis and I have barely begun working our case. And it has yet to be determined that the murders are even related."

"There, you see? Even your own detective thinks you're moving too fast," the sheriff argued.

Ignoring him, Lieutenant Bradshaw focused on Casey. "The M.E.'s preliminary report came back while you were out. The victim had been sexually assaulted prior to death. Which makes the MO identical to the first two cases. It's almost a given that all three murders were committed by one man.

"We need to catch him. And fast. Before he kills again. The task force will be made up of two officers from the State Highway Patrol, two from the sheriff's office, and you and Shannon. If you want to get help from the FBI, go ahead. You call the shots. I'm counting on you, O'Toole. Concentrate all your efforts on this until we nail the bastard."

"Whatever you say, boss," she replied without enthusiasm. For her own part, Casey would have preferred that she and Dennis continue to work their case alone, although she knew that a joint effort would probably yield results quicker.

Heading a task force would certainly look good on her record if they caught the guy. With extreme cases like this, it was normal for the various law-enforcement agencies to work together, but Casey knew that Charlie Crawford wouldn't see it that way.

If Dwight Henman still held the office of sheriff there would be no problem. Given his experience and record, he would probably have been put in charge of the task force, and that would have been fine with her. She admired and respected the man and had confidence in his abilities.

Sheriff Crawford was another story.

"Are we all on the same page now?" the mayor asked.

The sheriff appeared to be struggling to hold his tongue. After a moment he said in a tight voice, "I'll send the files over with the deputies I assign." He stabbed the air with his forefinger in the general direction of Casey and her boss. "But I'm warning you. If you don't produce some positive results quickly, I'm complaining to the governor."

"Don't worry. We will," Lieutenant Bradshaw assured him.

Casey bit her tongue and remained silent.

"And I'd better be kept informed of all developments as soon as they occur."

"Right." The lieutenant glanced around the room. "Okay, that wraps it up. We'll all meet downstairs in twenty minutes."

"Can you handle this dog-and-pony show without me?" Dennis whispered to Casey as they filed out of the lieutenant's office into the almost-empty squad room. "I'd like to get home to Mary Kate and Roger as soon as I can. Maybe pick up a bouquet of flowers on the way. That always seems to cheer her up."

Casey grinned. "Sure. Go ahead. And tell Mom and the others I'll be there as soon as I can. I still have the paperwork to complete."

"Will do. And thanks, Tiger. I owe you one."

"Hi, Casey."

Casey looked around and saw Danny Watson, Keith's younger brother, jump up from the bench in front of Monica's desk and look at her eagerly. She wanted to groan. Danny was a dear, but she didn't have time for him right now.

"Uh-oh." Dennis grinned devilishly and whispered, "Here's your ardent admirer. I'll just leave you two alone."

"Funny, Shannon. Real funny."

"How's it going, Danny?" Dennis said, pausing long enough on his way out to shake the young man's hand.

"Good, Detective Shannon. I'm doing real good."

"Great. I'm glad to hear that. I'm on my way home to my wife and son. I'll see you later, pal."

"See you later," Danny called after him in his slurred speech. As soon as Dennis disappeared down the steps, the young man's attention homed in on Casey again.

"I'm sorry, Danny, but if you're looking for Keith, I can't help you. I have no idea where he is."

"I know where he is. He's downstairs in the basement. In the property room," he supplied eagerly. "You want me to go get him for you?"

"No. No, that's okay."

"He said I could come up and say hi to you while he logged in some stuff. But I wasn't to disturb you if you were busy."

"Well. I'm glad you did." Casey patted the young man's arm. "I'm always happy to see you. I do have some reports to fill out, but you can talk to me while I do. How's that?"

"That would be real nice."

The chore would go quicker if he weren't there, but Casey didn't have the heart to tell Danny that she was too busy to talk to him.

A lot of the guys envied Keith his good looks, and others, like her partner, were irritated by his cockiness, but everyone on the force agreed that he was great with his mentally handicapped younger brother and admired him for the way he looked after Danny.

Her husband had been Keith's partner before he was killed. They had worked out of the Fifth Precinct. Tim had liked his partner, and he'd talked to Casey about Keith often. During those conversations she'd learned that Danny had an IQ of seventy and was therefore only mildly retarded. He could read and write at about a sixth-grade level, drive a car and take care of his own personal hygiene.

"Danny could probably function just fine in a supervised home with other people like himself," Tim had told her once. "But Keith won't even consider it. To him, that would be the same as abandoning him. Keith vows that as long as he's alive Danny will have a home with him. I tell you, sweetie, he may have his faults, but hey, you gotta admire a guy like that."

To his credit, Keith did all he could to help his brother develop as an individual. Four years ago, when Danny turned eighteen, Keith had set him up in a small fish-tank-cleaning business. The work involved was repetitious and something that Danny could handle, and it gave him a sense of independence and boosted his self-esteem.

As far as Casey was concerned, Keith's love for and devotion to Danny more than offset his less-endearing qualities. Added to that, she could never forget that Keith had shot and killed the scumbag who had murdered her husband.

Shortly after that incident, Keith had transferred to the Second Precinct, and consequently she had begun to see more of both him and his brother. They lived within walking distance of the station house, and Danny came by almost every day.

Through the cops' grapevine Casey had heard that Keith had transferred to the Second because he'd prom-

ised Tim before he died that he would look after her.
Though Casey appreciated the thought, she'd tried on
numerous occasions to make it clear to Keith that she
did not need a protector, but her protests had not made
a dent.

He was always hanging around her, showing up at
crime scenes she was working or dropping by her desk
several times a day. Once he'd actually had the nerve to
object when the boss sent her out on a potentially dangerous assignment.

She had set him straight in no uncertain terms, and
he'd apologized and backed off, but he still hovered at
a distance.

Glancing up at Danny's hopeful expression, Casey
sighed. No matter how mixed her feelings were toward Keith, she could not bring herself to disappoint
Danny. For some reason he was hopelessly smitten
with her.

It was a harmless crush, and he was well enough
aware of his handicap and their age difference to know
that nothing could ever come of it. But being around her
made him happy, so she went out of her way to be nice
to him. Besides, he was a dear.

"Did you have a good day?" Casey asked, sitting
down at her desk. She pulled up a blank form on her
computer and began typing in the case particulars.

"Oh, yes. I cleaned two fish tanks all by myself today.
And after we eat dinner, Keith's going to help me clean
another one. This one's too big for me to clean by myself,"
he explained with the big-eyed earnestness of a child.

"That's great, Danny. It sounds like your business is
doing well."

"Yeah." He shifted from one foot to the other and

looked at her as though she'd hung the moon in the sky just for him.

"Hey, there you are, sport." Keith sauntered into the squad room, grinning at his kid brother. "I figured I'd find you here, flirting with the prettiest girl on the force."

Danny turned red from his collar to the roots of his blond hair. He shuffled his feet and stared at the floor. "Ah, Keith, I wasn't…me 'n Casey…we were just talking," he stammered. "That's all."

Keith threw his arm around Danny's shoulders and gave him a rough but affectionate shake. "Hey, sport. Don't get all tongue-tied on me, okay? I was just kidding. I know how much you like Casey." He nudged Danny's side and waggled his eyebrows in an exaggerated leer. "I gotta say, kid, you got great taste in women."

With the two men standing so close, the resemblance between them was striking. Danny would be just as handsome as Keith, Casey realized, if only it weren't for that perpetual blank look on his face.

"Danny and I are about to head out and grab a bite to eat at Giovanni's. Why don't you join us?" Keith nudged Danny's ribs. "You'd like that, wouldn't you, sport?"

Danny nodded his head and turned red again.

"Sounds like fun, but I can't. My mom's expecting me for dinner. Plus, I've got to be downstairs for a press conference in exactly…" She shot back the sleeve of her blazer and glanced at her watch. "Oh, my gosh! I should be there right now. Sorry, guys, but I gotta run."

Grabbing her purse out of the bottom drawer of her desk, Casey took off, calling over her shoulder, "'Night, Keith! See you, Danny!"

Five

Casey maneuvered her car up the long, winding drive through the woods that led to her parents' rural home. The big, rambling house sat about a half mile off the highway on five hundred acres of mainly wooded land ten miles north of Mears. Reaching the clearing that surrounded the house, she noted that her brothers' vehicles were already parked in the circular area out front. No surprise there. News traveled fast among the ranks of the Mears Police Department, and a serial killer on the loose was big stuff.

She'd known that Will, Ian, Aiden and Brian, all Mears cops assigned to different precincts, would have already heard about the case and her appointment to head the task force, so naturally, they had come to offer their support and tell her how proud they were of her. And pump her for information.

Casey glanced toward the house and smiled.

Maureen Collins had radar where her children were concerned, she thought fondly. Her mother had but to take one glance at any of her children's faces or hear their voices over the telephone to gauge their emotions. She was waiting for Casey on the front porch.

She parked behind her brother Brian's pickup, got out of her car, climbed the steps and, with a sigh, walked into her mother's waiting arms.

"Ah, sweeting, what a day you must have had," her mother crooned. Stroking her daughter's hair, she rocked her from side to side. "What a terrible thing. That poor, poor girl. All those poor girls. You must be sick at heart."

Grasping Casey's shoulders, Maureen stepped back, her blue eyes full of understanding and compassion as she raised one hand and stroked her daughter's cheek. "I know it's weighing on you, Casey, love. You always did take things to heart, much more so than your brothers. But don't you fret, now. You'll catch the man who did those terrible things. I know you will. I have faith in you."

Like magic, some of the tension in Casey's neck and shoulders eased. Without her having to explain, her mother always seemed to know what she was feeling, and exactly what to say to make her feel better.

"I hope you're right, Mom. Dear God, I hope you're right."

The two women exchanged another warm hug. For that moment Casey gave herself up to the familiar comfort of her mother's embrace.

She was one of the lucky ones, she thought. No matter what grief or pain or responsibilities fate dealt her, she always had the security of knowing that her family was there for her, her one true safe harbor.

Becky Sue Belcamp would never know that comfort again. Nor would the two other unfortunate women.

Casey closed her eyes and took a deep breath, drawing strength and comfort from her mother's familiar scent, a wonderful, homey blend of smells—laundry soap, face powder, fresh-baked bread and lilac-scented talc.

"Well, come along inside," her mother said, slipping her arm through Casey's. "Mary Kate's bored with keeping her feet up and is dying for some girl talk, and the men are raring to speak with you, as well. You'll get no peace until they've heard every gory detail."

As her mother predicted, the barrage of questions began the instant they walked into the den, where everyone was gathered.

"Hey, Stretch!"

"It's about time you got here."

"What's the deal?"

"Yeah, c'mon over here, sweetheart, and take a load off and tell us all about it," her father, Patrick Collins, added, patting the arm of his recliner.

"Oh, no you don't," Mary Kate intervened. "I've been waiting all day to talk to Casey! I'm sorry, Uncle Patrick, but you and the rest of you bozos can grill her over dinner while I lie here all alone with my TV tray. For now she's mine." She grabbed Casey's hand. "Thank goodness you're finally here. You haven't visited since Sunday."

Seven months pregnant with twins and looking as though she'd pop if you stuck a pin in her belly, her cousin lay propped up on one of the room's two sofas like a beached whale.

"Sorry. I've been busy." Casey bent over the sofa and gave Mary Kate a hug. "Anyway, what's the problem? We talk on the phone every day. Just last night I talked to you for an hour."

"It's not the same," her cousin muttered, pouting. "I'm slowly going out of my mind with nothing to do."

Two-year-old Roger raced through the den with his arms outstretched, making "vroom, vroom" noises. Casey snagged him the second time he raced past her and gave him a smacking kiss. The squirming toddler giggled in protest, then squealed with delight when she tossed him up in the air and caught him. "There you go, little man," she said, setting him on his feet.

"Vroom, vroom!" and he was off again.

"How are you doing?" Casey sat down on the hassock next to Mary Kate. Even blimp-size, her cousin was a knockout. She had black hair, white skin and the big blue eyes that ran in the family. When not pregnant, her figure was a bit more curvy than Casey's, but they were the same height and size.

Ever since she and Mary Kate had been twelve years old and her cousin had come to live with them after her own father and mother, Maureen Collins's sister, had been killed in a car accident, they had been as close as sisters, sharing a room and clothes and their deepest secrets.

"Physically, the babies and I are doing fine," Mary Kate said, patting her enormous belly. "The problem is, the only time I get off this sofa is to pee."

"Which is about every fifteen minutes," her husband supplied, grinning.

"Yes, but Aunt Maureen makes me use the wheelchair just to get from here to the powder room."

"Just following doctor's orders, sweeting," Maureen called from the adjoining kitchen, where she and Casey's mother-in-law, Francis O'Toole, were putting the finishing touches on dinner. "Dr. Thomas said for you to stay off your feet, and that, my girl, is what you're going to do."

Among the Collins clan, Maureen was the eye of the storm, the source of calm and reason in a household filled with high-spirited Irishmen and constant cheerful chaos. As usual, she went about her work without batting an eye, unperturbed by her niece's grousing, her grandnephew's sound effects or the boisterous din created by her loved ones.

"An' 'tis lucky ya are to have your auntie to watch after ya, my girl," Granda Seamus Collins admonished, shaking his bony finger at Mary Kate. "We'll be wantin' those babies to get here healthy an' strong an' with all their parts, now won't we."

"Yes, Granda. I know." Mary Kate lowered her long lashes and gave the old man a penitent look. "I'm just bored."

"It's not easy on her, staying off her feet all the time, you know," Dennis defended. "Anybody would get restless."

Mary Kate gazed at him adoringly and blew him a kiss.

Dennis sat on the opposite end of the sofa from his wife, rubbing her swollen feet and legs and looking back at her with something close to worship in his eyes.

Her beautiful cousin could have had her choice of men. Everyone but Casey had been surprised when she had chosen big, burly, ordinary-looking Dennis Shannon. He, most of all.

Casey knew her cousin better than anyone. Though Mary Kate sometimes appeared to be a flighty, flirtatious sexpot, underneath that femme fatale veneer was a good person with a warm heart and plenty of down-to-earth common sense. Casey had known that good looks, money, power—all the things that beautiful women supposedly want—were not what her cousin longed for in a mate.

What drew her was what was in a man's heart. For all her former big talk about looking for a millionaire, it was basic goodness, kindness and unimpeachable character that mattered to Mary Kate. That was why, four years ago, after Dennis became Casey's partner and she'd gotten to know him, she had introduced him to her cousin.

"Okay, you lot, dinner is ready." Francis placed the last platter of food on the long table and took off her apron as everyone but Mary Kate took their places.

As often happened, Joe and Francis O'Toole and the Shannons stayed for dinner. No sooner had the blessing been said and the platters and bowls been passed around the table than the questions began.

Retired cops themselves, Casey's father, Patrick, and father-in-law, Joe O'Toole, were just as interested in the new murder case as her brothers.

"Is this guy really turning his victims loose and tracking them down?"

"Was your vic a prostitute? I got a buddy over at the sheriff's office who says that's Crawford's theory on the other two."

"Have you identified what kind of weapon the perp's using? Must be a helluva rifle. I heard he blew a hole in your vic big enough to put your fist through."

"Ian, for heaven's sake. Remember where you are," Maureen scolded her youngest son. She and Francis exchanged a long-suffering look, but both women knew that the reprimand was a waste of breath. They had learned years ago that such grisly discussions over dinner were par for the course when you were married to a cop.

"Sorry, guys, but I can't tell you much," Casey said when she could finally get a word in edgewise. She cast an apologetic glance around the table. "I'm under orders not to discuss the case with anyone outside the task force. There are things we don't want leaked to the press, and the fewer people who know, the better."

"See? I told you guys that we couldn't discuss the case." Dennis shot his partner an exasperated look. "They've been giving me the third degree ever since I walked in the door."

"The task force hasn't gotten started yet. Just tell us what you've got so far," her brother Brian coaxed, forking up a helping of roast beef.

"You heard her. Stretch can't discuss the case, so leave her alone," Will ordered.

The eldest and most serious of the Collins siblings, thirty-six-year-old Will had always been the leader. As lieutenant over the squad of detectives at the Fifth precinct, he was the highest in rank of any of them, including their father and Joe, who had both retired with the rank of Detective First Grade. Whenever the occasion warranted, Will didn't hesitate to exert his authority over his siblings.

Not that they took him seriously—not the brothers, anyway.

"Ah, c'mon. What's the big deal?" Brian groused. "We're just family here. It's not like any of us is going to run out and blab to the press."

Will waggled his fork in Brian's direction. "You see. There it is, right there. That kind of attitude is exactly why you haven't made Detective First Grade yet."

The youngest of the brothers, thirty-one-year-old twins, Ian and Aiden, elbowed each other and chuckled. Though Ian was still "in the bag," as they referred to uniformed cops—mainly because of his temper—and Aiden, the most easygoing of them, was only one rank higher as a Detective Third Grade, neither was in the least intimidated by their older brother.

"Yessir, Lieutenant, sir! Whatever you say, sir!" they mocked in unison. "Your wish is our command, sir."

Shaking his head, Will turned his attention back to the food on his plate. "Bunch of clowns," he muttered, but a reluctant grin tugged at the corners of his mouth as he dug into his mashed potatoes.

"Aye, 'tis barbarians they are, the lot o' them, an' that's the God's truth," Granda Seamus declared, glaring from one burly grandson to the next. Then he flashed a mischievous grin and spoiled the whole thing by adding, "An' isn't it just grand?"

The three younger Collins males hooted agreement and cheered the old man until their father stopped them.

"All right, settle down, all of you. And don't encourage them," Patrick ordered, shooting his father a chastising look, which the old man blithely ignored. "Your granda stirs up enough mischief without help from the likes of you three."

Casey ducked her head to hide her grin. It was true. Granda Seamus was an imp.

It was difficult to believe that the frail little wisp of a man was the patriarch of the robust Collins clan. She'd been told that in his youth Seamus Collins had been almost as big and muscular as his son and grandsons, but ninety years of living had worn him down.

However, though thin and stooped, his once-bright red hair now silver, his brain was sharp as ever, his blue eyes still twinkled, and he was spry and full of vinegar. And just in case anyone forgot that, he took great delight in flirting with the ladies and in general being a charming rascal.

Nor, unfortunately for Casey, was Seamus Collins above getting into the occasional donnybrook with his card buddies. Muldoon's, the Irish pub the old men and most of the guys on the force favored, was right around the corner from the Second Precinct station house, so it was always left to her to break up the squabbles that erupted and smooth everything over.

On the average of twice a month she received a call from the bartender at Muldoon's, informing her that she'd better get over there because "the old geezers were at it again." The episodes were a running joke around the Second.

"And your brother is right," her father continued. "We've no business prying into your sister's case. Now, eat your dinners."

After that, though the talk around the table still centered on the murders, the gist of it was confined to information that was general knowledge and speculation about the killer and what it was going to take to catch him.

Dinner at the Collins's home was a time for conversation and catching up with one another and was never rushed. By the time the meal was over, the dishes were done and everyone was again settled around the television in the den, the ten-o'clock news was starting.

Casey's parents, Granda Seamus and her in-laws, along with Dennis and Mary Kate, had already seen the live broadcast of the press conference on the six-o'clock news. Casey had hoped they could skip the ten-o'clock rerun.

Yeah, right, she thought. Fat chance of that happening with her family.

As expected, the first news story was about her case. On the screen a serious young female reporter stood on the forest road near the crime scene describing Becky's death.

"The police say Ms. Belcamp was released a bit farther up the road, just around the next bend. They believe that she was given a short head start, then hunted down by the perpetrator as though she were a trophy animal. Ms. Belcamp apparently did her best to evade the hunter by doubling back, but she only made it as far as this spot in the road.

"The similarities to last month's two murders are chilling, but the police are no closer..."

The young woman went on to take a few subtle digs at law enforcement's failure to apprehend the killer and speculate on whether or not he would strike again. The on-the-spot report was followed by a somber question-and-answer segment between the reporter and the news-show anchorman, then a clip of the press conference.

"Shush, all of you," Maureen said. "Casey's coming on."

"You heard your mother," Patrick commanded his boisterous sons. "Pipe down."

"Ah, there she is," Granda Seamus announced in his thick brogue, beaming and pointing toward the television. "There's our girl. I ask ya now, isn't it grand she is, standin' there all straight and important-like beside himself, the mayor? Ah, 'tis a sight ya are, Casey, darlin'. And 'tis proud we all are of ya."

Casey winced. No matter the reason, that one of his own was on the telly, as her granda called it, was a source of great pride for him.

Sitting beside Casey on the sofa, her father reached for her hand and gave it a squeeze. Recognizing the silent request for forbearance, she managed a smile and murmured, "Thank you, Granda. But I haven't done anything yet."

Seamus bristled. "Well, ya've not had time, have ya. What with that swaggering braggart doin' his best to poke a stick in your spokes at every turn."

"Oh, dear. The one time you're on television and you're wearing *that* blazer," Mary Kate bemoaned. "I've begged you to throw it away. Sweetie, that color does nothing for you. And just look at your hair. They should have given you time to take it down and freshen your makeup. Obviously this press conference was planned by a man," she added with disgust.

Brian rolled his eyes. "Wouldn't you know the only thing you care about is hair and clothes. Jeez, Mary Kate. This is an important press conference, not a style show. Anyway, nobody cares how Stretch looks."

"Oh! If that isn't typical—"

"Pipe down, everybody. I want to hear this," Will ordered, leaning forward in his chair.

Press conferences, in Casey's opinion, were a waste of time and of little value. They usually served merely as a venue for political posturing by those in elected office. This one was no exception.

The mayor, in his most serious and concerned voice, confirmed that a third murder victim had been found, and all indications pointed to a single perpetrator.

The announcement sent a ripple through the crowd of reporters. Several frantically raised their hands to ask a question.

Ignoring them, Mayor Guthrie forged ahead, announcing the formation of a task force—which he theatrically dubbed Operation Hunt for the Hunter—to be headed by Casey. Her appointment to head the task force piqued the attention of the crowd of reporters and again they all began yelling questions at once.

Taking advantage of the pandemonium, the sheriff stepped up to the microphone and took charge. "Now, now," he soothed, raising his hands for quiet. "As has been pointed out to me, Miss O'Toole is an experienced policewoman. I'm sure the little lady will—"

"Little lady?" Aiden yelped, jumping up off the sofa. "Man, you've either got a lot of guts or you're dumber than dirt, putting Stretch down that way. You're going to pay for that remark."

As if on cue, on the screen Casey leaned into the microphone and interrupted. "Correction, Sheriff, but it's *Detective* O'Toole. Not Miss or little lady."

"Woo-hoo!" her three youngest brothers whooped in unison. "Go get him, Stretch."

On the television a few beats of uncharacteristic silence followed, during which the reporters exchanged glances. Like bloodhounds catching the scent, they perked up their ears and turned their attention on the sheriff.

"Whoops," he replied with such patent insincerity that even now, hours later, Casey still itched to throttle him. "Dang it all, I keep forgettin' to do the politically correct thing. I guess I'm just a good ole country boy. In my world, pretty young things like Miss…ah, *Detective* O'Toole, are delicate flowers to be protected. We don't send them out to catch a cold-blooded woman killer."

That produced angry protests and colorful and inventive slurs on the sheriff's ancestry from all the men in the room. Not even Will could contain his resentment any longer.

Untouched by the vilification, on the screen the sheriff continued with a smirk, "But that decision has been made, and we're all just going to have to live with it. I'm sure the little lady will—dang it all, there I go again. What I meant to say is, I'm sure *Detective* O'Toole will do her best to apprehend the killer. And if she has trouble, all she has to do is call on me for help. I won't let her stumble."

"You jackass!" Brian snarled at the screen. "*You're* going to help her catch the killer? You couldn't find your own rear end with both hands."

"Yeah, my friend at the sheriff's office says Crawford is a royal pain in the butt and a total bust as a lawman," Aiden said. "He swaggers around the sheriff's headquarters and insists on running every investigation. Every move the deputies make has to be cleared through him first. According to Dan, the guy knows bupkus about detective work. Their clearance rate has dropped like a stone since he took over from Sheriff Henman."

Will sent Casey a serious look. "Watch your back with this guy, Stretch. It's obvious that his aim is to discredit you." He nodded toward the muted TV screen. "He's already trying to make you look like you're a weak little twit of a female with fluff for brains."

"I know. Don't worry, I'll be on guard." Getting to her feet, Casey raised her arms over her head and stretched. "But for now I'm going home and get some rest."

"But, sweeting, it's so early," her mother protested. "Can't you stay a bit longer?"

"Sorry, Mom, but tomorrow promises to be another stressful day. Anyway, I'm pooped."

"Aye, 'tis time I put these old bones to bed, as well."

Granda Seamus hauled himself up out of his recliner with the help of his walking stick and a hand from Will. He winked at Casey and whispered, "Don't let the bastard grind ya down, darlin'."

"I won't, Granda." She kissed his papery cheek, and he patted hers, his eyes twinkling affection.

Immediately the others followed her lead. By the time Casey had kissed her parents and in-laws goodbye, Brian and the twins were heading out the door.

Will draped his arm around her shoulders. "C'mon, Stretch, I'll walk you to your car."

Though it was June, when the sun went down in the mountains, so did the temperature, and their breath fogged in the cold night air the instant they stepped out onto the front porch. Down the long drive, one by one, three pairs of taillights disappeared into the woods, heading for the highway, a half mile away.

Neither Casey nor her brother spoke as they strolled down the walkway. Still, when they reached her car Will seemed in no hurry to part company.

Casey could tell that he had something on his mind, something more than the serial killings or Sheriff Crawford's scheming. She also knew that it would do no good to prod him. Will would work around to the subject in his own sweet time.

He leaned his hips back against the front fender and crossed his arms over his chest. The pale glow of the front porch light barely illuminated his face, but she could see the concern in his eyes.

"I meant what I said about Crawford, Stretch. Keep your guard up. He's a devious bastard, and he doesn't care whose career he trashes, as long as he can make himself look like a hero.

"A high-profile case like this doesn't happen in our part of the world very often. Crawford knows that since he squeaked into office last fall, people have been having second thoughts about him. If he could take credit for solving the murders and catching this guy, he'd be a shoo-in come the next election, and he knows it."

"I know. Don't worry. I'll be careful." She leaned back against the car, as well, and when Will draped his arm around her shoulders again she edged closer to his warmth. Strangely, though Will was the oldest of the Collins siblings and she the youngest, she had always felt closest to him. Maybe it was because, of the five of them, they were the serious ones.

For the most part Brian was happy-go-lucky and took few things seriously. The twins were artistic at heart, though both vehemently swore otherwise. Aiden, the most easygoing of all of them, was a talented painter and sculptor, and Ian, though he'd never had a single music lesson, could play any instrument he picked up. He also had the voice of an angel, and when pushed, the devil's own temper.

She and Will, however, were the ones who had worked hard in school, the ones who thought things through and weighed the pros and cons before acting. They were deliberate and intuitive and analytical. And, to the others, probably dull as dishwater.

But they understood each other, and had a bond that the others did not share, though they all loved one another dearly.

Casey breathed in a deep draft of frosty air and let it out slowly, her gaze on the star-strewn sky. Last night's full moon had barely begun to wane. The glowing orb appeared so close Casey felt as though she could reach up and touch it. A sense of peace and contentment settle over her. "God, how I love it here," she murmured.

"Mmm. Yet you won't consider moving back."

She shrugged and shook her head. "I can't. Everywhere I look I see Tim. It hurts too much. Yet...I can't stay away. I don't *want* to stay away. This is home. I draw strength from this place. From my family."

"Yeah, we all do," Will agreed, giving her shoulders a brotherly squeeze. "This place is our bedrock, the foundation of our lives. It's where we grew up feeling safe and loved and never alone. It's comforting to touch base with that security now and then. That's why we're all drawn back here and to one another."

It was true. Whenever anything impacted any of them, whether the event spelled trouble or triumph, the Collins clan instinctively came together, as they'd done tonight, without being summoned. And invariably their gathering place was the family home in the woods.

Joe and Francis O'Toole came out of the house and headed toward their home next door, waving and calling good-night, their flashlight beams bobbing as they walked arm in arm. Casey and Will waved back.

The front door opened again and Dennis emerged, carrying Mary Kate in his arms. "'Night," their cousin called, waving to them over her husband's shoulder. "Call me tomorrow, Casey. Okay?"

"I will. Good night."

Patrick Collins walked behind the couple with their toddler draped over his shoulder like a limp rag, sound asleep.

"'Night, all. See you in the morning, Tiger," Dennis called once his family was ensconced in the car. She and Will watched the vehicle circle around to the back of the house and follow the narrow gravel road that led to the cottage, nestled out of sight in the woods behind the two main houses.

Gradually the O'Tooles' bobbing flashlight beams disappeared and the pop of tires on gravel faded. After waving another good-night to his daughter and eldest son, Patrick Collins went back inside. A comfortable silence descended.

"You were just a baby when we moved in here," Will continued in a reminiscent voice, as though the interruptions had not occurred. "So you wouldn't remember all the weekends and evenings the families spent out here while Dad and Joe were building the two families' houses. Mom and Francis usually cooked dinner here in the clearing on a campfire so the men could work until dark. Once electricity was hooked up Dad and Joe rigged lights and often worked until late into the night. We kids were put to bed in sleeping bags in the back of Dad's pickup.

"Sometimes buddies from the job lent a hand, but Dad and Joe did most of the work. It took them five years to finish both houses, but they did it," he said with pride.

"Mmm." Casey and Will gazed at the rambling house and the surrounding forests. She'd heard the story many times before, but she never tired of it.

In the distance a pack of coyotes yipped, and another group on the other side of the valley answered. Close by, a rustling in the undergrowth announced the presence of a forest creature. Probably a deer, Casey thought. Or a bear.

She glanced toward the shadowy line of trees on the east side of the clearing that separated the Collinses' home from the O'Tooles', and the spot where her in-laws had just disappeared down the path that cut through the forest, connecting the two homes. The houses were about a hundred yards apart, screened from each other by the trees but close enough that the old friends and former partners and their wives could enjoy one another's company.

As kids, the five Collins offspring and Tim, the O'Tooles' only child, and later, Mary Kate, had run back and forth at will between the two homes, beating the well-worn path through the woods.

"When Dad and Joe pooled their resources and went into debt to buy this five hundred acres of wilderness land all those years ago, plenty of people thought they were crazy," Will rambled on. "But the joke's on them. These days, with Mears growing like it is, this is considered prime land. Hardly a week goes by without them receiving an offer from a developer to buy the whole parcel. They could make a fortune if they accepted an offer."

Small wonder, Casey thought. Except for the three structures that her Dad and Papa Joe had built—their own homes and the cottage for her and Tim—the property was pristine.

"Mom and Dad will never sell," Casey said with confidence. "Neither will Joe and Francis."

Patrick Collins and Joe O'Toole had been best friends since they were boys. When Patrick had joined the Mears Police Department, Joe had followed, and the two had spent most of their careers as partners.

These days both men were comfortably retired and happy with their lives. This was where they'd sweated and worked together for five years to build their homes. This was where they'd raised their children to adulthood and seen them leave to start lives of their own, and in Tim's case, to die. This was where the two old friends would live out their days.

"Naw," Will agreed. "This place suits them right down to the ground. Of course the house is too big for just Mom and Dad and Granda, but they're waiting for us to give them grandchildren to babysit."

"Huh. With none of us married, that's not likely to happen anytime soon. Mary Kate's kids have taken a bit of the pressure off of us, though. Thank goodness."

"Which brings me to something I wanted to talk to you about."

Ah, here it comes, Casey thought. She'd known that Will had something on his mind. "What's that?"

"When are you going to start living again?"

"Pardon me? What are you talking about?"

"I'm worried about you, Stretch. All you do is work, visit the family and go home to your empty town house. I know you loved Tim. But, honey, he's been gone for more than a year. It's time for you to get on with your life. Get out there. Start dating again."

"Again?" Casey gave a dry chuckle. "When have I ever dated?"

She and Tim had both known since they were about fourteen that they would marry. She could not recall him ever actually asking her out. It had always just been assumed that they would spend their free time together, although, more often than not, they had been accompanied by one or more of her brothers.

"You know what I mean."

"Yes, well, in order to date, someone has to ask you out. That hasn't happened."

"Only because you give off an 'off-limits' vibe.

Lately several guys on the job have asked how you're doing, and I could tell they were interested. They're just waiting for you to give the signal that you're available."

"Yeah, right. And I'm supposed to know how to do that?" She shook her head. "To tell you the truth, I haven't given the matter any thought. Anyway, I'm too busy for a social life right now."

Nor was she interested. Grief had a way of anesthetizing you. She had been numb to any kind of emotional or romantic attraction ever since that awful day when Tim had been killed.

Well…there had been that moment of sizzling lust she'd experienced when Dr. Adams had walked into his office earlier today. But, hey! When a man was that gorgeous and sexy a woman would have to be blind or dead not to respond.

Besides, he was safe. Sort of like having the hots for a movie star. You could let your hormones go berserk and even indulge in a harmless fantasy or two with no harm done because you knew that nothing would ever come of it.

Dr. Mark Adams was in the same category. There was no way a man like him would be interested in her.

"Then make time," Will insisted. "It's not healthy to bury yourself in work. Everyone needs a private life."

"Oh, really?" She shot him a droll glance. "You seeing anyone lately?"

"Nice try, Stretch, but we're talking about you, not me."

Right, Casey thought. No one ever dared discuss Will's private life—not with him, anyway. Any poor fool who tried got cut off with a sharp word and a lethal look that would scared the pants off Lucifer himself.

For the last ten years, ever since Will had been left literally standing at the altar by his high-school sweetheart, Constance Nelson, he had avoided serious relationships.

Casey had led a sheltered life for the most part, but she had no illusions that her big brother lived like a monk. He did, however, confine his dating to women who wanted nothing more from him than he did from them: occasional companionship and sex. Period. The women he dated were not the kind he would ever consider bringing home to meet his family.

"And I want more for you than the solitary life I have," he continued. "You deserve more." He straightened away from the car and opened the door for her. When she'd slid in behind the wheel, he bent and tweaked her straight little nose. "Just promise me you'll think about what I said. Okay?"

Casey huffed out a long sigh. "Okay, okay. I'll think about it. Happy now?"

Mark Adams put down the medical journal that he'd been reading and turned on the TV to watch the ten-o'clock news. As he expected, Becky's murder was the headline item. The young woman reporting from the crime scene had barely begun to speak when the doorbell rang.

Still listening to the news report, he went to answer the summons. He looked through the peephole and opened the door. "Hey, Matt! I didn't expect you back until late."

"I finished up sooner than I expected and caught an earlier flight. Where's Jennifer?"

Mark's twin brother stepped inside and put his suitcase down on the floor of the foyer and headed for the living room. In a hurry to see Jennifer, he'd obviously not taken the time to stop by his own apartment next door.

Mark followed, smiling. Matt's devotion to his daughter never failed to warm his heart—or to make him envious.

"Jen's in her room, watching a movie."

Matt's import-export business required that he travel a lot. When he was gone Mark looked after his niece, so the girl had a room in his apartment as well as in her father's. Mrs. Otis, Matt's live-in housekeeper, looked after Jennifer whenever Mark was called out for a late-night emergency, but thankfully that did not happen often. Both he and Matt preferred that Jennifer be with family as much as possible.

"I'll go let her know that I'm here," Matt said, and headed down the hall.

"Daddy!" came Jennifer's delighted squeal a moment later, bringing another smile to Mark's lips.

He went to the bar and poured two glasses of wine, and when Matt returned a few moments later, he handed one to him.

"Thanks. Jennifer will be out in a minute. The movie she's watching is almost over."

"How was Belgium?" Mark asked, returning to his easy chair.

"Hectic." Sipping his wine, Matt sat down on the sofa and, like Mark, turned his attention to the television screen. "This must be about that woman who was murdered this morning. I heard about it on the radio on the drive from the airport. That makes three in less than two months. This is getting serious."

"Mmm."

The press conference started, and both men listened in silence to the mayor's announcement of the formation of a task force.

Mark stared at the television screen, but it wasn't the mayor who had captured his interest. His gaze fixed on Detective Casey O'Toole, standing behind and slightly to the left.

"They're appointing a *woman* to head up this investigation?"

Mark shot his brother a wry look. "Don't look now, but your chauvinism is showing."

"No, it's not that. It's just that I'm surprised, is all. These murders have all been gruesome. I assumed it would take someone with experience and a tough hide to handle them. I mean, *look* at her. With those big, innocent blue eyes and red hair she looks about nineteen. Hardly the picture of a hard-boiled veteran officer."

"Don't sell her short. Detective O'Toole is bright and determined, and probably very intuitive. My guess is she's the best choice for the job."

"You know her?"

"I met her. Today, as a matter of fact."

"Hmm." Matt conducted a closer study of Casey. "She plays down her looks so they're not obvious at first, but she's quite pretty, really."

"Yes. I noticed," Mark replied quietly, his gaze still fixed on the screen.

Matt took a sip of wine to hide his smile, then turned a sly look on his younger brother. "So, are you going to ask her out?"

"I don't think so. At least…not yet. It's not a good time."

"Why not?"

"Because right now I'm her prime suspect."

"What?" A startled laugh burst from his twin. "Are you serious?"

"Uh-huh. The woman who was killed this morning was a patient of mine. Apparently I was one of the last ones to see her alive."

"You *are* serious. This Detective O'Toole actually thinks you killed those women?"

"Looks that way."

Matt studied his brother. "Did you?"

Tearing his gaze away from the television screen, Mark turned his head and fixed his twin with a hard stare.

Six

Casey read through the first page of the case file on victim number two with growing disbelief. "Your second victim is still a Jane Doe?" She shot a hard look at the sheriff's deputy who had turned over the two files to her. "Why don't we have an ID on this woman yet? It's been a month since she was killed."

Deputy Detective Lewis Manning shrugged. "We checked the missing-persons reports for this county and all the surrounding counties. No one matching her description has been reported missing. We also fingerprinted her and ran it through all the national databases, but we didn't get a hit."

Seated with Casey, Dennis and Lewis around the long table in the conference room, which had been assigned to the task force, were Travis Kemp, the other sheriff's deputy, and state troopers, Hugh Longmont and Hector Comal.

"That's it? That's all the effort you made to identify her?"

"What did you want us to do, go door-to-door showing her picture? There's more than a hundred thousand people in this town and the surrounding county. We don't have that kind of manpower. Like the first vic, she had no identification on her."

Casey flipped open the file on victim number one and scanned the first page. "It says here her name is Selma Hettinger. How did you ID her?"

"One of our deputies recognized her. Plus we got a match on her fingerprints. She'd been arrested a few times."

"For what?" Casey asked, grinding her teeth. If she was going to have to pull every scrap of information out of this guy, he wasn't going to be of much help. Which was probably the sheriff's plan.

Again, the deputy shrugged. "The usual stuff—turning tricks, disorderly conduct. She was a hanger-on. When she didn't have a boyfriend to support her she sometimes worked as a bartender in one of the dives around town. Occasionally she strolled over to Congress Avenue."

"So from that the sheriff assumed that the second victim was also a hooker? The first one was, so it followed that the second had to be, as well?"

"Hey, it's logical. Serial killers usually go for the same type. Look at Ted Bundy. If you line up pictures of his victims they all look like sisters."

That was true, as Casey and every other law enforcement officer in the country knew. Still…her gut told her that hooking for a living was not what the women had in common.

For one thing, Becky Belcamp had been a hardworking young woman from a stable and decent background. Also, the lack of a fingerprint match meant the second vic had never been arrested. She looked to be between thirty-five and forty. With a hooker, the chances of reaching that age without an arrest were almost nil.

Casey continued to flip through the two files. "I don't see anything in here showing that the victims' clothing was sent to the state forensics lab to be tested."

"What's the point? Except for the blood, which was her own, there wasn't anything on the clothing."

"Maybe nothing visible to the naked eye, but there could be foreign fibers, or semen, or other trace evidence. That's what crimes labs are there to determine. I want all the clothing in the first two murders tagged and bagged and sent in for a thorough forensics workup."

"I'll take care of it," Hector volunteered.

"Good. Now, I want you guys to get a list from the DMV of every white, tan, gray or silver van on the western slope. Split the list up between the four of you. Track down the owners and find out where they were at the time of the murders."

"Oh, man," Lewis groaned. "There must be at least a thousand. I hate grunt work."

"That's what most detective work is, Deputy. So let's get busy. You four can work here in the conference room. There are plenty of phones and you won't be disturbed or overheard. While you make calls, Dennis and I will work at our desks. I want to go over these files again to see if there is anything that might have been overlooked."

"I gotta fortify myself with some coffee first," Lewis said, heading for the break room.

"Yeah, me, too," Hugh agreed, and he and Hector followed him while Travis lingered behind.

Casey and Dennis began to gather up the files and the

boxes of the victims' personal belongings that she had checked out of the sheriff's property room.

"Detective, could I speak to you a second?" Travis asked when he was certain the others were out of earshot.

"Sure."

He looked around to be sure no one was listening. "I just want to warn you to be careful what you say to Lewis. He's one of Sheriff Crawford's cronies, one of the guys he brought in after he won the election. I'm not sure he's ever even worked law enforcement before."

"I see. How long have you been with the sheriff's department, Travis?"

"Eleven years. Like most of the men, I don't think much of our new boss, but I've got too many years on the job to chuck it all and go somewhere else.

"I thought you should know that the sheriff ordered Lewis and me to pass along to him anything we learned from working here, and to keep you in the dark if we uncovered anything useful. I won't do that. I won't spy for him or undercut this investigation. You have my word on it. But the thing is…Lewis will."

"Thank you for the information, Deputy. I appreciate the heads up. I'll be sure to watch what I say around Deputy Manning." *And you*, she added silently.

"That's definitely a good idea." He nodded, gave her a grim smile and left the room, presumably, like the others, in search of coffee.

"What do you make of that?" Dennis asked. "Do you believe him?"

"About Lewis? Oh, yes. The only question is whether or not Travis is lying about his own loyalties."

"You think he's setting you up?"

"Who knows? He could be telling the truth. But then

again, the sheriff isn't stupid. He has to know that I don't trust him or his men. Travis's helpfulness and his supposed dislike of the sheriff could be a clever ploy to get me to trust him."

"So what're you going to do?"

"Play it safe. We'll watch what we say around both of them and reveal information on a 'need to know' basis."

"Gotcha. Keep them in the dark as much as possible."

They toted the boxes and files into the squad room and placed them on their desks. Casey fetched them both some coffee, then settled in her chair and picked up a file.

"Before I start on this, I'd better check out Dr. Adams's alibi," Dennis announced, picking up the telephone.

A half hour later, after being transferred from one person to another and being left on hold repeatedly, Dennis hung up the phone with a sigh. "Well, it looks like Dr. Adams is in the clear. St. Mary's Hospital confirmed that he was performing surgery there from four-thirty yesterday morning until after nine. He couldn't have murdered Becky."

"I'm not surprised. That would've been too easy." She stared at several of the crime-scene photos taken of the second victim, flipping back and forth through them, her mouth pursed thoughtfully. "Something is not right here. This woman is no hooker," she mused out loud.

Looking up, Dennis glanced at the photos spread out on her desk. "What makes you say that?"

"She's too well dressed."

"I hate to burst your bubble, Tiger, but there are some high-priced call girls out there."

"I know. But not even the classiest wears Umbrago

shoes." She tapped a photo showing the victim's feet. "Look at these. I drooled over that very same pair of shoes in an ad in a high-toned magazine just last month. That brand runs from eight hundred to two thousand dollars."

"For a pair of shoes!" Dennis squawked.

Casey picked up the telephone.

"Who're you calling?"

"Your wife. She's the savviest shopping maven I know."

Mary Kate picked up on the first ring, and Casey had to smile. Her cousin was so desperate for diversion she kept her cell phone on the end table right beside the sofa, along with various other necessities like the TV remote, her manicure set, makeup bag, hand mirror and a bag full of saltwater toffee, which she craved constantly.

"Hello?"

"Mary Kate. Good. I'm glad you're home."

"Oh, very funny, Casey."

"Sorry, I couldn't resist. Listen, sweetie, I need your help."

"With what?"

"My case, actually."

Before her cousin said another word, Casey could sense her perking up. "Really? You need *my* help with your murder case? Oh, this is exciting. What can I do?"

"This is a long shot, but it's worth a try. I've got a vic wearing Umbrago shoes. I'm hoping that she bought them locally. Is there any place in Mears that carries them?"

"Only two stores," Mary Kate replied with certainty. "Vanders carries a few of their ready-mades, but if you want the custom-fit variety—you know, the kind where they make a mold of your feet, send them to Italy and they hand-make the shoes—you have to order them through Panache. Both kind are expensive, but we're talking really big bucks for the customs. You'd have to be loaded to afford them. And I mean filthy rich."

"Thanks. That's a big help. Talk to you later."

She hung up the receiver, gathered up the pictures and slipped on her blazer. "C'mon, let's go."

"Where're we going?" Dennis asked, already following her.

"Shopping."

"May I help you?" the clerk asked, but her tone and haughty expression as she checked out Casey's dark brown trousers and blazer and green knit tank top and Dennis's off-the-rack suit clearly indicated that she thought they were in the wrong store.

Panache was the only truly chichi shop in Mears. It had opened for business about five or six years earlier to cater to the wealthy retirees and high-powered entrepreneurs and business types who had moved to the area in recent years and now made up the new country-club set.

The inside of the store was pure opulence—lots of marble pillars, plush sapphire-blue carpet and accessories in various gradations of sapphire with accents of silver. An exotic scent wafted through the air, along with the muted strains of classical violin music.

Casey had never been inside the place before. On a cop's salary she doubted that she could afford to so much as press her nose against the window glass. So, apparently, did the clerk.

The woman's snooty attitude raised Casey's hackles, but she held her tongue. Vanders department store had yielded zip. This was their only other hope.

"I hope so," Casey replied. She showed the woman

her badge and introduced herself and Dennis. Instantly, the clerk's expression changed from haughty to shocked.

She splayed her hand against her bosom. "Oh, dear. You're…you're that woman detective who's investigating those murders, aren't you? The one who was on the news last night. I…I can't imagine how we could possibly be of any help to you, Detective."

"I need you to look at a photo and tell me if this woman is a customer here," Casey said, withdrawing the snapshots from the inner pocket of her blazer.

She handed the clerk a head shot of victim number two, and the woman gasped. "Why, that's Mrs. St. Martin. She's one of our best customers. I'm the store manager, but I personally wait on her. She looks… Oh dear, is she one of those murdered women?"

Casey took back the photo. "Do you happen to have an address for Mrs. St. Martin?"

The woman wrung her hands, her shocked gaze glued to the photos until Casey slipped them back into her inside blazer pocket.

"Uh…yes. Yes we do. I'll…I'll get it for you."

The address was located in the most exclusive neighborhood in Mears. Mountain Laurel was a gated community of enormous homes, each estate consisting of ten acres or more of land.

The guard at the gate was at first dubious about letting them inside, even after Casey and Dennis showed him their badges.

Annoyed, Casey reached for the door handle, but Dennis was quicker.

"Sit tight, Tiger. I'll handle this."

He climbed out of the car, straightened to his full height and squared his shoulders. The man's eyes widened, his expression changing from autocratic, to shocked, to one of naked fear.

Bending from the waist, Dennis got in the man's face and scowled. "Listen, you self-important little twit. You've got five seconds to open that gate. Otherwise I'm going to arrest you for obstruction of justice. Got it?"

"Ye-yes, sir."

"Good. I'm glad we came to an understanding." He climbed back into the car and put it in gear.

"Nice work, Hulk," Casey teased her partner as he drove their unmarked car into the heavily wooded neighborhood.

"Thanks. Every now and then, being built like a tank makes this job a heck of a lot easier. I hardly ever have to get physical to put the fear of God into someone. You, on the other hand, would've had to kick that guy's butt for him to take you seriously."

"Hey. I can be intimidating."

"Oh, yeah, right. With those big, innocent blue eyes and that angelic face? Tell me another one."

Casey flounced back in the seat and folded her arms, her face sullen. "I get the job done."

"That, you do." He glanced her way. "C'mon, Tiger, no offense intended. Actually, in some ways your girl-next-door looks are an advantage. You've got the element of surprise on your side. The bad guys never suspect that a sweet young thing like you is capable of giving them a grade-A ass-whuppin'."

Casey slanted him a look out of the corner of her eye, a reluctant smile tugging at her lips. "That's right. And don't you forget it."

"Oh, don't worry, partner. I keep that thought in the back of my mind at all times.

"Ah, there's the house," he said, and turned into a driveway flanked by two marble pillars, one of which bore discreet gold house numbers. The property, at least what they could see as they headed up the drive, was surrounded by a tall privacy hedge. Evidently, the home owners felt the twelve-foot stone wall around the entire neighborhood and the guard at the gate provided all the security they needed.

"Would you look at this place?" Dennis murmured as they climbed the steps to what looked like a French palace, set against the backdrop of craggy mountains. "I bet their gardener makes more than we do."

"Probably," Casey agreed. She rang the doorbell, and they could hear the series of melodious notes echoing through the interior of the house. A moment later a Hispanic woman in a maid's uniform answered the door.

"Sí?"

"Police," Casey said, showing her badge. "We're looking for Mr. St. Martin."

"The *señor,* he ees not here."

At least now they knew there was a Mr. St. Martin, Casey thought. "Do you know where we can find him?"

The woman held up one finger. *"Uno momento."* When she returned she handed Casey a business card. "Señor St. Martin's office," she said, pointing to the card.

"Thank you. Is Mrs. St. Martin home?"

"No, no." She shook her head. "Gone on trip."

"When did she leave?"

The woman shrugged her shoulders in the classic "I don't know" gesture.

"I see. Well, thanks for your help."

"What did *that* mean?" Dennis asked when they returned to the car. "That she didn't understand the question, or that she didn't know when Mrs. St. Martin left? And if it was the last, how could that be?"

"I have no idea. Maybe Mr. St. Martin can enlighten us. I'm interested to know what kind of husband doesn't report his wife missing when he hasn't seen or heard from her for more than a month."

The address on the business card took them to the Powers Building on Bridger Boulevard, the same building in which Dr. Adams's office was located. "Well, well," Casey murmured. "Isn't this interesting?"

"Could be a coincidence," Dennis offered.

"I suppose. Except I don't believe in coincidence."

They took the elevator to the third floor and located the office. The gold-leaf sign on the door read Jason St. Martin, Investment Broker. Inside, the woman sitting at the desk painting her long fake nails looked as though she'd stepped from the pages of a girlie magazine—blond, busty and vacuous. Her reaction when Casey and Dennis showed their badges and asked to see Mr. St. Martin deepened the impression.

She didn't turn a hair, merely looked at the badges, blinked her fake eyelashes twice, then, with a resigned sigh, pressed the intercom button.

"Yes, Monique?"

"There are a couple of cops here to see you."

"The police? Here? What for?"

"They didn't say. Should I send them in or what?"

"Yes. Yes, of course. Send them in."

Jason St. Martin stood up and introduced himself when they entered, reaching across his desk to shake their hands. He looked to be in his forties, fairly fit and nice-looking, in a patrician sort of way.

"I must admit, I'm a bit shocked," he said when they'd all taken their seats. "I've never been visited by the police before. How may I help you, Detectives?"

"We won't take up much of your time, Mr. St. Martin. We just have a few questions to ask regarding your wife."

"Madeline? Is she in some sort of trouble?"

"There's no easy way to say this. Sir, we believe that your wife has been the victim of foul play."

Jason sat forward in his chair. "Wh-what do you mean? Are…are you saying that Madeline is…is dead?"

"We have some photos we'd like for you to take a look at and tell us if you recognize the woman."

He looked as though he might be sick. "A…a dead woman? You think it's my wife?"

"Yes. Are you up to that?"

"Just a minute." He closed his eyes and took several deep breaths. "All right. I'm ready now."

Casey withdrew the photos from her blazer pocket and spread them out on the desk, and immediately Mr. St. Martin groaned. "Ah, God, no. Maddy. Oh, my poor Maddy." He touched one of the photos tenderly. "Ah, Maddy what did you do?"

"So this *is* your wife?"

"Yes. Yes, that's Madeline. What happened to her?"

"She was shot. We believe she was the victim of a serial killer."

"Oh, my God! Are you talking about that monster who is hunting women down like animals? Everyone is talking about those cases and it's all over the news."

"Yes, I'm afraid so."

Covering his face with his hands, he began to sob.

"Oh, my poor Maddy. What she must have gone through."

"Mr. St. Martin, your wife was killed more than a month ago. We find it curious that you haven't filed a missing-persons report on her."

He pulled his hands away from his face. Casey had to give him credit. His eyes were moist and red-rimmed, and tears streamed down his cheeks. "I can explain that. My wife and I have been going through a rough patch lately, so we agreed to…well, I guess you'd say…take a break."

"A break? From what?"

He spread his hands. "From each other, from our marriage. It's worked in the past. After a few months apart, we are always happy to be back together. Our relationship is revitalized."

"When you say you take a break from marriage, does that mean that you both see other people?" Casey asked.

"It means, Detective, that for that specified period we are both free to pursue whatever interests we choose. Whether or not my wife was involved with someone else, I couldn't tell you. We never question each other about our time apart. But if she was, I promise you, it wasn't serious on her part."

"And that doesn't bother you?" Dennis asked in an incredulous voice. "That your wife might be sleeping with other men during your so-called breaks?"

Standard procedure for cops was to maintain a neutral demeanor during an interview. Casey was certain her partner did not realize that his face was screwed up in a grimace of revulsion. Being a solid, true-blue husband and family man, Dennis found the whole idea of an open marriage like the St. Martins' distasteful and foreign. So did she, for that matter.

"I tried not to think about that. Detective, I realize that you are probably shocked by our arrangement, and I admit, it is unconventional, but it works for us. My wife is—was—a restless spirit. I've always known that. And I must admit, to some extent, so am I. But we do—did love each other.

"This time we agreed that we would have no contact for three months. So naturally I wasn't concerned when I didn't hear from Maddy. Quite the contrary, I would have been surprised if I had."

"Can you tell us why her maid believes that she's on a trip?"

"When Isabella called to ask me where Madeline was, I assumed she'd picked up and gone on one of her jaunts, so that's what I told her."

"And you don't think it's strange that your wife would leave on a trip without telling her maid?"

"Not really. Whenever the mood struck her, Madeline would simply pick up and go. As I explained, she was a free spirit. A free spirit with the means to go wherever she pleased and do whatever she pleased." He closed his eyes and seemed to be fighting off pain. "And now that adventuresome bent of hers has gotten her killed. Oh, God, how will I go on without my Maddy?"

Mr. St. Martin put his head in his hands and succumbed to a few more moments of sobbing. Finally, taking a monogrammed handkerchief from his pocket, he dabbed at his eyes and struggled on. "You have to understand, Maddy didn't like to feel tied down or that she had to answer to anyone. A few times in the past she left without even telling me, and she seldom bothers to tell her maid where she's going or when she'll be back. You can ask any of our friends. They'll all confirm that was Maddy's way."

"I assume that you don't live at your Mountain Laurel address during these…breaks," Casey said.

"No. I own a house out on Black Bear Lake. Actually, it's more of a hunting cabin, but it's comfortable. I'm staying there."

"I see. Are you a hunter, Mr. St. Martin?" she questioned, striving to keep her tone neutral. The one thing that was obvious from their investigation so far was the killer was an expert tracker and hunter.

"Not a serious one," he replied absently, his mind clearly not on her questions. "But I've bagged my share of deer and elk."

"We're going to need directions to your cabin and a telephone number there, if there is one. Just in case we need to contact you again about your wife's case."

Jason St. Martin stared into space, his red-rimmed eyes unfocused, lost in thought. It took a moment for Casey's request to register. "What? Oh…certainly. I'll, uh…I'll give you my cell number, as well." He scribbled down the information and handed the sheet of paper across the desk to her. "I want whoever killed my wife caught. I'll do whatever I can to assist you to do that. If you think it will help, I'll post a reward."

"We appreciate that, Mr. St. Martin, but hold off on the reward for now. That usually brings out the crackpots and con artists and causes more trouble than it helps.

"But if you truly want to help, perhaps you could tell us where you were on the evening of May 2 through the morning of May 3?"

"May 2 and 3? Off the top of my head, I can't say for certain, but I can check my calendar. Why do you want to know?" In the middle of punching his Palm Pilot with a stylus, he stopped and stared at Casey with horror. "Oh, dear Lord. Is that when...when Maddy was...?"

"Yes," she replied as gently as possible.

"And you suspect *me?* You think *I* killed my wife?"

"At this point we're looking into all possibilities. If you are innocent, I'm sure, as a grieving husband, you'd want us to leave no stone unturned. All you have to do is account for your whereabouts the nights before and through the dawn hours of April 3, May 3 and June 1, and we can eliminate you as a suspect."

"I see," he said, his voice tight. "I do recall that on April 1 Madeline and I attended an April Fools Charity Ball at the country club. I was extremely hungover and sick as a dog for two days afterward. I remember I counseled a client on the third feeling as though the top of my head was going to blow off any second."

"What time on April 3 did you meet with your client?"

"Around noon. We had a business lunch at the Timberline."

"And where were you the previous evening until dawn?"

"Sleeping."

"Is there someone who can verify that?"

"My wife—" He closed his eyes. "No. I guess not."

"How about your maid?"

"She has Sundays and Mondays off. That particular week she had gone to visit her sister in Grand Junction."

"I see. And the other days I mentioned?"

"April 30 was when my wife and I decided to take the break from each other, and I moved to my hunting cabin. I assume that I was there since there are no social engagements noted on my calendar for those evenings. I can't recall with any degree of certainty what happened on specific days that long ago, but I've spent every night at my cabin since I moved out of our Mountain Laurel home."

"Can anyone corroborate that you were at your cabin?"

He raked his fingers through his hair, his face pale and haggard. In the few minutes they'd been there he seemed to have aged ten years. "I doubt it. No one saw me. My closest neighbor out at the lake is at least a mile away. Not even the lights are visible through the woods."

"So, in essence, you have no alibi for the times of any of the murders."

"I suppose not. Look, Detectives, I realize that when a married woman is murdered the husband is always the first one you suspect, but why in God's name would I murder two strangers? It doesn't make sense."

"Serial killings never do."

"Do you know of anyone who would want to harm your wife, Mr. St. Martin?" Dennis asked.

Jason sighed and pulled his hand down over his face. "No, not really. Maddy could be sharp with the servants, and I guess a bit overbearing at times. There are some among our set who refer to her as Rich Bitch Number One, but that's mostly jealousy. I can't imagine any of them harming her."

After a few more routine questions, to which they received seemingly straightforward if distracted answers, Casey and Dennis left.

"Well? What do you think?"

Dennis punched the down button for the elevator with more force than necessary. "I think I need a shower. Those people are sick. They call that a marriage? If that's how the rich live, then I'm glad I'm middle class."

The elevator doors opened and Casey started to step into the cubicle, then hesitated when she saw who was inside.

"Detectives," Dr. Mark Adams said, smiling pleasantly. "This is a surprise."

Seven

Casey had forgotten what an impact Dr. Adams had on people. Or at least, she'd refused to think about the impact he had on *her*. It wasn't merely his looks, though they were stunning. There was a magnetism about him, an aura of intense masculinity that reached out and enveloped you. Her first glimpse of him took her breath away and kicked her heart rate up several notches.

The medical smock was gone. In its place he wore a charcoal-gray suit, crisp white shirt and a charcoal-silver-and-wine-striped tie. Merely looking at him made her mouth water.

The cop in Casey told her to step inside the elevator and take advantage of the opportunity to question the doctor further. At the same time, the woman in her immediately went on red alert, urging her to keep her distance, to make an excuse and wait for the next elevator.

Before she had a chance to act on either impulse, the decision was taken from her when Dennis placed his hand on the small of her back and nudged her into the elevator.

"Hiya, Doc," her partner said amiably. "How's it going?"

All Casey could manage was a nod.

"Actually, this is turning out to be a very good day," Dr. Adams responded, his gaze fixed on Casey. "And how are you, Detective O'Toole?" The corners of his eyes crinkled when he smiled at her, and amusement gleamed in the silvery gray depths, as though he knew something funny that she didn't.

Dammit! No man had a right to be that attractive, Casey thought. There ought to be a law that men like him had to wear a sign that read, Women Beware—May Be Dangerous To Your Emotional Health.

"I'm fine."

Disgusted with herself for letting him get to her, she turned and stared in silence at the floor indicator and tried to pretend he wasn't there. Not many things flustered Casey, and it irritated her that Dr. Adams seemed to have such an unsettling effect on her.

"Were you on your way to see me, by chance?" he asked.

"No. We had business with someone else in the building."

"That's too bad. I was hoping you'd come to tell me that my alibi had checked out and I was no longer a suspect."

Casey glanced at him over her shoulder. "I could have picked up the telephone and done that. Actually, your whereabouts yesterday morning was confirmed. However, we don't notify suspects when their alibis check out. If you don't hear from us again, you can safely assume that you've been eliminated from the suspect list."

"So…have I?"

"Not quite. We're also looking at two other murders. If you can tell us where you were from the evening of April 2 through around dawn the next day, and from the evening of May 2 until dawn on May 3, you will be in the clear on all counts."

"Wonderful. I'll get that information to you as soon as I can."

"Fine. There's no rush."

"Maybe not for you, but I have a personal reason for wanting to be taken off your suspect list."

The statement hung in the air, sending out tiny shock waves, like the reverberations of a struck gong. Casey could feel his gaze on her profile, and she knew that he was waiting for her to ask what his reason was, but she remained silent. Some things you were better off not knowing.

The elevator stopped in the lobby, and Dr. Adams held the door open. "Go ahead. I'm going down to the parking garage."

With a nod, Casey stepped out.

"See ya, Doc," Dennis said, following her.

"Right. I'll phone you soon, Detective O'Toole," the doctor called after them.

Casey beat a hasty retreat across the lobby and out the door, a tingle prickling down her spine as she felt Mark Adams's gaze on her back.

"What did you do that for?" Dennis asked, hurrying to keep up with her. "If we're certain the killer in all three cases is the same man you know the doc can't be guilty of the first two murders."

"I know. But it won't hurt him to sweat a little."

"Well, number one, I don't think the doc's worried. He knows he's innocent. And number two, why have you got it in for the man? He seems like a nice guy to me."

"I'm sure he is. He just makes me nervous, that's all."

"Oh, really?" Grinning, Dennis put his hands into his trouser pockets and jingled his change as he ambled along beside Casey. "I've never known any man to make you nervous, Tiger. I'd say that bodes well for the doc. At least he's got your attention."

"Oh, shut up, Shannon."

Casey and Dennis spent the remainder of the day interviewing the St. Martins' friends and neighbors, both those in the Mountain Laurel development, and the few who lived full-time at Black Bear Lake.

The St. Martins' friends and acquaintances were, for the most part, happy, some even eager, to talk about the couple's unconventional marriage. Apparently the arrangement raised eyebrows even among the privileged, who were accustomed to a lifestyle of self-indulgence. However, they all agreed that despite their bizarre marital arrangement, Jason St. Martin and his wife got along well.

Before returning to the station house, Casey and Dennis also canvassed the staff at the country club and verified that Jason and Madeline had, indeed, attended the charity ball together on April 2.

However, when it came to revealing anything of a personal nature about the members of the club, the manager was circumspect and protective to the extreme. The man obviously knew that when working for the wealthy, discretion was a requisite for job security. It took the threat of arrest for obstruction to get him to answer Casey's questions, and even then she had to drag the answers out of him.

If the man was to be believed, throughout all the years the St. Martins had been members, he had never witnessed any signs of friction between them. He also reluctantly confirmed Jason St. Martin's story that on the night of the charity ball both he and his wife had left the country club in the early hours of April 2 in an inebriated state.

"What do you think?" Dennis asked when they headed for the station house at the end of their shift.

Casey leaned her head back on the seat and sighed. "That we've put in an awful lot of legwork with little to show for it. Tomorrow is Friday, review day. The boss definitely isn't going to be happy."

That was putting the situation mildly.

Storming into the task-force room the next morning, Lieutenant Bradshaw barked, "Okay, people, tell me what we've got so far." He sat at the head of the long table, his sharp gaze skewering Casey, who occupied the hot seat at the other end.

"Not much," Casey admitted. She glanced at Lewis, seated halfway down the table from her, and saw his lips twitch in a smirk. "We've identified the second victim, at least."

Lewis's smirk collapsed. "How'd you do that?"

"Old-fashioned detective work," Casey replied, and had the satisfaction of seeing the deputy's jaw tighten and angry color climb his neck.

"Her name is Madeline St. Martin. Wealthy, married, though the marriage was on hold at the time of her death."

"On hold? What does that mean?" the lieutenant growled.

Casey explained the St. Martins' unusual arrangement, and got the same reaction from the others around the table that she and Dennis had experienced.

"The husband has no alibi for the times of any of the murders, but there's nothing to tie him to any of them, either.

"I did some checking into the St. Martins' finances. Jason has a small investment firm, but from all accounts he isn't a big player. It's his wife who has money. Lots of it. They've been married for twelve years. No children. He stands to inherit, provided no long-lost relatives appear to challenge the will. That gives him a possible motive to kill his wife, but not the other two women. There's no connection there that I can find."

"Maybe he killed the other two to throw us off the scent," Deputy Kemp offered. "So we'd blame his wife's death on a serial killer, instead of looking at him as a greedy husband."

"Perhaps. But that's a stretch. We need hard evidence to make a charge like that stick.

"From all accounts Jason and his wife got along well. He had free access to her money to live whatever kind of life he wanted. He even had occasional periods of freedom to cat around if he was so inclined. If he has a girlfriend on the side, someone he cares enough about to want to bail out of the marriage and take Madeline's money with him, Dennis and I have yet to discover her, and believe me, we've looked. We spent the entire afternoon questioning his friends and neighbors. They all claim the St. Martins were happy together."

"What about the lead on that doctor?" the boss asked.

Lewis gave her a sharp look. "What lead? You didn't tell us about any doctor."

"It turned out to be nothing. Becky Belcamp had an appointment with a doctor on the day she disappeared, but she returned to her health studio afterward, and the doc had an alibi for the time of her death."

"You should have told the rest of us, anyway," Lewis complained.

"Why? As I said, the lead was a dead end. I'll decide what is relevant and what's not. I'm not going to waste time relaying every false lead that Dennis and I run down."

She turned her gaze back to the lieutenant. "I may be wrong, but I don't think Jason St. Martin committed these murders. No more than Becky Belcamp's father or one of her brothers. We've got three victims—one a hooker, one a wealthy socialite and one a decent young woman from a middle-class background. They have nothing in common."

"Well…there is one thing," Dennis interjected almost reluctantly. "Reading through the files, I noticed that they all had red hair. Dyed, in all three cases, but red all the same."

Casey had noticed the same thing. The discovery had sent a chill down her spine and made her strangely uneasy. She'd told herself that it meant nothing. It was just coincidence.

Except, as she had repeatedly told her partner over the years, she didn't believe in coincidence.

Lewis chuckled. "Better watch out, O'Toole. With that flaming mane of yours, you may be next."

A beat of uncomfortable silence followed, during which the others shifted in their seats or cleared their throats, looking anywhere but at Casey or the lieutenant. All, that is, but Dennis.

"You jerk," he snarled, rising halfway out of his seat.

Casey put her hand on his arm. "No, don't," she whispered. "Let it go."

"Sit down, Shannon!" the boss barked.

Dennis clenched his jaw and glared across the table at Lewis, but he sat back down.

When the lieutenant was certain peace had been restored, he focused on the deputy. "If that's your idea of a joke, it's not funny. I don't want to hear any more remarks like that in this office. Got it?"

Lewis folded his mouth into a thin line and nodded.

Lieutenant Bradshaw looked around the table at the other men. "How is the canvass on the light-colored vans going?"

"There turned out to be more than eighteen hundred light-colored vans in this and the surrounding counties. We've barely made a dent in the list," Hector replied. "Of the ones that we checked out, we haven't been able to place any of them in the vicinity of Ms. Belcamp's exercise studio two days ago at the time of the abduction. But we'll keep plugging away. Maybe we'll come up with a possible perp."

"Do that." The lieutenant's gaze zeroed in on Casey again. "So what's your next move?"

"I had hoped that we could wrap up this case on our own, or that we'd at least be further along by this point, but since we aren't, I don't think we have any choice but to bring in the FBI. I'll give them a call and see what help they can give us.

"Once that's set up, I'd like to take a look at the first two crime scenes. I know that the sheriff and his men have already gone over both sites, but who knows. Dennis and I may spot something that didn't turn up the first time around. It's worth a shot."

"Do it," the lieutenant said. "The rest of you keep plugging away at that DMV list."

Following protocol, Casey put in the call to the local FBI office. They stalled her, saying they'd have to run the request by the regional office in Denver. Denver, of course, had to contact FBI headquarters in Washington, D.C. It was almost noon when Casey finally received a call back.

She talked to several different department heads and specialists in the field of serial killers. Every person to whom she spoke had to be convinced that they were, indeed, dealing with one. She spent hours describing over and over each of the cases and their similarities. It took the remainder of the morning to convince the powers-that-be at FBI headquarters to send someone to assist them, but finally she succeeded.

When she got off the telephone, Casey stuck her head into the lieutenant's office. "I just finished speaking with FBI. The only help they can give us is on the forensics and profiling. For them to take over the case we'd have to have evidence that the perpetrator had killed in other states, which would make his spree an interstate crime."

"So where do we stand?"

"I told them that we'd take whatever help we could get. Apparently there are a lot of serial killers at work right now. It'll be ten days to two weeks before they can send us a profiler.

"In the meantime Dennis and I will keep going over the files and photos. Right now we're going to grab a bite of lunch, then we'll take one of the deputies, probably Travis, and have him show us the first two crime scenes."

The lieutenant nodded. "Your call, O'Toole. Just keep in mind that we've got every politician and petty bureaucrat from the governor on down breathing down our necks."

"I'd like to see Detective O'Toole," Mark said to the sergeant at the front desk.

The burly uniformed officer pointed with the eraser end of his pencil to a set of stairs against the far wall on his left. "Second floor. Top of the stairs."

"Thanks." So this was what a police station looked like, Mark thought. He looked around as he crossed the room and headed up the stairs.

The main lobby was smaller than he'd expected and was filled with uniformed officers going about their business. Two unsavory-looking characters sat handcuffed to the bench across from the sergeant's desk, and an officer holding a cursing, scuffling, handcuffed man by the back of his shirt collar manhandled him through a door marked Holding Cells.

This was a rough, raw, gritty environment, a slice of life that few saw, or could handle. Most would not even want to try. What, he wondered, would draw a woman to such a life? Especially a delicate, feminine woman like Casey?

He smiled to himself. That was part of the attraction, he realized. The mystery of Casey O'Toole.

From the moment he first saw her he'd felt this irresistible attraction. It was stronger than anything he'd ever felt for any of the women with whom he'd been involved. He couldn't stop thinking about her. It was as though she'd grabbed hold of his heart and mind and wouldn't let go.

Maybe it was because she was unlike any female
he'd ever met. She was obviously intelligent and competent, otherwise she would not have made detective at
such a young age. He guessed her to be twenty-six or
twenty-seven, tops, even though she looked about nineteen. Feisty, independent and strong, she brimmed with
a confidence that radiated from within her.

Not to mention she was downright adorable. With all
that flaming hair, skin as flawless and cool as cream, and
big blue eyes, she almost glowed. And that trim, taut
body immediately brought to mind erotic thoughts of
hot, sweaty nights; cool, wrinkled sheets and a pair of
long, silky legs wrapped around…

Whoa, Adams, slow down. You're getting ahead of
yourself, Mark cautioned with a chuckle, shaking his
head to dislodge his X-rated thoughts. Way ahead. You
don't even know the woman yet.

But he intended to.

On the second-floor landing, a hallway led off to the
right and the stairs continued up to the third floor. A uni-
sex restroom sign marked the door to his immediate left
and straight ahead an open doorway led into a large
room crowded with desks. Just inside the room, a young
woman sat at a desk positioned at a right angle to the
door. Beyond her Detective Shannon lounged back in his
chair before a desk that was butted, face-to-face, against
another one just like it. There was no sign of Casey.

"I'm looking for Detective O'Toole," he told the
young woman. "My name is Mark Adams."

The young woman glanced up, then did a double
take, her eyes widening as she focused on him.

"Uh, she's…uh…"

"Hey, Doc. What brings you here?" Dennis said,

looking up from his file. He waved him over. "Come on in. Have a seat."

Mark sat down in the chair next to Dennis's desk. "I was in the neighborhood, so I thought I'd stop by with that information for Detective O'Toole. And to tell you the truth, I've never been inside a police station before and I was curious."

Dennis chuckled. "Well, it ain't much. Not as fancy as your office, that's for sure. But we're used to it."

"Is Detective O'Toole around?"

"She's stepped out. She'll be back in a minute." They both knew that Mark could just as easily give his information to Dennis, but neither man mentioned that.

The burly detective eyed him. "You know, Doc, you look real fit. Are you, by chance, a runner?"

"Yes, I am. I try to run a few miles every day."

"I thought so. You have that lean look." Folding his hands over his midriff, Dennis assumed a bland expression and added, "You know, Casey's a runner, too."

"Is that so?"

"Yes. She gets up every morning at the crack of dawn and runs three miles through Arvada Park."

"Really?"

To anyone observing they were merely having an innocuous chat to pass the time, but a look of silent communication passed from Dennis to Mark, and the message could not have been more clear if it had been flashed on a neon sign: Dennis knew what he was up to and approved.

"That's not far from my apartment building. I live about five blocks south of there."

"Is that so?" Dennis replied. "Casey lives on Beeker Street at the north end of the park."

"In that row of neat town houses right across the street from the park?"

"Yep. Those are the ones. Hers is the redbrick with white trim. The colonial model, second from the east end."

"Yes, I know the one." Thanks for the info, his gaze added.

A door along the front wall, which obviously connected to the same bathroom as the one in the hallway, opened, and Casey walked into the squad room, her head down, rubbing lotion onto her hands. "By the way, Dennis, I forgot to tell you, after lunch we have to swing back by here to pick up Travis. He's going with—" She looked up and came to a halt. "Dr. Adams. What're you doing here?"

She quickly schooled her features, but not before Mark caught the flustered look that raced across her face.

He smiled. Oh, yes, she was aware of him, all right. And it was more than the superficial attraction that most women felt for him. He got under her skin, the way she did his. She tried to fight the reaction, but it was there all the same. He could see it in her eyes.

"Hello, Detective. I stopped by to give you my whereabouts on the dates we discussed. I've written the information down for you," he added, holding up a slip of paper.

"You could have given that to Dennis, or called the information in. It wasn't necessary to make a trip over here."

"No problem. It's not that far from my office to here. Besides, as I mentioned before, I have my reasons for wanting to get this matter cleared up as soon as possible." He waited a beat, hoping she'd ask why, but, as before, she merely nodded.

"All right." She took the slip of paper. "I'll have someone check this out right away."

Mark watched her sit down at the desk that faced her partner's. She looked up at him and widened those big blue eyes. "Was there anything else, Doc?"

Mark's lips twitched. It was a clear dismissal—no chitchat, no flirting, no effort to get him to hang around. He had to admit, her response to him was a novel and refreshing change. Still…he wouldn't mind a *little* encouragement.

"Not yet," he replied. "I'll check with you later, Detective, to see if I'm cleared." He nodded at her partner and said, as though they were old buddies, "See you around, Dennis."

Casey looked up, disquieted by his remark. What did he mean, "not yet"?

Keith came in the door as Mark was going out, and both men murmured an "excuse me" and stepped aside to let the other pass. For a moment they stood side by side, the two most fantastic-looking men that Casey had ever seen. Why, she wondered, did the sight of one do funny things to her insides, while the other evoked merely an abstract sort of appreciation? She shook her head. One of nature's mysteries, she supposed.

"Who was that guy?" Keith asked, stopping by her desk.

"Just a material witness in a case of mine."

"Oh. I thought for a minute there that maybe you had a boyfriend."

Her partner opened his mouth to speak, but Casey stopped him with a warning look. Giving a little snort, she rolled her eyes. "Hardly."

"Did you need something, Watson?" Dennis asked when the other detective hitched one leg and sat down on the corner of Casey's desk. "If not, Casey and I are kinda busy. We were about to head out."

"Actually, I just wanted to ask this lovely lady if she'd have a drink with me and Danny at Muldoon's after work. It's his birthday, and I promised him that I'd invite you. Several of the guys will be there. Oh, and you're welcome, too, Shannon," he added as an afterthought.

"It's Danny's birthday? I wish you'd told me earlier."

"Why, do you already have plans?"

"No, it's not that. At least...none I can't adjust a bit for Danny. I would just liked to've had time to get him a nice gift. Of course I'll be there."

What she wanted to do was go home, take a long, hot soak, have her customary telephone chat with Mary Kate, then climb into bed with the book that she was currently reading. But even if it weren't Danny's birthday, she couldn't do that. It was her in-laws' anniversary, and the family was planning a celebration. She would have to leave Danny's party early in order to make an appearance at Joe and Francis's party.

She wished that she could skip the birthday party. Muldoon's was not only her granda's favorite hangout, it was the preferred watering hole for the cops of the Second Precinct. Occasionally Casey stopped by the bar after a difficult shift for a beer with the guys, or to celebrate the retirement or promotion of a fellow officer, but tonight she wasn't in the mood. If it were anyone but Danny, she would beg off.

"Great," Keith said. He grabbed her hand and kissed it before she could stop him. "See you there, doll."

Casey waited until she heard Keith's footsteps disappear down the stairs. Then she pointed her finger at her partner. "Don't even think about bailing on this, boyo. If you think I'm going to Muldoon's alone, think again. You call Mary Kate right now and tell her you're going to be a little late."

Expecting an argument from him, she braced to counter any excuse he gave. Instead he surprised her.

"I'm not planning to bail on you, Tiger. I like Danny, too. Besides, I don't trust Watson where you're concerned. I've got a hunch he'd like to add you to his long list of conquests, and I mean to see to it that doesn't happen."

"Oh, for Pete's sake. First it's Dr. Adams, now Keith. Why, suddenly, have you got it in your head that every single man I know is lusting after me? Did my fairy godmother fly in when I wasn't looking and wave her magic wand to make me irresistible? Jeez, Shannon. Get a grip."

"All right, all right, maybe I'm wrong. But I'm going to Muldoon's with you tonight, anyway. Now, gimme that," he said. Standing, he leaned across their desks and snatched up the slip of paper the doctor had given her.

"That can wait."

"Oh, no, you don't. You've kept the doc on tenterhooks long enough. It's time to give the man a break."

Casey fidgeted while Dennis made a few calls, checking her wristwatch frequently and tapping a pencil against her desktop, but her partner ignored her impatience. When he finally hung up the receiver he had a peculiar look on his face. "You're not going to believe this, Tiger."

"What?" she asked. Tossing the pencil onto her desk, she glanced at her watch again.

"On the evening of April 1, the doc was attending the April Fools Ball at the country club."

That caught Casey's attention. "That's the same ball the St. Martins attended."

"Yep. Though I suppose it makes sense. The doc's probably loaded, too, being a successful plastic surgeon and all."

"Hmm. I guess. What about his alibi for the other date?"

"He was attending a medical convention in New York. I called the hotel. The desk clerk verified that he was there. He paid by credit card."

"Well, that lets the good doctor off the hook, but I still have a gut feeling that he's somehow connected to these murders. Something just isn't right."

Eight

Happy hour at Muldoon's, especially on a Friday night, was not for those seeking a quiet retreat from the workday world. The instant Casey and Dennis stepped inside, the din hit them almost like a physical slap. Raucous laughter combined with shouted conversations, the clack of billiard balls, the clink of glasses, waitresses shouting orders to the bartender and the cook back in the kitchen, and the blare of the jukebox all combined at a decibel level Casey figured to be roughly comparable to a jackhammer going full bore.

During the daytime hours that her granda and his cronies favored, the atmosphere was more subdued and peaceful, except when the "over the hill gang" of geriatric bridge players got into one of their periodic rumbles, that is.

Friday evenings, however, were when the hardworking first shift of the MPD let off steam. The owner, Paddy Muldoon, himself a retired cop, welcomed any man or woman "on the job," past or present. He went so far as to give a special discount to his former comrades in blue, and the place was the favored watering hole of the Second Precinct.

"Jeez, what a racket," Dennis complained.

"I know," Casey shouted over her shoulder, squeezing through the crowd. "I'm only going to stay long enough to be polite and give Danny our gift."

The place smelled of beer, burgers and Muldoon's Friday-night special, fish and chips. Overlaying it all was the scent of human flesh—mostly male—a hint of leather and pool chalk and the occasional whiff of cigarette smoke.

On their way back from the second crime scene, Casey had talked her partner into stopping long enough to buy the birthday gift. They had splurged a bit, getting the complete set of DVDs of the original *Star Trek* series, but she and Dennis had split the cost. Anyway, Danny was special and he loved the show.

"Good." Dennis craned his neck. "I think I see him and Keith over there by the bar."

They changed course and headed that way.

"Hey, birthday boy, how's it going?" Dennis shouted over the noise when they reached the bar.

"Hi, Detective Shannon," Danny replied, but he barely glanced at Dennis before turning his attention to Casey. He gave her a shy smile. "Hi, Casey. I was worried you forgot."

"What? Forget your birthday bash? Not a chance. Happy birthday, handsome." Going up on tiptoe, she kissed his cheek, and Danny blushed.

Keith clapped his brother on the back. "See? Didn't I tell you she'd be here? She promised. He's been fretting for the past hour. He was sure you had changed your mind."

"Don't be silly. I wouldn't miss your birthday for the world. Here. This is from Dennis and me."

"A present!" Danny's eyes lit up like a child's on Christmas morning. He stroked the gift-wrapped box, his face filled with awe. "Look, Keith. Casey brought a present. It's for me."

"Yeah, buddy. That's great."

"I wonder what it is?"

"There's only one way to find out. Open it."

Danny looked at Casey with wide-eyed wonder. "May I? I don't want to mess up the pretty package."

"Don't worry about it, sweetie." She leaned in close and confided, "I'll tell you a secret. Whenever I receive a gift I rip into it."

"Really?"

"Sure. That's the best way. Go ahead. Go for it."

With unrestrained delight, Danny attacked the gift, popping the ribbon loose and tearing the paper to shreds. At his first glimpse of the cellophane-wrapped set of DVDs, he sucked in a sharp breath.

"*Star Trek!* Look, Keith! Look, everybody! Casey gave me *Star Trek!*" He clasped the package tight against his chest and rocked from side to side, his eyes growing moist. "I love it. I love it. Thank you, Casey. Thank you. You're so wonderful."

"Hey, sweetie, don't cry," she whispered in his ear, hugging him. "It's no big deal. You just enjoy watching them, okay? And don't forget, they're from Dennis, too."

"I won't." Danny sniffed and wiped his eyes with his sleeve. "Thank you, too, Detective Shannon."

"You're welcome, pal."

Keith took a sip of his beer, but he watched his younger brother with a look of tenderness.

Quietly observing him as she sipped the beer he had ordered for her, Casey experienced a warm sensation in the region of her heart. All of the arrogance and cockiness, the swagger that Keith usually displayed, seemed to melt away whenever he focused his attention on Danny. It was too bad he didn't allow that softer side to surface more often, she mused. Caring and tenderness held much more appeal, at least to her, than cockiness.

"Hey, sport, since it's your birthday, why don't you celebrate by asking Casey for a dance?"

Danny's gaze darted to Casey. The look that raced across his slack face was a combination of panic and longing. "I, uh…I c-can't."

"Sure you can. Go ahead."

"Keith, I'm not sure that's a good idea," Casey said.

"See. She doesn't want to dance with me."

"Oh, sweetie, it isn't that. It's just that it's kind of crowded in here for dancing." The truth was, she wasn't in the mood. All she wanted was to drink a little beer and go home, but she could not bring herself to hurt Danny's feelings.

"Hey, that's easy to fix." To see over the crowd, Keith stepped up on the brass rail that ran along the bottom of the bar. Sticking two fingers in his mouth, he gave a piercing whistle that captured the attention of most of the patrons and brought the noise level down to a dull roar. "All right, you bozos, clear the dance floor. Danny's going to have a birthday dance with his favorite girl."

A chorus of catcalls and shouts and wolf whistles went up from the crowd of cops.

Casey glanced at her partner for help, but Dennis

merely mouthed, "Don't look at me. It was your idea to attend this shindig, remember?"

Pasting a smile on her face, she slipped her arm through Danny's, who had turned the color of a beet, and they made their way to the postage-stamp-size dance floor in front of the jukebox.

The music switched from pulsing rock to a slow ballad. Danny put one hand on the side of Casey's waist and held her other arm straight out to the other side. He moved to the beat with all the wooden grace of a toy soldier, concentrating fiercely while looking down at his feet and counting under his breath. At least a foot of space separated their bodies.

"Woo-hoo!"

"Way to go, Danny!" the crowd called out.

"C'mon, Danny! Pull her close. Whisper sweet nothings in her ear."

Casey shot the guy who had yelled the last comment a dagger look, and he grabbed his chest and staggered back as though mortally wounded.

"Pay no attention to those clowns, Danny. You're doing great."

He continued to stare at his feet and count, and she realized that he hadn't heard a word she or any of the others had said.

When the song finally came to an end, she smiled at him. "Thank you, Danny. That was nice."

He looked relieved and immensely pleased, like a puppy whose master had just lavished praised on him. "Did I do good?"

"Yes, you certainly did. You're a very good dancer."

"Keith taught me."

"Well, he did a good job."

"Thanks," Keith said from just behind her.

Startled, Casey turned, and in a move as smooth as silk, Keith slipped his arm around her waist and pulled her close. "Since you think so, you get to dance with his teacher. You don't mind if I steal her for one dance, do you, sport?" he asked his brother, even as he began to twirl away with her in time to the music.

"I don't mind. And don't worry, Casey," Danny called from the sidelines. "He's a real good dancer."

"Uh, look, Keith, do you mind if we don't do this? I'm really tired. It's been a tough week."

"Relax. Just lean on me."

"Keith, you're holding me too close."

He leaned his head back and looked down at her with that smoldering look she'd seen him give so many other women, and then he murmured in his sexiest voice, "Baby, I don't think that's possible. Just relax and go with the flow."

Casey sighed. She didn't seem to have much choice unless she was willing to make a scene, and she couldn't bring herself to upset Danny. Resigned, she gave in. She didn't even bother to protest when Keith rested his jaw against her temple and pulled her closer still.

She had to admit, he was a wonderful dancer. If their relationship had been one of a romantic nature, she might have enjoyed the experience. They moved as one with the music, their bodies plastered together from shoulder to knee, swaying with a sensual rhythm that suggested an intimacy that did not exist.

The number finally ended, but Keith did not loosen his hold on her one iota.

"Keith, let go."

"Relax, babe," he whispered in her ear, swaying in place. A second later another song began, and he picked up the rhythm without missing a beat.

From the corner of her eye, Casey could see some of the other cops watching them, occasionally murmuring comments and elbowing one another.

Over Keith's shoulder, she caught Dennis's eye and mouthed, "Help me."

Her partner downed the last of his beer and waded through the crowd and out onto the dance floor. He tapped Keith on the shoulder. "Sorry to interrupt."

"Go away, Shannon."

"No can do. Casey and I have to go. If we're going to make it to your folks' in time for dinner, we'd better get going."

Frowning, Keith stopped dancing and Casey stepped back out of his arms. "What do you mean, go? You can't go now. You just got here."

"I know. And I'm sorry. If I'd known sooner that this was Danny's birthday I wouldn't have made other plans, but I can't miss this dinner. My in-laws are celebrating their thirty-fifth wedding anniversary."

"I see." Keith frowned, and his voice had an angry edge. "Danny's going to be disappointed."

"I know, but I'll make it up to him somehow." She thought fast, groping for something to offer as an olive branch. "I know. Why don't you and Danny come to my folks' for our annual Fourth of July cookout?"

Behind Keith's back, Dennis waved his arms and frantically shook his head no, but it was too late to take back the invitation.

"Sounds like fun, and I'd like to accept, but I can't. I'm on duty that weekend."

"Oh. Well…how about if Danny comes? I can pick him up and bring him home afterward."

"You don't mind? He can be a handful at times. When he gets moody he's kinda tough to deal with."

"Oh, I think we can manage. He'll have a great time."

Keith glanced at his brother and his face softened. "Yeah, he'd love that. Okay, you got a deal. Thanks, Casey. That's real nice of you."

"No problem. I'll go tell him goodbye and let him know." She gave Keith's arm a friendly squeeze. "I'll see you Monday."

Danny was crestfallen when she told him they were leaving, until she broke the news about the cookout. He got so excited he jumped up and down and asked one question after another.

He wanted to know exactly how many days he had to wait until the Fourth of July, what time she would pick him up, how long he could stay, what he should bring with him, what they were going to do. She finally kissed his cheek, told him they'd talk about it another time, waved goodbye, then she and Dennis hightailed it out of the bar.

The instant they stepped outside, her partner started in on her. "I can't believe you invited Watson to our Fourth of July. Man, you've almost ruined my holiday weekend, and you know how much I look forward to our family cookouts."

"Well, I'm sorry, but I had to do something to make up for leaving the party so early. Anyway, what are you complaining about? He won't be there."

As they talked, they walked around the corner and back to the station house, where they'd left their cars.

"Yeah, well, it was pure luck his rotation came up that weekend. You dodged a bullet with that one. What were you thinking, Tiger? I've been telling you that Watson's got the hots for you, and you wouldn't listen. Well, tonight proved it."

"How? Just because we were dancing?"

"Dancing, my foot. He was all over you like ugly on an ape."

Casey rolled her eyes. "That didn't mean anything. Flirting is a reflex for Keith. He can't get around a female without going into Casanova mode."

"I'm telling you, Tiger, the guy's got you in his sights."

"First the doc, now Keith. What *is* it with you lately?"

"What is it with me? You're the one with the problem."

Unlocking her car, she opened the door, stopping to grin at him over the top before climbing in. "Oh? And what, exactly, is my problem?"

"You're inexperienced. Marrying the boy next door, someone you'd known all your life, you never had a chance to learn about men in general. You're a great cop, Tiger. You're intelligent and well trained, and you've got that woman's intuition thing going for you. But when it comes to reading when a male is on the prowl, you might as well be in a coma."

"So you keep telling me. But I still say you're wrong. Anyway, I'm safe now. I'm not likely to see the doc again and Keith won't be attending the cookout."

"Hmm. Just to be on the safe side, I think I'll have a heart-to-heart with the boss the first thing Monday morning and ask him not to let Watson trade days with anyone. It would be just like him to try. Hell, I'll get down on my knees and beg the lieutenant if I have to."

The soles of Casey's running shoes slapped the asphalt path in a steady rhythm. The only other sound was her breath rushing in and out through her mouth in time with the beat, forming little puffs of vapor in the frosty mountain air. Filtering through the tall trees of the park, the predawn light had a pearly cast that made the scene almost surreal.

When she ran in the early-morning hours, it felt as though she were the only person in the world. Nothing stirred but her and a few forest creatures that had tiptoed in during the night to nibble the shrubbery and perhaps drink from the creek that meandered through the park.

In the interior, among the trees, Casey spied a doe and her two spotted fawns trotting daintily away, heading back into the forest that surrounded the town. Up ahead, a squirrel raced across the running path, then scolded her from a nearby tree as she pounded by.

Sometimes she welcomed the solitude. It gave her a chance to unwind, to soak in the peace, and, for a short time, to forget about whatever cases she was working and let her mind float free.

At other times, however, the deserted feeling of the park was a sharp reminder of how alone she was, how her life had narrowed down to a fixed routine that hardly ever varied.

Except for being preoccupied with the serial murders, the weekend that had just passed had been a rerun of all the others that had slipped by this past year. Friday evening she'd gone home to her empty town house, had a long soak, read a few chapters of the novel she'd started the weekend before, then gone to bed.

Saturday after her morning run she'd cleaned house, showered, done her grocery shopping for the week, run a few errands, then come home. After dinner, she'd watched a sappy movie on TV and had another early night. As always, she attended church with her family on Sunday and afterward had gone home with them to spend the day.

Now it was Monday morning and another week stretched ahead. But at least she was working an important case that required all her focus.

No matter how loose running made her, Casey never completely relaxed on the early morning outings. There was always that part of her that was alert to her surroundings. On some level she heard and noted every sound, every movement around her.

At the southeast end of the park, the running path curved ninety degrees to the west. Following the arcing turn, Casey maintained her pace. Out of the corner of her eye to the left she spotted another runner crossing Monarch Street to enter the park.

It was unusual for her to encounter anyone at that hour, but once in a while it happened. Behind her, she heard the rhythmic slap-slap of his running shoes when he joined her on the path. The sound grew closer as he gained ground on her, and she moved over to one side to let him pass.

At the same time she braced herself, her muscles tightening ever so slightly and her mind switching to full alert. Attacks on female runners in the parks around Mears were rare, but they did happen.

The runner moved up beside her, and Casey tensed.

"Good morning, Detective."

The rumble of that familiar voice in her ear startled her so much she missed a step and would have fallen if he hadn't reached out and steadied her.

"Whoa. Easy there," Dr. Adams said. "I didn't mean to give you a scare."

Somehow Casey managed to regain her balance and keep going, and the doctor matched his pace to hers.

Shooting him an annoyed look, Casey demanded, "What are you doing here?"

"Running. The same as you."

"I've never seen you in this park before."

"Really? Maybe you didn't notice me because you didn't know who I was."

She slanted him a dubious look. That was possible, she supposed, but not likely. What woman wouldn't notice a man who looked like him? Even with his hair plastered to his head and dripping sweat, he looked scrumptious.

The front of his sweatshirt had a damp blotch across his chest, and his muscular legs glistened, even though the temperature hovered in the midthirties at this early hour. How far had he run before reaching the park?

Covertly, she inspected his running shoes and shorts and the Texas Tech University sweatshirt he wore. All showed signs of hard use, a good indication that he really was an experienced runner.

Her gaze encountered his, and she realized that he'd caught her looking him over. He grinned, and her gaze snapped forward. She could feel heat flood her face and silently prayed that she was already so flushed from exertion that he wouldn't notice her embarrassment.

"Actually, I have to admit, I've only run here twice before. Just this past Saturday and Sunday. I didn't see you either day, though."

"I run a bit later than this on Saturdays. That's my only day to sleep in. Sunday I take a break from running."

"Ah, that explains it."

Now that the shock of seeing him here in the park had

worn off, Casey felt acutely self-conscious. At the best of times she had no illusions about her looks; she was passably attractive, cute most would say, but that look depended on the help of beauty aids and good grooming.

At this hour, after running for almost a mile and a half, wearing no makeup—not even lip gloss—her wild mane of curls tied back with a rubber band and damp with perspiration, she knew she looked as though she'd been jerked through a knothole backward.

Casey hoped Dr. Adams would pull ahead and leave her behind. With his longer stride, even at an easy pace, he would cover more ground than her. Instead he continued to match his steps to hers.

They ran without talking for several minutes. Casey kept her gaze fixed straight ahead and tried to ignore the occasional brush of his sleeve against her arm, the heat emanating from his body, those big feet pounding along beside her much smaller ones.

"You don't mind if I run here, do you?" he asked after they had traversed the short side of the park and turned north on the west side.

"It's a public park."

"Do you always run alone?"

"Yes."

"Isn't that a little dangerous for a woman?"

She slanted him a dry look out of the corner of her eye. "I can take care of myself. Actually, you're probably in more danger than I am."

His expression said he doubted that, but he kept the opinion to himself, and they ran on in silence.

The park was rectangular-shaped, the two long east and west sides measuring one mile each, the short sides a half mile each. Casey's daily three-mile run consisted of once around the park. She and Dr. Adams ran in silence until the path curved back to the east, parallel to Beeker Street, where Casey lived, which ran along the short north side of the park.

Spotting her town house in the distance, Casey experienced a mix of feelings. On the one hand, it was nice to have someone by her side to keep her company while she ran. The doc didn't chatter away incessantly like some people, or crowd her or do anything to interrupt her rhythm.

On the other hand, the man made her…not nervous, exactly, but…well…edgy, she guessed you could call it—keyed up and too aware of her own body. It wasn't a comfortable feeling.

She had no idea why he had that effect on her. He wasn't pushy or aggressive, nor did he strut and preen or flirt nonstop like Keith, yet every cell in her body seemed to sit up and take notice when he was around.

Which was just plain silly. Like was drawn to like, and a man as drop-dead gorgeous as the doc would hardly be attracted to someone like her. She was no troll, it was true, but neither was she in his league.

And then there was this feeling she had about him that she couldn't shake, this gnawing in her gut that told her that, despite his alibis, he was somehow connected to the three murders.

"By the way," he said out of the blue, as though he'd read her mind. "Have you taken me off your suspect list yet?"

"Yes. Your alibis checked out."

"Great. Now I can pursue that personal matter I mentioned. I'd like to ask a favor of you."

Casey's heart did a little flip. Oh, Lord, was Dennis

right about the doc? *Was* he going to ask her out? If he did, what would she say?

"Oh?" she replied without looking at him. Another hundred yards and they'd be directly across the street from her town house. Sanctuary. Unconsciously, she increased her speed.

"Yes. You see, I coach my thirteen-year-old niece's softball team. They're a great bunch of young girls, and I was wondering if you could come talk to them after a game some evening about career opportunities for women on the police force, maybe give them some tips on how to keep themselves safe from attackers. That sort of thing."

They drew even with her house. At this point Casey usually stopped running and did her cool-down stretches, but that would have to wait until she got inside. She jerked to a halt and gaped at him while he ran on a few feet, then doubled back and ran in place beside her.

"That's it? That's what you wanted to ask me?"

"Yes."

Pulling out the towel that she'd hung through a loop on her jogging suit, she buried her sweaty face in its folds and bent over, laughing. So much for her partner's romantic notions about the doc and her.

"Is something funny?" he asked in a perplexed voice.

"No. No." She shook her head and got herself under control before lowering the towel. "I just remembered something amusing, is all. As for your request, I suggest you call our PR department. I'm sure they'll be happy to arrange for someone to talk to your team."

"The problem is, it's you that the kids want. Especially my niece, Jennifer. You see, I told her about you, and she thought it was really cool that I knew a real live woman detective. She's anxious to meet you." He gave her a cajoling look. "C'mon, Casey. Help me out here. If you do me this favor, I'd earn some serious points with the girls. And I'd owe you one."

Looping the towel around the back of her neck, Casey held on to both ends and glanced longingly at her house across the street. "I don't know...."

"At least promise me you'll think about it. Okay?"

She looked away toward the interior of the park. Hadn't she just been thinking about how dull and routine her life had become? And despite what her gut was telling her, he wasn't a suspect any longer.

"All right, I'll think about it. But I'm not making any promises."

Later that day, Casey sat at her desk, deep in thought, reading through the M.E.'s report on the St. Martin case and absently sipping her fifth cup of coffee. When she reached the end, she turned back to the first page of the file and started over.

Dammit. The answer was here somewhere, she told herself. She could feel it in her bones. What was she not seeing?

"Which file are you reading?" she asked Dennis.

"Belcamp."

"Here, trade with me. I've read through this one too many times. I need something fresh to look at."

"Good idea."

They traded files, and both went back to reading. Halfway through the second page, Casey stopped and glanced up at Dennis, an arrested expression on her face. "Have you got the Hettinger file over there?"

"Yeah."

"Give it to me," she said.

Her partner complied, his attention caught by her tone and the sudden urgency in her movements as she paged through the file. "What've you got?"

"A link. According to the medical examiner's report, Selma Hettinger had breast-enlargement surgery, approximately a year ago." Barely able to contain her excitement, she switched back to the Belcamp file and flipped through the pages until she found the notation she was looking for on the M.E.'s report. "And our girl Becky had rhinoplasty not too long ago. She was still healing."

"Rhino what?"

"A nose job. That's why she went to the doc for a checkup the day she was abducted."

"Ah, I see where you're going." He picked up the St. Martin file and searched through the pages. "Here it is. Madeline St. Martin had a face-lift and a tummy tuck."

Casey's gaze locked with her partner's. "What do you want to bet they were all patients of Dr. Adams?"

Nine

Less than ten minutes later, Casey and Dennis walked into Dr. Adams's offices.

The waiting room was empty, but the doctor stood behind the sign-in counter, talking to his nurse and the receptionist.

"Detectives. I didn't expect to see you again this soon," he said, his gaze zeroing in on Casey.

"We were hoping that you'd still be here. We need to talk to you," Casey said.

"Excuse me, Detectives, but it's late. The office is closed," the receptionist informed them.

"It's all right, Jolie. I'll see the detectives. Come with me. We'll talk in my office. Jolie, you and Martha can call it a day. We'll catch up on those files in the morning."

"I'm sorry about that," the doctor said once they were seated in his office. "My staff tends to be protective of my time. And I must admit, when I told them that you suspected me of being the serial killer they were outraged on my behalf. I'm afraid you two are not their favorite people at the moment."

The doctor leaned back in his chair. "What can I do for you?"

"Do you have a patient by the name of Selma Hettinger?" Casey asked.

"The name doesn't ring a bell. Let me check my files. I'll be right back."

In less than a minute he returned with a file. "Yes. I performed surgery on Ms. Hettinger about fourteen months ago."

"Breast enlargement, right?"

"Yes. How did you know?"

Ignoring the question, Casey asked, "Do you also have a patient by the name of Madeline St. Martin?"

"Now, that one I know. Yes, Maddy is a patient. I've performed surgery on her a couple of times."

"Face-lift and tummy tuck, right?"

"Right again."

"Correct me if I'm wrong, but I get the feeling that you know Madeline St. Martin as more than a patient."

"I do."

Casey tried to keep her expression neutral, but the revulsion she was feeling must have shown in her eyes. The doctor cocked one eyebrow. "Not, however, in the way you're probably thinking. I've known both of the St. Martins for years. We all belong to the country club. I also know about their…unusual marriage, which I assume you've learned of by now. And before you ask, no, I was not one of Maddy's lovers."

"Did she want you to be?" Dennis asked.

Dr. Adams hesitated, frowning. "If you're asking, did she come on to me, the answer is yes. Several times. But how serious she was, I don't know. You'll have to ask her. In any case, I rejected her advances—politely, of course."

"Of course," Casey said.

"What is this about, Detective?"

"Ms. Hettinger and Mrs. St. Martin were the first and second victims of the serial killer."

"What?"

Watching closely for his reaction, Casey saw his eyes widen and what looked to be genuine shock ripple over his face.

"Good Lord. Madeline is dead? Murdered by this madman?" He shook his head. "That's terrible. I thought she was gone on one of her trips. I could swear that's what Jason told me."

His gaze met Casey's again, and he frowned.

"Why are you looking at me like that?"

"I don't believe it's merely chance that all three murdered women were patients of yours."

"What are you saying? That you still think I had something to do with these killings?" For the first time since she'd met him, Casey saw real anger in Mark's face. He set his jaw and his silvery eyes turned icy. "Now, see here, Detectives, when you first accused me, the very idea was so ludicrous it was almost a joke, but this is no longer amusing in the least. I did *not* kill those women, nor did I have anything to do with their deaths."

"Relax, Doc," Dennis said. "We know that you didn't do the murders."

Mark looked at Casey. "And how about you, Detective? Do you agree?"

"Yes. Nevertheless, I believe that these murders are all connected to you in some way. If only two of the victims had been patients of yours, maybe I could chalk it up to coincidence, but all three? I don't think so."

"You think someone is targeting my patients?" he asked, his voice and expression incredulous.

"It looks that way."

"But why? Why would anyone do that?"

"That's what we have to figure out," Casey replied. "Can you think of anyone who would want to harm you by sabotaging your career?"

"No. Of course not. Why would you even ask such a thing?"

"Because if the press gets wind of this information and reveals it to the public, your practice will go down the tubes."

"Aw, hell." Leaning his elbow on the desktop, Mark cupped his forehead with one hand. "I hadn't thought about that."

"We'll do our best to keep that from happening," Casey assured him. "This information falls into the category of something only the perpetrator would know, so it's a legitimate piece of evidence to withhold from journalists. I don't think I'll have any trouble convincing my boss of that."

"Thanks. I appreciate that."

"But you're going to have to help us. Are you absolutely sure there is no one who would try to get to you in this way?"

"Yes. I'm sure."

"Take your time, Doc, and think about it," Dennis advised.

"What about rivals?" Casey prodded. "Some other doctor who may be jealous of your success? Or a dissatisfied customer? Has there been anyone who was unhappy with the results of their surgery? Any who had complications? Have there been any deaths as a result of your surgeries?"

Wearily, Mark pulled his hand down over his face and rubbed his chin. The friction of his fingers against his five-o'clock shadow made a raspy sound. With his heavy beard and dark hair he was probably one of those men who had to shave twice a day, Casey thought absently.

"There are only a handful of plastic surgeons in Mears," Dr. Adams said. "Trust me, between accidents, birth defects and baby boomers wanting to turn back the clock, there's plenty of patients to go around.

"As for disgruntled customers, there is always going to be the occasional patient who is unhappy. The unrealistic kind who expect miracles, and they're disappointed that the surgery didn't make them look twenty-five again or movie-star beautiful. But I've never deformed anyone or botched a job.

"Nor have I ever lost a patient. And certainly none of my patients has ever been displeased enough to go out and kill three women just to get back at me. A person would have to be a real sicko to do something like that."

"Exactly. That's why he's a serial killer," Casey pointed out.

"Do you have any enemies outside your practice, Doc?" Dennis asked. "Anyone at all who would have reason, real or imagined, to seek revenge on you? Perhaps you were involved in an investment deal that went bad? Or maybe there's a jealous husband who'd like to see you leave town in disgrace? Or a jealous ex-lover?"

"No, nothing like that. Detectives, I'm telling you, you're going down the wrong road. There has to be some other reason why this creep is singling out my patients."

"Hmm." Casey considered that for a moment. "You could be right. Maybe his reasons have nothing to do with you personally. Could be he doesn't approve of plastic surgery in general. Or maybe he just disapproves of women who artificially enhance their looks. That's what all three victims did. Maybe, in his mind, that makes them cheats or liars."

"That still doesn't explain why all his victims are patients of the doc's," her partner said.

Casey mulled that over. "Could be his are the only files to which our perp has access." She looked at Mark. "My family doctor can use his computer to access the hospital's records and pull up the results of any tests or ER visits I've had. Do you share that sort of patient data with the hospital and your patients' other doctors online?"

"Yes. If you have hospital privileges you can access your own patients' records, no matter the attending physician. The person must be registered as one of your patients, however. And the system is supposed to be secure."

"I'm not sure there is such a thing as a one-hundred-percent-secure Internet site." Casey jotted down a note on her pad. "Dennis and I will check it out.

"How about direct physical access?" she continued. "Are your files locked up when no one is here?"

"No. There's no reason. The office is locked, and there's a building night watchman."

"Who besides you has a key to these offices?"

"Well, let's see." Mark leaned back and began ticking off on his fingers. "There's my nurse, Martha Harvey, my receptionist, Jolie Graver, the building manager, the night watchman, and the building cleaning service. I believe that's all."

"Are either of the women who work for you married?"

"Yes, both are. Why do you ask?"

"Because it's possible that their husbands may have access to the key, as well."

Dr. Adams looked stunned. "You can't suspect Martha's or Jolie's husbands? That's crazy. I know them both. They're decent guys."

"I hate to disillusion you, Doc," Casey said. "But serial killers don't have horns and forked tails. They usually look and act just like everyone else. At this point the suspect list is wide-open. The one thing we know for sure is there's a common thread here somewhere. We just haven't figured out what it is yet. Which means we have to check out all the possibilities.

"I'd like you to think really hard and make a list of anyone, anyone at all, who may be angry with you or jealous of you or simply doesn't like the way you wear your hair or the brand of shampoo you use—anything, no matter how trivial it seems to you."

"All right. I'll work on that and have it for you in a few days. Anything else?"

"No, I think that's it for now. If you think of anything that may be of help, give Dennis or me a call."

They all stood, preparing to leave, but as Casey and Dennis headed for the door, Dr. Adams said, "By the way, Detective, have you given more thought to my request?"

Casey shot a glance her partner's way, and as she expected, Dennis's ears had perked up like a hunting dog's on point. He looked back and forth between Casey and Mark, curiosity crackling from him.

"No. Sorry, I haven't had time."

"I understand. No rush."

"What was that all about?" Dennis demanded the instant they stepped out of the doctor's office into the hallway.

"Nothing."

"Don't give me that. What was he talking about?"

The elevator doors opened and Casey stepped inside. Dennis followed right on her heels. Any hope she had that he might let the matter drop was quickly squashed.

"C'mon, Tiger. What kind of request did he make of you? Did he ask you for a date?"

"No. Of course not."

"Don't tell me he wants you to fix a ticket."

"No, nothing like that."

"Then what?"

Casey sighed. "You're not going to let this go, are you?"

"Nope," he replied cheerfully.

This time she rolled her eyes. "You're as bad as my brothers. If you must know, the doc coaches his niece's softball team, and he wants me to attend a game one night and talk to the girls afterward about career opportunities for women on the police force."

"Hey, that's a great idea."

"Yeah, well, I haven't agreed to do it. I just said I'd think about it. Actually, I probably won't."

"Why not?"

"For one thing, I haven't cleared it with the boss. For another, I'm pretty busy right now, in case you haven't noticed."

"The boss won't mind, and you know it. As for this case, you can't let it occupy your thoughts every waking moment. You'll burn out in no time that way. When you leave the station house you need to leave the case there and have a life of your own."

"Now you really do sound like a brother. Will, to be exact."

"If he's nagging you to get a life, then I'm all for him. Go to the game and watch the girls play. Then afterward give 'em a pep talk about how great this job is. Get your mind off this case for a few hours. Trust me, there's nothing like being around a bunch of youngsters to shake off what's bugging you for a few hours."

"If I don't do this, you're going to nag me about it forever, aren't you?"

"Damn straight."

Casey exhaled a defeated sigh. "All right, all right. I'll run it by the boss. If he's okay with it, I'll do it. Satisfied?"

"Sure." He poked her arm and grinned. "Now, that wasn't so hard, was it?"

Two hours later, after returning to the station house, filling in the boss and making a dent in the daily paperwork, Casey turned her car into her driveway. Without conscious thought she automatically followed the prescribed safety rules for a woman living alone, casting a quick look around the interior of the space to be certain she was alone, then closing the garage door with the remote before unlocking her car door and getting out.

Gathering up her purse and the plastic bag containing the milk and bread she'd picked up at the market on the way home, she entered her town house through the door connecting the garage and the kitchen. The instant she stepped inside she heard her telephone ringing.

Depositing her things on the kitchen counter, she hurried into the living room and picked up the receiver.

"Hello?"

"Hey, Stretch, it's Will."

"Well, hi. This is a surprise." Then it occurred to her that none of her brothers ever called just to chat, and she frowned, gripping the receiver tighter. "Is something wrong? Is it Granda? Is he ill?"

"He's fine. Unless you count tottering around the

den shaking his walking stick and threatening to beat the living daylights out of the sheriff as ill."

"Oh, dear. What's happened?"

"Happening. Do you have your TV on?"

"No. I just walked in."

"You better turn it on. The sheriff is holding a press conference."

"What! He's not authorized to do that. Hold on a sec." Still holding the receiver to her ear, she picked up the remote and turned the set on, and Sheriff Crawford's jowly face filled the screen.

"...don't mean to criticize," he said in his most patronizing tone. "I'm sure Detective O'Toole is doing her best, but she's been running the show for almost a week now, and the killer is still at large. We need to catch this man before he kills again."

"Someone needs to remind Crawford that he had the first two cases for more than a month without so much as getting an ID on the second vic," Will grumbled in Casey's ear.

In the background, she could hear her granda shouting dire threats and describing the sheriff's ancestry in colorful and unflattering terms.

"Has Detective O'Toole made any progress at all on the cases?" one of the reporters on the TV screen shouted.

"Only that the killer drives a light-colored van and all of his victims have been redheads. I'd advise all redheaded women to be very careful. Maybe even visit their hairdressers and go blond," the sheriff said with a "good ole boy" grin. "Also, I've heard, off the record, that a local doctor is under suspicion."

"Oh, my Lord!" Casey gasped. "That idiot! That

bombastic, glory-seeking, pea-brained idiot! He just gave away the most useable pieces of evidence we had to work with and possibly set an innocent man up for potential ruin. Just wait until I get my hands on that jackass. I'll personally sew his mouth shut if that's what it takes to keep him quiet."

"Take it easy, Stretch," her brother advised. "Don't go flying off the handle. And don't confront Crawford yourself. Take your complaint to your boss and let him handle it."

Casey ground her teeth and counted to ten. The advice was vintage Will. He was a by-the-book cop. He followed the rules, went through the proper channels, kept his formidable Irish temper under strict control and his nose clean. As a result, he'd made lieutenant by age thirty-two. And for those exact same reasons, it was doubtful that he would advance any further.

Sometimes, Will's strict adherence to the rules got under Casey's skin.

In many ways they were alike. They were both serious and hardworking, both disciplined and dedicated to the job, and—though her brother would deny it—they both possessed a strong sixth sense.

Some called it ESP or intuition or psychic ability, but what it boiled down to was a gift for sensing things that weren't obvious to others.

When investigating a case, Casey would often get a feeling about a person or a situation. It would sometimes manifest itself as a gnawing sensation in the pit of her stomach, or a tingling all over her body that wouldn't go away, as though every nerve ending had sprung to vibrant life. Or sometimes it was as though she had suddenly sprouted invisible antennae that picked up warning signals.

To Casey's way of thinking the ability was the most useful and formidable tool a cop could have, and she had made use of the gift throughout her career and went with her hunches.

Will, on the other hand, rejected the very notion that such a thing as extrasensory perception existed, and most certainly not in him, even though, as children, both he and Casey had experienced the phenomenon on numerous occasions.

By adulthood he had turned his back completely on the gift with which he'd been born. He'd joined the police force, determined to make his mark using only good, solid, tried-and-true police procedures. None of that hocus-pocus stuff for William Harrison Collins.

His stubborn refusal to follow his instincts sometimes made Casey want to strangle her eldest sibling, but—as much as she hated to admit it—this time she knew that Will was right.

"Did you hear what I said, Stretch?" her brother asked in response to the tense silence on the telephone line.

"I heard you."

"So you'll let Lieutenant Bradshaw handle this?"

"Yes," she agreed, gritting her teeth.

"You swear?"

The press conference ended, and Casey switched off the TV and began to pace the room with the telephone pressed to her ear. She was livid. Nothing in the world would have pleased her more at that moment than to be able to give her temper free rein and let fly at Sheriff Crawford, but the rational part of her knew if she did that she would probably permanently derail her career.

"Stretch?" Will prodded again.

"All right, I swear."

But, oh, how she ached to publicly tell off the big blowhard and let the chips fall where they may.

The next morning, for the first time in years, Casey skipped her morning run. A restless night had done little to dampen her temper, and when she stormed through the front doors of the station house, the officers who usually called a friendly greeting either eyed her warily or were prudent enough to suddenly have business elsewhere.

The mob of reporters waiting to pounce on her, however, possessed no such common sense.

Casey had made it only halfway across the lobby of the station house when someone called out, "There she is!"

Pandemonium broke loose. Like a swarm of bees, the press swooped down on her and she found herself being jostled and crowded by reporters and cameramen, and people sticking microphones in her face.

"Detective! Detective! What do you think of the sheriff's allegations?"

"Is it true, Detective, that you suspect a local doctor of being the Hunter? Do we have a Jack the Ripper roaming the streets of Mears?"

"Excuse me. Let me pass, please," Casey said through clenched teeth, trying to shove a path through the crush of bodies.

"Detective O'Toole, in his press conference last evening Sheriff Crawford as much as said that you and your task force are no closer to catching the Hunter than you were a week ago. He intimated that you should be replaced. Any comment?"

"Sheriff Crawford is entitled to his opinion."

"But is he right? You must admit, it's been almost a week, and you have no one in custody."

Casey narrowed her eyes at the aggressive woman and snarled, "If you stick that microphone in my face one more time, I'll feed it to y—"

"I'm afraid you're ignoring facts, ma'am," a familiar voice interrupted. At the same, time a big hand spread across the small of Casey's back. "Serial killers rarely know their victims. They are picked at random, which makes catching the perpetrator extremely difficult. If you'll recall, it took years to get Ted Bundy."

Dennis squeezed in beside Casey and used his bulk to plow through the crowd.

"Are you saying this investigation will probably go on for years?"

Dennis steered them to the foot of the stairs. "I'm just suggesting that you and the sheriff have a little faith and exercise some patience. Everything that can be done at this point is being done."

"Thanks," Casey muttered to her partner, taking the stairs at a run. "I was ready to deck that know-it-all woman."

"I know. Why do you think I intervened?"

Reaching the second floor, Casey cut through the squad room with single-minded purpose, oblivious to the wary looks cast her way by her fellow detectives. Dennis followed along behind her at his usual ambling pace. She marched into Lieutenant Bradshaw's office with blood in her eye, but he was ready for her. Raising his hand, he forestalled her tirade before she had a chance to utter the first word.

"Whoa. Hold it right there. Before you explode all over me, let me just say that I saw the press conference, too, and I'm on it. I've called the mayor and the county commissioners and we're going to meet with Crawford in less than an hour. I'll see to it that he issues a public apology to you, *and* that he makes no more unauthorized statements to the press."

"Oh, great. Another chance for Crawford to grandstand. You get that guy near a microphone and he'll use it to his advantage."

"Not this time he won't. He answers to the county commissioners, and they're as angry as we are. Apparently, last night's press conference is just the latest in a long list of unorthodox and unauthorized things he's done since taking office. Crawford seems to have the mistaken notion that getting elected sheriff is the same as being made grand potentate of the county."

"Somehow I doubt that receiving a slap on the wrist by you and the commissioners is going to change his attitude," Casey said. "Or get him to retract his statements."

"Oh, he'll retract, all right. Trust me on this. I've already prepared his statement and he'll read it verbatim or I'll put a muzzle on him myself."

The promise took some of the wind out of her sails, but Casey was not yet mollified. "Fine. But I want Lewis and Travis taken off the task force. Today. One or both of those bozos leaked that information to the sheriff."

"I can't do that, O'Toole, and you know it. Crawford will scream that he's being cut out of the investigation. He'll make political hay out of that for sure.

"Anyway, he has a right to the info. He just didn't have the right to blab it to the press without checking with you first."

"That idiot gave away our only advantage," Casey objected. "By now the perp has gotten rid of that van or at the very least had it painted, and every redheaded woman in the area is panicking.

"And hasn't Crawford got any better sense than to implicate someone without a shred of proof? If the press gets hold of Dr. Adams's name, it won't matter that he's not guilty, or not even under suspicion, his practice will be ruined. And we'll be extremely lucky if he doesn't sue the city. And the MPD. And the sheriff's department," she railed.

"I know, I know. Trust me, I'll make sure the sheriff knows just how badly he messed up and set our case back. But you have to let me handle this. I know you, O'Toole. When you're this riled that temper of yours takes over. It's going to get you in trouble one of these days."

"Fine. You handle the situation. In the meantime, what are Dennis and I supposed to do? There's a pack of reporters downstairs howling for blood."

"I'll speak to them on my way out. You and Shannon just keep plugging away. Interview the doc's staff and everyone else with access to that building. And if you don't hear from Dr. Adams soon, press him for that list of less-than-pleased patients. Go about your business as usual and ignore the press. Remember—I've got your back."

"You got it, boss," Dennis assured the older man. Moving over to stand directly behind Casey, he put his big hands on her shoulders and steered her out into the squad room.

Casey's temper wasn't the only one on the boil.

Mark waited by the water fountain at the southeast corner of the park, where he'd intercepted Casey the day before. Impatient, he paced back and forth, keeping an eye out for her and checking his wristwatch every so often.

Where was she?

Determined not to miss her, he'd arrived at the park before daylight. He checked his watch again. He'd been waiting almost an hour with no sign of her.

Had she gone for her run somewhere else to avoid him? he wondered. It was beginning to look that way. Funny, he would never have pegged her for a coward.

He waited five minutes longer, then, muttering an oath, he took off down the jogging path.

Driven by anger, he ran at a punishing pace. At the northeast end of the park, acting on impulse, he cut across Beeker Street and ran up the walkway to Casey's front door. Running in place, he rang the bell twice and pounded on the door, but she didn't answer and there was no sound coming from inside. Finally, accepting that she wasn't home, he recrossed Beeker Street to complete the last leg of his run and head home.

The moment he arrived at his apartment, he pulled Casey's card from his wallet and punched in her office number.

"Detective Squad. May I help you?" a young woman said.

"I'd like to speak with Detective O'Toole, please."

"I'm sorry, sir, Detective O'Toole is not in the office at the moment. She's out working on a case. May I take a message?"

Damn, Mark thought. He rubbed his forehead and considered leaving a terse message. "Uh, no. No, I'll call back later, thanks."

Casey and Dennis spent all that day conducting interviews. They talked to the building manager, the woman who operated the janitorial service and the four women who did the actual cleaning. Toward the end of their shift they were in the middle of interviewing the night watchman for the Powers Building when Dennis's pager went off.

He checked the instrument and sent Casey a panicked look. "It's your mother. Something must be wrong."

Before the words were out of his mouth, Casey's pager went off. "Mine's Mom, too."

"Oh, God. It's got to be Mary Kate. She's in trouble."

"Stay calm, okay, and let me call Mom," she ordered, already punching in her mother's cell-phone number.

Maureen answered on the first ring. "Casey?"

"Yes, it's me. What's up?"

"Sweeting, your father and I are in the car, on the way to the hospital with Mary Kate. She's gone into early labor. You and Dennis meet us at the emergency room entrance, okay?"

"Right. We're on our way."

"It's Mary Kate, isn't it?" Dennis demanded the instant she pushed the off button.

"Yes. I'm sorry, Mr. Britton," she said to the night watchman. "We have a family emergency. We have to go." She grabbed Dennis's arm. "C'mon, I'll explain on the way. And I'll drive."

"Oh, God, it must be bad if you don't trust me to drive."

"Just get in the car."

Dennis was so distraught he was like a shell-shock victim. She had to guide him to the car and stuff him inside.

Using the siren, Casey got them to the hospital, which was only a couple of blocks from the Powers Building, in less than two minutes, beating her parents and cousin.

However, when she brought the car to a screeching stop in the ER entrance, her partner shook himself out of his panicked stupor and took control. While Casey parked the car he ran inside, alerted the staff and commandeered doctors and nurses and hustled them outside. Casey's father pulled up to the ER entrance moments later to find her and Dennis waiting with a team of medical people.

One by one over the next few hours Casey's brothers arrived. Joe and Francis had followed her parents in their car, bringing Roger and Granda with them. There was nothing they could do but wait and pray and comfort one another, but not one of them gave a thought to leaving, nor would they until they knew that Mary Kate and the babies were out of danger.

Finally, around eight that evening, a weary-looking Dennis walked into the waiting room. In an instant they were all on their feet, pelting him with a barrage of questions.

"It's good news," Dennis said, holding up his hands for quiet. "Mary Kate and the babies are okay. The doctors gave her something that stopped the labor," he continued when the collective sighs of relief died down. "They're going to keep her overnight to be sure, but if all goes well we can take her home in a day or two. She's been transferred to a private room, so you can all go see her now."

Lying propped up in bed, looking tired but beautiful, Mary Kate beamed at the relieved group as they tromped into the cramped room. They all took turns kissing and hugging her and teasing her about scaring them.

"'Twas a nasty fright ya gave us, Mary Kate," Granda scolded in his heavy brogue, which was all the more prominent due to the emotional situation. He shook his bony finger at her. "In the future ya'd best remember, I'm an old man. Me poor heart won't take many more scares the likes o' that. So ya'll be showin' a little consideration for your poor old granda and no be doin' such again. Ya hear?"

"Yes, Granda." Mary Kate kissed his papery cheek, then lowered her eyes and pretended to be duly chastised, but a small, pleased smile tugged at her lips. Though, technically, Granda Seamus was Casey's paternal grandfather and not related by blood to Mary Kate, the dear old man had accepted his daughter-in-law's niece as one of his own from the day she'd joined the Collins family.

For a while they visited with the patient and one another, but when Roger started getting cranky Francis announced that it was time to take him home and put him to bed.

Getting the okay from his parents and grandparents, she asked the toddler, "Roger, sweetie, how would you like to spend the night with Auntie Francis and Uncle Joe?"

The cranky little boy's eyes lit up and his whining immediately changed to shouts of joy. "Yeth! Yeth! I thay wiff Auntie Fancis and Unble Thoe," he declared.

Shortly after the O'Tooles departed with Roger and Granda Seamus, Casey's brothers began to take their leave, until soon only Dennis and Casey and her parents remained with Mary Kate.

"Can I get you something before I go?" Casey asked her cousin.

"You're leaving, too?" Mary Kate looked hurt and stared down at her beautifully manicured fingernails, which were plucking the coarse thermal cotton blanket that covered her. "Can't you stay a little longer?"

Casey chuckled. Whenever Mary Kate assumed that pathetic pout, Dennis invariably caved like a sand castle at high tide, but Casey was made of stronger stuff. She'd shared a room with her cousin for four years before going away to college, and she knew all her wiles.

Leaning over the bed, she kissed Mary Kate on the cheek. "Sorry, love, but I'm starving. Now that I know you're going to be okay, I'm going home to have dinner."

"Oh, all right. But we will see you for dinner tomorrow night, right?"

"You bet. I wouldn't miss Mom's home cooking." Casey kissed her parents and went to the door and pulled it open. Looking back over her shoulder, she waggled her fingers and stepped outside, then slammed into a hard chest as the door swished shut behind her.

"Whoa, there."

A pair of masculine arms encircled her and pulled her tighter against the broad chest, and Casey's senses were suddenly bombarded with the feel and scent of male.

"Well, well, if it isn't Detective Casey O'Toole," a deep voice rumbled with a hint of amusement, just above her head. "You know, we're going to have to stop meeting like this."

Ten

Casey's head jerked up. "What are you doing here?"

Mark grinned. For an instant Casey was distracted by the way the skin at the corners of his eyes crinkled attractively. "That's funny, I was about to ask you the same thing. I work here, remember? I just finished an emergency surgery."

Duh, Casey thought, mentally giving herself a whack on the forehead with the heel of her hand. Some detective you are, O'Toole. For Pete's sake, the man is dressed in hospital scrubs.

Her gaze wandered over his torso, and her heart gave a funny little thump against her rib cage. The garment's loose V-neck partially exposed the mat of short black hair on his chest, and beneath the capped sleeves his upper arms were muscular, the forearms sprinkled with more of the short, silky hair. As always, he smelled of antiseptic soap and his own personal manly scent. Who would have thought the two would be such a heady combination?

Her gaze wandered over his broad shoulders, up

the strong column of his neck to his jet-black hair. It still bore the marks of a scrub cap and was slightly mussed.

It wasn't fair, she thought peevishly. How in the world did he manage to look mouthwateringly sexy wearing a baggy pair of cheap puke-green cotton hospital-issue scrubs? It simply wasn't fair.

"Casey? Are you okay?" Mark asked, jarring her out of her daze.

"What? Oh, uh…yes, I'm fine. So, uh, was there another car accident? Was that your emergency?"

A troubled look flickered over his face. "No. This was a domestic assault. During an argument a man sliced his wife's face with a knife. I was called in to try to minimize the scarring."

"Oh. I see." Casey understood his sudden gloom. She hated domestic-assault calls, herself. She'd worked a few as a uniform cop, and that was plenty for her. Never in a million years could she work the domestic-assault squad on a regular basis.

Mark seemed to shake off his grim thoughts, and the twinkle returned to his eyes. "You still haven't told me what you're doing here."

"Oh." She gestured toward the door behind her. "My cousin, Mary Kate, who is also my partner's wife, is expecting twins in about seven weeks, but she's gone into early labor and was admitted this evening."

At once concern replaced the devilish humor in Mark's face. "I'm sorry to hear that. How's she doing?"

"Better. Her doctor gave her something that stopped the contractions."

"Who's her obstetrician?"

"Dr. Thomas."

Mark nodded. "She's in good hands. He's one of the best."

The mention of hands brought Casey back to earth with a thump. Belatedly, she realized that Mark's were still splayed against her back, holding her pressed against him.

Before she could move, a nurse came out of the room across the hall. She jerked to a halt when she spotted them, her eyes widening. Like a guilty child caught with her hand in the cookie jar, Casey jumped back out of Mark's arms.

He chuckled as the woman hurried away toward the nurses' station. "This place is a hotbed of gossip. By morning the rumor mill will have us engaged."

"Oh, great," Casey snapped to cover her unease and the undeniable dart of excitement his words produced. "I'm glad you find it funny." Gradually, however, her scowl turned to a reluctant grin. "I know what you mean, though. It's the same way at the station house. The least little thing and—"

The door behind them opened and Dennis stuck his head out. "I thought I heard your voice, Doc. What're you two standing out here in the hall for? Bring him on in, Casey." He held the door wide and waved for both of them to come inside. "C'mon, Doc. I want you to meet my wife and Casey's parents."

Casey tried to stammer out an excuse to leave, but with Mark's hand on the small of her back, propelling her back into the room, she wasn't given much of a choice.

She saw Mary Kate's eyes widen when she got her first look at Mark.

"Uncle Pat, Aunt Maureen, I'd like you to meet Dr. Mark Adams. Doc, meet Casey's parents."

While Dennis made the introductions, Mary Kate's gaze bounced from the doctor to Casey, then back, her expression changing from gaga to calculating.

Casey was instantly uneasy. Oh, Lord. She knew that look. Mary Kate was hatching up something.

"So, you're Dr. Adams," her cousin practically purred when Mark shook her hand. "My husband has been telling me about you."

"Has he, now? Well whatever he told you, they were lies, all lies. Don't you believe a word."

Mary Kate giggled. "Oh, don't worry, it was all good. He likes you a lot."

"Whew! That's good to hear. When someone carries a badge and a gun I've always found it wise to stay on their good side."

"Does that include Casey?" Mary Kate asked slyly.

Mark looked at Casey, and something in his eyes made her chest tighten. "Especially Casey," he murmured.

Turning serious, he asked, "How are you feeling, Mrs. Shannon? Any more pains?"

"No, none. And, please, call me Mary Kate."

"Dr. Thomas said she's responding well to the medication he gave her. If all continues to go well we may be able to take her home tomorrow," Dennis said hopefully.

"I assume he's restricted you to complete bed rest." Mark commented, cocking an eyebrow at Mary Kate.

Immediately her pretty mouth turned sulky, and she flounced back against the pillows with her arms folded over her turgid belly. "Yes. I'm not allowed to do anything anymore."

"Inactivity doesn't sit well with my wife," Dennis explained, patting Mary Kate's arm. "She's an energetic, vibrant woman, so this is difficult for her."

"Thank you, darling." Mary Kate's pout dissolved as she took her husband's hand and cupped it against her cheek. "You understand me so well."

"I know it's tough," Mark continued. "But every day that passes increases those babies' chances of survival and good health. I'm sure you agree that's worth the sacrifice."

"Of course. I'll do anything for my babies."

"How long have you been practicing in Mears, Dr. Adams?" Casey's father asked.

"I opened my office here eight years ago, immediately after I finished my specialty training. My brother and his daughter live here, and since they are the only family I have left, I wanted to be near them."

Casey could see her father using the information to mentally calculate Mark's age, while her mother looked concerned.

"Oh, dear. You have no other family at all?" Maureen's expression held something akin to horror. She had come from a large family, and so had Casey's father. The very idea of not having that broad base of unconditional love and support seemed tragic to them.

"No, ma'am. My twin brother and I were late-in-life babies. Our parents passed away several years ago, within six weeks of each other."

"Oh, you poor thing. But surely you have aunts or uncles? Or cousins, perhaps?"

"Not that I know of. Both my mother and father were only children of only children."

"Oh, how sad for you." She turned to her daughter with a determined look. "Casey, love, you must invite this young man to one of our family gatherings some time. I know, why don't you and your brother and niece join us on the Fourth of July?"

"Uh, Mom, I don't think—"

"That sounds wonderful, Mrs. Collins," Mark said. "Thank you for inviting us. We'd love to join your family."

"Good. It's settled, then," Maureen said with satisfaction.

Casey didn't know what to do. She couldn't uninvite him. She wasn't even certain that she wanted to. Which was what concerned her most.

It was foolish to entertain any romantic illusions where she and Mark Adams were concerned. Talk about your mismatch.

To begin with, she had no idea if he was interested in her. Dennis thought so, and he'd infected Mary Kate with the notion. Casey's mouth twitched. Which would have been about as difficult as slipping on ice. Her cousin thrived on romance and playing matchmaker. If a man so much as smiled at a woman, she smelled love in the air and went into action.

Casey, however, wasn't convinced. A few times the doc had seemed to be flirting, but she couldn't be sure. In any case, he might be the type who flirted with every woman he met.

Heck, even if he *was* interested, it wouldn't work, she told herself. He was a well-to-do doctor, part of the country-club set. She was a cop from a big, boisterous middle-class, first-generation Irish-American family of cops. They had nothing in common.

And to top it all off, he was drop-dead gorgeous and no doubt experienced.

Tim had been the only man she'd ever been involved with romantically, and their courtship had been carried on under the watchful eyes of two sets of old-fashioned parents, a grandfather and four protective older brothers. Tim had thought she was beautiful, but as everyone knew, love was blind. Not that she was a gargoyle or anything, but she would never be an exotic beauty like her cousin. She certainly wasn't in Dr. Mark Adams's league.

All else aside, the man was undoubtedly adept at avoiding commitment. He hadn't reached his midthirties and remained single by accident, not with his looks—not to mention his position and wealth. Beautiful women probably threw themselves at him on a daily basis.

No doubt, the good doctor wouldn't object to having a brief, torrid affair with her, if the opportunity fell into his lap, but no way would he be seriously interested in someone like her.

The plain truth was, with her background and upbringing, she wasn't cut out for an affair. She'd feel so guilty and gauche she'd be sure to botch the whole thing up within twenty-four hours.

Besides, if she ever got up the nerve to carry on an affair and her brothers found out, they'd skin Mark alive, never mind that none of them lived like a monk.

Casey sighed. It was a double standard, but she had given up fighting against it at some point during her teens. That was just the way it was when you grew up in a household with four protective older brothers. The sexual revolution may have changed the way society in general looked at premarital relations between consenting adults, but to the male of the species that standard did not apply to a sister. Particularly a baby sister.

Poor things. They couldn't help it. It was bred into their bones—something to do with that primitive, tes-

tosterone-driven need to keep the females of their tribe
safe and inviolate.

Everyone else in the room burst into laughter, rein-
ing in Casey's drifting thoughts. Looking around, she
realized that Mark had said something that the others
found hilarious.

"Oh, Mark, you're terrible," Mary Kate sputtered
through her giggles.

Still guffawing, Dennis stood bent over, holding his
side, and Casey's parents were both wiping away tears
of mirth.

Casey forced a smile and pretended to get the joke
but remained silent.

Paying closer attention, she realized that during those
few minutes while she'd been lost in thought Mark had
succeeded in winning over her parents and cousin. They
were all now chatting as though they'd known one another for years.

Though she knew she was being irrational, she couldn't
help but feel betrayed somehow. Didn't they know that
this man was a danger to her emotional well-being?

Apparently not. The next thing she knew, Mark was
asking her to have a cup of coffee with him, and everyone else was urging her to accept.

"I'm hoping to twist her arm some more and per-
suade her to give a talk to my niece's softball team," he
explained, glancing around at the others.

"Really? A talk about what?" Casey's father asked.

"Several topics, actually. Career opportunities for females within the police department. Safety for women.
That sort of thing."

"That's a great idea," her cousin declared. "Casey,
you should do it."

"I think so, too," her mother seconded.

"I'm, uh…I'm thinking about it."

"Then let's go have that coffee and give me a chance to convince you."

"No, really. I can't," Casey insisted. "I have to go. Actually, I was on my way home when I bumped into you."

"C'mon, Tiger, since when do you turn down a cup of coffee? Anyway, it's about time for your next fix. You haven't had a cup for about an hour." Dennis shot Mark a confiding look. "Casey's addicted to coffee. Consider this fair warning. She turns into a snarling, wild-eyed, raving maniac when the caffeine level in her blood gets low."

"Oh, come *on*. I'm not that bad," Casey objected, but her offended tone was wasted on her family.

They broke into a chorus of groans and laughter.

"Oh, no?" Dennis looked at Mark again. "For example, at one time the brass thought it would be cheaper and less messy and time-consuming to install vending machines at each precinct station house rather than collecting money from everyone to stock our refrigerator with goodies and making our own coffee. Sounds like a good idea, right? Right. The vending-machine coffee was lousy, of course, but then all station house coffee is, so no one complained too much.

"Well, one day Casey begins to have withdrawal symptoms, so she puts a quarter in the coffee machine and—"

"Dennis, I'm sure Dr. Adams isn't interested in this," Casey protested.

"Oh, no. I'm fascinated," he insisted, grinning. "Please, go on, Dennis."

"Well, the cup comes down, topples over, and all the coffee goes down the drain. She snarls a few unprintable words and tries again. Same thing happens. By now, her teeth are gritted and steam is coming out of her ears and everyone within hearing or visual range is looking for cover. On the third try, with her last quarter, mind you, the cup topples again and Casey loses it.

"She grabs hold of the machine, which has to weigh a couple of hundred pounds, and she's yelling all sorts of colorful curses and kicking the thing and shaking it back and forth until it's rocking so hard it eventually topples over and crashes to the floor, spewing hot coffee and spitting out cups like quarters out of a slot machine. She might have been crushed if she hadn't jumped out of the way in time."

By then Casey could feel her cheeks burning and the others were laughing, but Dennis wasn't through. Like most Irish, he was a born storyteller, so he waited for the laughter to die down, then grinned and delivered the punch line.

"The next day the coffee machine was removed and we've been making our own brew ever since."

"Yeah, and my daughter received a chewing-out from her boss, which she richly deserved, and had to reimburse the vending-machine company for the repairs," her father added.

"And the story of how Casey killed the coffee machine has become legend at the MPD," Maureen put in.

"Wow." Mark looked at Casey with laughter still dancing in his eyes. "You actually *destroyed* a vending machine?"

She shrugged. "I wanted a cup of coffee."

"Ah, I see. Well, I certainly wouldn't want you to have a caffeine fit here. I'm not sure the hospital would be so forgiving if you destroyed one of their machines. So, c'mon, let me buy you a cup."

"Go on," Mary Kate urged. "It's not as though you *have* to go home. All you're going to do when you get there is make a pot of coffee and have dinner in front of the TV like you always do."

"You haven't eaten? In that case, let me take you to dinner."

"Oh, no, I couldn't do that. I'm not dressed for going out to dinner."

"Neither am I, but don't worry. You look fine." Mark took her elbow and began to steer her toward the door. "Where I'm taking you, there's no dress code. In fact, it's close, so they're used to doctors in scrubs dropping in."

At the door, he stopped and smiled back at the others, who were watching them with avid interest. "Nice to meet you all. I'm looking forward to July 4."

"The hospital cafeteria? *That's* where we're eating?" Casey said moments later when they stepped off the elevator.

"I told you it was casual. I have to stick around for a while to monitor my patient. C'mon, grab a tray. For hospital food, it's not bad."

As they went through the serving line, Mark joked with the women servers and the cashier. Casey couldn't help but notice that they and everyone else in the cafeteria were eyeing her with interest.

He picked a corner table as far away from the other people as they could get, but that didn't stop the curious glances.

"I missed you at the park this morning," Mark said when they were settled at the table.

A dart of surprise shot through Casey. With all the hubbub of the last few hours she'd temporarily forgotten about the events of the past twenty-four hours. She shook out a paper napkin and spread it in her lap. "I had to skip my run this morning. There was a problem at the station house that I had to take care of," she explained.

"Putting out the brush fires the sheriff started with his news conference, right?"

She looked across the table at him with a contrite expression. "You saw that, huh?"

"Yeah. I have to admit, at first I was plenty ticked off at you and Dennis. Then I saw the retraction and the reluctant apology to you that the sheriff gave this afternoon with all the county officials standing behind him. That's when I realized that sheriff had acted on his own and had been just shooting off his mouth, as usual." Mark chuckled. "Crawford wasn't a happy man. Eating crow doesn't set well with him."

She met Mark's gaze across the table. "Just so you know, I would never give the sheriff information vital to our case. Neither would Dennis. Only three people connected to this case know your name—me, Dennis and our boss, Lieutenant Bradshaw, and he's as reliable as the tides. He's also not a fan of the sheriff."

"That's good to hear. Thanks."

For the next few minutes they ate in silence, then Mark said, "I had no idea that Dennis was married to your cousin."

"I had no idea you were a twin, so we're even. Are you identical?" The very thought that there could be another man who looked like him was mind-boggling.

"No, we're fraternal. You can tell we're brothers, but that's it. How long have Dennis and Mary Kate been married?"

"A little more than three years. Dennis made detective about four years ago and was assigned as my partner. After we'd worked together for a while I introduced him to my cousin. No one else thought he stood a chance with Mary Kate, her being so beautiful and all, but they hit it off right away."

"So you played matchmaker," Mark said with a grin, and stabbed a bite of salad.

Casey's fork paused halfway to her mouth. "I just introduced them and let nature take its course." A chuckle bubbled from her. "You should've seen Dennis's slack-jawed expression when I introduced them. Poor thing, he looked like he'd taken a zap from a stun gun. I should have been prepared for his reaction. Most men are bowled over by Mary Kate's beauty."

"Mmm. Your cousin is attractive."

"Attractive!" Casey's spine stiffened. "Do you have trouble with your eyesight? She's gorgeous. And, though she can be a pill at times, and a terrible flirt, she's as sweet and kind as she is beautiful."

Mark swallowed the bite of food in his mouth and grinned. "Damn. No wonder Dennis calls you Tiger. You really jump to the defense of the people you love, don't you?"

Feeling foolish, Casey looked down at her plate. "I guess I do. Sorry."

"Hey, don't be. I admire that." He leaned forward. "But let's set the record straight, okay? I didn't mean to insult or slight your cousin. Mary Kate is, as you say, a beautiful woman, and I can see why Dennis was bowled over, but she's just not my type."

Casey stared across the table at him, dumbstruck, her glass held suspended halfway to her mouth. She blinked, then blinked again. "Not your type?" She'd never encountered a male over the age of fifteen who wasn't entranced by Mary Kate.

"Not really. Sultry good looks and overt sexuality are a real turn-on for some men, but I find wholesome beauty much more appealing."

Casey didn't know what to say. That a man could be exposed to Mary Kate's undeniable beauty and not fall even a little bit in love with her was such a new and novel concept she could barely grasp it. Nor did she know if his last comment was a reference to her or merely a general statement.

Confused, she looked down and tried to concentrate on her meal.

After a while Mark said, "I like your family."

Happy to be on safer ground, Casey looked up and smiled. "Thanks. I like them, too, but maybe you'd better reserve judgment. You haven't met even half of them yet. My grandfather, Seamus Collins, lives with my folks, and he's a rascal. Then there are my four brothers. They're all Mears cops, too. So were my father and father-in-law, Joe O'Toole. He and his wife, Francis, live next door to my parents and are part of the family, too."

Mark's fork clattered against his plate. "You're *married?*"

"I was. My husband was on the force, too. He was killed in a drug raid a little over a year ago."

The shock on Mark's face melted away, changing to compassion. "Aw, hell, Casey, I'm sorry. That must have been tough."

"Yes. It was. It still is at times, but the pain eases a little with each day that passes." She stared at her plate and fiddled with the handle on her coffee cup for a moment, then drew a deep breath. "Somehow, you have to find a way to move on. Otherwise the grief will consume you."

"Does it help to talk about him?" Mark asked quietly.

"I haven't had a chance to find out. My family and friends all avoid even mentioning Tim's name. Even my in-laws, and I know they're hurting, too. I think everyone's afraid it will upset me to talk about him. Instead, not talking about him makes me feel as though they've forgotten him, or want to pretend that he never existed, and that makes the pain worse."

"I'm sure it does. So...how did you two meet?"

"I don't know."

"Excuse me?"

Casey chuckled, the tightness that always squeezed her chest when she thought about Tim easing a bit. "Tim was six months old when I was born. He and his parents have always lived next door to us, so he was a part of my life from the beginning."

She went on to explain how their fathers had been partners on the job and lifelong best friends, how, as young men, they'd invested in the rural piece of property together and built their homes side by side.

"Sounds like a great way to grow up," Mark commented when she explained how, as kids, they'd all run wild on the five-hundred-acre property.

"It was." Nostalgia flooded Casey as the memories came rushing in. "We fished and hunted, built tree houses and rope swings. Once we built a raft. We were going be like Tom Sawyer and pole it downstream to the next town—wherever that was." She laughed and shook her head. "We hadn't allowed for differences between the Mississippi River and a Colorado mountain stream. We hadn't gone a hundred yards before we went over a small waterfall and the raft broke up on the rocks. The creek was shallow, but it's always icy cold and swift-running. I couldn't swim or gain my footing and would've drowned if my oldest brother, Will, hadn't hauled me out, shivering and choking. Believe me, we all got in trouble for that escapade."

"When did you know that you were in love with Tim?"

"Oh, I knew before we started school. Being a typical little boy, it took him a while longer," she replied with a laugh. "When he was about fourteen he informed me that when we got out of high school we would get married."

This time it was Mark's turn to laugh. "Just like that?"

"Just like that. And we did. With our parents' help, and both of us working, we graduated from Colorado University four years later and we both joined the Mears Police Department." The laughter faded from her eyes and her voice dropped to a husky pitch. "We'd just celebrated our tenth anniversary when Tim was killed."

"Any children?"

She shook her head. "No. We wanted kids, but it never happened. I regret that so much. If I'd had a child, at least a part of Tim would have lived on. His parents and I would have that much."

"Mmm. Sometimes it's difficult to know why things happen the way they do," Mark said gently. "All we can do is accept."

"I know." She gave him a wan smile. "I'm trying. Thanks for letting me ramble on. It does help."

"Anytime."

Mark finished his meal and took a sip of his coffee. "So you never dated anyone but Tim before you married?"

"No. Actually, I doubt that you could classify our

courtship as dating. We just sort of grew up together, and we were nearly always chaperoned by one or more of my brothers."

"How about during this past year? Have you gone out with anyone?"

"Heavens no. To tell you the truth, the very idea of dating for the first time at my age is intimidating. I'm in no rush."

"I can sympathize with you there," Mark said with a laugh. "After you pass about twenty-five or -six the whole singles scene loses its appeal. You just want to find someone you can love forever and share life with."

Casey picked up her coffee cup and cradled it between both hands. She looked at Mark over the rim. "So, why haven't you?"

"I could say there wasn't time, what with my medical studies and getting established in a practice and all, but the truth is, I've just never met the right person. I've always had this feeling that when I did, I would know it."

"Hmm." She took a sip of coffee. "I guess it could happen that way. I hope you find her soon."

"Oh, I intend to," he said, staring at her in that intense way that made her stomach feel fluttery.

Then he cleared his throat, signaling a change of subject. "My niece's team has a game tomorrow night. Do you think you could make it?"

"Tomorrow night? I'm sorry. I have dinner at my parents' house every Sunday and Wednesday."

"*Every* Sunday and Wednesday."

"Uh-huh. The first one of us kids to move out of the house was my oldest brother, Will. Ever since then it's been a tradition in our family that we all meet for dinner on those two nights."

"I see. That sounds nice. But you don't think they would understand if you missed just one time to do this?"

Probably, Casey thought, given the way her parents had responded to him, but she wasn't going to admit that. "Maybe, but I don't want to risk hurting Mom's feelings."

"Well, let's see, this week the team is scheduled to play Wednesday, Thursday and Friday nights. How about Friday night?"

"I could probably make it then, as long as you don't mind me being late. After work on Tuesdays and Thursdays I do my martial arts training at the police gym. I missed my workout this evening because of Mary Kate's problem. I need two sessions a week to stay in shape so I'd planned to make it up on Friday night."

"I see. Okay, sure. That'll be fine. The game doesn't start until six and usually lasts until around eight. Just show up anytime before it's over. We play at the civic center. Jennifer's team is called the Trailblazers, and their uniforms are green and white."

"Fine. I'll find you."

Mark reached across the table and squeezed her hand, and Casey felt a tingle run up her arm.

"I really appreciate your doing this, Casey."

"No problem." She saw the earnestness in his eyes, and silently chastised herself. Idiot. The man's not interested in you. He's just devoted to his niece, is all. "You must really love your niece to give up so much of your free time to coach her softball team."

"I do. She's a great kid. You'll like her. My brother is a widower. It's difficult to bring up a daughter without a mother to guide her. Plus, Matt has to travel a lot in his business, so I try to give him a hand with raising her."

"I see." Score another point for the doctor, Casey thought. Family loyalty was high on her list of endearing traits in a man.

Mark glanced at her almost empty cup. "Would you like a warm-up on that coffee?"

"Oh, no thanks. I've had enough. Actually, I'd better be—"

"Dr. Adams. Dr. Mark Adams. Please report to Recovery," a voice on the PA system requested.

Mark blotted his mouth and tossed his wadded-up napkin aside. "That's me. Look, I'm sorry, but I have to go. My patient is probably in need of some heavy-duty painkillers about now."

"Oh, don't worry about me. I should be getting home, anyway."

As they stood up, Mark took her arm. "C'mon. I'll walk you out."

They rode the elevator in silence, and on the first floor he stepped out into the front lobby with her.

"Don't let me keep you, Doc. My car's just a few feet outside the entrance," Casey said, but he paid no attention.

"Then it won't take long to walk you there, will it? It's late, and that parking lot isn't that well lit."

Casey slanted him a dry look. "Doc, I'm a cop. I can take care of myself."

"So humor me."

In only seconds they left behind the light spilling from the hospital entrance. The deserted parking lot was dark except for the pools of amber cast by the parking lot lights. A steady stream of vehicle headlights passed by on Johnson Avenue, which ran in front of the hospital, and the distant sound of traffic floated to them. Overhead one of the stanchion lights buzzed.

An involuntary shiver ran through Casey, but the chilling night air seemed not to bother Mark, even though he wore only the thin hospital scrubs.

They reached her car and Casey unlocked the door, climbed in and started the engine, then lowered the window. "Thanks for dinner. You were right, it wasn't bad."

"It was my pleasure."

"And thanks for letting me ramble on about my husband and family."

Bracing his forearms along the window opening, Mark bent down until their faces were level and only inches apart. His slumberous gaze roamed leisurely over her face, finally settling on her mouth. He stared at her lips, and Casey thought she saw something flicker in his eyes. Something hot and hungry.

Her heart began to pound.

Then he reached out and flicked the end of her nose with his forefinger. "Drive careful. And I'll see you in the morning at the park."

He turned and jogged away through the rows of cars, leaving Casey staring after him with her mouth agape.

Eleven

On her run the next morning Casey reached the southeast corner of the park and found Mark waiting for her. With only a friendly "Good morning," he fell in step beside her.

Casey wanted to be annoyed, but she couldn't muster a good reason to be. Mark neither crowded her nor distracted her with chatty conversation. Side by side they followed the path, the slap of their shoes in unison against the ground, creating a rhythmic beat, their deep, raspy breathing in sync. There was no tension or awkwardness. They simply ran through the serene stillness of the park at dawn in the companionable silence of two dedicated runners.

While Casey did not feel she needed protection, she had to admit it was nice to have someone to keep her company, to feel somehow connected to another person.

Throughout the entire run neither spoke until they reached the point directly across from her town house, where they parted company with a casual "See ya."

The day turned out to be a calm one. Mary Kate called in a snit because the doctor had still not decided whether or not he would let her go home. Casey listened to her cousin's complaints and finally managed to calm her and promised that if she had to stay in the hospital another day she would stop by on her way home.

She picked Dennis up from the hospital a little before noon and drove him to the station house to pick up his car. He went home and showered, shaved, changed clothes and picked up fresh ones for the next day, just in case Mary Kate did not get to go home that afternoon.

After lunch Casey and her partner spent most of the day canvassing the rest of the St. Martins' neighborhood and the businesses in the strip mall in which Becky Belcamp's studio was based. It was tedious, fruitless work. No one, it seemed, had seen anything.

The next morning Mark again joined her on her run and they again circled the park in silence. Slowing to a stop across the street from her house, Casey began her cool-down stretches. "I'd like to talk…to your nurse and…your receptionist today," she said, doing forward lunges, first on one leg, then the other. "At the station house."

"Fine," Mark agreed, running in place beside her. "I can't spare…them both at once…though. I'll send Martha…this morning and Jolie…after lunch."

"Okay. Thanks."

"No problem. See ya." He waved and took off again along the jogging path, leaving Casey doing slow side-to-side stretches and staring after him.

An hour and a half later, about twenty minutes before her shift officially started, Casey walked into an empty squad room. She could hear Keith and his partner in the coffee room shooting the breeze with the night-watch guys, but no one sat at the desks scattered throughout the room.

Casey went into the detective squad's bathroom/dressing room and stowed her purse away in her locker. When she came out a few minutes later, the rest of the detectives still had not arrived.

She glanced at Lieutenant Bradshaw's office, not surprised to see him already at his desk, talking on the telephone.

The pressure was on, and the entire squad was feeling the heat.

The news media was demanding answers and keeping the citizens of Mears stirred up with daily broadcasts and articles, consisting mostly of speculation and rumors.

Lieutenant Bradshaw was bombarded daily with telephone calls and visits—from the brass, the mayor, councilors and every other petty functionary who could talk his way past Monica, who was doing her best to screen all calls and visitors.

Day by day, the lieutenant grew more brooding and grouchy, like an old grizzly with an impacted tooth. Casey knew he was probably taking a lot of flack about the lack of progress on the case, though he had not passed the criticism along.

She felt bad that he was taking all the blame, when it was her case and her task force. Common sense told her to count her blessings and leave the matter alone, but she was curious about what was being said and what the sheriff was up to. Knowing now would probably be a good time to talk to him, while the squad room was all but empty, she went to the door of his office and knocked. "May I talk to you a minute, boss?"

"What is it, O'Toole?" he growled. "And make it quick. I'm busy."

"Well, sir, I…I couldn't help but notice that you've been getting a lot of calls, and the mayor came to see you yesterday, and Monica told me that the sheriff dropped by, too, while Dennis and I were in the field."

Actually, what their civilian aide had said was that Sheriff Crawford had stormed into the station house on Tuesday morning and closeted himself in the task-force room with his two deputies for almost an hour. Afterward he stomped into Lieutenant Bradshaw's office, and the two men had engaged in a shouting match.

"So? What's your point?"

"It's just that…well…I know that you're under a lot of pressure from the brass and others to get this case solved, and I wondered if there was anything I could do to take the heat off of you? If you want me to answer their questions or explain what's being done, or offer to step down…."

"Dammit, O'Toole! You don't worry about any of that. I told you I had your back, and that's all you need to know. You just concentrate on catching this scumbag. I'll pick off the snipers and handle the stuff that rolls downhill. Got it?"

"Yes, sir."

"Okay, then. Now get out of here."

Caustic as his words had been, Casey left the lieutenant's office feeling marginally better about things. She knew the gruff statement was his way of saying that he had faith in her ability and knew that she'd do all that was humanly possible to capture the killer. And that he'd take whatever heat was aimed at her.

Keith was bent over her desk, scribbling on a notepad, when she walked back into the squad room.

"Hey, beautiful, I was just leaving you a note," he said when he straightened and saw her.

"'Morning, Keith. What's up?"

"Your phone was ringing when I came in. Evidently Monica isn't here yet, so I took a message for you. Dennis is at the hospital with his wife. He said to tell you that he'll be here as soon as he talks to the doctor."

Concern marked his handsome face. "I hope your cousin is okay? Dennis didn't give me any particulars."

"Mary Kate is having difficulty carrying the twins to term," she explained absently, wondering if she could call and check on her cousin before she started work. "She went into early labor two days ago and had to be hospitalized, but the doctor was able to stop the contractions.

"I wonder why he didn't call me on my cell phone?" She pulled the instrument out of her blazer pocket to check it. "Oh, damn. I forgot to turn the darn thing on. Did Dennis seem worried? Did he want me to call him back?"

"No. He seemed his usual self."

"Hmm. Well, I guess everything is still all right or he would be calling in the family."

"Yeah, I'm sure you're right. That's one of the really great things about your family. You all stick together. It must be nice to grow up in an atmosphere like that."

Struck by something in his tone, Casey really looked at him, and it occurred to her for the first time that she knew very little about Keith's background. "It is. I take it you didn't have that?" she asked cautiously.

"Me? Naw. Our mother died when Danny was just a toddler. And our father, well...when he wasn't working he was drunk. So mostly Danny and I looked after ourselves."

Meaning he looked after Danny, Casey thought. That explained a lot, like the closeness between the two of them, and Keith's protective attitude toward his handicapped younger brother. Possibly even Keith's almost obsessive neatness. That was one thing he could control. "I'm sorry. I had no idea."

"Hey, don't worry about us. Danny and I managed fine. It's just that sometimes I think it would be nice to have a big, close-knit family like yours."

The wistfulness in his voice, which he probably did not realize he was revealing, tugged at Casey's heartstrings. She put her hand on his arm. "All the same, I wish life had been a little kinder to you both."

Keith looked down at her hand. He put his own hand over hers and gave it a squeeze, his warm gaze returning to her face. "Thanks. You're sweet. Say, why don't you join me for a drink at Muldoon's after work?"

"Sounds good, but I can't. I've got a martial arts workout scheduled, then afterward I'm going to my folks' house if Mary Kate gets released from the hospital today. You know how it is with my family."

"Yeah. I understand."

"Excuse me, Detective O'Toole. I was told you wanted to speak to me."

Casey pulled her hand from beneath Keith's and turned to find Mark's nurse standing just inside the door, looking stiff and resentful.

"Mrs. Harvey. Yes, thank you for coming in."

"I can't for the life of me imagine why you would want to talk to me," the gray-haired woman said in a belligerent tone. "You surely don't think that *I* took a rifle and shot those poor women?"

"No, Mrs. Harvey, I don't." Striving for patience, Casey sent up a silent prayer that Dennis would get there soon. With his plodding, genial manner, he could usually have a recalcitrant female like Mrs. Harvey eating out of his hand within minutes. But it looked like she would have to handle this interview alone.

Casey forced a smile. "However, without knowing it, you may have some information that could be helpful. Why don't we talk in the coffee room. It'll be more private in there."

The interview yielded nothing of importance. Martha Harvey cooperated, after a fashion, but she was huffy and irritable, and Casey had to pull every scrap of information out of her.

At the end of the interview Casey rose and shook the nurse's hand. "Thank you for your help, Mrs. Harvey. I'm sure the doctor has cautioned you, but let me remind you not to talk to anyone about this. We're doing all we can on this end to keep his name out of the news, but you have to careful, as well. If word gets out that all the victims were your boss's patients, it could ruin his practice."

Martha Harvey looked at Casey with a hint of new respect. "Well. I'm glad to hear that his reputation concerns you. But don't you worry about me," she said, scraping her chair back to stand up. "I wouldn't for the world do anything to hurt Dr. Adams."

On her way out, Mrs. Harvey passed Dennis coming in.

"Sorry I'm later than I said I'd be. Dr. Thomas was late making his morning rounds." He plopped down at his desk and nodded toward the stairs that Mrs. Harvey had just descended. "I see you've started the interviews. Did you get anything we could use from that nurse?"

"Not really. She claims that no one but she and her husband have access to her office key, and that they were both home on the nights of all three murders. The doc's receptionist is suppose to come in after lunch. Maybe we'll get something from her. How's Mary Kate?"

"Doing great."

After spending only one night at the hospital with his wife, Dennis looked a little frayed around the edges, but happy and relieved.

"If all continues to go well, I'll check her out and take her home around four this afternoon."

"Terrific." Casey checked her wristwatch. "Time for the daily briefing with the task force. I want to find out where we stand on the van checks. Also, Hugh Longmont got a tip from an informant that he was going to check on. I want to hear how that panned out.

"If we get through early enough I want to go talk to the crime-lab people. We should have some forensic results on the victims' clothing by now."

"Sounds good to me."

Despite the nagging sense of urgency that ate away at Casey, the day moved along at a frustratingly normal pace. She could not shake the feeling that there was something she was overlooking, or the more ominous sense that if they didn't get a break soon another woman would die.

The trip to the forensics lab had to be put off until after lunch as the meeting with the task force ate up most of the morning. Trooper Longmont's tip turned out to be bogus—a snitch with a drug problem looking to score some informant money with a made-up story.

"I suspected from the get-go that he was stringing me along," Hugh said. "He was coming down off a high and desperate to make a buy. But I had to check out his story."

"Right," Casey agreed. "We can't afford not to look into every possible lead. It's not like we have a lot to go on." Tips poured in daily. So far, none had led anywhere, but they all had to be checked out.

Running down false leads and rumors ate up time and manpower and got them nowhere. Merely checking the snitch's story had taken Hugh a day and a half.

The team had a few more possible suspects from the van list to run down, but nothing red-hot. More and more, that avenue was looking like a dead end.

They discussed the cases from every angle, exchanging ideas and theories and suggested strategies and possible lines of investigation, but nothing viable emerged. In the end the only thing left to do was continue to check out every tip and at the same time dig in and go back over what they already had—revisit crime scenes, go over all the case files again, and reinterview everyone connected with the victims.

In the case of the first victim, that meant trying to locate friends and family. The sheriff's investigation had turned up almost nothing on the woman other than her name and arrest record. Casey could not help but wonder if the sheriff would have pursued the case with more vigor had she not been a part-time prostitute.

As promised, Dr. Adams's receptionist, Jolie Graver, arrived at the station house. The interview with her turned out much the same as the one that morning with Martha Harvey, yielding little and causing the subject to bristle with resentment.

Whether the women were still smarting on behalf of their boss, or their animosity stemmed from personal affront, was a toss-up.

Unlike Martha, Jolie could not recall what she or her husband had been doing on two of the three of the nights when the murders had taken place. Since an alibi provided by a spouse was not considered the most reliable, neither of the women nor their husbands could be ruled out entirely. However, with nothing directly connecting any of them to the crimes other than access to the patient files, neither could they be considered strong suspects.

After grabbing a couple of corned-beef-on-rye sandwiches at Muldoon's, Casey and Dennis returned to the station house after lunch and found that the medical examiner had left a message for her to come to the lab, that she had something to show her.

Casey informed the lieutenant, then she and Dennis drove to the state-of-the-art forensics lab that was part of the new morgue/medical examiner's facility on the southern edge of town. In addition to serving Mears and the county, the complex serviced most of the small towns along the western slope.

"What have you got for us?" Casey asked Dr. Betty Beaudreaux the moment they walked in through the swinging double doors.

"Another piece to the puzzle, I think," the middle-aged medical examiner replied. "One of our technicians scraped all the clothing from all of the victims and came up with something I think you'll find interesting."

"Please tell me it's seminal fluid. Or at least skin scrapings or hair. Anything we can use to get a DNA profile."

"Sorry. Either we're not that lucky or our perp isn't that stupid. The presence of latex powder indicates he used a condom with each victim, and there was no tissue under the victims' fingernails. However, present on the skin and clothing of each victim were some very distinctive fiber samples."

She led them to a workstation and placed a slide between the specimen holders on the stage of a microscope and adjusted the focus. "Take a look at this," she said, stepping back.

Casey peered through the eyepieces. "They're bright green fibers. So what?"

"Notice the shape?"

"They're triangular."

"Right. That's a very unusual shape for fibers. Combine that with the neon-green color and you narrow your search. They're synthetic, and also fairly long and twisted. My guess is they're carpet fibers, probably a shag made for a vehicle. There can't be a lot of manufacturers who make that particular carpet in that particular color."

"So we're looking for a light-colored van with neon-green carpeting."

"Looks like it."

Casey straightened and Dennis took a look at the strands.

"There were an unusually large number of the fibers on the clothes and skin of each victim," the M.E. continued. "My guess would be that they were picked up from the perp's trunk or the back of his van while he was transporting them."

"You're probably right," Casey agreed, trying not to imagine the terrified women, bound and gagged, lying in the dark on the putrid-green shaggy carpet. "Anything else?"

"Nope. As far as science goes, that's it, given the evidence we have to work with. I did as you asked and ran every test possible on all three victims. Here are the updated files. The results are all in there.

"However, if you want a personal opinion, I noticed that with each victim the killer is inflicting more damage, getting more vicious. My guess is, he's enjoying killing." The usually unemotional M.E. put her hand on Casey's arm, and her voice dropped, taking on an urgent edge. "Get this guy, Casey. You get him. He's a bad one."

"Yeah, I know. Believe me, Doc, I'm trying."

By the time they returned to the station house it was time for Dennis to leave to go to the hospital. Mary Kate had called earlier with the good news that Dr. Thomas had given the okay for her to go home.

After Dennis left, Casey went over the new information with the lieutenant, and they decided to keep it to themselves, fearing the killer would replace the distinctive carpet if the new lead got out to the media.

Back at her desk, she gave the files a cursory look, but it was already past the end of the shift so she locked the updated M.E.'s reports away in her desk.

Leaving the station house, Casey felt frustrated and depressed over the lack of progress on the case and irritated by the constant niggling feeling that there was something she wasn't seeing, something just out of reach. It didn't help that the moment she reached the bottom of the stairs she was met by a gaggle of reporters and photographers, all jostling to stick a microphone in her face and yelling questions.

Replying "No comment," Casey put her head down

and shouldered her way through, sending the sergeant behind the front desk a silent plea for help as she passed.

He nodded and signaled to a group of uniform cops, who "accidentally" blocked the way while Casey escaped out the door. By the time the group of news people made it outside she was driving away from the station house.

Casey would have preferred to go home and curl up on her sofa and think, but she was too self-disciplined to skip her workout, and family-dinner night had been postponed twenty-four hours to celebrate Mary Kate's release from the hospital. With a sigh, Casey turned onto the northbound highway out of town.

She was the last to arrive at her parents' home that evening. Mary Kate was ensconced on the den sofa, holding court and being fussed over by Casey's mom and mother-in-law. The moment Mary Kate saw Casey, she wanted to hear all about what had happened between her and Dr. Adams at dinner two nights ago, and she pouted when Casey brushed aside her excitement with a casual "It was no big deal, so don't get your hopes up. He's not interested in me."

"Fiddle-dee-dee. I saw the way he was looking at you that night. He couldn't keep his eyes off you."

"You're imagining things. Again. But I love you, anyway." She bent and kissed her cousin's forehead, then turned to her mother. "What's for dinner?"

"Casey Collins O'Toole, you get back here this minute and talk to me," her cousin demanded.

Casey rolled her eyes. "What? There's nothing to talk about. Nothing happened. We had dinner in the hospital cafeteria and talked about ordinary stuff. Nothing romantic."

Mary Kate sighed. "What am I going to do with you? You take a perfect opportunity and blow it. At least tell me that you agreed to talk to his niece's softball team."

"Yes, I did. I'm going to go to their game either tomorrow or Saturday evening, depending on how things go at work. I'll talk to the girls after the game. Satisfied?"

"Not really, but at least it's something."

"Good. Now can we eat dinner?"

Throughout the meal, the three youngest of Casey's brothers badgered her for the latest on the serial-murder cases, but Casey just shook her head and kept eating. After a while Will and her father ordered them to knock off the questions. Casey was so preoccupied she barely noticed.

After dinner she helped with the dishes, but her mind wandered and she found it difficult to follow the chatter of the other women. When they were done, instead of settling in the den with the rest of the family for a visit like always, she made an excuse to leave.

"Wait a second," Mary Kate said. "Before you leave, at least tell me what you're going to wear on your date."

"What do you mean, what am I going to wear? Whatever I wear to work, of course. If it even turns out that I can go tomorrow night. I'm going to the training center after my shift and work out. After I shower I'll go to the game from there."

"Oh, for heaven's sake. You can't go dressed like that." Her cousin looked to the two other women for support. "Will one of you tell her?"

"Casey, sweeting, Mary Kate's right. Your trousers and blazer look very nice and are perfect for work, but they're not exactly appropriate attire for a date," her mother said.

"It's not *a date!*"

"You are so naive," Mary Kate declared with a wave of her hand. "Of course it's a date. You just haven't figured it out yet."

"What's this?" His ears suddenly perking up, Will looked from one woman to the next. "Stretch has a date?"

Earlier, Casey's brothers had been embroiled in a heated discussion about which professional baseball team was going to win the World Series this year and hadn't heard her and Mary Kate talking about Dr. Adams.

"Hey, sis, way to go," Brian chimed in.

"Who is he?" Aiden asked. "Do we know him?"

Putting in his two cents' worth, Ian said, "Yeah. What precinct does he work out of?"

"He's not a cop. He's a doctor," Mary Kate informed them with barely contained excitement. "A very good-looking, very charming, very successful doctor."

All of her brothers looked shocked, even sensible, serious Will. You would have thought her cousin had announced that Casey was going out with an alien from another planet. They could not conceive of her being interested in any man who wasn't a cop.

Granda Seamus, however, seemed pleased. "Well, now, tisn't that grand. A doctor, is it? What with the cost of health care these days, we could use a good doctor in this family."

"Now see what you've done," Casey scolded the other women. "Granda, listen to me. I'm not going out with a doctor. And I'm certainly not about to marry one just so you can have free medical care."

"Of course you're not, Casey, darlin'," he said, patting her cheek. "That's just a bonus."

"Granda—"

"What's this guy's name?"

"Where did you meet him?"

"How old is he? Are you sure he's single? Sometimes married guys lie, you know."

"Yeah. You need to be careful. A young widow like you would be ripe pickin's for one of those slick types."

"You'd better let us check him out before you go out with him. I'll run his name through the system in the morning."

"You'll do nothing of the sort," Mary Kate declared, cutting off the brothers' barrage of questions. "And don't you dare tell these Neanderthals his name," she ordered, sending Casey a warning scowl. "They'll scare the poor man away."

"Hey! She's *our* sister. We've got a right to protect her," the youngest, Ian, declared.

"Will you people please listen to me?" Casey yelled, and pressed the heels of her hands against her temples.

In an instant you could hear a pin drop. Everyone in the room—her brothers, her parents, Granda, Joe and Francis O'Toole, Mary Kate and Dennis, even little Roger—gaped at her with a combination of surprise and chagrin on their faces.

"Good. That's better. Now, I want you all to listen to me. I don't have a date. I'm going to talk to a team of thirteen-year-old girls about careers for women on the job, and maybe, if there's time, about safety practices for women. That's it. Our starry-eyed cousin here has merely blown the whole thing up into something it isn't. Got it?"

They all nodded and mumbled apologies. Satisfied, Casey turned to go. She was halfway out the door when Mary Kate called after her, "All the same, Casey, prom-

ise me you'll come by here tomorrow after your workout and let me help you get ready. I have the perfect
summer sundress for you to wear."

Stopping dead in her tracks, Casey closed her eyes,
ground her teeth and prayed for patience.

"Promise me, Casey, or I swear, I'll get off this sofa
and come and get you."

She wouldn't, and they all knew it, nevertheless the
statement sent up a collective gasp from all around the
room, and Maureen admonished, "Mary Kate, you'll do
nothing of the kind! You know what the doctor—"

"I will, too, if Casey refuses to let me help her."

"All right, all right," Casey surrendered. "I'll do it.
I'll be here tomorrow evening. I promise."

With a self-satisfied little smile, Mary Kate reclined
back against her mound of pillows and crossed her arms
over her belly, and the others relaxed, as well.

Casey's narrowed gaze swept the room. "But it's *not*
a date."

Twelve

The next day went much the same as the one before. The only difference being that when Casey emerged from her town house for her morning run Mark was waiting across the street beside the park bench. She didn't ask why and he offered no explanation, merely fell in step beside her as usual.

"Did you get what you needed from Martha and Jolie yesterday?" he asked when they'd been running for about ten minutes.

"I guess. I'd hoped for more, but I knew that was a long shot."

"Hmm," he replied, and after that they ran the three-mile course in silence, then again parted with a friendly "See ya."

Watching him go, Casey felt more certain than ever that all Dr. Mark Adams wanted from her was friendship. His general attitude toward her was casual and pleasant, but not by any stretch of the imagination would she call it flirtatious. If once in a while she felt a spark of excitement when he got close or she looked into those sexy gray eyes, that was her problem.

Anyway, it meant nothing. Mark was a fantastic-looking man and she was reacting to his physical beauty. That was all.

On Casey's arrival at the precinct she and Dennis spent the first hour with the task force. In the last twenty-four hours a half dozen more tips had been called in anonymously. Each of the other four men on the task force were assigned one to check out and she and Dennis took the other two.

Casey listened to the men's discouraging reports and suggestions. She then instructed them to widen the search to include every van owner in the entire state and to go back over the ones they had already checked out and dig deeper into the background of anyone who had been in the vicinity of any of the crimes on the nights they were committed. She also asked them to check out anyone about whom they had a gut feeling.

Casey and Dennis, meanwhile, followed up on the two tips. Both turned out to be dead ends. After lunch they began the tedious process of reinterviewing. By the end of the day, they were weary and discouraged.

"Damn," Dennis muttered, leaving the apartment of one of Becky Belcamp's employees. "We're getting nowhere fast. I don't know about you, but I'm going to call it a day."

"We might as well," Casey agreed. She rolled her shoulders to loosen the tension in her back. "I'm heading for the gym. What I need is a no-holds-barred match with Leo."

"Uh-oh. I'd better give him a call and warn him. When you're stymied by a case, you're dangerous."

"Very funny."

Leo Chang was the martial arts instructor at the po-
lice-training center. He had trained Casey, and since
her graduation had been her regular sparring partner.
Leo was the best. He had lightning-quick reflexes and
lethal moves. Even so, she had fought him to a draw a
few times, mostly when she'd been working off frustration and anger.

"And don't forget you're supposed to go to that game
tonight. So come by when you finish playing kick-butt
with Leo. Mary Kate will be expecting you. We'll be at
your folks'."

"Oh, thanks so much for reminding me," Casey
drawled.

The match with Leo was fast, furious and aggressive,
and just what she needed. Several times she drove her
former instructor to the edge of the mat and knocked
him on his keister. He had to call upon all his skills to
counter her attacks and score some points of his own.
When the ref finally called the match a draw, Casey and
Leo bowed to each other, both panting and exhausted,
their skin glowing with a sheen of sweat.

"Very good, Detective," the small Asian man said
with pride.

"Th-thanks. One…one of these…days I'm going to
beat you," Casey replied, burying her face in a towel.

"Of that I have no doubt. You are my best student. You
have the heart of the Tiger that your partner calls you."

At the mention of Dennis, Casey's gaze darted to the
clock on the far wall. "Sorry, Leo, but I've got to run."

She dashed out, grabbing her gym bag and clothing
on the way. A little after six she drove into the clearing,
parked in front of her parents' home and ran inside.

Maureen accepted her daughter's quick kiss on the cheek, then pointed toward the stairs. "Mary Kate is up in your old room, waiting for you."

"Poor Dennis. She made him carry her all the way up there?"

Her mother laughed. "You know Dennis. Mary Kate's wish is his command."

Casey took the stairs two at a time and dashed into the big corner room that she and her cousin had shared for four years. The bedroom was still as it had been when she and Mary Kate were teenagers—pink rosebud wallpaper, white-painted furniture and mint-green accents.

"It's about time you got here," Mary Kate scolded. "I was getting ready to send out a search party."

"I told you I had a workout scheduled. I got here as soon as I could."

"Who won the match, Tiger?" Dennis asked.

"It was a draw."

"I knew it! I knew you were going to kick butt."

Mary Kate lay propped up against a mound of pillows on the twin bed that had been hers. Dennis sat beside her, and their toddler played on the floor with one of the stuffed animals from Casey's childhood.

"Never mind that martial arts stuff. My goodness. Look at you," Mary Kate said, wrinkling her nose. "You're a mess."

"I know. Just let me take a quick shower."

"Well, hurry up. You're late already," her cousin called after her.

Fifteen minutes later Casey poked her head out of the bathroom. Her face was scrubbed and shiny clean, her wet hair wrapped in a towel. "Is the coast clear?"

"Yes, come on out. Dennis took the baby outside to

play. There's your outfit. Aunt Maureen fetched everything from the cottage for me earlier this afternoon."

Clutching the towel she'd wrapped around her body, Casey padded barefoot across the room to her old bed. "You've got to be kidding. *That's* what you picked out for me to wear? Who wears an outfit like that to a softball game?"

"A smart woman who wants to knock the socks off a certain handsome doctor, that's who," Mary Kate fired back. "And don't look at me like that. It's not as though I'm asking you to wear a ball gown or anything inappropriate. That outfit isn't even very dressy. It's just a feminine skirt and top. Now, hurry up. You don't have much time."

"I never said that I *wanted* to attract Dr. Adams."

"Don't be silly. Of course you do. Now, get dressed."

"Uh, don't you think something more casual, say a pair of slacks or capri pants, would be a better choice?"

"No, I don't. This is casual enough."

Casey groaned. "C'mon, Mary Kate. I'm going to stand out like a sore thumb in this get-up."

"My point, exactly. The stands will be full of moms in their jeans and shorts and crop pants and scruffy athletic shoes. In that lavender you'll look like a lilac in a weed patch. I know what I'm doing, Casey, so will you just quit arguing and get dressed?"

"Oh, all right. Just don't expect anything to come of this. Okay? I keep telling you this isn't a date. Mark isn't interested in me that way. And quit nagging me about the time. He knows that I'm going to be late."

"Oh? Well, I suppose it wouldn't hurt to keep him waiting for a little while in any case. And that'll give us more time to work on your hair and makeup."

Casey knew better than to argue. When Mary Kate had that look in her eye you just went along and hoped for the best.

With a defeated sigh, she dropped the towel, stepped into the ecru bikini panties and matching lace bra she'd brought with her and put on the clothes. "The skirt and top I'll go along with, but do I have to wear these?" she asked, dangling the strappy high-heeled lavender sandals from her forefinger.

"Of course you do. They complete the outfit. Oh, Casey, sweetie, that color is glorious on you. I just knew it would be. Go look in the mirror."

Casey finished slipping on the sandals and went to stand in front of the full-length mirror attached to the inside of the closet door. At the first glimpse of herself, her eyes widened. A blazer, cotton tee and slacks made up her usual work attire. On Sundays for church she sometimes wore dresses, but they were of the sedate variety. It had been years since she'd dressed in this kind of feminine clothing. She had to admit, wearing the ultra "girlie" outfit made her feel beautiful.

The gored, deep lavender trumpet skirt hugged her waist and hips, then flared out at midthigh into a flirty little flounce that swished around her knees with the slightest movement, drawing attention to her legs, which, she had to admit, looked darned good in the strappy high heels.

The two-inch ruffle around the bottom of the button-down-the-front overblouse barely covered the waistband of the skirt. Made of a silky floral material in several shades of lavender and purple, it had a ruffle-trimmed sweetheart neckline, a fitted bodice and three-quarter sleeves with six-inch ruffle flounces at the bottoms that fluttered around her wrists and forearms.

"What do you think?" Mary Kate asked.

"It looks good," Casey replied.

"See. I told you that I know what I'm doing. When will you learn to trust me?" Not expecting an answer, Mary Kate waved Casey over to the bed. "Now, come over here and let me do your makeup. I have my kit right here."

"Mary Kate, I can put on my own makeup," Casey protested, sitting down on the bed beside her cousin.

"I know, but I can do it better. Now, turn this way."

Giving in, Casey sat semipatiently on the side of the bed and let her cousin work her magic.

"There. You look gorgeous," the other woman announced finally. "Now, take off that towel and let's do something with your hair."

"That's okay. I'm just going to twist it up in a bun," Casey replied, pulling the damp towel off her head. Her thick mane tumbled down her back in a mass of bright red corkscrew curls.

"You most certain are *not!* I didn't go to all this trouble to make you look gorgeous and sexy, just to have you spoil the whole effect with an old-maid bun. You have the most gorgeous hair. Why you insist upon slicking it back I'll never know."

"It's easier to manage that way. It stays out of my way and the style is more appropriate for my job."

"Well, you're not on the job tonight, so you're going to wear it down."

"Down? But it's a wild mass of curls if I don't tame it in some way."

"Yes, and it's lovely. And sexy. And any man with an ounce of red blood in his veins will want to run his hands through it."

Casey gave her cousin a dubious look. "And that's a *good* thing?"

Mary Kate rolled her eyes. "Honestly. You are such an innocent when it comes to men. Trust me, that's definitely a good thing. Now, scoot closer and turn around, while I put this styling gel in your hair."

Casey felt ridiculous. Why in the world had she let her cousin talk her into getting all gussied up like this? she wondered, standing behind the backstop, scanning the bleachers for an empty seat. Every other woman there was dressed in jeans or shorts or something equally casual. Dr. Adams would probably see through her cousin's ploy in a heartbeat, only he'd think that she was the one trying to snare him.

A bat cracked and the crowd of parents went crazy, jumping up off the bleacher seats, shouting and whistling. Casey looked around in time to see a slender, dark-haired girl in a green-and-white uniform toss her bat aside and race for first base while the runner on third took off for home plate.

The batter rounded first and kept going as the left fielder scooped up the ball and threw it to the shortstop. She spun and rifled the ball to the catcher, but the runner from third beat the catch by at least a second and scored.

The batter, in the meantime, rounded second and kept going, arms and legs pumping for all she was worth.

The other team's catcher threw the ball to third.

"Slide! Slide!" the crowd yelled.

The dark-haired girl dove and slid in low.

"Safe!" the ump yelled, signaling the call.

The crowd behind Casey went wild, while the peo-

ple in the bleachers behind the other dugout reacted
with groans.

Casey couldn't help but be infected by the excitement
and clapped along with the others. The bleacher in which
she stood was draped in green-and-white crepe paper,
so she figured she was cheering for the Trailblazers.

That was confirmed a moment later when she heard
her name called. Looking around, she saw Mark heading
her way. He approached the chain-link fence backstop and
waved for her to come around the barrier and join him.

"You made it. I was beginning to worry that something
had come up and you wouldn't," he said when she reached
him. His gaze ran over her in a quick once-over, and a subtle change came over his face, the look in his eyes going
from genial welcome to pure male appreciation.

"Wow. You look fantastic," he murmured. His gaze
traveled over her hair, and to Casey's surprise, he
reached out and lifted a handful of soft curls and let the
fiery strands slither through his fingers, his pupils growing darker and wider as he watched the silky curls fall.
"I like your hair this way," he continued in that deep,
mesmerizing tone. "It's beautiful."

For the first time in her life, Casey felt out of her
depth, as though she were trying to tread water with
weights tied around her legs. No amount of willpower
would stop the flush that crept up over her chest and
neck and spread over her face, but Mark was gentleman
enough to pretend not to notice.

"Uh, thanks. I, uh…I wear slacks to work every day,
so I thought I'd wear a skirt tonight," she stammered,
using the first excuse that popped into her head. She
hoped the explanation did not sound as lame to his ears
as it had to hers.

"You should wear them more often. You look fabulous. C'mon, sit with me and the team. I brought a thermos of coffee with me in case you need a fix."

"Really?"

Casey's face lit up and Mark laughed and took hold of her arm. "I thought you'd like that." He pointed to the scoreboard. "We're in the bottom of the eighth inning with two out. There's only one inning left. Just half an inning if we can hold on to our lead."

"Oh, dear. I'm really sorry to be so late—" Casey started, but he cut her off.

"Don't worry about it. You made it. That's all that's important."

As they drew near, Casey saw an attractive blond woman in the dugout watching them. Uh-oh, Casey thought. Whoever she was, she did not look happy.

Mark introduced her as Debra Neelly, his assistant coach. "Debra fills in for me whenever I have an emergency," he explained.

The woman was barely civil, giving Casey a clipped "Hello," before turning away, ostensibly to watch the game, but a muscle worked along her jaw, and her lips were folded so tight they almost disappeared. Casey had a hunch that the only thing about softball that interested Debra Neelly was Dr. Mark Adams. And she viewed her as competition.

"This is Debra's daughter, Rebecca," Mark went on, indicating the girl sitting at the end of the bench. "She plays second base." He introduced all of the players except for his niece. "That's Jennifer on third base, the one who just hit that triple," he explained. "And the girl going up to bat is Eva Smith."

Mark poured coffee from his thermos into a paper

cup and handed it to Casey. "Here you go. Have a seat on the bench if you want."

"Excuse me," Debra interjected. "She can't sit here. The dugouts are for the players and coaches, not spectators."

"Oh, sorry." Casey shot to her feet, abandoning the seat she'd just taken. She gave Mark an apologetic look and gestured toward the bleachers. "I'll, uh…I'll just go sit in the stands."

"Stay right where you are." He narrowed his eyes on Debra. Though soft, his tone left no doubt of his annoyance. "Casey is here at my invitation. Lighten up, Debra. This is a regional girls' softball game, not the big leagues."

The woman sniffed and raised her chin a notch. "I just think we should obey the rules, is all."

"Let me worry about the rules. If anyone complains, I'll handle it. I want Casey here with me."

Casey winced, wishing he hadn't put it quite that way.

Though it hadn't seemed possible, Debra's jaw grew even tighter. If she's not careful she's going to crack some teeth, Casey thought.

Mark turned back to Casey, his expression relaxing. "Do you know anything about softball?"

"Are you kidding me? I played all through my teen years. For this league, actually. I've been in this very dugout hundreds of times."

"Really? Hey, that's great. The girls will be happy to know you're an alumni."

The girl at bat popped a high fly ball and the crowd erupted again, drawing their attention back to the field. The center fielder caught the ball to retire the side, but not before Mark's niece crossed home plate and scored another run.

"Okay, girls, we're ahead, so get out there and hold 'em," Mark coached as the team poured out of the dugout and took to the field. "Let's wrap this game up."

His niece, Casey noticed, took her position on first base. She appeared to be alert and really into the game, keeping a sharp eye on the batter while keeping up a running stream of encouraging chatter to bolster her teammates. The pitcher was a slender, almost delicate-looking girl, but she had a wicked arm on her. Her windup and pitch were lightning-fast and lethal, and the ball whizzed by the batter like a bullet for a strike call.

The ump called the second pitch a ball, the third a strike, and on the fourth the batter took a vicious swing at the ball and hit nothing but air, striking out. The next batter did the same, and the girls on both teams grew tense as the third batter walked up to the plate.

The first pitch was low and outside. The batter swung at the next two so hard she spun around, nearly augering herself into the ground. The next two pitches appeared to be just within the strike zone, but the ump called them balls.

With two out and a call of two and three, every player on both teams left their benches and stood at the edge of their dugouts, waiting for the next pitch. The delicate pitcher wound up and let fly. The batter swung, getting a piece of the ball, and hit a low grounder that was scooped up by the shortstop and whipped to first, and the Trailblazers won the game.

The team went wild, the girls on the field were jumping up and down and embracing one another, while their teammates poured out of the dugout to join them. When they finally calmed a bit, they came trotting back to the dugout full of good spirits and excitement.

Mark's niece, Jennifer, turned out to be a vivacious, typical thirteen-year-old, full of energy and teenage dramatics. She had dark brown hair and brown eyes, but Casey could see a slight resemblance to her uncle in her finely molded features. The girl would be a beauty someday, Casey decided. As Mark introduced them, Jennifer's excitement grew.

"Oh, Detective, I've been dying to meet you ever since Uncle Mark told me he'd met a policewoman. I saw you on television, and of course I've heard a lot about you from Uncle Mark. You're even more beautiful than he said. The TV didn't do you justice, either," the teenager gushed. "I just *love* your hair! It's *awesome.* And your eyes are so *blue!* They're *gorgeous!*"

The compliments took Casey by surprise, especially the part about Mark describing her as beautiful, and for a few seconds she was at a loss for words. "I…um…well, thanks. I'm happy to meet you, too, Jennifer."

The girl flashed her uncle a grin. "You're right. She is as nice as she is beautiful."

Casey was still trying to absorb that when Mark winked at his niece and raised his voice to be heard over the excited chatter of the girls, who were still congratulating one another on their win. "Okay, girls, get your gear and let's all go inside to the gym. Detective O'Toole is going give you a short talk."

"Rebecca and I are going home," Debra announced in an icy voice.

"But Mo-om! I want to hear what Detective O'Toole has to say."

"Don't argue with me, Rebecca. We're going home."

"If you don't want to stay, we can take Rebecca home afterward," Mark offered.

"No, thank you. Rebecca doesn't need information about joining the police force. I'm sorry," she said, glancing at Casey, but the coldness in her eyes belied the apology. "But I want more for my daughter than that."

Casey shrugged, letting the insult roll off of her like water off a duck's back. The woman was jealous and angry and lashing out. She supposed she could understand that, although, in Casey's view, she was getting herself worked up over nothing.

"That's all right, Ms. Neelly. Although there are those on the force who would argue that law enforcement is the best job in the world, and I'm one of them, I do recognize that it isn't for everyone."

Mark looked as though he wanted to throttle Debra, but seeing the embarrassed reactions of the girls, particularly Rebecca Neelly, he opted for diplomacy.

"I think you're wrong, but if that's how you feel, it probably would be best if you left." He turned to the red-faced teenager and tugged her ponytail. "Sorry you'll miss out, Becca. See you Saturday, okay?"

"Well, I'm glad she's gone," Jennifer said the moment Debra and her daughter were out of sight. Carrying bats, balls, mitts and base pads, the group headed for the civic center building, with Jennifer walking beside Casey and Mark. "Becca is okay, but her mother is a skank."

"Now, Jen," Mark warned. "That's not nice."

"But it's true. The only reason she volunteered to help coach is so she could spend time with you, and you know it. She sure doesn't know anything about softball. That woman's been throwing herself at Uncle Mark ever since she met him about a year ago," the teenager explained to Casey, making a disgusted face.

"Um. I see. I imagine that your uncle has to contend with that sort of thing a lot, being an eligible bachelor *and* a successful doctor."

"And don't forget handsome," the teenager reminded her.

Casey laughed and slanted Mark a teasing look. "And handsome. I'm sure he has to beat women off with a stick."

"Hey! Do you two mind?" Mark protested, holding open the door to the civic center for them. "I'm right here, you know."

With a mischievous twinkle in her eye, Jennifer looped her arm through Casey's and leaned in close as they passed her uncle and stepped into the building. "Don't mind him. He always gets embarrassed when you talk about how good-looking he is."

From behind them came a low, warning rumble that sounded like a cross between a groan and a growl.

Casey kept her talk brief. She stood at the edge of the gymnasium floor in front of the bleachers where the girls had gathered. At first she felt self-conscious and conspicuous in her frilly outfit, but as she got into her topic and the girls responded with genuine interest, she forgot about everything else.

She told them that the department preferred applicants with at least two years of college, but having a degree, particularly in criminology or law, would greatly increase your chances of being accepted. Under certain circumstances they would consider someone with less education, provided they scored high on all the tests.

Explaining the rigorous training—dealing with criminals and the public, spotting trouble, investigative techniques, marksmanship, firearms safety and physical endurance and strength that a recruit received—Casey then stressed to the girls the necessity of keeping fit.

"It's particularly important for women on the job. Men have the natural advantage of being physically stronger than most women. We have to offset that by staying in tip-top shape and knowing how to defend ourselves and how to disarm a suspect in a critical situation."

She explained how the role of women on the force had changed, how they had managed to break through the "glass ceiling" and climb to the highest ranks. "In some cities there are even women who have made it all the way to the upper echelon, in a few cases as far as chief of police," she said with an ironic smile. "Not in Mears, yet, but the day is coming. The point is, do a good job, hone your skills, and the opportunities are there. One thing is certain, there will never be a shortage of bad guys."

When she opened the discussion for questions, the first one was from Jennifer.

"Do you think you'll be chief of police someday, Detective?"

"I'd like to think it's possible," she replied, grinning at the girl's eagerness. "Next question."

The girls responded with enthusiasm, asking intelligent and relevant questions. By the time they called it quits Casey was glad she'd agreed to give the talk.

"We always go out for pizza or burgers after a game," Mark told her when they stepped outside and he locked up the building. "Why don't you come with us?"

"Oh, please say yes, Detective," Jennifer squealed. "That would be so cool."

"Oh, I…uh…"

"You haven't already eaten, have you?" Mark asked.

"Well, no—"

"Good, it's settled, then." He shot Casey a teasing grin. "The coffee there is great, too."

"You convinced me."

Not that it had taken much convincing. Casey was starving. A workout like the one she'd had with Leo Chang earlier always left her ravenous, and usually she went straight home and had dinner. Plus, she liked Jennifer and the lively group of teenagers. Having pizza with them and Mark held much more appeal that eating her mother's leftover stew alone in front of the TV.

"Good. Let's do it. Okay, girls, stop horsing around and let's go," he called to the teenagers in a friendly but authoritative voice, hustling them all toward the parking lot.

There were only two vehicles left in the lot, Casey's car and an extralong white van. Both were on the same row with one empty space between them.

Approaching the other vehicle, Casey felt a chill ripple down her spine. "You drive a van?"

He hit the remote button and a chirp sounded as the doors unlocked. Chattering and giggling, the girls tossed their gear into the back and crowded around the doors to climb in.

"Not all the time. This baby belongs to my brother, Matt. He has an import-export business, and the van is one of his company vehicles. He lets me use it after hours to haul the girls and equipment around."

"I see."

"Why? Is something wrong?"

"No. No, I was just curious. It, uh…it didn't seem your style, is all."

"You mean it looks too domesticated? Like its owner would be a settled family man?"

"Something like that, I guess."

"Let me guess. You probably pictured me driving something like a red Corvette. Or a Jaguar. Right?"

"No, but I didn't think you'd drive a van."

Actually, to her chagrin, he had read her thoughts to the letter. She was a detective, for Pete's sake. She knew better than to jump to conclusions based on appearance—Mark Adams was a young, handsome, successful doctor, ergo he must be a playboy in possession of all the toys that go with the stereotype. For Pete's sake, O'Toole, she silently scolded. A rookie knows better than to make that kind of snap judgment.

"I've got news for you, Casey. You're looking at a man who can't wait to settle down with the right woman, buy a house in the suburbs and a van, and fill both with kids. It won't bother me in the least to be thought of as domesticated. Becoming a husband and family man is my dream."

Casey stared at him, not knowing what to say. Luckily she was spared the need to say anything when Jennifer and another girl piled out of the van and interrupted.

"Uncle Mark, may Susan and I ride with Detective O'Toole to the pizza parlor? We've never ridden in a police car before. Please, please, please. May we, please?" she wheedled.

"Well now, I don't know. It's up to Casey." He turned to her with a questioning look. "Is it okay if they ride with you?"

"Sure. No problem."

"Yay!" The two girls ran across the empty space and

scrambled into the squad car as though they were afraid she might change her mind if they waited around too long.

Chuckling, Casey started after them. "I'll be right behind you," she called over her shoulder to Mark.

Despite the cheerful chatter of the girls in the back seat, her lighthearted mood faded as she drove out of the civic center parking lot behind Mark and the other girls.

Driving with one hand, Casey scribbled the license number of the van down in her notepad and made a mental note to run the number with the DMV. And while she was at it, she'd do a background check on Mark's brother, Matt.

Thirteen

Sharing pizza with thirteen lively and vocal teenage girls turned out to be a lot more enjoyable than Casey had anticipated. Coming off an important win, the girls were full of high spirits and giggles and were just plain fun to be around.

Mark bought eight different large pizzas and several pitchers of soft drinks, which they passed around. Casey was agog at the amount of food, certain that he'd gone overboard, but the girls attacked the pies like a pack of hungry wolves, and within minutes every slice was devoured.

Everybody talked at once. It was pure chaos around the table, but Mark appeared impervious to the din.

Watching him, Casey noted that he was always friendly and patient with the teenagers, but firm. He gave them a sort of offhand, avuncular affection that was in no way threatening or suspect. He laughed at their silliness and joked with them and seemed to genuinely enjoy their company, while always maintaining just the right balance between buddy and confidant and authority figure.

. Around nine o'clock parents began arriving to pick up their daughters. Soon Mark and his niece and Casey were the only ones left.

"Casey and I are going to visit the ladies' room before we go," Jennifer announced out of the blue.

She grabbed Casey's arm, giving her little choice but to go along. As soon as they were inside the tiled facility, Jennifer turned to her almost in tears and wailed, "Please, Casey, you have to help me. You just have to."

"Whoa. Slow down. Of course I'll help you if I can, but first you have to tell me what's wrong."

"I *desperately* need to shop for…well…you know." She waved her hand vaguely and gave Casey a hopeful look.

"No, I'm afraid I don't know. What is it you need?"

Beginning to look frantic, Jennifer wrung her hands and shifted from one foot to the other. "You know…" She looked around, then wrinkled her nose and whispered, "That…feminine product." When Casey still looked blank she added almost in a panic, "For the monthlies."

"Ah, I see. Okay, but what do you need me for? There's an all-night pharmacy right next door? If you don't have any money I'm sure your uncle will pay."

"That's just it. I can't tell Uncle Mark. I just *can't!*"

"Why not?"

"He's a man."

"He's also a doctor. He'll understand."

"But he's my *uncle!* I can't talk to him about *that.* I would just *die!*"

"Surely he knows that you've begun to have your periods?"

"No! Oh, heavens, I hope not!"

"How about your father? Does he know?"

"No. He's gone as much as he's here. Anyway, Dad still thinks I'm about six years old."

"Have you talked to anyone about this?"

Jennifer shrugged. "Not really. This is only the second time it's happened. Anyway, the only woman around is Mrs. Otis, our housekeeper, and she's really *old.* At least fifty.

"Please, Casey, all I need you to do is distract my uncle for a few minutes. Tell him you want to pick up something at the drugstore—a birthday card, maybe. Then I'll act like I just remembered something I have to get for school. While you keep Uncle Mark busy I'll go buy what I need."

Casey sighed. She didn't like to be part of a subterfuge, but she could empathize with the girl. She remembered what it was like to be thirteen and budding into womanhood surrounded by a house full of rough-and-rowdy brothers. At that age everything was a big deal, and something as private and mysterious as bodily functions was a source of unbearable mortification. However, at least she'd had her mother and Francis to guide her.

"All right. I'll help you, but only on one condition."

"What condition?"

"That you sit down and tell either your father or your uncle about this."

"Eeew! That's so gross. I can't do *that.* I just can't. Please, Casey, don't make me. Please, please, please!"

"All right, sweetie, calm down." She gave the girl's shoulder a squeeze. "I won't force you. But your father and uncle need to know. They are your family, your caretakers. But if you can't tell them, then how about if I talk to your uncle for you?"

Jennifer grabbed Casey's hands and looked at her as though she were an angel from on high come to earth. "You'd do that for me?" The girl lunged forward and threw her arms around Casey and hugged her tight. "Oh, thank you, Casey. Thank you so much. You're so wonderful. I just *love* you."

The girl's gratitude tugged at Casey's heartstrings. Poor little motherless child. She hugged her back and stroked her dark hair. "I'm fond of you, too, Jen. And I understand how you feel, but you must realize that some things have to be dealt with, no matter how unpleasant or embarrassing. That's part of growing up. Okay?"

"O-kay," the girl agreed with glum reluctance.

"Good. Now, let's go get you some supplies."

Mark accepted their story without hesitation, and when they entered the pharmacy Jennifer took off for another part of the store while Casey pretended to look for just the right card for her mother.

"What kind of card are you looking for? Humorous or flowery?"

Casey raised her chin at a haughty angle. "I suppose you'd call the type of verse I'm looking for flowery. I prefer to think of it as heartfelt and loving. My mother happens to be a very special woman and she deserves to be told so on occasion."

He grinned. Slipping his hand beneath her hair, he cupped the back of her neck and gave her a playful little shake. "Don't get your back up, Red. I was only kidding. I like your mother a lot and I've no doubt at all that she's a wonderful woman. In fact, I'm looking forward to getting to know her and the rest of your family."

"Careful what you wish for, Doc," she warned, sending him a dry look.

An odd mix of disappointment and acceptance washed through Casey. All evening, as always, his demeanor toward her had been teasing and lighthearted— exactly the same as that of her brothers'. So much for Mary Kate's attempt at matchmaking.

Well, what did you expect?

Casey sighed. More of a reaction than she'd gotten, she admitted to herself, feeling foolish. No matter that she'd tried to convince Mary Kate, and herself, that she wasn't interested in Mark, that she didn't have a chance with a man like him, so why bother? But deep down there had been that little kernel of hope.

Honestly. Did you really think that he'd take one look at you in this "girlie" outfit and be bowled over? Yeah, right. Face it, O'Toole, you're not the type to short-circuit a man's brain and fill him with lust. You're cute— the girl-next-door type that guys think of as a buddy.

"How about this one?" Mark asked, interrupting her silent lecture. Putting his hand against the small of her back, he leaned across in front of her and pulled a card from the bottom row of the rack and opened it.

Casey's breath caught. Through the silky material of her blouse, she felt the warmth of his hand as though it were a branding iron. His shoulder grazed her breast and set off a tingle that rippled through her entire body. She stared down at the back of his head, at the short, clipped hairs along his nape, the way his black hair glistened beneath the fluorescent lights with the blue-black sheen of a raven's wing, and her heartbeat took off like a snare drum roll. The clean male scent of him drifted to her nose and made her head spin.

"Here, read this." Straightening, Mark handed her the card.

At first Casey simply stared at the fancy greeting card decorated with lace and flowers and tiny bluebirds, not sure what to do with it.

Fortunately for her, Jennifer's arrival snapped her out of her daze.

"I've got what I need," the girl announced, holding her bagged purchase in a death grip. "Are you guys ready?"

"Casey hasn't decided on a card yet."

"No, this one's fine. I'll take it," she said quickly, snatching the envelope from the rack. Shaken by her reaction to Mark, all Casey wanted to do was pay for the card and get the heck out of there, and away from him. Oh, Lord. How could she be so stupid, to let herself fall for a man like Mark Adams?

And that was exactly what she'd gone and done. Lately she'd been so preoccupied with the murder cases and her problems with the sheriff that, without realizing what was happening, she'd let herself be drawn in by Mark's fantastic looks. And his character. And his great personality. And his delicious masculinity.

Casey barely stifled a groan. You idiot.

"Are you sure you want this one?" the object of her self-berating thoughts asked. "You haven't even read the inside yet?"

"Oh, uh…you're right." She opened the card and scanned the flowing script without comprehending a word. "Yes, it's perfect."

Stepping away from Mark, she headed for the checkout counter, but when she started around the end of the aisle she came to a halt, so abruptly that Mark slammed into her back.

"Whoa. Sorry, I—"

"Shh. Get back," Casey commanded over her shoulder. For good measure, she turned and splayed her hand across the center of Mark's chest and pushed him, and Jennifer, who was behind him, back down the aisle. "Get down and stay down," she whispered. "No matter what happens."

"What is it? What's wrong?"

"I think the store is about to be held up. Just do as I told you and stay down. And take care of Jennifer."

The girl gasped and clutched the sack she was carrying to her chest, her eyes round with fear.

"Held up? You mean robbed? Hey, where are you going?" Abandoning his crouched position, Mark grabbed Casey's arm. "You can't go out there. We have to call the cops."

"I *am* the cops. Now, get back there and take care of your niece like I told you. Stay out of sight. I'll handle this."

"Dammit, Casey—"

Glaring, she signaled for him to be quiet and get back, and drew her service revolver out of the ridiculous little purse of Mary Kate's that her cousin had insisted she carry. The bag was barely big enough to hold her revolver, a pair of handcuffs, a lipstick and some money. Holding the gun close to her right shoulder, pointed at the ceiling, she edged back down the aisle.

Using extreme caution, Casey peeked around the end of the shelves. Sure enough, second in line at the counter was Leroy Bertrum, a petty thief and holdup man whom she had arrested several times.

In that split second when she'd first come around the end of the aisle she had spotted him, and her training had kicked in. She'd noticed several things at once—

that Leroy was acting nervous, constantly looking around to see who was in the store and where they were, that he had no purchases in his hands, and sticking out of the pocket of his windbreaker was the butt of a gun. None of which boded well, given his record.

The little weasel was probably out on parole. Even if he'd served his latest sentence, being a convicted felon, she could bust him for having the weapon in his possession.

While she looked around, checking the position of the other customers in the store, the man in front of Leroy took his package and left. Casey was about to step out from behind the shelves and arrest Leroy when a woman carrying a package of disposable diapers in one hand and a whining toddler on her opposite hip came around the end of the next aisle over, heading for the checkout counter. She was so harried and distracted by her fussy baby she didn't notice Casey's gun until she was almost even with her. The young mother jerked to a halt and gave a little yelp of shock, which fortunately was drowned out by the baby's wails.

Before she could yell again Casey grabbed her arm and pulled her into the aisle. "Police. Get back there with the others and stay down," she ordered, shoving the frightened mother down the aisle toward Jennifer and Mark. He reached out to her and drew her down to huddle together with him and his niece.

Gritting her teeth at the delay, Casey took another peek around the end of the shelves and saw Leroy draw his gun. Damn. She'd hoped to make her move before things got this far.

"This is a stickup," he yelled, pointing the barrel of the gun at the cashier's nose. "Gimme everything you got in that register. And keep your hands where I can see 'em."

Casey stepped out from behind the row of shelving, her gun held at arm's length in a two-handed grip. "Police. Drop the gun. Now."

Leroy tensed. The young clerk behind the counter froze, her eyes big as saucers.

Casey braced, her gun held steady.

Every cop knew that this was the most dangerous few seconds in any arrest. She could almost smell the fear and indecision coming off Leroy, could almost hear his thoughts—*Do I take the risk and whirl around and fire, or do I give up?*

"Drop the gun, Leroy, or I'll drop you," she warned. "You know I'll do it."

"Aw right, aw right. Don't shoot. Look. I'm putting the piece down."

"Nice and easy, Leroy. Don't try anything cute."

Slowly, he lowered the gun and placed it on the counter.

"Now back up a step. You. Pick up the gun and move back," Casey ordered the clerk.

The girl's face turned even paler. "Me? I can't—"

"*Do it.*"

The girl jumped at the barked order but obeyed. Grimacing and using two fingers, she picked up the cheap "Saturday night special" and backed away.

"Now, you! Down on the floor and spread 'em," she ordered the man.

He obeyed.

Out of the corner of her eye, over the row of shelves, Casey saw the top of Mark's head and knew that he was coming around the end of the aisle, but she was too occupied to order him to get back.

She returned the gun to her purse and pulled out a pair of handcuffs. She was about to bend over and snap them on Leroy when Mark yelled, "Casey, look out!"

She looked around in time to see another man running up behind her. Before she could move he clamped his arm around her neck in a choke hold. With his other hand the man knocked the cuffs and purse out of her hand.

"I got this bitch, Leroy. Git up and git the money an' let's git outta here."

Struggling with the man, Casey half turned them around and saw Mark disobey her orders and start forward.

Before he could take two steps, she stomped down on her attacker's instep with her four-inch stiletto heel and at the same time jabbed him in his midsection with her elbow.

The man shrieked in pain. Losing his hold on Casey, he stumbled backward, hopping on one leg.

Casey whirled and in lightning-quick moves delivered three punishing kicks, the first two to his chest, and the third to his knee, which sent him staggering back against the first row of shelving. Cans and bottles of soft drinks crashed to the floor, bouncing and rolling, some spewing their frothy contents every which way.

The man shrieked again and grabbed his leg. With a growl of rage, he heaved himself away from the shelves and lunged at Casey.

She stood her ground, and when he was close enough she finished him off with an upward blow to his nose with the heel of her hand, followed by a two-fisted downward chop to the back of his neck that laid him out, facedown on the floor.

"Are you all right?" Mark asked anxiously, reaching her side.

"I'm fine. Hand me those cuffs, will you?"

Mark fetched the manacles and her purse and handed them to her.

Straddling the second perp's legs, Casey snapped the cuffs on him. Out of the corner of her eye she saw Leroy stealthily climb to his knees.

"Don't even think about making a break for it, Leroy," she warned. "If you do, I'll just have to chase you down. And I swear, if you make me run in these heels, I'll kick that bony butt of yours all over that parking lot."

Leroy flopped back down on his belly like a dropped pancake.

"What can I do?" Mark asked. "Should I call your station house for help?"

Pulling out her gun again, she aimed it at Leroy. "I've got some flexcuffs in the glove box of my car. If you'll go out and get a pair for me, I'll truss this one up, then I'll call my dispatcher on my car radio." She looked around. "How is Jennifer?"

"I'm okay," the girl said.

Turning her head, Casey saw the teenager standing at the end of the aisle where she'd left her and her uncle. Right behind her stood the young mother and her toddler. The baby was still whining and oblivious to the goings-on around him, but the two females appeared shocked and pale.

"Jennifer, you stay with Casey while I go get the cuffs," Mark said.

"Okay." Clutching her sack to her midriff with both hands, Jennifer cautiously came forward, her wide-eyed gaze fixed on the two men lying spread-eagled on the floor. "Golly, Casey, you were fantastic," the girl said in an awestruck voice. "I never saw anyone move so fast."

"You saw what happened?"

"Uh-huh. Me 'n Uncle Mark sorta watched from the end of the aisle."

"I thought I told you both to stay where you were."

"I know, but…well…Uncle Mark thought you might need help, and I followed him to the end of the aisle so I could see what was going on." Jennifer bit her lower lip. "You're not angry with us, are you?"

Casey sighed. "No, I'm not angry." Although she would have preferred that neither the child nor her uncle had witnessed the takedown.

Mark came running back inside. "Here's the cuffs you wanted."

"Thanks." She handed him her gun and instructed, "Keep this trained on these two while I cuff Leroy."

When she had the second man restrained, she took Leroy's gun from the clerk. "I'm going out to my car and put this in an evidence bag and call my dispatcher. I won't be long. Just keep your eye on those two."

Within minutes of Casey's call several patrol cars that were in the vicinity arrived. She explained what had happened, and the two men were taken into custody by the uniformed officers to be booked and jailed. The officers took the names of all the witnesses and a statement from each.

Through it all, Jennifer chattered away, wide-eyed with awe and admiration for Casey.

"Wait until I tell all the other girls on the team. They'll be so jealous that they missed all the excitement," the teenager gushed.

Mark, however, seemed less than thrilled with all that had transpired. While talking to the officers and walking them through the scene, Casey could not help but notice that he seemed withdrawn, almost angry.

Was he, like most men, put off by her ability to defend herself? she wondered. In her limited experience, she'd found that the male of the species liked to think of himself as the protector.

At last, the officers left and all the hubbub died down and there was only Casey, Mark and Jennifer left standing outside the pharmacy.

"Well, that was more than any of us bargained for tonight," Casey said to break the awkward silence.

"Yes. It was that," Mark agreed in a flat voice.

"I thought it was exciting," Jennifer said. "I've never seen anything like it before."

"And I hope to God that you never do again. Tell Casey good-night. It's time I got you home, young lady."

"Yay. For once I'm glad. I can't wait to tell all my friends what happened." The girl gave Casey a quick hug. "Night, Casey. And thanks for everything."

While his niece climbed into the van, Mark turned to Casey, his expression still remote. "I'm sorry there wasn't time tonight for you to speak to the girls about safety."

"Perhaps I can speak to them another time," she suggested.

"Perhaps. I'll check our schedule and call you."

Sure you will, Casey thought. His distant demeanor and the coolness in his voice told her more clearly than words that she had seen the last of Dr. Mark Adams. He had been thoroughly revolted by the display of violence and her skill at martial arts.

"Good night, Casey. And thank you for talking to the girls."

"No problem." Hurt and disappointment settled over her as she watched him climb into the van and drive away. She got into her own car and drove out the opposite exit. It was too bad to have their friendship nipped in the bud before it had really gotten started, but it was probably for the best. She was what she was—a cop. And a darned good one. If Mark couldn't accept that, it was his loss.

She pulled out onto Pinion Avenue and immediately had to stop at a traffic light. Only then did she notice that her cousin's skirt was ripped up one side, halfway to her hip. Well, that explained the leering grins on the faces of the patrol officers.

"This is just great," Casey muttered to no one in particular, banging her forehead on the steering wheel. Just perfect. It was bad enough that the evening ended in shambles. Mary Kate was really going to be furious with her now.

Fourteen

Casey wasn't surprised when Mark did not join her Saturday morning on her run, but she was disappointed, much more so than she'd expected to be.

She should have known better, she supposed. The general consensus among people on the force was that most civilians could not cope with the day-to-day realities of police work. Most of her fellow officers advocated marrying someone on the job or, at the very least, in a related field.

Not that marriage was ever part of the future for her and Mark. However, she did regret losing his friendship. She had grown accustomed to having him around.

Of course, it could be that he'd had another emergency that kept him away. But intuition told her otherwise.

The weekend passed in the usual uneventful way. As Casey went about her usual routine, she told herself she wasn't listening for the telephone to ring or for a knock on the door. Which was just as well, as neither occurred.

Monday morning she arrived at the station house and noticed while climbing the stairs that it was quiet in the squad room. Unusually so. Reaching the second-floor landing, she poked her head inside the door to see what was up, but all seemed normal. All the detectives were there and busy at their desks and Monica was filing.

The instant she walked in, however, without missing a beat or looking up from their work the guys broke into a raucous, off-key rendition of the old Irish ditty, "Clancy Lowered the Boom," only they substituted Casey for Clancy.

"Ohhh, that Casey. Ohhh, that Casey. Whenever they got her Irish up, Casey lowered the boom, boom, boom, boom."

"All right, knock it off, you clowns."

"Hey, Tiger," Keith called out. "We heard all about that little fracas you had the other night. Peterson said you really kicked ass. Single-handedly laid two robbers out cold. And in a skirt and high heels, to boot."

"Yeah," one of the other detectives put in. "I didn't know you even owned a skirt. Or a pair of high heels."

"Stuff it, Murphy."

"Oh, and by the way, the guys said to tell you that you have great legs."

"Very funny. Now that you've had your laugh, will you knock it off? Some of us have work to do. That bust Friday night added at least an hour of paperwork to my load that I don't need," she muttered to the room in general. "Damn that Leroy."

Grumbling, Casey sat down at her desk and called up the required form on her computer and began the tedious task of filling out an arrest report on Leroy Bertrum and Tyrone Rudmann.

Dennis grinned at her across the tops of their desks.

"Hey, Tiger, lighten up. The guys were just having a little fun. You know how stories spread in the department."

"I know," she mumbled.

Dennis looked around, then, leaning closer, asked, "I didn't get a chance to ask you yesterday. How'd it go Friday night?"

"Fine."

"C'mon, Tiger. I need more than that. Mary Kate is in a huff because she couldn't get anything out of you yesterday."

Casey could believe that. Somehow she'd managed to evade her cousin's questions and shameless probing the day before, mostly by keeping as far away from her as possible. By the time Casey had left, Mary Kate had been so frustrated she was practically foaming at the mouth. Casey was surprised that she hadn't called as yet.

"Before I left the house this morning, my wife insisted that I find out what's going on. If I don't have a full report for her when I get home she's going be impossible. You wouldn't do that to me, would you?"

Casey stopped typing and looked at the ceiling, as though seeking help from above. "For the last time, it *wasn't* a date. I simply gave a talk to a bunch of adolescent girls. You and Mary Kate can forget about anything happening between me and the doc. He treated me like a pal all evening."

"Really?"

"Yes, really. Even if he had been interested in me—which I assure you, he wasn't—after seeing me mop up the floor with Tyrone Rudmann he changed his mind."

Dennis groaned and held his head in his hands. "Ah, jeez, Tiger. You mean the doc and his niece were there?

They saw you take down those guys? I thought that happened after you left them."

"No, they were there. Jennifer was impressed, but by the time the whole thing was over the doc's manner had gone from friendly to frosty. He also didn't show up at the park Saturday morning, or this morning, for a run. I think that pretty much says it all, don't you? So please, will you and Mary Kate lay off me about the doc? It isn't going to happen."

Dennis looked crestfallen. "I guess you're right. Guys like to think of themselves as the protector. It's kinda hard to be a knight in shining armor when your woman can whup up on you. I guess I misjudged the doc. I was kinda hoping he was a better man than that, the kind who won't let his male ego get in the way."

"Yes, well…I guess you were wrong."

Trying to ignore the little ache in the region of her heart, Casey went back to work on the arrest report.

When she had finished the paperwork, she ran a check on the license plate for Matt Adams's van and ran his name through the system. Everything came back clean—no arrests, no prints on file, no criminal history of any kind.

Casey then called up the playing schedule for the Mountaineers Softball League. The Trailblazers had been playing games on two of the nights in question, but that still left plenty of time after the game for someone to pick up a woman, hold her captive until dawn, then commit the murders.

Pulling out her updated copy of the DMV list, she found that Trooper Longmont had already checked out Matt Adams's van and crossed it off. A notation beside his name read, "Owner out of country on dates of murders."

"Well, that answers that," Casey muttered. "Damn." Heaving a disgusted sigh, she tossed the list onto her desk. She was relieved for Jennifer's sake but frustrated beyond bearing. The case was going absolutely nowhere.

At that moment an attractive middle-aged brunette walked into the squad room.

"I'm Helen Moran, special agent with the FBI. I'm here to see Detective O'Toole."

"I'm Detective O'Toole." Casey stood up and shook the woman's hand. "This is my partner, Detective Dennis Shannon. I'd introduce you to our boss, but he's upstairs in Anti-Crime right now. Why don't the three of us talk in the coffee room." Grabbing up the crime folders from her desk and Dennis's, Casey led the way.

Before she introduced the agent to the others on the task force, she wanted to get a sense of the kind of person the woman was and how she worked.

"Coffee?"

"Yes, please. Black," the other woman said as she plopped her briefcase on the scarred table and pulled out a chair.

Casey poured two cups of coffee, one for the agent and one herself.

Agent Moran took a sip and grimaced. "Hmm. One thing never changes. No matter the branch of law enforcement, we make the lousiest coffee in the world."

Casey glanced at her mug with a puzzled expression and took an experimental sip. "It tastes fine to me."

Dennis rolled his eyes. "Pay no attention to her. Her taste buds were numbed years ago. She's addicted to the stuff. As long as it's hot and black, even if it's thick as sludge and vile, she'll drink it."

The agent gave a husky laugh. "Me, too. You sound like my kind of cop. Now, what have you got for me?"

Casey laid out the three files in front of her and gave a verbal account of each case. As she talked, Helen paged through the files, pausing occasionally to examine crime-scene photos closely.

Casey explained the steps they had taken so far and what the forensics lab had turned up.

"So you have no body fluids and no hairs?" the agent asked.

"No. Just the unusual triangular-shaped carpet fibers found on the bodies of all three victims, a tire impression, boot impression, a couple of bullets and a vague description of a light-colored van spotted near the last crime scene."

"Any common thread among the victims?"

"Two things. They all have dyed red hair, and…" Casey glanced at her partner. She hated to bring Mark to the agent's attention, but she had no choice. "And all three women had at one time or another had cosmetic surgery performed by the same plastic surgeon. A Dr. Mark Adams."

"I assume you've checked him out?"

"Yes. He has airtight alibis for the times of all three killings. To protect his reputation we're keeping his connection to the vics strictly need-to-know. Not even the other task force members are privy to the information, so we'd appreciate it if you'd respect that."

"Sure. Still…there has to be something there."

"I know. But so far, I haven't found anything."

"The women didn't know one another," Dennis put in. "Except for the red hair, they couldn't be more different. The first vic sometimes worked as a prostitute, the second was a wealthy socialite, and the third was apparently a sweet, hardworking girl from a middle-class family."

"Ages?"

"The youngest, Ms. Belcamp, was twenty-eight," Casey supplied. "We don't have an age on Selma Hettinger, but the M.E. puts her around thirty-seven or thirty-eight, though she looked older."

"Not surprising," the agent commented. "That kind of life can do that to a woman."

"Madeline St. Martin was a well-preserved forty-eight who could've probably passed for ten years younger."

"I'd like to have a firsthand look at the crime scenes," the agent said.

"Of course. But first let's introduce you to our lieutenant. He should be back by now. And you need to meet the rest of our task force."

They spent the morning with Lieutenant Bradshaw and the other men.

Agent Moran questioned them about the vehicular search. So far they hadn't had any luck identifying the brand of tire. She suggested they send the tire impression to the FBI expert at headquarters for identification of the manufacturer and the model and any wear patterns. "They may look similar, but every tread design is unique to a particularly manufacturer," she explained. "Our guy's the best in the field. If you've got a tread impression six inches long he'll identify it for you. The manufacturer can tell you how many were shipped to Colorado and to which retailer."

She questioned the deputies about the sheriff's department handling of the first two investigations. Every good detective knew that the way an investigation was conducted, particularly during those critical first few hours, could make or break a case. Though Helen made no accusations, her unspoken message was clear to everyone in the room: the job done by the sheriff's department did not pass muster.

As usual, Lewis reacted to the questions with surly resentment. "We worked that case by the book. But once we identified the Hettinger woman, the sheriff saw no reason to waste a whole lot of manpower and taxpayers' money to solve the murders of a couple of hookers. I mean, who cares?"

"A lot of people. Particularly the families of the murdered women. And Detective O'Toole tells me that only one of the women was a hooker."

"Yeah, well…we didn't know that at the time."

The level look she gave him said plainer than words that it was his job to find out. "That, Deputy, is why you give every case your best shot."

"Look, I don't know why you're even here," Lewis snapped. "We sure as hell don't need some hotshot federal agent coming down here telling us how to do our jobs."

"All right, Manning, that's enough," the lieutenant began, but Agent Moran held up her hand to silence him.

"No, that's all right, Lieutenant. Deputy Manning, I wouldn't have been called in on this case if you didn't need help, but I'm here to lend a hand, not to take over the investigation. My job is to work up a psychological profile on the perp that will tell you the kind of man you're looking for and hopefully narrow your search."

"Ah, that stuff's nothing but mumbo jumbo."

"No, Deputy. Like fingerprints or ballistics, and other

forensics, a profile is a tool. Nothing more, nothing less. A smart investigator makes use of every tool in his or her arsenal. Whether psychological or geographical— a profile won't solve a case for you. People solve cases. But they can point you in the right direction and save time and legwork. And quite frankly, we're in a race to catch a killer here. We don't have time for this kind of foolish wrangling."

Lewis slumped back in his seat, his jaw tight, and Casey had to fight back a grin.

With a few well-chosen words and a "don't mess with me" attitude, Agent Moran had put the deputy in his place. He sat through the remainder of the meeting in tight-lipped silence.

After lunch, Casey and Dennis took the agent to the crime scenes, beginning with the first. All three sites were in the same area. The spots where the bodies of victims one and two were found were only a couple of hundred yards apart.

"We think he released them all from this point," Casey explained, showing her the exact point along the side of the road where they'd found the tire print. "Selma Hettinger, the first vic, made it farther than the second woman. But then, Madeline St. Martin was a pampered socialite who had probably never been in the woods before. Plus, at the time of her murder, she'd been wearing a cocktail dress and high heels, not the best outfit for running for your life through the wilderness."

"Hardly."

"Becky Belcamp was the smartest. She doubled back on him," Dennis said. "Came darned close to making it, too."

"Yeah, well, unfortunately for Ms. Belcamp, close only counts in horseshoes," the agent murmured.

"True, but that was our killer's first slipup. The only time he left any evidence behind."

"Mmm." Agent Moran stood in the middle of the dirt road with her hands on her hips and stared up at the tree-covered mountain. "It was clever of him to kill his victims in a known hunting area where any recovered bullets or shell casings could be attributed to hunters. And this penchant he has for hunting down his victims is a new twist I haven't seen before. There's sure to be something behind that behavior."

"I agree," Casey said. "It's sick and twisted and risky. What if one of the women had gotten away? Becky almost did. Why take that chance? The compulsion to hunt them down like an animal must be strong."

"Yes," the agent agreed. "And it's just going to get stronger."

It was past the end of the shift when they returned to the station house. On first entering the squad room, Casey was surprised to find all of the other detectives still there, lounging around, shooting the breeze. The moment she entered the room, however, they stopped their conversation and stared at her expectantly.

"What? Why are you all looking at me that way?"

Keith nodded toward her desk. "Those came for you about ten minutes ago."

Turning, Casey saw a bouquet of spring flowers on her desk. The bright blossoms looked so incongruous in the dull, utilitarian office that she had to blink twice to make sure she wasn't seeing things.

Casey walked over to her desk and touched a velvety petal. She'd never received flowers before in her life and couldn't imagine who'd be sending them now. She glanced at the expectant faces around her. At least now things made sense. The bunch of nosey parkers were waiting to find out who had sent her flowers.

"There's a card with them," Murphy supplied helpfully.

She sent him a droll look. "So I see."

Casey removed the small envelope from the bouquet and pulled out the card.

"Who're they from?" Keith asked. "Do you have a boyfriend we don't know about?"

"Hardly. I hate to disappoint you guys, but these are from the girls on the softball team. You know, the ones I talked to the other night about joining the force. Here, see for yourself."

Keith took the card from her and read aloud, "'Thank you for taking time out of your busy schedule to speak to us. The Trailblazers.'" He scratched his chin. "Well, I'll be damned. They really are from a bunch of girls."

"Ah, hell. We stayed late for *that?*"

"Yeah, I thought we were going to get some good dirt."

One by one the guys called a good-night and filed out the door, still grousing and grumbling.

When they were gone, Casey picked up the card again and stared at the message. There was no doubt in her mind that Mark had sent the flowers. He had the means and it was the sort of polite gesture he would make, but he'd been careful to keep the note impersonal. He hadn't even included himself in the thanks.

And that, Casey decided, was that.

Agent Moran spent two weeks in Mears, working mainly with Casey and Dennis. She went over every word and every photograph in each file, plus all of the notes that Casey and Dennis and the other men on the task force had taken. They visited the crime scenes several more times, and discussed the cases endlessly among themselves.

Helen Moran's insights and the information she mined from the killer's every action fascinated Casey. From the most minute detail she could discern the killer's motives and rationale, twisted though they may be.

"There are two kinds of serial killers," Helen told her one day during one of their discussions. "There's the organized killer and the disorganized killer. The first plans his murders, often stalking a victim for weeks to learn her routines. When he strikes he knows exactly how, when and where he's going to commit his crime and he is prepared, bringing with him everything he needs.

"The disorganized killer is a creature of impulse. He doesn't plan. In fact, he may have no intention of killing anyone, until something or someone triggers his rage and he is seized by an irresistible compulsion. He uses any weapon of convenience he can get his hands on, or he may simply use his hands.

"Generally speaking, the disorganized killer is the easiest to catch, precisely because he doesn't plan, and therefore often leaves clues. The organized killer is another story. He's extremely difficult to catch because he plans so carefully and chooses his victims seemingly at random, and they're nearly always women who have no connection to him. Unfortunately, from what I've seen so far, that's the kind you're after."

During Helen Moran's stay in Mears, Casey joined the agent for dinner most evenings. Spending her time learning from someone like Helen was preferable to sitting at home alone, eating a frozen TV dinner in front of the television and torturing herself, brooding about Mark Adams.

When Casey's parents heard about the FBI agent, they insisted that Casey invite her to dinner the following Wednesday.

Missing her own family, Helen accepted. She was fascinated to learn the history of the Collinses and the O'Tooles and that, except for Casey's mother and mother-in-law, that they were all cops or former cops.

Helen asked as many questions of Casey's family as they asked of her, and she seemed to enjoy the evening, though the talk around the table was mostly about police work.

Casey learned a tremendous amount from Helen. At the end of the agent's second week in Mears she was sorry when the other woman announced that she'd finished her profiles and would be flying home that evening. Before leaving, Helen sat down with Casey and the rest of the task force and the lieutenant and explained the profiles she had worked up.

"It's my opinion that your killer is a white male, between the ages of twenty-five and forty. Probably clean-shaven. He's neat and organized. Methodically so. That's probably the only way he is able to operate in society and appear normal. He is rigid and has a black-and-white outlook. There are no shades of gray in this man's world. He likes to do things by the book. He probably makes lists for everything.

"He has issues with his mother. My guess would be that she abandoned him as a child. That's probably why he hunts women down to kill them. Symbolically, he's hunting his mother and punishing her for leaving him.

"I strongly suspect that his mother was preoccupied

with her looks and her figure. Therefore the killer targets women who have had plastic surgery."

"How about the red hair?" Hugh Longmont asked. "Where does that figure in?"

"That would be another part of the vanity angle. His mother may have dyed her hair red. Or it could have been a woman with whom he was once involved. Or perhaps a woman he wanted who rejected him. He most likely doesn't relate well to women at all."

"So? What are we looking for here? A geek? A loner? What?" Hector Comal asked.

"On the contrary. I expect he's at least average, probably nice-looking. Well groomed and friendly on the surface. He knows all the right things to say, all the right moves. But like everything else about him, it's methodical, a programmed response. He maintains a good facade, but he's incapable of true closeness or sustaining a relationship—romantic or otherwise. Emotionally, he's empty."

"Sounds like a real nice guy," Travis Kemp drawled.

"I also worked up a geographical profile." Helen tacked a map onto the bulletin board. "The blue circles on this map represent the crime scenes. As you can see, the three are a very tight grouping. This area is one of his comfort zones. He probably knows these woods like the back of his hand.

"Each green square is one of the victims' residences, and in Ms. Belcamp's case, her place of business. All of these sites are in the north part of town, within a very confined area. And all are within or adjacent to this precinct. Another familiar area for him.

"Organized serial killers tend to like a comfort zone. They commit their crimes in areas they know well and where they feel at home. Even ones who move around a lot, like Bundy or the interstate killer, scope out the area before making a move. Your man probably lives and/or works in this section, where the map is highlighted in red. He usually won't operate really close to his home, but he won't go too far, either. It's probable that he travels these streets daily," she said, indicating the yellow highlighted areas.

"And that's it. My job here is done, at least for now. With the information that you've given me, that's all I can glean. If you turn up anything else, give me a call and I'll see if it alters the profile."

Helen had a flight out that evening, and when the shift ended she and Casey parted company outside the station house.

"I like your style, Casey. I think you should consider joining the bureau. You've got what it takes to make a great agent, and I'd be happy to put in a good word for you."

"Thanks, Helen. I appreciate that, but I'm happy here. Besides, I don't think I could stand being away from my family for very long."

"I understand. You've got a great support system there. But if you ever change your mind, let me know. You've got my card. E-mail me sometime. I'd like to keep in touch. And if you ever need help from the bureau again, forget protocol. Just give me a call."

"I will. Thanks."

After stopping by the market for a few items, Casey arrived home just before dark. The answering machine contained chatty messages from her mother and Francis, a sharp demand from Mary Kate for Casey to call her back, and a reminder from her dentist's receptionist that she needed to set up an appointment for a cleaning. There was nothing from Mark.

Annoyed with herself for being so disappointed, she hit the erase button with more force than necessary. "Idiot. Did you really think he would call?" she muttered. "And say what? 'I really admire the way you beat up on those two thugs.'"

Casey snorted. "Yeah, right. In your dreams, O'Toole. It's time you started believing what you've been telling others all along. Dr. Mark Adams is not for you."

Determined to put him out of her mind, she forced herself to eat a light dinner, watch TV for a while, then go to bed early. The next morning she followed her usual Saturday routine and went for a run, cleaned the house, took a shower and ran errands. That evening she had just kicked off her sandals and settled on the sofa with the book she was reading when the doorbell rang.

What now? she wondered, stomping barefoot to the door. Probably one of her brothers had found himself without a Saturday-night date and, at loose ends, had decided to pay little sis a visit.

Though fairly certain she was right, her ingrained sense of caution made her take a peek through the peephole before opening the door. When she saw who was standing on her front porch she gasped and stepped back. Just as quickly she leaped forward again and opened the door.

"Mark. What're you doing here?"

Fifteen

Wearing jeans, a casual crew-neck cotton sweater and a light suede jacket against the evening chill, Mark stood with one hand braced against the door frame, the other hooked over the top of his hip bone, his open jacket thrust back.

"Hi." His gaze took her in, from her bare feet and legs, up over her cotton wrap skirt and scoop-neck tee to her loose hair. His somber gaze met hers again. "May I come in?"

"Oh. Yes, of course." She stepped back and held the door wide. Her foolish heart began to boom like a kettledrum. What was he doing here? She hadn't seen him or heard so much as a peep out of him in more than two weeks.

Mark stepped past Casey, bringing with him the cool freshness of the Colorado night. Mingled with the crisp smell was his own manly scent. Inhaling the heady combination, she felt almost woozy.

In the small foyer he peeled off his jacket and hung it on the antique hall tree, then, without a word, strolled into the living room. He looked around at her home with interest. "Nice place."

"Thanks. I'm just renting now, but the owner has offered to sell it to me. I'm thinking about it." She laced her fingers together in front of her, then realized how nervous she looked and pulled them apart. "Uh, would you like something? Coffee? A soft drink? I'm sorry, but I don't keep anything stronger."

"No thanks, I'm fine." He continued to amble around the room, looking at the oil painting above the fireplace that her brother Aiden had painted, the photos of her family scattered around the room.

He picked up a framed photo from one of the end tables. "Is this your husband?"

"Yes, that's Tim."

"Looks like a pleasant guy."

"He was."

He put the photo down, stuffed his fingers into the back pockets of his jeans and continued his aimless inspection. The soft cotton sweater draped over his shoulders, emphasizing their breadth, the muscles that banded his back. The sleeves were pushed up to his elbows, revealing his strong forearms and broad wrists.

Casey watched him, growing more antsy by the moment.

"Would you like to sit down?" she asked, gesturing toward one of the overstuffed chairs flanking the fireplace.

He glanced at her over his shoulder. "Sure."

Ignoring the chairs, he joined her on the sofa, leaving an empty cushion between them. He sat slumped down on his spine, his long legs stretched out in front of him and crossed at the ankles, and stared straight ahead at the unlit fireplace. Another thirty seconds ticked by in silence.

"You must have had a whole string of emergencies. I haven't seen you for a couple of weeks," Casey said to fill the void.

"No emergencies. I ran somewhere else."

"Oh. I see." She felt as though she'd been slapped. Which was just plain silly, she told herself, fiercely fighting back the tears that threatened to fill her eyes. The man was free to run anywhere he liked. And he certainly didn't owe her an explanation.

Like Mark, she fixed her gaze on the fireplace.

Out of the corner of her eye, she saw him turn his head and stare at her profile. "I had some thinking to do."

Casey continued to stare straight ahead, blinking rapidly. She didn't trust herself to speak.

"About us," he added quietly.

She looked at him then. "Us?" Her heart was beating so hard she could barely breathe.

"Yes. I had to decide if I could handle a serious relationship with you."

"A serious...?" Casey shook her head. "What are you saying? I had no idea...you've never... The way you've acted around me, I thought you just wanted us to be friends."

"I do want us to be friends. And someday—soon, I hope—I'm hoping we'll be friends and lovers."

Speechless, all Casey could do was blink.

Mark chuckled at her stunned expression. "And for your information, I flirted a bit at first, you just didn't notice. I thought you were playing hard to get until that night at the hospital. When I learned your history and realized how inexperienced you are, I realized that I needed to change my approach.

"You'd known Tim all of your life. You felt at ease

with him. I've been trying to give you time to get to know me better and get comfortable around me."

"I see." Casey looked down at her hands, which were clasped together in her lap. "Then you saw me take down those two holdup men, and you were repulsed by the whole thing."

Out of the corner of her eye she saw Mark's entire body stiffen. "Repulsed?" Astonishment gave his voice a grating edge. He sat up straighter on the sofa and turned sideways. Crooking his left leg on the cushion that separated them, he draped his arm along the top of the sofa back. "Hell no, I wasn't repulsed. Stunned, yes, at least at first, then proud and amazed, but most of all I was scared out of my mind. I was so terrified that you would get hurt or killed that I was shaking inside.

"For the first time it occurred to me—actually it hit me like a ton of bricks—that this was the sort of thing you did on a regular basis."

"But…you've always known that I was a cop."

"A detective. I never really gave it much thought, but I suppose, in the back of my mind, I assumed all detectives operated like Sherlock Holmes. You'd go to the scene, gather clues and sift through them, then announce, 'By George, Watson, I think I've got it!'"

"Really?" Casey said, smiling for the first time since his arrival.

"Well…maybe not *exactly* like that. At least not with the phony British accent," he conceded, a tiny smile tugging at his lips, as well. "My point is, I never pictured you having to get physical with the bad guys. I guess I assumed that once you figured out who committed a crime, someone else went out and arrested him."

They had started the discussion at opposite ends of

the sofa, but somehow, without her being aware of him doing so, he had moved closer, Casey realized. His left knee nudged her hip, and with his hand on the back of the sofa he picked up a handful of her hair and winnowed his fingers through the curly mane.

His silvery eyes darkened and grew languid as he watched the fiery tendrils twine around his fingers as though they had a life of their own. "I wasn't repulsed by what you did, Casey," he murmured in a velvety voice that raised goose bumps on her arms and scalp. "Just terrified out of my mind when I realized that your job puts you in harm's way on a daily basis."

Casey sobered and returned her gaze to her twisting hands. "I see. So…after doing all that thinking, what did you decide?"

A small, mirthless sound, somewhere between a laugh and a snort, escaped Mark. "It turned out to be more a matter of what I learned—about myself, mostly.

"Gradually, I came to realize that I really didn't have a decision to make. It was too late for that. I was already serious about you, and there was no going back. The past sixteen days without seeing you has been pure, unadulterated hell."

The fingers in her hair delved deeper and stroked the back of her neck. The tips of his fingers were warm and caressing against her sensitive nape. Casey shivered and closed her eyes. She had to fight to suppress a groan. Until that moment she'd had no idea that the back of her neck was an erogenous zone.

Exerting the gentlest of pressure, Mark turned her head until she was forced to meet his gaze. "I'm in love with you, Casey."

Shock widened her eyes. She didn't know what she'd

expected him to say. Maybe that he wanted to get to know her better and see what happened. Or maybe even that he wanted to make love to her. But she certainly had not expected a declaration of love.

"Wh-what? Mark, you don't mean that. You can't be in love with me. You barely know me. It's only been three weeks since we met."

"Three weeks, three days, four hours and—" he glanced at his wristwatch "—seventeen minutes, to be exact," he said with a grin.

"I may not know what kind of breakfast cereal you like, or if you prefer opera or bluegrass music, or if you put the cap back on the toothpaste, if you're a morning person or a night person, but I know the things that count. I know that you're sweet and smart and honest and loving, that you're dedicated to your family and your job. I know that you are intuitive, analytical, hard-working, that you respect your body and take care of your health and work to stay fit. And most of all, I know you're so lovely you take my breath away."

"I…I…I don't know what to say."

"You don't have to say anything. I don't expect you to love me back right now. I know that with you the process takes longer, and you're not there yet. All I'm asking is that you give me a chance to win your love."

Casey stared at him, her heart thrumming. She had to admit, the idea of being courted by Mark was exciting. And tempting. What she could not figure out was, why her? How could a drop-dead-gorgeous man like Mark, who could have almost any woman he wanted, be in love with a girl-next-door type like her? It didn't make sense.

"Mark, I don't want to get hurt, and I certainly don't

want to hurt anyone else. I'll admit, I'm attracted to you. Very attracted. But I'm not ready to put a name to those feelings. And I just don't understand how you can be so sure of yours so soon."

"That's because we're different in that way. Your love for Tim grew slowly over time. You told me your-self that you couldn't remember exactly when or how you fell in love, it just evolved.

"I, on the other hand, am a person who instantly knows what I want and I go after it. I've always thought that when I met the woman who was meant for me, I'd recognize her."

Taking Casey's hand in his, he looked deep into her eyes. "I believe that you were meant to love Tim and marry him and bring joy to his short life. But I also be-lieve that you were meant to build a life and family with me, to grow old with me. I think that's why I've remained single. I didn't know it, but I've been waiting for you to fulfill the first part of your destiny and come to me."

Casey's heart did a little flip-flop in her chest. She felt as though she were melting inside. How could any woman resist a declaration like that?

Looking into his silvery eyes, she saw only sincerity and adoration, and she felt her puny resistance crumbling.

"Since that first day when I walked into my office and saw you sitting there with your back to me, I haven't been able to get you out of my mind," Mark continued. "The first thing I noticed was all that beautiful red hair twisted into a knot on top of your head. Then I spied those fiery baby curls that defied control, clinging to your neck along your hairline. I had an almost over-whelming urge to bend and nuzzle my nose in them."

Casey's jaw dropped. "It's a good thing you didn't," she declared indignantly. "You'd have found yourself flat on your back on the floor in a New York second."

"Yeah, I know," he said with a chuckle. "Then I walked around and sat down at my desk and you looked at me with those big, serious blue eyes, and I was a goner. I felt as though I'd been struck in the solar plexus with a battering ram. I could barely breathe. And every time I've seen you since, my feelings have just gotten stronger."

He leaned in closer. She could feel the moist warmth of his breath feathering over her cheek, see every individual black eyelash that framed his eyes, the spokes of darker gray that radiated from his pupils. "Will you give me a chance, sweetheart?" he whispered.

Casey looked at those beautifully chiseled lips, just inches from her own, and a longing deeper than any she'd ever known trembled within her.

Mixed with it was fear and uncertainty. She wanted to take a chance with Mark. Everything within her, every cell in her body urged her to do so.

But what if things didn't work out between them? She'd never been hurt in love before, never experienced a broken romance and the heartache that came with it. She wasn't at all certain that she could handle that kind of pain, especially so soon after losing Tim.

Still, if she didn't explore the possibilities, she knew she would always regret not doing so.

Raising her trembling hand, she cupped Mark's face. "All—all right. But if things don't work out—"

"Shh." He put his forefinger over her mouth. "Don't fret. We'll be fine." He leaned closer still, until their lips were almost touching, and whispered, "Just relax, sweetheart, and let it happen."

And then his mouth settled over hers.

The kiss was luscious. A soft, tactile exploration, trembling with hunger and emotions and a fierce restraint. His mouth rocked over hers with exquisite gentleness and simmering passion that seemed to set her soul aflame.

It was the most voluptuous experience of Casey's life. She'd had no idea a simple kiss could be so consuming, so utterly sensuous and arousing. She responded to the tender caress with every beat of her heart, with every breath she took. Nothing else existed for Casey. Nothing else mattered. For that moment in time the world was well lost.

Worries, doubts, all thought and reason vanished. All she could do was cling to this man, touch him, revel in his warmth, the taste of him, the wonderful scent of him that enveloped her and set her head to spinning.

Only vaguely, as the kiss went on and on, was Casey aware of Mark lifting and turning her until she lay cradled in his arms across his lap. She didn't mind. As long as he continued to kiss her like this, to hold her in his arms, she didn't care what he did with her. She was a smart, competent woman. Her body was well honed and strong, and in a physical confrontation she could wipe up the floor with most men, but held in Mark's arms she felt small and helpless. Utterly feminine. And it felt heavenly.

When the kiss finally ended and Mark raised his head to look at her, she was breathless and limp, her poor heart chugging like a Model T in need of a tune-up.

He smiled down at her, his gaze caressing her face, a gleam of humor twinkling in his eyes as he took in her puffy bare lips and dazed expression.

"You see? I told you we'd get along fine." He touched the corner of her mouth with his forefinger and his voice dropped to a husky pitch. "I've been wanting to do that since the moment I first saw you. It was even better than I dreamed it would be."

Lying across his lap, breathing hard, Casey gazed back at him, struggling to clear her head and gather her thoughts. There was something she had to say before things went any further. "Mar—" Her voice cracked, and she had to stop and clear her throat. "Mark, there's something I should tell you."

"Sure, go ahead."

"I…I—" she felt embarrassed color rising in her cheeks and blurted out the rest before she lost her nerve "—I don't have affairs."

Mark threw his head back and laughed. The rich, full-bodied sound came from deep in his chest and filled the cozy room.

Casey frowned. "What's so funny?"

"You." He grinned at her and stroked his finger between her eyebrows, smoothing away the creases there. "Sweetheart, I've known that since that night at the hospital. It doesn't matter. I mean—sure it matters. I want to make love to you. Very much. But after meeting your parents and hearing about the way you grew up, I realized that having intimate relations before marriage was probably not an option for you. I wouldn't want to push you into anything that you weren't comfortable with, or that went against your upbringing or your religious or moral convictions. I can wait."

He could wait? Casey's chest tightened. Did that mean he intended to *marry* her?

The question hovered on the tip of her tongue, but she lacked the courage to ask.

"And I'll admit, there is one other thing," he added with a wry grin. "I don't want those brothers of yours coming after me with tar and feathers."

Casey wrinkled her nose. "They'd do it, too. But how did you know? You haven't even met them."

"Because if you were my sister—God forbid—I'd do the same to any man who tried anything."

Casey rolled her eyes. "Oh, great. Now I'm in a relationship with a guy who thinks just like my brothers."

"I guess you're just the lucky one," Mark murmured, and bending his head, he kissed her again.

This kiss was harder, less controlled, devouring. Casey lay in his arms and twined her own around his neck, her entire body humming.

Just when she thought surely that Mark would lay her down on the sofa and make love to her, he broke off the kiss and pulled back.

Passion darkened his face. Breathing hard, he shook his head and gasped, "We have to stop now, while I still can. Otherwise I'm going to break the promise I just made."

Casey experienced a stab of acute disappointment and frustration. A part of her wanted him to give in to what they both were feeling, to take things out of her hands and sweep her away on a cloud of passion, past that point of no return where restraint and denial were unobtainable, where all that existed were desire and need and that primal drive for fulfillment.

Immediately she was ashamed of herself for the moment of weakness. She prided herself on being a responsible adult. She made her own decisions and accepted the consequences of her own actions. She did not put the onus on someone else.

Casey wouldn't have traded her old-fashion upbringing and the solid values her parents had passed on to her for anything. Still, she had to admit there were times, like now, when she wished she could take a more casual view of sex. It was the twenty-first century, after all, and the sexual revolution had already been fought and won. Most people of her generation thought nothing of indulging in an intimate relationship with someone for whom they had deep feelings. They didn't necessarily have to be in love to make love.

Casey sighed. Unfortunately, she did.

She just did not feel right about sharing the most intimate of acts with someone unless it meant more than merely satisfying a hunger. For her, there had to be a deep connection, a melding of hearts, of souls. There had to be a commitment.

There were other considerations, as well. Besides the caveman reaction her brothers were sure to have, there would be her parents' disappointment to face. And she didn't even want to think about what Father Mike would say when she went to confession.

"Here we go," Mark said, lifting her off his lap and plunking her down on the sofa beside him. "As much as I enjoy kissing you and holding you, I think we're going to have to be careful if we're going to abide by your rules."

"It's not a matter of arbitrary rules. It's more—"

"Shh. Sweetheart, I was just kidding. Anyway, you don't have to explain to me. I understand. Really, I do. And it's okay."

"Really?"

"Really," he said with finality. "And now that we've got that settled and defined our relationship, what would you like to do tonight? Have you eaten?"

"Uh…yes. I have."

"Good. So have I, but I'd take you out to dinner if you were hungry. Would you like to go out? There's a nice little jazz club over on Laramie. Or if you'd like we could go to a late movie."

In the end, when Mark discovered Casey's DVD collection, they decided to stay home and watch a movie. Casey made popcorn, and when she returned to the living room with the huge bowl, she found that Mark had loaded the disk into the player, kicked off his shoes and settled into one corner of the sofa with one leg stretched out on the cushions. She started to sit down at the other end of the sofa, but before she could he hooked his arm around her waist and said, "Come here," and pulled her down and snuggled her between his outstretched legs.

With her back resting against his chest and one arm around her waist, he reached around her, grabbed a handful of popcorn, rested his chin on top of her head while he ate, then started the movie.

At first Casey was too tense to relax. She was aware of Mark with every fiber of her being. Against her back his chest was warm and broad, and she felt each rhythmic rise and fall as he breathed. The strong arm encircling her made her feel cherished and protected. With his sex snuggled tight against her bottom and his strong thighs flanking her hips, scissor fashion, the position left no doubt that he was as aware of her as she was of him, yet he seemed engrossed in the movie and supremely relaxed. Every now and then he'd reach around her, grab a handful of popcorn and feed her a bite before tossing the rest into his mouth.

Gradually, the tension began to drain out of Casey as the position became more familiar and the fatigue of the day of chores caught up with her. By the end of the movie she lay cuddled back against Mark, limp as a cooked noodle and half-asleep.

"Okay, I can take a hint," he teased, shifting her so that he could stand up. "It's time for me to go so that you can go to bed."

"I'm awake," she mumbled.

"Mmm. Sure you are." He tipped her chin up with his forefinger and gave her a quick kiss, then headed for the door.

Yawning, she padded barefoot after him into the foyer.

Mark took his suede jacket from the hall tree hook and shrugged into it. "Will I see you tomorrow?" he asked, slipping his arms around Casey's waist, lacing his fingers together at the small of her back.

"Tomorrow? Oh, sorry. I always spend Sunday with my family."

She could see in his eyes that he was waiting for her to invite him along, but something held her back. Maybe it was because everything had happened so fast, or because their relationship was too new.

Despite Mark's assurances, she still had reservations about the two of them. Common sense told her that there were no guarantees in this life, especially where emotions were concerned, but she didn't want to set herself up for heartbreak if she could help it.

She was attracted to Mark. And if she was going to be completely honest, she had feelings for him, as well—deep feelings, but she wasn't ready to call them love. Casey knew what it was like to love someone with all your heart and soul, then lose them. Until she felt more confident of Mark's love, she wasn't going to risk that pain again.

Her mother had invited him and his brother and niece to the family Fourth of July cookout, but if she showed up with him at a family dinner she might as well announce their engagement. Casey knew her family. Her mother, probably with help from Francis and Mary Kate, would start planning the wedding before the meal ended.

"I see," Mark said, and she had the unsettling hunch that he did. "Well then, how about keeping next Friday and Saturday nights open for me. Okay? Friday, the team is playing, but there's a charity ball at the country club on Saturday. The proceeds go toward building a new neonatal wing, so I'm sorta obligated to attend. Wear something formal."

All trace of drowsiness vanished. Casey was instantly wide-awake and on the verge of panic. "A ball? At the country club? Oh, Mark, are you sure you want to take me? I've been interviewing those people about the murders. Some of them weren't too happy about it."

"Tough. They'll just have to get over it."

Leaning back in his arms, she nibbled on her lower lip and plucked at the nubby weave of his sweater. "I'm not exactly the country-club type, you know. I wouldn't want to embarrass you."

"Embarrass me? Sweetheart, you couldn't embarrass me if you stripped naked and danced on top of the table in front of the Queen of England. I'm proud of you."

Despite her best effort to hold it back, a wry smile tugged at the corners of her mouth. She gave him a light sock on the arm. "I wouldn't do anything *that* gross."

"Then it's settled. I'll pick you up at seven-thirty."

Casey sighed. "Oh, all right."

"And while we're making plans, how about Monday and Thursday nights, too? Jennifer has games every night next week but Tuesday, but I know your Wednesdays are booked. Wanna join us on the other nights?"

Now, that was more her style. Besides, she liked Jennifer.

Uh-huh, her conscience whispered. And you know that the child will serve as a buffer.

Ignoring the feeling of guilt, she smiled at Mark. "I'd love to. I'll have to meet you at the park, though, like before. I never know exactly when I'll get off if I'm working a lead. Plus, I work out on Tuesdays and Thursdays after my shift."

"Sure. Whatever works for you."

The mention of Jennifer reminded Casey of her promise to the girl. When she'd thought that her friendship with Mark was over she had intended to write him a letter, but since he was there, she decided that she might as well get it over with.

"There's something I have to tell you. Something I think you should know. It concerns Jennifer."

"Jennifer?" In an instant Mark's smile changed to a frown and he tensed and released Casey. "What about her? Did she confess something to you that she won't tell me or Matt?"

"Well…in a way."

"What's she done? Oh, God, don't tell me some creep has victimized her? I'll kill him—"

"No! It's nothing like that. For heaven's sake, calm down and listen."

Calmly, and as matter-of-factly as possible, Casey explained to Mark that his niece had begun her monthly cycles and she was embarrassed to tell him or her father. By the time she finished, Mark's jaw hung agape.

"*Jennifer? Our* little Jennifer? But that can't be. She's just a child."

"She's thirteen."

"Barely. Her birthday was just last month."

"Granted, she may be a little young, but it happens to some girls a lot younger than that. You should know."

Mark raked his hand through his hair and paced the small foyer. "I don't understand. Why didn't she tell me? I'm a doctor, for Pete's sake."

"I suggested that, but apparently she thinks of you as an uncle first. And a male. And she's thirteen. That's an extremely sensitive and self-conscious time for a girl. At that age, as much as I love him and as close as we are, I would have been mortified to tell my father something like that."

"I can't believe it," Mark said mournfully. "Our little Jennifer is growing up. Matt is losing his baby girl."

Casey looked heavenward. "Men and their daughters. No wonder Jennifer wanted me to tell you."

"Aw, hell. Now *I* have to tell Matt. He's going to be crushed."

"Poor babies." Casey patted Mark's arm. "Don't worry. You'll live through it."

"So how are we supposed to handle this? Do we make some casual remark to let her know that we know? Do we pretend we don't know? What do you suggest?"

"I think it would be best if I let her know that I told you. Then, if she wants to discuss the matter with you or her father, it's up to her.

"However, I do think she needs some guidance from an older woman. How about, when you're at my folks' place for the Fourth of July, my mother and Francis and I have a talk with her?"

"Oh, sweetheart, that would be great." He put his arms around her again and smiled into her eyes. "You're going to be good for her. And me."

Sixteen

"Look at victim number one's ankle through a magnifying glass."

Reaching across the desk, Dennis took the crimescene photo from Casey and did as she asked. "It's a tattoo. So?"

"Isn't that the insignia of that biker gang that call themselves the Barbarians? The ones that hang out at that dive out on the Grand Junction Highway?"

"I know the place you're talking about. Skinny's, isn't it?" Dennis took a closer look. "I think you're right. That is their insignia."

"Which means she must have been part of the gang at some point." Casey mulled that over, tapping her forefinger against her pursed lips. She stood up and shrugged into her blazer. "I'm going to check with the rest of the team to see how they're coming along following up on the tips, then you and I are going to check out Skinny's. Someone there may know something about Selma Hettinger."

Dennis groaned and held his head with both hands.

"You want to go to a dive and question a bunch of motorcycle-gang lowlifes?"

"Do you have a better suggestion? Sheriff Crawford was in here Monday throwing a hissy fit. He threatened to go over everyone's head and hold another press conference. Tuesday, two commissioners paid the boss a visit, and yesterday the mayor was here. He's taking all kinds of sniper fire over these cases. And to top it all off, the media is in a feeding frenzy. If we don't come up with a viable lead soon, the brass and the politicians are going to nail all our hides to the barn door."

"I know, I know." Dennis raked both hands through his hair. "I just hate to get you anywhere near those guys. They're always looking for an excuse to fight. You walking into that bar is tantamount to throwing a lit match into a gunpowder factory."

"Hey. Are you saying I start trouble?"

"No, Tiger." Lumbering up out of his chair, Dennis clamped his large hand around the back of Casey's neck and steered her toward the conference room door. "You just finish it."

An hour later Casey parked the police car on a remote dirt road south of Mears, across from a run-down mobile home.

The buckled vinyl siding on the trailer had come loose in places, most of the windows were cracked and held together with duct tape, and rust coated the bare wheels a bright orange.

Weeds grew up around the base of both the dwelling and the derelict pickup that sat on cinder blocks next to it. The dilapidated wooden steps leading up to the small porch and front door leaned dangerously to one side.

Rusty auto parts, scrap lumber, a roll of chicken wire, several plastic buckets, empty beer cans and bottles and various other junk littered the semi-cleared area that passed for a yard surrounding the mobile home.

On the dirt trail leading up to the place, a man stood bent over a motorcycle, tinkering with the engine. He looked to be over six feet tall and at least three hundred pounds. A rubber band held his stringy hair in a ponytail, and he had fastened two more bands around his chest-length beard, presumably to keep it from getting caught in the engine of the bike.

He wore no shirt, merely a leather vest and faded, dirty jeans that rode so low on his hips they were in danger of exposing much more of the man's backside than Casey cared to see. The enormous beer belly that hung over the top of his pants in front was covered with tattoos and hair, as were his beefy arms.

Another man, this one tall and skinny and just as grungy-looking, leaned against the side of the trailer, watching and swilling beer from a bottle.

"Charming place," Dennis muttered.

"Mmm. One of that pair has to be our man."

"Wanna bet it's the big guy?"

"Are you kidding? With a moniker like Attila? No way."

Fortunately, at that hour, customers had been scarce at Skinny's Tavern when Casey and Dennis arrived. The bartender had not been a model of public-spirited cooperation at first—not until Casey had threatened him with inspections from the liquor-licensing people and the board of health.

Reluctantly, he had then told them that Selma Hettinger had been the "old lady" of the Barbarians' leader, a biker by the name of Attila, and that the couple had been together in the bar the night of Selma's murder and had gotten into a fight. After a bit more persuasion on Casey's part, the barkeep had supplied them with the location of Attila's mobile home.

"Well, there's no time like the present," Casey said, reaching for the door handle. "Let's go see what 'Billy Bob Badass' has to say."

As Casey and her partner climbed from the car and headed up the dirt driveway, the skinny man abandoned his lounging position against the trailer and nudged his friend. Looking around, the big man straightened and squinted at Casey and Dennis, wiping his hands on a rag.

"Are you Attila?" Casey asked as they drew near.

"Who wants to know?"

Both Casey and Dennis pulled out their badges and showed them. "Mears Police. I'm Detective O'Toole. This is my partner, Detective Shannon. If you're Attila, we'd like to ask you a few questions."

The man snorted. "Beat it. I don't talk to pigs." He turned back to his motorcycle and started tinkering again as though they weren't there.

The skinny man snickered and resumed his slouched position against the end of the mobile home.

"We're investigating a series of homicides. Your name has been linked to one of the victims. So you can either talk to us here or we can take you down to the station house. Your choice."

The big man turned back to them with a wrench in his hand. His expression—what she could see of it behind the beard—held sneering amusement.

"Oh, yeah? And just how're you gonna do that?"

Casey sighed. "By force, if necessary."

The man's gaze switched to Dennis, then back to her.

"You gonna sic your friend here on me, are ya?" He shook his head. "I don't think he can take me. He's big, but I fight dirty."

"When I have to, so do I."

"*You?* Why, you ain't nothin' but a puny lil' ole girl. Git, the both of you. You're stinkin' up my place with pig smell."

Dennis groaned and shook his head. "Oh, man, I wish you hadn't said that." At the same time he reached under his jacket and put his hand on his gun.

"Drop that wrench, Attila, and come with us," Casey ordered, taking a step forward.

"Sure, bitch." He threw the wrench at her. As she dodged the tool he whipped out a big-bladed knife from a scabbard on his belt and assumed a crouched position. "You ain't takin' me nowheres. I'm gonna cut you up like a Thanksgiving turkey, bitch," he snarled, waving the knife.

"Drop the knife! Now!" Dennis ordered, standing to one side, holding his gun in a two-handed grip, aimed at Attila.

Ignoring him, the man lunged at Casey. In a blur of motion she kicked his arm and sent the knife flying, then delivered a crippling kick to his groin.

"Aaaugh," the big man screamed, clutching his privates with both hands.

The skinny man took a step toward Casey and Dennis barked, "Hold it! Don't even think of joining in."

Grabbing the big man's beard, Casey brought her knee up beneath his chin in a blow that clacked his teeth together. Attila's eyes crossed, and he went down like a poleaxed ox.

Casey cuffed his hands behind his back and read him

his Miranda rights. When she was done she looked at his friend. "You. Get in the car."

"*Me?* Wha'd I do? I was jist standin' here."

"It's not what you did, it's the company you keep. I've got some questions for you, too. Now, unless you want some of what I gave your buddy, get in the car."

"I'll drive," Dennis said.

"Why? That little scuffle didn't tire me. I can drive."

"Not with that cut on your leg, you won't."

Casey looked down and saw that the leg of her trousers was slashed and blood was streaming down into her shoe from a long gash that sliced diagonally across her leg, between her knee and her ankle.

"Oh, dammit. These were my best trousers. Now just look at them. They're ruined. So are my shoes."

"Forget your outfit. That cut is worse than I thought. It's pretty deep. Here. Hold this handkerchief pressed against it. I'm going to call for some uniforms to take these two in and book them while I drive you to the hospital. You're going to need some stitches."

"And a tetanus shot," she added, wrinkling her nose. "I hate to even think about what kind of germs were on that knife."

It was almost seven by the time Casey left the hospital. Dennis fussed about taking her by the station house so she could pick up her car, but she insisted.

"You shouldn't be driving. The doc said go home and put your leg up. Let me drive you home. I'll pick you up in the morning and we'll interview our perps."

"I'm fine. Besides, I'll need my car over the weekend." Deliberately, Casey made no mention of having a date to meet Mark at Jennifer's game.

During one of their almost nightly telephone conversations, Mary Kate had wheedled it out of Casey that Mark joined her most mornings on her run. Presumably, her entire family knew that bit of information by now. However, she had not told either her cousin or her partner that she and the doctor were now dating, and she wanted to keep it that way for a while—at least until she felt more comfortable about the whole thing.

Her pager buzzed again. Casey sighed and checked the number and stuck the annoying instrument back in her pocket.

"Your folks again?" Dennis shot her an amused look.

"Yes." Whenever her pager went off during her shift it was almost always someone in her family. Being a family of cops, her parents respected their time. They knew the cell phones that Casey and her brothers carried were for police business. When her parents wanted to speak to one of their offspring, they paged them and waited for them to call when they had time.

For the last two hours her pager had been buzzing about every ten minutes, and each time it had been her parents. Casey knew that news of her little scuffle with Attila had reached her mother and father.

"Do me a favor. When the folks ask you about what happened today, play it down, will you? I don't want Mom and Dad upset."

"Okay. But you know that no matter what I say, they're not going to believe you're okay until they hear it from you."

Casey grimaced. "I know. I'll call Mom as soon as I get home and smooth the waters."

After picking up her car, then heading home to finally change out of her ruined clothes, Casey telephoned her parents. As she'd guessed, they had already heard about the incident, first from Aiden, who had heard about it at his station house. Then Will had called with the news, then Ian and Brian. Casey was not surprised. Whenever any cop got hurt on the job, the news spread among the various precincts like wildfire on the plains.

It took Casey fifteen minutes to calm her mother and father and assure them that she was fine. She gave them an extremely sanitized version of what had occurred and laughed the whole thing off.

"Are you sure you won't come stay with us this weekend so I can take care of you?" her mother asked.

"Thanks, Mom, but I can't. I have to go in to work in the morning and interview this guy. Anyway, it's just a little cut. It's no big deal. Really."

"At least promise me you'll go to bed early tonight and get some rest."

"I will. I promise."

"And don't do too much tomorrow."

"Mom. I'll be fine. Now, quit worrying. I'll see you Sunday at church."

She hung up, grabbed her keys and purse and hurried for her car. For the first time, she wore slacks to the game instead of a skirt. The bandage on her leg was huge, and she didn't want to draw attention to it.

She didn't know why everyone was making such a fuss. It was just a cut and it didn't hurt at all.

By the time Casey reached the civic center she had begun to revise her estimation of her injury. The local anesthetic the doctor had injected around the wound had begun to wear off, and when she climbed from her car and started for the stands, the pain in her leg seemed to grow worse with each step.

The game was well under way. She heard the crack

of a bat smacking a ball followed by the cheers of parents as she hobbled toward the field.

Briefly she had considered calling Mark on his cell phone and begging off, but she would've had to explain what had happened. She refused to start off their relationship by lying to him. And in her experience, unpleasant news was always best given in person. Anyway, what was the point; she couldn't hide the injury for long.

Nevertheless, as she neared the dugout she gritted her teeth and did her best not to limp. Mark was standing, watching the play on the field and didn't see her when she slipped inside.

"Hi. How're the girls doing?"

He turned at the sound of her voice, his face lighting up. "Hi, sweetheart."

Slipping his arm around her waist, he bent and kissed her on the lips, and, as always happened, Casey's heart did a little flip-flop in her chest. Mark ignored the giggles of the girls on the bench, but Casey felt her cheeks heat up.

During the Monday- and Thursday-night games and the meals that had followed, Mark had made their relationship obvious to everyone, but the teenagers still found the sight of their coach kissing his lady titillating.

The team's assistant coach was another story. Debra Neelly stiffened up and grew sullen and remote whenever Casey joined the team in the dugout, and immediately after each game she hustled her daughter to their car and took off.

"We're zero and zero in the bottom of the fifth," Mark informed her when the kiss was over. "It's an evenly matched game."

His attention returned to the field, but his arm remained around her waist. Casey was grateful. His support allowed her to take her weight off her injured leg without anyone noticing.

"Hi, Casey." Another arm slipped around her waist from the other side. Turning her head, she encountered Jennifer's smiling face. "I'm so glad you could make it again tonight. I was beginning to think you wouldn't."

"Sorry, sweetie. I just had a little trouble with a suspect."

Mark's head snapped around. "Suspect? You like someone for the murders?"

"It's too soon to tell. I'm letting him cool off in jail overnight before I interrogate him. Other than that, I really can't discuss the case. Let's just say, we picked up someone we're taking a hard look at."

"I don't like the idea of you being anywhere near that guy, but I hope he turns out to be the right man. These murders have the whole town on edge."

Casey responded with an "Mmm." He had no idea how much she hoped the same thing. Solving this case would not only be a feather in her cap, it would take the heat off herself and the boss and perhaps take the sheriff down a peg or two.

Although, knowing Sheriff Crawford, the blowhard would probably find a way to take credit for the bust himself.

While at the hospital she had gotten word that a background check had identified Attila as Marian Percival Posey and his sidekick as John Wesley Crow, respectively. Both men had extensive rap sheets, with arrests for everything from robbery to assault to suspicion of murder, so Casey was hopeful. The only thing that bothered her was that neither man fit Helen Moran's profile of the serial killer.

Still, Attila was the last person known to have seen Selma Hettinger alive.

The game turned out to be a nail-biter, with the Trailblazers winning one to nothing in the ninth inning. During the excitement Casey all but forgot about her injury. That is, until she and Mark and the girls headed for the parking lot, and each step she took gave her a sharp reminder.

A niggle of worry curled inside Casey. Something wasn't right. She'd had cuts before, but none that had hurt this much.

She knew it was too much to hope that Mark wouldn't notice that she was favoring one leg.

"You're limping," he said before they were halfway to the parking lot. "What's wrong?"

"It's nothing."

"Don't give me that. No one limps for nothing. Especially not you. What happened?"

"I had a little trouble when I tried to take the suspect in for questioning. He pulled a knife, and while I was disarming him—"

"He *cut* you?"

"Well…yes, but it's not serious."

"Did it need stitches? If it needed stitches, it's serious."

"Calm down, Mark. The doctor at the ER stitched it up and gave me a tetanus shot and a prescription for an antibiotic. I'm fine."

"How many stitches?"

"Mark—"

"How many?"

"Eighteen, but—"

"*Eighteen!* You've got eighteen stitches in your leg and you're walking around?" Cursing fluently, he swept her up in his arms and stalked toward the van.

"Mark! What're you doing? Put me down. I can walk."

"I'll put you down in the van. Then I'm going to take a look at your leg. With that many stitches you should stay off your feet—at least for tonight."

That was what Dr. Kendall in the ER had told her to do, but she had felt fine until the freezing had worn off.

"Mark, you're going to scare the girls."

"What's wrong with Casey? Why're you carrying her?" Jennifer asked, as if on cue.

"She was injured making that arrest today. She needs to stay off her feet for a few hours. Open the passenger door of the van for me. And get my bag. It's between the front seats."

Jennifer and several of the other girls ran ahead to do as he asked. Mark put Casey in the captain's chair on the passenger side and retrieved a flashlight out of the glove box. "Here, Jen, hold this for me. I want to take a good look at this wound."

"Mark—"

"Hush. I'm doing this." Mark raised his head, and his silvery gaze drilled into her at close range. Casey could see that he was upset and determined to see just how badly she'd been hurt. She wanted to be indignant, but instead his concern brought a lump to her throat. Wisely, she opted for silence.

Mark took out a knife and grabbed the hem of her slacks, but Casey jerked her leg back.

"Don't you dare cut my pant leg. I've already had one pair of slacks ruined today."

He hesitated, then nodded. "Okay, I'll roll them up."

When the bandage came into view Jennifer and the other girls gasped. "Oh, Casey, what *happened?*" his niece asked.

"The bastard cut her," Mark said through gritted teeth.

That brought a chorus of shocked exclamations from the girls, followed at once by a barrage of questions. The teenagers crowded in for a closer look, some hanging over the back of the seat and the rest standing behind Mark, craning their necks to see over his shoulders.

He removed the bandage as tenderly as possible, but the adhesive tugging the injured flesh caused Casey to cry out.

Gasps and "eeeewoos" went up from the teenagers, but Mark remained ominously silent, the muscles in his jaw rippling as he examined the gash that wrapped at an angle from one side of her leg to the other.

Casey bit her lower lip and stared at the top of his head.

"Hold that light still, Jennifer." He put on a pair of latex gloves and probed around the edges of the wound. Casey gritted her teeth and tried not to flinch.

"Let me guess," he said in a disgusted voice. "Dr. Kendall was on duty in the ER. Right?"

"Yes. Do you know him?"

"Yeah, he's doing his internship at St. Mary's. He's an excellent diagnostician, and one day he's going to make a helluva G.P., but the man is ham-handed with a needle. Thank God he isn't going into surgery."

Mark probed the wound some more, and Casey groaned. "I don't like the look of this. It's abnormally swollen and angry. I think you have internal bleeding going on. Either a severed blood vessel wasn't reattached securely or you've torn something loose in there by walking around. I'm going to take you back to the hospital and open up the wound and see what's going on."

"Is that really necessary?"

"Absolutely. You don't ignore a leaking blood vessel. Besides, this closure is a mess. Unless you want a big puckered scar across the front of your leg I need to restitch you. What kind of painkiller did Kendall give you and what time did you take the last one?"

"Um…he didn't give me any painkillers."

Mark's head jerked up. "None at all?" She shook her head and he muttered a curse under his breath, too low for the girls to hear. "Since we're going to restitch, that works in our favor, but you shouldn't have had to suffer any pain."

"It isn't that bad," Casey fibbed, keeping her fingers crossed behind her back. "Anyway, it's not the doctor's fault. I told him I didn't want anything that would put me out of commission."

"Now, why am I not surprised?" Mark shot her a pithy look that made her feel like a chastised child.

He taped the bandage loosely over the line of stitches and straightened. "All right, girls. Listen up. I have to take Casey back to the ER, so there isn't going to be any pizza tonight. Anybody with a cell phone, call your parents to come pick you up here, and tell them to hurry. If you don't have a phone you can use mine."

Casey expected groans of complaint, but the girls were surprisingly understanding and subdued. The calls were made and within twenty minutes everyone had been picked up and she, Mark and Jennifer were on their way to the hospital.

Overruling the woman on duty at the check-in desk, Mark bypassed the paperwork altogether. Telling her that he was simply going to correct a botched closure made by another doctor earlier that day, he carried Casey directly into a treatment cubicle.

His sudden appearance in the ER carrying a woman created a stir among the staff. No sooner had he placed her on the gurney than not one but three nurses came rushing into the cubicle to help.

Mark snapped orders to the women to get out a suture kit and several other items that Casey didn't recognize. "I need to get you into a hospital gown. Lift up your hips, sweetheart, so I can take your slacks off."

"Mark!"

The three nurses didn't miss the endearment, and Casey saw them exchange a knowing look.

"If you don't want those slacks cut off you're going to have to help me here. C'mon, love, don't be shy. I've seen you in less…" He paused, his eyes twinkling with mischief as Casey blushed, then added, "Every morning when we go for our run."

"Very funny."

"Dr. Adams, behave yourself. You're embarrassing the young lady," the oldest of the nurses admonished, elbowing Mark aside. "Here's a gown for you, darlin'," she said kindly, holding the faded floral garment up in front of Casey as a screen. "If you'll slip off your clothes and put this on I'll fasten the back ties for you."

Keeping one eye on Mark, who busied himself on the opposite side of the small room, Casey scrambled out of her clothes and into the hideous gown, and the gray-haired nurse covered her with a sheet.

One of the other women handed Mark a tiny paper cup containing a capsule, and he gave it to Casey along with a glass of water. "Here, take this. By the time I finish scrubbing you'll be nice and relaxed and drowsy."

She tried to give the cup back to him. "This isn't necessary. I can stand a little pain."

Bending over her, Mark brushed her hair away from her cheeks and spread the bright curls out on the coarse white hospital pillowcase. "I can see that during our life together I'm going to have to constantly remind you which one of us is the doctor."

Casey's heart stumbled to a halt, then took off again at a gallop. She forgot about the three women watching them. She forgot about the throbbing pain in her leg. She forgot about her decision to play it safe and see how things developed. All she was aware of was this gorgeous, caring man, looking at her with so much love in his eyes that she felt as though she were melting inside.

She blinked up at him and swallowed hard. "Are... are we going to have a life together?" she asked in a whisper, touching his cheek with her fingertips.

"If I have anything to say about it, we are."

Mark bent and kissed her, a slow, lingering caress that turned her insides to mush and made her feel better than any pill could have done. He didn't seem to care that they had an audience, or that gossip about them would surely fly through the hospital grapevine. It was as though he wanted everyone to know that he was serious about her.

When at last he raised his head, he smiled. "Now, take your pill like a good girl. There you go," he praised when she obeyed, docile as a lamb. "You just relax while I go scrub up."

He glanced at the three nurses, who were pretending to be busy, and said, "Take care of my lady while I'm gone."

"Oh, we will."

"You bet."

"It'll be our pleasure," the women chorused eagerly.

Casey closed her eyes and sighed. So much for taking things slow.

By the time Mark, Jennifer and Casey arrived at her town house, it was a little after eleven. On the way home, with the passenger seat reclined partway, Casey lay back with her eyes closed. She was tired, hungry and still feeling woozy from the medication that Mark had given her.

Parking the van in her driveway, he turned to her. "Do you have a spare bedroom?"

"I have two. Why?"

"Because Jennifer and I are going to stay with you for a couple of nights."

"Yay!" Jennifer yelled from the back seat. "This is going to be fun. We'll have a slumber party."

"Not tonight, sweetie," Mark said. "Casey needs to get some rest. Maybe tomorrow if her leg looks better." Before Casey could protest he bailed out of the car, trotted around the vehicle to her side and scooped her up.

"You need to stay off that leg for at least the next twenty-four hours and take antibiotics and a painkiller, which I couldn't help but notice tend to make you goofy. Cute, but definitely a little on the loopy side. You'll need someone with you. So…either Jennifer and I stay here or I take you to your folk's place. Your choice."

Some choice. Casey could imagine the fuss her family, particularly her mother and Francis, would make. Experiencing a mixture of frustration, helplessness, gratitude and a lovely, warm sensation of being cherished, all she could do was stare into Mark's pale eyes and whisper, "There are fresh linens for the spare beds in the closet at the top of the stairs."

"Good decision." He dropped a quick kiss on her mouth. "I was prepared to sleep on your sofa, but since you have two spare bedrooms, I won't have to."

He headed up the walk with her in his arms, and Jennifer scampered along behind them.

They were almost at the front steps when, out of the darkness, an angry voice demanded, "Where the hell have you been?"

Jennifer screamed and jumped forward and clutched the back of her uncle's shirt.

"What the hell!" Mark snapped. He jerked to a halt, tensing for flight as the dark shapes of four men materialized out of the shadows on the front porch.

"What's going on here? Who are you and why are you carrying our sister?"

"Will? Will Collins, is that you?" Casey demanded. She peered through the darkness at the others. "And Brian and Ian and Aiden, too. I should have known. What are you four doing skulking around in the dark? You scared us half to death."

"Hey! We weren't skulking," Brian protested. "We were waiting for you."

"Yeah," Ian concurred. "Mom sent us."

"That's right," his twin chimed in. "She was worried. She paged you and called both your home phone and your cell phone."

Casey could have kicked herself. In her rush to get to the civic center she'd left both in the pocket of the blazer she'd worn to work that day.

"When you didn't answer, she asked us to check on you."

Will glanced at Casey and nodded agreement, but his hard stare returned immediately to Mark.

Glancing over Mark's shoulder, Casey spotted her brothers' vehicles parked across the street. If she'd been more alert she would have noticed them when they drove up.

"You're lucky we didn't break your door down," Will added. "Mom was certain you were passed out on the floor. Fortunately for you, we looked in through the garage window first and saw that your car was missing.

"Now, back to my original question. Where the hell have you been. And who is this guy?"

"Not that it's any of your business, but we were at the hospital. This is Dr. Mark Adams. And this is his niece, Jennifer," Casey informed them in a haughty voice. "Don't be afraid, sweetie. These big lugs are just my brothers." Slowly, the frightened girl edged around to her uncle's side. "Mark and Jennifer, meet Will, Brian, Ian and Aiden."

Deliberately, Casey made no mention of the softball game. She was no fool.

"What's wrong?" Will demanded. "Why did you have to go back to the hospital? Damn, you must be hurt a lot worse than you let on if a doctor had to bring you home."

"There was a problem with the wound," Mark replied before Casey could. "I reopened it, repaired a couple of blood vessels and stitched her up again. She should be fine now, if she'll stay off that leg for the next forty-eight hours."

"Oh, she'll stay off of it, Doc," Brian said. "We can guarantee that."

"Right. If we have to, we'll take turns sitting on her," Ian said.

"That won't be necessary." Mark looked from one brother to another. "You see, my reasons for bringing your sister home are more personal than medical. Casey and I are dating. I'll be staying here tonight to look after her."

"The *hell* you will!" Hotheaded Ian charged forward, but Will held him back.

"Easy. Easy. You can't hit him while he's carrying Stretch."

"Damn you! You're sleeping with our sister," Brian charged.

Aiden took a step forward. "Doctor or no doctor, you can kiss your ass goodbye, you—"

"Stop it! Stop it right now. All of you." Casey glared at her brothers. "I will not have you starting a donny-brook in my front yard. And will you kindly remember that there's a young, impressionable girl present."

The brothers backed off, looking sheepish but no less angry.

"Casey's right," Will said. "Let's go inside before the neighbors start complaining."

"You're not going to fight in my house, either."

"Look, fellas. Why don't I take Casey upstairs and get her settled. Then I'll come down and we'll discuss this."

"There's nothing to discuss. I'm going to whip your sorry—"

"Can it, Aiden," Will ordered. He turned a warning glare on Mark. "We'll give you one minute. If you're not back by then we're coming after you. We'll be in the living room."

"Fine." Mark instructed his niece to get Casey's keys out of her purse and unlock the door.

"Oh, for Pete's sake. What do you think he's going

to do? Ravish me while the four of you are downstairs? And for your information, I'm a grown woman. I make my own decisions," Casey scolded her siblings over Mark's shoulder while they all trooped inside. "I don't need a bunch of Neanderthals running my life. If I want Mark to stay overnight, that's my business."

"Hush, sweetheart." Mark gave her a little shake. "You stay out of this. This is between me and your brothers."

Shock dropped Casey's jaw and silenced her tongue. The brothers exchanged a surprised look that held a touch of reassessment.

Upstairs, Mark carried Casey into her room and place her on her bed. "Jennifer, help her get ready for bed while I go talk to the brothers. I'll be back in a few minutes."

"Are you sure?" his niece asked, twisting her hands together.

"Mark, you don't have to do this. Why don't you just take Jennifer and go. My brothers will look after me."

He bent and kissed her forehead. "Stop fretting. It'll all work out."

Ht turned and left the room, and Casey shouted after him, loud enough for her siblings to hear, "Tell them if they lay a hand on you they'll answer to me!"

"Do you think he'll be all right?" Jennifer asked.

"Oh, sure," Casey said with a lot more confidence than she was feeling. "My brothers are more bark than bite."

With the girl's help, Casey hobbled to the bathroom for her nightly hygiene rituals. They left the door open and both she and Jennifer kept a sharp ear out for any sounds of violence from below, but all they heard was the murmur of voices—fairly calm voices, considering the situation.

Casey slipped into her nicest nightgown and gave her unruly hair a good brushing. She had barely returned to the bed when Mark reappeared.

She gave him a quick once-over. "I don't see any blood. What happened?"

"Nothing. We came to an understanding and everything's fine now."

"What does that mean? Where are they?"

"They've gone. Will and Brian took your keys. They're going to go pick up your car and leave it out front."

"They're *gone?* Just like that?" Flabbergasted, Casey stared at him with her mouth agape. Then she shook her head. "I don't understand any of this. You go downstairs and confront a pack of angry men, and scare Jennifer and me half to death, then a few minutes later you tell me that everything is fine. What happened? What did they say? What did you say to them to make them back off?"

Mark grinned and ruffled her newly brushed curls. "Never you mind. As I said before, my love, *that* is between me and your brothers.

"Now," he said with finality, "Jennifer and I are going to rustle up something to eat."

After a meal of scrambled eggs and bacon, Mark brought her another pain capsule and insisted that she take it.

"And if you wake up during the night in pain, which you probably will, call me," he ordered.

He sat down on the edge of the bed and kissed her good-night, a sensual, lingering kiss that made her pulse pound and her head swim. She wrapped her arms around his shoulders and returned the kiss with a hunger that she hadn't experienced in more than a year.

Maybe it was the situation, or the fact that she was in bed, dressed in her sexiest nightgown, or maybe it was merely more than a year of abstinence catching up with her, but the kiss was so arousing that, if Mark had pressed just the slightest, she would have thrown back the covers and welcomed him into her bed with open arms.

However, Mark did not press. When his control threatened to crumble, he reluctantly pulled back. His face was flushed with passion, and his hand trembled when he smoothed her hair away from her temple. He gave her a rueful smile. "Being a man of honor is tough. But I gave my word." He touched her cheek with his fingertips. "Good night, sweetheart. Call if you need me."

With that he left the room, leaving the door open so that he could hear her if she called to him.

Casey sighed and switched off the bedside lamp and turned onto her side, propping her throbbing leg up on a pillow. She had just found a comfortable position when she heard Jennifer in the hallway, tapping on Mark's door.

"Uncle Mark," she called in a small, frightened voice.

Casey sat up and turned the bedside lamp back on. At the same time a light came on in Mark's room. She heard the rumble of his voice as he talked to Jennifer, but she couldn't understand what he was saying.

"What is it? What's wrong," Casey called.

Mark and Jennifer appeared in her doorway. The girl was trembling. "Jennifer says there's a man across the street in the park."

"A man?" Casey glanced at her bedside clock. It was after midnight. What was a man doing prowling around in the park at that hour?

"Yes. I'd turned out the light and gotten into bed,

when I remembered I hadn't taken my contacts out. As I was going to the bathroom I happened to look out the window and there he was."

"What's he doing?"

"Nothing, really. He's just standing there, staring at your house."

Seventeen

Casey sat up in the bed. "I'd better find out what he's up to."

"Oh, no you don't. Don't even think about going out there," Mark ordered. "You're in no condition to get into another kickboxing match. I'll go."

"Neither of us will go." She reached for the telephone on the bedside table. "I'll call dispatch and get a patrol car out here to check the park."

Casey made the call and asked that someone call her back after the park was checked out. Only minutes later Jennifer and Mark watched from the front bedroom window as two squad cars cruised slowly around the perimeter of the park, shining spotlights into the interior, while several more officers walked through the area with flashlights.

"It doesn't look as though they found anyone," Mark called to Casey. "The officers on foot are returning to the squad cars."

A few moments later he and Jennifer returned to her room, looking disappointed. "They're taking off."

"The guy was probably gone before they got here. If he caught a glimpse of one of you watching him out the window, he probably figured the police were on the way," Casey said.

The telephone rang, and they all jumped.

Casey snatched up the receiver before it could ring a second time. "Hello?"

"O'Toole. This is Lieutenant Bradshaw. The men couldn't find anyone in the park, but just to be safe, there'll be a couple of squad cars parked outside your place—front and back—all night."

"That's not necessary, boss."

"It's my call, O'Toole, not yours."

"Sarge shouldn't have bothered you with this. I don't know why he called and disturbed you at home with something so trivial."

"He called me because I put the word out to every cop on the force that I was to be notified of any threat aimed at you. We've got a killer on our hands who's targeting red-haired women, and my lead detective has red hair. Now some creep is watching your house. The patrol cars stay."

His bark made Casey grimace. "Right. Whatever you say. Thanks, boss."

"Is everything okay?" Mark asked when she hung up the receiver.

"That was my lieutenant. They couldn't find anyone in the park, but he's posting patrol cars out front and in the alley out back for the rest of the night."

"He's that concerned?"

"Don't worry, he's just being cautious. We cops tend to look after our own. With all the media coverage I've been getting lately, and my red hair, well…" Looking sheepish, Casey shrugged and spread her hands wide.

"He's worried that the killer may have zeroed in on you," Mark finished for her in a grim voice.

Jennifer made a strangled sound and scooted closer to her uncle's side.

"Well…yes, but I think he's worrying for nothing."

"If we're in danger here—"

"We're not. The lieutenant is just being a mother hen. Even if he's right, no way will the guy attempt a break-in with patrol cars in plain sight. If you're worried, though, why don't you take Jennifer and go back to your place. I'll be fine here with my bodyguards."

The teenager tugged at her uncle's sleeve. "Please, Uncle Mark. Let's go."

"If Jennifer and I go, we're taking you with us," Mark said in a tone that brooked no argument.

"That's not a good idea. Believe me, we're a lot safer here with a couple of cops standing guard than we would be at your place. Plus I have a state-of-the-art security system and dead-bolt locks on all the windows and doors. No one is going to get in here unless I let them in."

She switched her gaze to Jennifer and smiled. "So you see, sweetie, you don't have to worry. You're perfectly safe."

Casey awoke the next morning to the sound of her partner's voice rumbling downstairs. Surprise darted through her when she glanced at the bedside clock. It was almost eight. Between the pain in her leg, all that had happened the previous day, and the awareness that Mark was sleeping just across the hall, she hadn't expected to sleep a wink.

Rubbing her eyes, she dragged herself out of bed

and headed for the bathroom, sucking in a sharp breath with each step she took.

After taking a quick bath with her injured leg hanging over the side of the tub, she dressed in her usual work attire, applied a little makeup and clipped her hair back at the nape of her neck. She strapped on her holstered gun, grabbed her purse and started hobbling down the stairs, carefully maneuvering one step at a time.

Mark appeared in the foyer at the foot of the stairs before she was halfway down. "Where do you think you're going?"

"To work. Dennis and I have to interview our suspect this morning."

Her partner appeared behind Mark, chomping on a bagel spread with a thick layer of cream cheese and jam. "'Morning, Tiger. I dropped by to pick you up. Hanson and Jones were just leaving when I got here. They told me about the guy in the park. They said to tell you it was quiet all night."

"I told the boss there was nothing to worry about."

"Maybe. Maybe not. Imagine my surprise when I found the doc here. We've been having an interesting discussion over breakfast. By the way, he makes an excellent pot of coffee. You oughta try some." He held up the steaming mug he carried in his other hand to tantalize her.

Casey caught a whiff of the brew and her mouth began to water. "I'll take some with me in a thermos. I don't have time for breakfast. I'd hoped to already be at the station house by now."

"You're not going to work today," Mark said.

"Oh, yes I am."

"Dammit, Casey. You need to stay off that leg."

"Hey, Tiger, there's no need for you to risk more injury. I can handle the interview alone."

"I know you can. But it's my case, and I'm going to be there." She narrowed her eyes at Mark. "Before we take this relationship one step further, you should know that I don't respond well to being ordered around."

"Sweetheart, that's not what this is about. I swear. You're hurt and I'm simply trying to take care of you. If you insist on going to work, then Jennifer and I will go with you."

"Oh, no you won't."

After more discussion, Casey and Mark reached a compromise. She agreed to stop by the medical-supply store and pick up a cane, which she would use until her leg was pain free.

Since the next day was Sunday, and Monday was July 4, Mark and Jennifer would go home and clean up, leave a note for his brother, Matt, who was due home the next night, pick up some extra clothes and meet Casey back at the town house in no more than two hours.

"Don't worry, Doc. I'll see that she doesn't overdo it," Dennis swore.

"So. You and the doc are a couple now, huh?" he asked Casey the moment they drove away from her town house.

"We're dating. Sorta." Uncomfortable talking about her relationship with Mark, she shifted restlessly.

"What does that mean? How do you 'sorta' date?"

Casey shrugged. "Mostly, we attend Jennifer's softball games and go out with the team afterward. Nothing serious."

"Do you want it to be?"

"No. Maybe. Oh, I don't know. It just all seems to be happening too fast. I haven't figured it out yet."

"What's to figure out? The doc's a great guy and he's crazy about you. You know what your problem is?"

"No, but I'm sure you're going to tell me."

Unfazed by her sarcasm, Dennis went on. "Your love for Tim evolved slowly over time, so you don't trust what you're feeling now for Mark because it's caught you by surprise. Well, I gotta tell you, Tiger, out in the real world, most of us get hit by a thunderbolt when we meet that right person." His expression turned dreamy and a bit sappy. "I remember the first time I saw Mary Kate. Oh, man, I was bowled over."

"I know. I was there. Look, could we drop this, please? I really don't want to talk about it right now."

"Sure. Just don't fret over this too long, Tiger. Emotions can't be analyzed like a case. You can't gather the evidence and put it all together like the pieces of a puzzle. You just thank the good Lord you found someone and enjoy the ride."

Two uniform cops were standing guard over the suspect when Casey hobbled into the interrogation room with Dennis.

Attila laughed when he saw her. "Looks like I hurt you real bad, bitch. I'd say I won that fight."

"Oh, I don't know about that. I'm not the one shackled to the table."

His arrogant smirk collapsed. "You can't hold me," he snarled.

"Wanna bet?"

Casey sat down in the wooden chair across from the suspect and hooked her cane on the edge of the table. "Now, then, Mr. Posey. Let's talk. Where were you on the night and through the following dawn hours of April 1?"

At the use of his real name the man's face turned the color of a beet. "Dammit, bitch, my name is Attila."

"Really? That's funny. Our records, and I believe your birth certificate also, lists you as Marian Percival Posey."

"Dammit—" He rose halfway out of his chair. Dennis, who had remained standing, took a step forward, but the uniformed cops on either side of the suspect put their hands on his shoulders and shoved him back down onto the chair.

"If you want to be called Attila, then start answering my questions. Where were you on the dates in question?"

"How the hell would I know? You think I keep a social calendar?"

"Do you know Madeline St. Martin or Becky Sue Belcamp?"

"Never heard of 'em."

"We have a witness who says that you were with Selma Hettinger on the night of April 1."

"What if I was? That don't mean I killed her."

"Our witness will testify that on the night of April 1 you and Selma got into a fight at Skinny's Tavern. That the disagreement turned physical."

"So I slapped her around a little. So what? She knew better than to mouth off at me. I showed her who was boss, that's all. Anyway, Selma always gave as good as she got."

"My witness also says that the two of you left together. That was the last anyone saw Selma alive. What happened when you left the bar?"

"The stupid cow was still givin' me lip, so I slapped her again and got on my bike and drove off. I left her standin' out front of the bar, screaming at me. I could hear her halfway down the block."

"And did she return to your place that night?"

"Naw."

"And you weren't concerned?"

"Why should I be? I was glad the bitch was gone. Good riddance, I say."

"I see. Where were you the next morning, around daybreak?"

"In bed. Sleeping off the beers I'd had the night before."

"Really? You didn't take Selma out into the woods and turn her loose, then hunt her down like an animal? You didn't shoot her in the back?"

"No," Attila snarled.

"I should warn you, we obtained a search warrant for your home, and in it we found a Remington hunting rifle chambered for the .300 Winchester Mag cartridge. The same type of ammo that killed Selma and the two other victims. We recovered the bullets that killed Ms. Belcamp. We're going to run ballistics test on your gun. If we get a match, you will be charged with three counts of first-degree murder."

"Go ahead and run your test. There won't be no match, 'cause I didn't kill those women. Then you're gonna have to let me go."

"Oh, I wouldn't count on that if I were you."

Picking up her cane, Casey stood up and hobbled toward the door.

"Hey! You can't pin those murders on me. You don't have no evidence, 'cause I didn't kill nobody."

Casey stopped at the door and looked back at him. "Maybe. Maybe not. We'll see. Regardless, there are plenty of charges I can file against you, starting with assaulting a police officer, assault with a deadly weapon and attempted murder. You, Mr. Posey, are going to jail. I guarantee it."

Casey and Dennis left the interrogation room and headed for the squad room to write up a report. "What do you think?" he asked.

"He's right. So far we don't have enough to charge him with murder. But at least he won't be able to skip town while we're looking for more."

"Do you think we'll find any?"

Casey grimaced. "Truthfully? No. I hate to say it, but I don't think he's our man. Not that he isn't capable of murder. I can see him killing Selma, but not the other women. Neither one of them was his type. Plus, he's about as far off Helen Moran's profile as you can get." Casey leaned back in her chair and sighed. "Anyway, it would be too easy if the perp turned out to be Mr. Posey."

By the time she arrived home, Casey was dragging. Mark took one look at her and ordered, "Okay, off to bed with you."

"I can't. I still have to clean the house and do my weekly grocery shopping. Plus I have a few errands to run."

"Too bad. You're going to rest. I saw your grocery list in the kitchen. Just tell me what else you need and I'll do your shopping while Jennifer cleans the house."

"Oh, Mark, I can't ask either of you to do my chores," she said, but they both knew it was only a token protest.

Mark put Casey on the bed and covered her with the colorful afghan her mother had crocheted for her. She was so exhausted she was almost asleep before he left the room.

After a couple of hours of dreamless slumber she awoke feeling refreshed and hungry and found her house spotless and all her shopping and errands done.

Jennifer, who seemed to have gotten over her fear, made cobb salads and tomato soup for lunch. Afterward, with Casey's leg propped up on a footstool, the three of them played Scrabble around the dining room table while a baseball game played on the television in the adjoining living room.

It occurred to Casey as they laughed and teased one another that she hadn't had that much fun in years. She hadn't realized how much she'd missed having someone with whom she could feel at ease, someone with whom she could share life's everyday simple pleasures. It was nice.

They were in the middle of the third cutthroat game when Casey's cell phone rang. The chirping sound gave her a start, and she glanced at Mark and saw that his expression had turned serious.

"O'Toole."

"Detective, I hate to call you at home on Saturday," a familiar voice said. "But the old geezers are at it again."

Casey groaned and cupped her forehead with her hand. "Okay, Harry, thanks. I'll be right there."

"You'll be right where? You're not going to the station house again, are you?"

"No, this is family business."

"What's wrong? Is someone ill."

"No. I have to go break up a fight."

"What?"

"Oh, cool! Can I go, too?" Jennifer asked, bouncing in her chair.

"That's up to your uncle." Casey made a rueful face at Mark. "My grandfather and his cronies have gotten into a rumble and are tearing up Muldoon's bar."

Mark gaped at her. "Your *grandfather?*"

"Yes. You're going to have to drive me down there. I hope you don't mind."

"What? Oh. No, of course not."

They drove Casey's car. As soon as they were on their way, Mark cast a sidelong look at her. "How old is your grandfather?"

"Ninety."

"Ninety!" Mark threw his head back and laughed, deep rumbling guffaws of pure mirth. "Good for him."

"You wouldn't say that if he was your grandfather."

Still grinning, he shot her another curious glance. "Why? Does this sort of thing happen often?"

"Are you kidding? At least once a month. Every payday everyone in the family pitches in twenty dollars to cover the damage he does. We call it Granda's Restitution Fund."

"Oh, man, this is rich. I can't wait to meet him."

"Well, you're about to. There's Muldoon's just ahead."

"Jen, you stay in the car," Mark ordered as he and Casey climbed out.

"Oh, bummer." The teenager flounced back in the seat and crossed her arms, her face sulky. "It's not fair. I miss all the good stuff."

"Neither of you have to come inside. I can handle Granda."

"Are you kidding?" Mark replied. "I wouldn't miss this for the world."

The sound of crashing glass from inside the saloon

made Casey wince. "I'd better get in there before he
trashes the place." She hobbled for the door, leaning
heavily on her cane.

Inside, the scene that greeted them brought a delighted grin to Mark's face and caused Casey to shake
her head.

In the middle of the floor, several tables and chairs
were overturned, and the customers had vacated the
area. They all stood back watching as Seamus Collins
and his best friend and card-playing buddy, Marcel
Petrantonio, circled each other, shouting insults and
dire threats.

Frail and stooped, the two old men tottered around
like two wobbly scarecrows. Marcel was using his aluminum walker as a battering ram, while Casey's grandfather shook his walking stick in the air and every now
and then took a swipe at his friend. Each time he missed
the other man by a foot or more, but he managed to take
out two Tiffany-style light fixtures and clear a table of
a pitcher of beer and several mugs.

For once, the two other old men in the foursome, Saul
Morganthal and Eddy Cook, were not taking part in the
fight. They stood to one side, taking bets on who would
emerge the winner.

"What are they fighting about this time?" Casey
asked Harry Donovan, the bartender.

"Something about who was the greatest warrior of all
time, Conn of a Hundred Battles or Caesar."

"Figures." Casey shook her head. "I knew it would
be something of earth-shattering importance. I guess I'd
better break it up before blood is drawn." She made her
way through the small crowd of patrons and stepped in
between the two old men.

"All right, you two, knock it off. Put your weapons down and back away before someone gets hurt."

"The devil ya say," Seamus bellowed. "I'm going to tear him limb from limb."

"Granda, stop it. Right now. And you, Marcel, put down that walker. You ought to be ashamed of yourselves, carrying on like this. Again."

"It was his fault," Marcel charged, shaking his fist at Seamus. "The old fossil doesn't know squat about history."

"Fossil, is it? I'll show ya, fossil, ya sorry son of an egg-sucking—"

"Stop it!" Putting her palms on each man's bony chest, Casey shoved them apart, gently so as not to upset their precarious balance and topple them over.

From the corner of her eye she saw Mark standing at the front of the crowd with his arms crossed over his chest, grinning, and out front Jennifer had her face pressed up against the plate-glass window with her hands cupped around her eyes.

"Harry, who started this brouhaha?" Casey called to the barkeep.

The group of old men had a deal. Whoever started a fight paid sixty percent of the damage and the defender or defenders paid forty.

"I'm afraid your grandfather struck the first blow. He lathered Marcel good with his cane before the old guy could get up on his feet."

"'Tisn't a cane, ya nincompoop!" Seamus shouted, shaking the item in question at the barkeep. "'Tis a walking stick. A Blackthorn walking stick from the old country. 'Twas me granda's and his granda's before him. I'll thank ya to show a little respect."

Harry held up both hands. "Sorry."

"An' well ya should be. Ya call yourself an Irishman," the old man grumbled. "A disgrace to the name Donovan 'tis what ya are."

"All right, Granda, that's enough. You've defended the old country enough for one day. And had a pint or two too many, I suspect. Time to go home."

She put her arm around the dear old man and steered him toward the door. Mark followed them. "Figure up the damages, Harry, and I'll write you a check."

"Will do, Detective. Say hello to your dad and Joe for me."

"I will."

They were outside on the sidewalk before Seamus noticed Mark.

"An' who might you be?" he demanded with a touch of belligerence.

"This is a friend of mine, Granda. His name is Mark Adams. Dr. Mark Adams." Casey gently helped her grandfather into the back seat of her car. Once she and Mark were settled in the front, she looked back and added, "And this is Mark's niece, Jennifer Adams."

Turning on the charm, Seamus picked up the girl's hand and held it between his two bony, age-spotted ones. "Well, now, 'tis pleased I am to meet ya, young lady. My, my, aren't you a little beauty."

Jennifer giggled and turned red, but she remembered her manners enough to murmur, "Nice to meet you, too, Mr. Collins."

Seamus leaned back and studied the back of Mark's head. "So, 'tis a doctor ya are."

"Yes, sir," Mark replied, glancing at the old man in the rearview mirror.

"Well, now, 'tisn't that just grand. As I told me darlin' Casey here, just a few weeks ago, we could use a good doctor in this family, what with the high cost of medical bills these days."

"Granda!" Casey covered her face with both hands. When she glanced at Mark he was biting the insides of his cheeks to keep from laughing.

During the remainder of the ride Seamus entertained Jennifer. He told her that she reminded him of a girl back in Ireland whom he'd been sweet on as a lad.

"Her name was Colleen. Ah, she was a beauty, she was," he reminisced fondly. "Eyes the color of the bluest sky and hair black as coal. An' her skin, ah, 'twas like white rose petals in the mornin' dew."

Jennifer listened, rapt, as he regaled her with stories of the things he'd done to get Colleen to notice him: walking by her cottage every morning on his way to work, just in the hope of catching a glimpse of her, though it was over a mile out of his way; writing her poems and love notes; leaving bouquets of wildflowers on her doorstep.

"I even entered a local bare-knuckled boxing match, just to impress her. Backfired on me, though. Got the stuffin' beat out o' me that day." Seamus heaved a dramatic sigh. "I tell ya, child, me poor heart ached for that lass."

"What ever happened to her?" Jennifer asked, wide-eyed.

"What happened? Why, I married her. We came to this country, had a fine, fine son and a good life. Then, four years ago last March, my Colleen passed away, just after our sixtieth wedding anniversary. An' I miss her with every breath I take."

Casey directed Mark where to turn into her parents' long driveway, then looked out the side window, her heart clenching at the memory of her sweet, beautiful Gram.

Colleen Collins had been the exact opposite of her high-spirited, rough-and-ready grandfather. The gentle, steady woman had been the grounding force in Seamus's life. Everyone in the family missed her sorely, and they knew that their own pain was nothing compared to his. Which was why they put up with his shenanigans. Getting into mischief was just a way of distracting himself from the pain of missing his beloved Colleen.

Casey glanced back and saw that Jennifer had tears in her eyes. "Oh, I'm so sorry, Mr. Collins."

Seamus took the girl's hand again and patted it. "Ah, don't be, child. 'Tis a lucky man, I am. I've had a good, long life and sixty wonderful years with the woman I loved. No man could ask for more than that."

Another glance into the back seat confirmed that Jennifer was just as choked up as Casey. The girl bit her bottom lip and looked out the window, blinking back tears.

They drove into the clearing surrounding the Collins' home and Mark exclaimed, "Wow, what a great place."

Whether the remark was a deliberate attempt to break the emotional tension or not, Casey could have kissed him. Surreptitiously, she wiped her eyes and turned her attention to the big rambling house that her father and Papa Joe had built with their own two hands.

"And what a perfect spot to raise kids. You must have had a wonderful childhood, growing up here."

"Yes. Yes, I did. We all did."

Mark helped Seamus out of the car, but when Casey started to climb out, too, he waved her back. "Don't trouble yourself, darlin'. Ya just take care of that injured leg o' yours. Besides, I don't need help gettin' up a few steps and into the house."

"I know you don't, Granda," she said, humoring him. "I was just going to run in and say hi to Mom and Dad."

"Well, don't bother. They've gone to Haviland Lake to go fishin'. Them and Joe and Francis."

"Will you be all right on your own?"

Seamus gave her an indignant look and stood as tall as his stooped body would allow. "Of course I will. I'm goin' to park me old bones in front of the telly until your folks get home. Now, go along with ya."

"Why don't I just see you inside, Mr. Collins," Mark suggested. "Since you have the wisdom of years, I'd like your advice on something."

"It's advice you're wantin', is it? Well, ya've come to the right place. By the way, what kind of doctor did ya say ya are?"

"I didn't." Mark took the old man's elbow and led him slowly up the walkway. "But I'm a plastic surgeon."

"A plastic surgeon!" Seamus said with undisguised disgust. "Ah, well, you'll be no use to this family. All me children and grandchildren are beautiful."

"Oh, Lord," Casey moaned, and slid down low in the front seat of the car and covered her face with her hands.

Mark threw his head back and laughed. "You know, Mr. Collins, you're absolutely right."

He was gone about ten minutes. When he slid back in behind the wheel, he looked pleased and smiled at Casey. "What are you doing scrunched down like that?"

"Hiding. Now that you've met all of my family, except for my in-laws, are you sure you want to get involved with me? I have four overprotective brothers, loving but hovering parents, and a rascal for a grandfather."

"I *like* your grandfather," Jennifer piped up from the back seat. "He's sweet."

"That he is. And I adore him, but he can be a trial sometimes."

Casey turned back to Mark, her expression serious. "The point I'm trying to make is, when you get involved with any of us, you have to take the whole clan. We're sort of a package deal. With your background, I'm not sure you can handle so much family."

Mark leaned across the seat and gave her a quick kiss. When he raised his head, his eyes were warm and caressing. "Sweetheart, you worry too much. Your family is delightful. The more I see of them, the crazier I am about you."

Eighteen

Mark's admiration for her family seemed to be mutual. The next morning at church, they all greeted him as though he were an old friend.

Even Joe and Francis seemed pleased to meet him. Casey had been concerned about how her in-laws would feel when they saw her with another man, but as everyone shuffled in the aisle to get the family seated, Francis pulled Casey aside and murmured in her ear, "Dr. Adams seems like a very nice young man. You'd do well to hang on to him, love."

"You don't mind that we're seeing each other?" Casey asked, giving her mother-in-law a searching look.

"No, of course not. Oh, child, you haven't been holding back because of us, have you? Dearest, we loved our son dearly, but we love you, too. I'll admit that Joe and I would have liked nothing better than for you and Tim to have had a long, happy life together, but things didn't work out that way. Tim's gone, but you're a vibrant young woman who has her whole life ahead of her. You deserve to be happy.

"Whoever you marry, whether it's Dr. Adams or someone else, you will have our blessing." She smiled and patted Casey's cheek. "You're our daughter as much as you are Maureen's and Patrick's. If in the future you have children, we will look upon them as our grandchildren. And if he will let us, we will look upon your husband as our son."

Tears welled in Casey's eyes. She surged forward and hugged the older woman. "Oh, Francis, you're so good to me. I love you so."

Returning the embrace, Francis patted Casey's back. "I know, love. I know. I love you, too. But come now, we'd better take our seats. The service is starting."

Casey slid into the pew and sat down between Mark and Jennifer in the space he'd saved for her. Sniffing, she pulled a tissue from her purse and blotted her eyes, and struggled to swallow the lump in her throat.

"Is something wrong?" Mark whispered.

She blinked her tear-drenched eyes at him and shook her head, too emotional to speak.

Throughout the service Mark held Casey's hand, something that escaped no one in her family. They nudged one another and exchanged smiles and knowing looks.

As little as a few weeks ago Casey would have been uncomfortable with the contact and the depth of involvement tacit in the simple gesture, particularly in front of her family. Oddly, now she couldn't work up a single objection. His touch felt natural, comforting even.

He's wearing me down. Chipping away at my defenses, she thought wryly.

After church Casey was not surprised when her mother insisted that Mark and Jennifer join them for

Sunday dinner, even though they were coming to the cookout the next day. No sooner had the invitation been issued than the others seconded the idea.

"Sounds great," Mark replied, which did not surprise Casey, either. "Just give us time to make a couple of quick stops by Casey's place, then mine, so we can change out of our Sunday duds, and we'll be there," he told Maureen.

The day could not have been more ideal. Mark and Jennifer fit right in, as though they had always been a part of the family. Baby Roger immediately captured the teenager's heart, and she spent most of the day playing with the toddler and talking to Mary Kate, who lay in her customary place on one of the den sofas.

After dinner Casey and her mother and Francis spent the rest of the afternoon preparing for the Fourth of July cookout the next day. Sitting at the long trestle table with her injured leg propped up on another chair, Casey peeled and chopped vegetables, iced cakes and cookies, and stuffed celery, while the other women made potato salad, simmered beans and made pies.

Outside in the driveway, Mark and her brothers were shooting hoops while the older men watched a baseball game on television. Every now and then her granda Seamus tottered into the kitchen to tease the women and swipe a goody or two.

While she worked, Casey's gaze was drawn out the windows to Mark. He charged and feinted as Will and Ian tried to guard him. Then in a lightning move he spun around and went in for the layup. The basketball rolled around on the rim once before dropping through the net. Mark gave a yell and, in a typical male gesture, pumped his fist in triumph.

Like her brothers, he wore jeans shorts and sneakers. Already sweating profusely, he paused for a moment, peeled off his shirt and tossed it aside. Casey stared at his broad chest, with its inverted triangle of black hair, his flat belly and bulging biceps, and felt her mouth go dry. Lord, he was a beautiful man.

She had been struggling to define exactly what it was that she felt for Mark. She was attracted to him, certainly. What heterosexual woman wouldn't be? Just looking at the man sent a tingle all over her body and made her chest feel as though it were being squeezed in a vise.

However, what she felt was more that mere physical attraction. From that first morning run in the park, she had felt—not at ease, exactly—but a sense of rightness, a deep-down awareness that being with him made her feel happy. She enjoyed his company, his sense of humor, his intelligence. As well, his compassion and caring never failed to tug at her heartstrings.

She and Mark had talked a lot during the past ten days or so, and everything she'd learned about him so far merely increased her admiration for his character and ethics, and deepened her emotional connection to him. His moral compass was definitely pointed in the right direction.

All those things combined made her feel warm and happy inside. Even with the serial-murder case to worry about and the pressure from the bosses and the media, since meeting Mark she had walked around with a funny, bubbly sensation in her chest, a feeling of anticipation and joy that she hadn't experienced in such a very long time.

But was that love? She resisted that idea. It just didn't

seem possible. She had been in love only once, but it had been a deep and abiding love that had grown slowly, developing over time. Wasn't that the way it was supposed to happen? Surely it didn't hit like a lightning bolt out of the blue, as Mark claimed it had for him. At least, she didn't think so.

Though she admitted to almost no experience with men, she considered herself a good judge of character, and not for a minute did she think that Mark was merely stringing her along. He truly believed that he was in love.

But what if what he was feeling was infatuation, or he was merely intrigued because she was so different from other women he'd dated, and he'd mistaken those feelings for love? If she let herself fall for him, and then they broke up, could she deal with the pain?

Of course she could, she admitted. She was a strong woman, and she would always have her family to comfort her. Still, her instinct was to play it safe and protect herself, to hold back and see what developed before opening her heart all the way.

By that evening, when she, Mark and Jennifer and her brothers piled into their cars to leave, they were all pleasantly tired.

"How's the leg feel?" Mark asked.

"It aches a little when I put weight on it, but it's better. I think I can leave off the painkillers tonight. Actually, there's no reason you and Jennifer have to stay with me any longer. I'm sure I'll be fine."

He shot her a dry look. "Trying to get rid of me?"

"No. It's not that. I...I just don't like imposing on people, is all."

"I'm not 'people.' I'm the man who's crazy about you. The man who's hoping to become a permanent part of your life soon. And Jennifer and I are staying with you again tonight. No arguments."

Casey's heart gave a little jump. A permanent part of her life? What did that mean? He wanted to marry her? He wanted to have a long-term affair? What? He had alluded to a future with her on several occasions, but he'd never come right out and said exactly what he intended that to be.

Worse, she wasn't sure how she would respond to either scenario if he did.

When they arrived at Casey's town house there was a message on her answering machine from Jennifer's father.

"Hey, Mark. Sorry I'm so late. My plane out of Heathrow was delayed and I missed all my connections after that. Anyway, it's so late, I won't pick Jennifer up tonight. I assume we're still going to the Collins's for the Fourth, so I'll come over to Casey's town house at eight in the morning. By the way, bro, that was a cryptic message you left. I want to hear more about your lady getting hurt, and that prowler. See you in the morning."

"Should I call Daddy back?" Jennifer asked in a sleepy mumble.

"No, it's late. He's probably sleeping off jet lag. We'll see him in the morning."

"'Kay," the girl said over a huge yawn. "Then I'm going to take a shower and go to bed. I'm pooped. I had no idea that two-year-olds could be so rambunctious."

Smiling fondly, Mark watched her climb the stairs. "She must really be tired if she's willing to wait until morning to see her dad. She's always ecstatic when he comes home from a trip."

He turned to Casey and touched a flyaway curl at her

temple. "You look tired, too. Why don't I carry you up-stairs and let you get to bed."

"You don't have to do that, I can make it— Ma-ark!"

He swooped her up in his arms and started up the stairs. "We're going to have to work on that habit you have of automatically refusing my offers of help. Don't get me wrong, I admire your spunk and independence, but this isn't the time to assert them."

"Sorry. It's habit, I guess." She looped her arms around his neck and settled back in his arms to enjoy the ride, ruefully aware that just a few short weeks ago she wouldn't have dreamed of doing so.

In her room Mark sat her down on the side of the bed.

"You sure you don't need a painkiller tonight? You don't have to be a hero and tough it out, you know."

Casey looked up at him and shook her head. "No, I'm fine."

He smiled and touched an errant curl at her temple. "You're so lovely," he whispered.

Casey shook her head and made a sound somewhere between a snort and a chuckle. "How can you say that? I'm just ordinary-looking. That's what I can't under-stand about all this. Why me? Why would a man like you pick me?"

"Ordinary?" Mark gaped at her with disbelief. Then he swooped her up in his arms again and stood her on her feet in front of the full-length mirror in the corner. Standing behind her, he circled her waist with his hands.

"Has growing up with four brothers and a cousin whom you mistakenly think is more beautiful than you made you blind? Look at yourself," he prodded almost angrily. "You have skin like cream and the biggest, blu-est eyes I've ever seen, and they're surrounded by absurdly long lashes most women would kill for. Your bone structure is lovely and in perfect balance. Your lips are full and luscious. And you have the most gorgeous hair in the world. Not to mention a tight, fit little body that drives me wild.

"For Pete's sake, Casey, how can you look at yourself and not see how beautiful you are? Trust me, I make a good part of my living improving women's looks, and I know what constitutes beauty. Sweetheart, every time I see you, you take my breath away." His gaze met hers in the mirror. "Don't you ever again say you're ordinary."

He turned her carefully and wrapped his arms around her. Slowly, his gaze roamed her face, touching on every feature. "There isn't a thing about you that I would change," he murmured in a husky voice. "Not one single thing."

"Not…not even my freckles?" she asked in a subdued voice.

Mark smiled and touched the bridge of her nose with his forefinger. "*Especially* not your freckles."

His gaze zeroed in on her lips and his eyelids began to droop as his head lowered. "I adore every one of them," he whispered against her lips an instant before his mouth touched hers.

The kiss was rife with emotion and need, and just a hint of anger. It was hot and openmouthed and so sensual Casey could do nothing but cling to him, trembling. Their bodies pressed together from shoulders to knees. Her breasts were flattened against his hard chest, and her nipples throbbed and ached almost painfully.

With every breath, she drew in his wonderful male scent. Mingled with it was a hint of the sweat that had dried on his skin. Casey could feel his sex, pressing against the apex of her thighs, and the desire he couldn't disguise. She felt on fire, her body awash with yearning.

It had been so long. So very long.

She was lost in a cloud of passion, and it took her a few seconds to realize that Mark had ended the kiss. Slowly, she opened her eyes and found him watching her. A dark flush tinted his face and his breathing was ragged, labored. The look in his eyes bordered on desperate. "Damn. If you don't make up your mind soon how you feel about me, I'm not going to make it. You're killing me, sweetheart."

Mark's brother, Matt, arrived at Casey's town house at precisely one minute to eight the next morning, and he was greeted at the front door with joyous affection from his daughter.

Casey had been curious about Mark's twin. There was a strong resemblance between the two men, but it was obvious at first glance that they were fraternal twins. Matt was perhaps an inch taller than Mark's six foot one, but they had the same lean-muscled, rangy build and the same ultramasculine way of moving. Where Mark's hair was black as coal, Matt's was a dark, dark brown. Though their facial features were similar, Matt's had a more rough-hewn look.

Casey quickly realized, however, that Mark's brother was just as charming as his twin, and if the twinkle in his eye was any indication, just as mischievous.

After Mark introduced them, Matt held Casey's hand between both of his and grinned wickedly. "Damn, bro. No wonder you're so smitten. If I'd met her first, you'd be outta luck."

"The hell you say." Elbowing his brother aside, Mark

put his arm around Casey. "Get your own woman," he growled, only half teasing.

Because Casey was on standby duty on the Fourth, they went in two vehicles, Mark and Casey in her car, followed by Matt and Jennifer in his company van. At his request, Matt had driven over in Mark's car, which they left parked at the curb in front of Casey's town house.

Before leaving her place, Casey explained to Mark, Matt and Jennifer about Danny. "He's slow, but he's a dear. He's starved for attention and family, and he's been looking forward to this picnic for weeks. He and his older brother, Keith, live near the station house, which is a little out of our way, but it won't take long to swing by and pick him up. I'm sure he's ready and waiting right now."

"No problem," they all agreed.

Ten minutes later they pulled up in front of the Watsons' small bungalow and found Danny sitting on the front stoop, waiting for them with a duffel bag at his feet.

"Oh, dear. He's probably been sitting there since daybreak," Casey said.

The instant he saw her he jumped up and ran to the car, a wide grin splitting his face.

"Hi, Casey. I've been waiting for you for so long." He stopped short when he saw Mark behind the wheel. "Who's that?"

"Hi, sport. Get in and I'll introduce you."

Danny scrambled into the back seat and sat clutching his duffel bag in his lap, looking at Mark with suspicion as she made the introduction.

"Mark is a friend of mine. And behind us in that van are his brother, Matt, and Matt's daughter, Jennifer." Danny twisted around on the seat for a look. "They're going to be joining us for the cookout, too," she explained gently.

Distracted by the reminder, Danny grinned at her again. "I can't wait. I've been ready since last night. I've brought extra clothes, in case I spill something on me, and my allergy medicine, and my toothbrush and floss, 'cause Keith says you have to take care of your teeth and brush after every meal. And I have my blanket, in case I get tired, and a whole bunch of other stuff."

"Well, that's fine, Danny. It sounds as though you're prepared to enjoy yourself."

"Yeah. I've been waiting and waiting for this day."

Preparations were well under way when they arrived at the Collins's home. On the back patio Patrick and Joe had two huge cookers smoking, each of the brothers and Dennis were cranking the handles of old-fashioned ice-cream makers. Inside the house, Maureen and Francis scurried about the kitchen taking care of last-minute details. Even Mary Kate had been assigned a job. She lay on a padded chaise longue under the shade of a clump of aspen trees, rolling utensils in napkins.

"Hey, Danny," Dennis called out. "You're just the man I wanted to see. This ice cream is almost ready. Come over here and sit on this freezer while I finish cranking it."

"Sure!" Delighted to be included, Danny scurried over and plopped down on the freezer, which was covered with a thick folded blanket.

"Hey, no fair," Ian protested. "Who's gonna sit on ours?"

Casey rolled her eyes at her other guests. "They do this every year. It's always a race to see who can finish first. We might as well be their anchors, otherwise we'll never hear the end of their complaining."

"Hey, if it means homemade ice cream, I'm game," Matt said. "C'mon, Jennifer, pick a freezer."

They ate outdoors on the shaded patio. As usual when they all got together, the conversation was lively and boisterous, with a lot of good-natured ribbing and laughter.

Casey had been worried that Mark and Matt might be a bit overwhelmed by her family, but they joined right in, bantering back and forth with her brothers as though they'd all been friends for years.

Seamus was in fine form, spinning yarns for the newcomers about his youth in Ireland. The family had heard it all before, but Seamus had a way with words and a great talent for embellishment, and they were as enthralled as their guests.

Everyone made an effort to include Danny, and he seemed to be having the time of his life.

Afterward, while they were cleaning up the mess and putting away the leftovers, Casey's dad pulled her aside.

"It was nice of you to invite Danny, child. You've a good heart."

"Thanks, Dad."

"But I hope you'll take a word of warning from your old dad. Be careful. The lad has a tremendous crush on you. Don't let him read too much into your kindness. You don't know how he'll react."

"I know." She glanced out the back screen door at Danny. He was arm wrestling Brian, who was letting him win. "It's just that I feel sorry for him. He's so sweet. He and his brother practically grew up on their own. Keith is all he has, and he craves attention."

"I know. Just be careful."

"I will."

A while later, Casey realized just how prophetic her father's warning had been.

After the meal, when everyone had rested for an hour, they began a croquet tournament on the back lawn. Danny had never played croquet before, but then neither had Jennifer, so Casey was able to explain the rules to the two of them in detail without making Danny self-conscious.

The only way Mark would agree to let Casey play was if she carried an aluminum lawn chair around with her and rested between her turns.

They were on opposite teams, and when she knocked his ball out of bounds and laughed, he growled, "Why you competitive little devil. Just for that, you're going to pay a penalty."

Giggling, Casey tried to run away, but he grabbed her and planted a long, passionate kiss on her lips.

"Hey! Hey! Watch it, Doc," Aiden yelled. "Kiss our sister like that in front of the family and you have to marry her."

Mark raised his head and grinned at her brother. "Fine by me. I'd marry her today if I could get her to say yes."

"Noooo!"

Stunned, they all turned and gaped at Danny. He stood beside the third wicket, rigid and shaking. His face was beet-red and he had a wild look in his eyes. Without warning he slung his mallet as hard as he could and charged toward Mark and Casey.

"Look out!"

Both Matt and Will had to duck to keep from being coldcocked. The mallet whizzed over both men's heads, hit a pine tree and split into three pieces.

Danny slammed into Mark, running full tilt, shoved

him back into a tree and began to hit and kick. Making no effort to strike back, Mark held his arms up and did his best to fend off the blows.

"No! You can't marry Casey! You can't!"

"Danny, stop it! Stop it!" Casey yelled. She tried to pull him away from Mark, but he was surprisingly strong. It took the help of two of her brothers and Matt to end his assault. While they held him she clasped his face with both hands. "Danny. Danny, calm down. You have to calm down."

Mark brushed himself off and added in a coaxing voice, "Casey's right, Danny. Just take deep breaths. Nice and slow. And when you collect yourself we'll talk about this calmly."

"No! I don't want to talk to you. I hate you!"

With that he pulled away from Brian and Aiden, dodged Matt's attempt to grab him and took off for the house.

"Danny, wait!"

Paying no attention to Casey's plea, he ran inside.

Speechless, they all stared after him as the screen door banged shut behind him.

"Are you all right, Mark?" Casey asked.

"Yeah." He rolled his shoulders experimentally. "I'll have a bruise or two, but I'm okay."

"I'll go see after Danny," Patrick said, but Casey put her hand on her father's arm.

"No, Dad, I'll go."

"Casey—"

"I'll be all right, Dad. Danny won't hurt me. This is my fault. I should have anticipated something like this. I'll straighten it out."

She found Danny pacing the front porch and mumbling to himself. He gave her a sulky look when she joined him. "I want to go home. I don't like it here anymore. I want to go home."

"Okay, if that's what you want, I'll take you home in a little while."

"I want to go *now.*"

"I think we should talk first, Danny. Come over here and sit down on the swing with me. We'll talk. Just the two of us."

With a complete absence of good grace, he did as she asked, plopping himself down at one end of the porch swing with his arms tightly crossed over his chest and a sulk on his face. He kept his head down and stared at his sneakers.

"Danny," Casey began cautiously. "We're friends, right?"

"Yeah."

"And friends can be honest with each other, right?"

"I guess."

"Then can you tell me why you're so angry with Mark?"

"I don't want you to marry him." He turned his head and gave her a pleading look. "I love you, Casey."

"Oh, Danny. I love you, too. Just not in a marrying kind of way."

"Oh, I know you can't marry *me.* I'm not smart enough for you." Grabbing her hands, he went on in a rush, his gaze beseeching, "But you could marry Keith and come live in our house with us. Then I'd get to see you every day."

Caught completely off guard, for a moment Casey could only stare, dumbfounded. Of all the things that he might have said, she hadn't expected that.

"Oh, Danny. Sweetie, I'm so sorry, but that's just not

going to happen." She patted his shoulder and smoothed a lock of hair off his forehead. "I'm not in love with Keith."

"But couldn't you be, if you tried really, really hard?" he asked hopefully.

"I don't think so. Emotions don't work that way. We can't make ourselves fall in love. It just happens."

"Do you love Mark?"

"Maybe. I'm...not sure yet. But Danny, no matter what happens, you and I will always be friends."

He stared down at his sneakers again, but after a while he cut his eyes around at her. "Promise?"

"I promise. Cross my heart and hope to die," she swore, drawing an imaginary *X* over her chest. She ruffled his hair. "Now, then. Now that we've got that settled, why don't you come back to the backyard with me."

"No! I can't go back there. They all hate me now."

"No one hates you, Danny. I promise."

He nudged one of her mother's potted plants with the toe of his sneaker. "Not even Mark?"

"Not even Mark. No one hates you, Danny. Everyone is just concerned about you, that's all."

She stood up and held out her hand. "C'mon. Let's go have some more fun."

Danny took her hand and they went back inside, cutting through the house to the back door. "First, though, I think it would be a good idea if you apologized to Mark."

Danny stopped in his tracks. "I can't do *that*."

"Sure you can."

"But why do I have to?" he whined.

"Because, it's the right thing to do. You're a man, Danny, and a real man always tries to do the right thing."

She squeezed his hand. "And everyone will think even more of you for it."

She could see him mulling that over, methodically putting each piece of information together. Finally he nodded. "Okay. I'll do it."

The only fireworks after that were the sparklers that they lit at dusk for the benefit of Roger and Jennifer, and of course, Danny.

Worried about setting a forest fire, Patrick and Joe had decreed from the beginning that there would be no other fireworks on the property. The edict was no great hardship. As kids, Casey and her brothers and Tim had always had so much fun on the holiday they hadn't missed the pyrotechnics.

By the time the last sparkler burned out, Roger was cranky and rubbing his eyes.

"I think it's time for us to load up and go home," Dennis announced. "It's past someone's bedtime."

That was the cue to end the party, and they all began to rouse themselves, murmuring about what a good day it had been while they folded lawn chairs and gathered up paper cups and other party debris.

"Oh, dear. Oh! Oh!" Mary Kate sat forward in the lounger and grabbed her turgid belly with both hands, a look of shock on her face.

Dennis went into instant panic mode. "What is it? What's wrong? Are you having pains?"

She looked up at her husband with a bewildered expression. "I...I think my water just broke."

"Ah, hell. Okay, okay. Hold on. Everything's going to be fine." He shoved the fingers of both hands through his hair and tried to think. "Uh, uh...somebody run up to the cottage and get Mary Kate's hospital bag."

"I'll do it," Ian volunteered, and took off.

"And here's my keys," he said, handing them to Brian. "Bring my car around, will you?"

"Sure."

"What's happening?" Danny asked, looking frightened.

"Don't worry. It's nothing bad," Maureen assured him. "Mary Kate is going to have her babies, that's all."

"Now? Oh, cool."

"Dennis." Mary Kate tugged on her husband's pant leg. "Dennis, the babies are coming."

"I know, love, I know. Just hang on. We'll have you at the hospital in no time."

"No. You don't understand. They're coming *now.*"

Nineteen

Mark squatted down beside Mary Kate's lounge chair and put his hand on her stomach. "You're having a contraction. Are you in pain?"

"I think—I think it's starting. Yes, here it comes. Yes! Oh! Ooh!"

"Easy. Easy," Mark coaxed.

Mary Kate moaned and clutched her husband's hand so hard he grimaced.

"There, the contraction is beginning to ease." Mark kept his gaze on his wristwatch and his hand on Mary Kate's stomach.

Dennis shifted from one foot to the other, raking his free hand through his hair. "Dammit, what's taking Ian and Brian so long?"

"Here's Brian with the car," someone yelled.

"To hell with the bag," Dennis muttered, and tapped Mark on the shoulder. "Doc, would you mind getting out of the way? I've gotta get her to the hospital."

Mark didn't budge. "Just a sec. Here comes another contraction."

"C'mon, Doc. We gotta go!"

"You won't make it to the hospital. As your wife said, these babies are coming now."

"What? Oh, Lord. Oh, man. What are we gonna do?"

"I suggest you get her into the house, while I go get my medical bag and scrub up."

"*You're* going to deliver the babies? But…but…do you know what you're doing? No offense, Doc, but you're a plastic surgeon."

"Unfortunately, I'm all you have right now."

"But…have you ever delivered a baby before?"

Mark chuckled. "It's been a while, but I delivered my share during my internship."

"Oh, for heaven's sake! We don't have time for this!" Mary Kate yelled. "Quit arguing with the man and let him get on with it or these babies are going to be born right here!"

"Oh, this is so exciting," Jennifer squealed, tugging on Casey's arm.

Mark stood up and ordered, "Okay, guys, grab the lounger—two on each end—and carry her inside. I'm going to get my bag out of the van."

Aidan, Will, Brian and Matt hurried to comply. With Granda Seamus tottering along beside, giving orders, Dennis on the other side, holding his wife's hand while she yelled through another hard contraction, the women running ahead to open the door and everyone else following, they scurried into the house.

"Easy with her. Easy," Granda barked. "Kindly remember 'tis precious cargo ya got there, ya big oafs."

"Bring her in here to our bedroom," Maureen ordered. "We don't want to take her upstairs. Francis, will you come help me put a plastic sheet on the bed, please?"

"You bet. And we'll need a bunch of clean towels and cotton sheets, too. And maybe some string to tie the cord."

Accustomed to working together, the two women had both sheets on the bed before the men maneuvered into the room and set the lounger, with their writhing, panting burden, beside the bed. Mark and Casey appeared right behind them.

"All right, guys, lift her onto the bed," he ordered. "Put her close to the end."

"Hang on, sweetheart," Dennis crooned. White as the sheet on the bed, he looked ready to faint.

Mary Kate arched her back and let out a blood-curdling scream.

"Holy sh—"

All the men, with the exception of Mark, jumped back a step and exchanged a look of universal male terror at the prospect of imminent child birth.

"C'mon, guys, we don't have much time. Move her. Casey, you stand by with some blankets to wrap the babies in."

"Ya heard the man," Granda blustered, to cover his own fear. "Do as he says."

The brothers and Matt exchanged another look, gathered their courage, stepped forward and shifted their cousin onto the bed, then nearly knocked one another down getting out of the room. Shuffling after them, Seamus said, "I'll be just outside if ya need me."

"Hurry, Doctor, hurry," Mary Kate screamed. "They're coming!"

"Looks like I won't have time to scrub." Mark snapped on a pair of latex gloves and called over his shoulder, "Seamus, do me a favor and telephone for an

ambulance. Mother and babies will have to be transported to the hospital as soon as they're born."

"Don't ya be worrin' none about that, now. I'll see
'tis done. An' I'll station Ian out on the highway to direct them in."

Maureen and Francis removed the mother-to-be's
underwear, shoved her maternity sundress up and covered her with a sheet.

"Oh! Oh! Oooh!" Mary Kate cried out. As the last
word dissolved into a scream, Mark dropped to his
knees at the end of the bed.

"You were right. We're in the home stretch. I see a
head. Give me a push, Mary Kate. C'mon, one really
hard push. That's all we need."

Casey watched her cousin, her heart pounding, awed
by Mary Kate's courage and the miracle that was taking place.

"C'mon, baby, you can do it," Dennis coached. "It's
almost over."

With her husband standing beside the bed holding
her hand and Maureen kneeling on the mattress at her
other side, wiping her sweaty face with a cool, wet
cloth, Mary Kate sucked in a deep breath, held it and
bore down with all her might.

"Great. You're doing great. And…you've got a beautiful baby daughter." With quick efficiency, Mark
cleared the baby's breathing passages, dealt with the
cord and handed the baby to Casey, who swaddled her
tight and placed her on her mother's chest.

For a moment, while Mark worked in silence, the
parents cooed over their new daughter, who kept up an
indignant wail, letting the world know of her displea-

sure. Silent tears streamed down Dennis's face while Mary Kate laughed and cried at the same time.

Watching them, Casey became so choked with emotions she could barely draw breath.

The respite was a brief one. When the pain returned even harder, Casey took the baby and handed her to Francis, who disappeared with her into the bathroom to clean her up.

"Here we go. Round two," Mark said in his deep, soothing voice.

Three hard contractions followed. During the third one, the Shannon's second baby girl slid into Mark's waiting hands.

Casey watched him perform the same after-birth routine that he had on the first twin, mesmerized by the calm efficiency with which he worked, the way his big, capable hands handled each tiny infant with such gentleness and care, and something inside her melted.

She was in love with this man, she realized in a blinding bolt of stunning awareness. Deeply, completely, irrevocably in love.

"Here you go." He turned and handed Casey the second baby, but when he saw her expression he cocked one eyebrow. "You okay?"

Casey swallowed hard and nodded. "It's... It's just all so beautiful."

He smiled. "Yeah. It is, isn't it?"

At that moment the ambulance came roaring up the drive, and within seconds the paramedics rushed in with a gurney. They were surprised to find Mark there, and even more surprised to learn that he had just delivered the twins.

"Hey, Doc, nice job," one of the crew said.

With so many people talking at once and everyone crowding into the room to get a look at the new arrivals, it was bedlam in the house for a while. After a few minutes the paramedics rolled a beaming Mary Kate, holding a baby daughter in the crook of each arm, outside to the waiting ambulance. Everyone followed, waving and calling encouragement as the attendant closed the doors and the ambulance made its way down the winding drive through the trees.

Mark took hold of Casey's hand and turned to his brother. "Matt, I have to go to the hospital and keep an eye on Mary Kate and the babies until her doctor arrives. Would you mind taking Danny home?"

"Be glad to. No problem."

"You don't mind if Matt takes you home, do you, Danny?" he asked. "Casey has to go to the hospital to be with her cousin."

"I don't mind. Oh, man, this was so exciting. Wait'll I tell Keith. Did you really help Mary Kate have those babies?"

Mark grinned at Danny and lowered his voice, pretending to confide in him, man-to-man. "Just between you and me, sport, she did most of the work. But don't tell anybody."

"Don't you believe him, Danny." Matt clapped Mark's shoulder. "My little brother is a terrific doctor. You did a great job tonight, bro. I've never seen you in action before. I'm proud of you."

"Thanks."

He turned back to Danny and said, "By the way, sport, don't pay any attention to that 'little brother' stuff. He's just two minutes older than me. Matt and I are twins, too."

"Really?" Danny's face lit up. "I've never known any twins before. And tonight I've met two sets. That's so cool."

Casey told her parents where she and Mark were going and kissed them goodbye, but when they turned to leave, Granda Seamus stopped them.

"Mark, me boy. Before ya leave, I've somethin' to say. 'Tis an apology I owe ya," the old man declared.

"Oh? How's that?"

"Forget what I said about ya being no use to this family. 'Tis a fine doctor ya are, an' that's a fact. An' 'tis proud we'd be to claim ya as one o' our own."

It was after eleven when Mark brought Casey home. They were both exhausted from the day of physical activity and emotional upheaval. He parked the car in her garage and they went inside through the connecting door so that he could gather his and Jennifer's things. Casey was planning to return to work the next day, as was Mark. Reluctantly, they had agreed that she no longer needed assistance.

At the front door he kissed her good-night, doing a slow, thorough job of it. When the kiss ended, he held her close. For several minutes they stood in silence, arms around each other, Casey's cheek pressed against Mark's chest, his resting against her crown. "It's been a good day," he murmured. His warm, moist breath skated over her scalp and stirred her hair, and she shivered.

"Mmm. It was a wonderful day. Despite Danny's little blowup."

"Yeah, but he came around. I think by the end of the day he even started to like me." Mark rubbed his jaw against the top of her head, catching her hair in his beard stubble. "I hope we have many more days like today."

Casey blinked several times and smiled. "We will." She almost told him then that she loved him, but they were both so tired, she decided to wait.

Mark released her and opened the door. "Be sure to lock up tight after I'm gone. I'm still not convinced that guy prowling around in the park the other night was just a vagrant." He gave her another quick kiss and stepped outside. "I'll call you tomorrow."

"Okay." Holding the door open, Casey watched him stroll down the front walk toward his car, one hand holding the duffel bag filled with his things, the other in the pocket of his windbreaker. His gaze was focused on the starry sky overhead. The mere sight of him excited her, she thought, heaving a deep sigh. She felt like a love-sick teenager.

Casey started to close the door, but at that moment she heard a car engine turn over, followed instantly by the squeal of tires. The dark shape of a boxy vehicle came careering around the corner with no headlights. The driver was in shadows, but she saw his left arm lift and the flash of something silver in his hand.

"Mark! Look out!"

Turning, Mark looked back. "Wha—"

Casey saw the muzzle flash and heard the loud pop of the gun.

Mark's body jerked, and he let out an agonized, "Aaaugh!"

"Mark!" Casey screamed as he fell facedown onto her small front yard.

She grabbed her purse from the foyer table, pulled out her revolver and hobbled outside as quickly as she could move. Holding the gun in a two-handed grip, she assumed a firing stance and took aim at the barely visible dark shape as it raced away, but she couldn't see it well enough to get off a good shot. In any case, with so many homes around the park, she couldn't afford to shoot blindly.

Dropping down beside Mark, she saw a bloodstain spreading across his upper back, soaking his shirt. She stripped off her cotton sweater, wadded it up and pressed it to the wound. Placing her fingers on the side of his neck, she searched for his pulse. When she felt the steady beat she sagged with relief. "Mark. Mark, can you hear me? Talk to me."

He moaned and tried to lift his head. "Yeah, I'm…still…with you. What…what happened?"

"You've been shot. Hold on just a second, I'm going to get my cell phone."

She hobbled back inside and retrieved the phone from her purse, then hobbled back out again, dialing 911 on the way. "This is Detective Casey O'Toole with the police department. A man has been shot. We need an ambulance right away."

She gave them her address and dropped down beside Mark again, placing her revolver on the ground beside her leg within easy reach. Using one hand to press her sweater tight to his wound, she dialed dispatch with the thumb of her other hand and reported what had happened. All the while her gaze swept the area in case the shooter returned.

"Why…why would anyone…shoot me?" Mark gasped.

"I don't know. But I'm going to find out."

He shifted and groaned.

"Just lie still. Help is on the way."

And they'd better get here soon, she thought, scanning the shadows. The shooter could have parked around the corner and cut back through the park. Even though she'd turned off the porch light, there was a streetlight on the corner and more light pouring out through her living room windows. She and Mark were sitting ducks out on the lawn.

To her relief, she heard the sirens in the distance. Two patrol cars arrived first. One after the other they screeched to a stop at the curb. The officers bailed out with guns drawn, sweeping the area for potential threats. A moment later a third, unmarked car arrived, and Keith jumped out, gun drawn. "I was coming home from a date when I heard the call," he said. "You all right?"

"I'm fine, but Mark's been shot."

All around, lights were coming on in the other town houses and a few brave neighbors stepped outside in their bathrobes to see what was happening.

"You okay, Detective?" Officer Kaslowski from the night shift asked as he approached.

"Yes, but my friend has been hit. Where is that ambulance, for Pete's sake?"

"Don't worry. Here it comes now. And if I'm not mistaken, that's Lieutenant Bradshaw's car right behind it."

The paramedics were the same ones who had transported her cousin to the hospital. They did a double take when they saw her, but when they squatted down and got a good look at the victim, one of them blurted out, "Holy Mary, mother of God. It's Dr. Adams."

"You're kiddin' me," the other medic said.

Casey stood up and stepped aside to give them room to work as her boss came striding across the lawn.

"What the hell happened here, O'Toole?"

As succinctly as possible, with Keith hovering close by her side, Casey recited the chain of events that had led up to the shooting. All the while she spoke she kept her eye on Mark. "I couldn't risk returning fire with all the houses around."

"Did you get a look at the shooter?"

"Not really. He may have had on a ski mask." One of the paramedics cut off Mark's shirt and pulled the material away from the wound, and he made an agonized sound, drawing her attention. "How is he?"

"Not too bad. Looks like the bullet hit his shoulder blade at an angle then ricocheted off. He's got a nasty graze, though."

"Which means the bullet is around here someplace. Where was the shooter when he fired and which way was your friend facing?" Lieutenant Bradshaw asked Casey.

She supplied him with the information, and he ordered several men to look for the bullet. "Make yourself useful, Watson. Give 'em a hand." The lieutenant turned back to Casey. "Anything else?"

"Yes. I didn't see the shooter, but I did get a glimpse of his vehicle when he drove by. It was a light-colored van. I don't think that was a coincidence."

Her boss's gaze sharpened. "You think this shooting has something to do with the serial murders?"

"I don't have any solid evidence, but that's my gut feeling."

"Could he have been shooting at you?"

"Maybe. But I doubt it. I was standing in the doorway in plain sight with a light at my back, but he aimed straight at Mark."

"Still, this has to be connected to you in some way.

I don't believe in coincidence, either. This was no random shooting."

"I agree. He was lying in wait over there around the corner of the park."

"Lieutenant, we found the bullet." A uniformed officer trotted over and dropped the piece of lead into the lieutenant's hand. "It embedded itself into the trunk of that aspen over there by the front window. Lucky for us, that's soft wood. It's in surprisingly good shape."

"Good. Get me an evidence bag for this."

"Yes, sir."

"You found the slug, huh?" Keith said, rejoining Casey and the lieutenant.

"Yeah. I'm going to wake up the ballistics guy and have him meet me at the forensics lab. I want a ballistic test run on this bullet tonight. I'll call you as soon as we have the results."

"Good." Casey saw the paramedics transfer Mark to a gurney and raise it. "Is there anything else you need from me? If not, I'm going to the hospital with Mark."

"Go ahead. But you're going to have a couple of uniforms with you."

"I'll go with her," Keith volunteered.

"Naw. You've been on duty all day and you work again tomorrow. These guys just started their shift and are fresh." Lieutenant Bradshaw scowled at Casey. "Until we catch this guy there will be two patrol cars on guard out here, one in front and one in the alley out back. Got it?"

"Okay by me," she agreed. "Just as long as Mark has protection, too. That guy intended to kill him. I want at least one officer with him during the day when he's working. At night he'll be staying with me."

Both men raised their eyebrows at that, but all the

lieutenant said was, "Right. Good idea. An officer will be here first thing in the morning. He'll accompany your friend to his office and stay with him all day."

"Thanks."

While following the ambulance, Casey first called Matt, then her partner, who was already at the hospital with his wife and new daughters, and told them what had happened. Dennis was waiting for them when she walked into the ER beside Mark's gurney.

Mark was immediately whisked away to a treatment room, and Casey and her partner and the two uniformed officers were left to cool their heels in the waiting area.

Matt and Jennifer arrived a short while later. "Any word yet on his condition?" he asked the instant he spotted Casey.

"No. Not yet."

"He's only been gone about ten minutes. You may as well have a seat. I imagine it'll be a while," Dennis said.

To Casey the wait seemed interminable. She paced the lounge area, pestered the receptionist for a report of Mark's condition and drank one cup of coffee after another, which Jennifer, bless her, fetched for her from the vending machine down the hall. Several times Matt tried to calm her, reminding her that the paramedic had told her that Mark's wound wasn't life threatening.

She wanted to snarl back, "Yeah, right. What do they know?" but she held her tongue for Matt's and Jennifer's sakes. There was no point in planting a seed of doubt in their minds.

"When she's like this the best thing to do is to just leave her be," Dennis advised. "Trust me, Matt. I've worked with the woman for years. You don't want to get into a cage with a pacing tiger."

"At least sit down for a while," Matt urged. "Give yourself a chance to relax."

"If my pacing is bothering you I'll go out in the hall," she snapped. Dammit, she couldn't sit. Her nerves were eating her alive.

The two uniformed officers started to stand up to go with her, but before they could Matt jumped to his feet and pulled Casey into his arms. "C'mon, Casey. I didn't mean that. I just hate to see you so upset, that's all. Trust me, he's going to be okay. Mark is tough."

"Man, I can't leave you alone with my girl for five minutes without you trying to beat my time."

"Mark!" Casey spun around. Joy exploded inside her at the sight of him, standing just inside the waiting room beside another man. She hurried to him and grabbed his hands, her eyes searching his face. "Are you all right? How do you feel? What did the doctor say?"

Mark laughed. "Whoa, sweetheart. One question at a time." He pulled her into his embrace and Casey went willingly, slipping her arms around his waist and laying her head against his chest. The strong, steady beat of his heart beneath her ear was the most wonderful sound she'd ever heard. "I am happy to know you were worried about me, though," he murmured.

The man beside them cleared his throat. Mark released Casey from the embrace, though he kept one arm around her waist and held her close to his side. "Everyone, this is my good friend, Dr. Jon Sorensen. He's the one who patched me up, so I'll let him tell you how I'm doing."

"Let me start by assuring you that Mark is going to be fine. As his friends and loved ones know, he's too ornery to kill."

Everyone chuckled, as he had intended, then the doctor turned serious.

"Fortunately for Mark, the bullet struck his shoulder blade at precisely the right angle to slide off instead of fracturing the bone," he said, demonstrating with his hands. "Unfortunately, it plowed a nasty six-inch furrow across his back.

"Actually, he's extremely lucky that he turned when he did, otherwise the bullet would have struck him in the heart.

"His wound is ugly and I'm sure it hurts like hell, but with the right treatment and a little TLC it will heal. As long as he sticks to just consulting with his patients, there's no reason why he can't return to work tomorrow. Although, I recommend that he give himself three or four days to heal before he attempts to perform surgery on anyone."

"Thanks, Doctor," Matt said. "We'll see to it that he follows your orders."

The doctor excused himself, and Dennis announced that he needed to get back upstairs to his wife and daughters. He shook Mark's hand. "I'm glad you're okay, Doc. And don't you worry. We'll get the bastard."

As they trooped outside, Mark looked over his shoulder at the two uniformed officers. "What's with Frick and Frack?" he whispered to Casey.

"Get used to them. Until we catch the shooter, we both are going to have police protection."

"What? I can't work with a policeman following me around."

"If I can, you can, so don't argue. I'm not going to give this guy another chance to get you."

"Casey's right," Matt agreed. "As long as this madman is running loose, you're in danger. Take the police protection."

"But—"

"The matter isn't up for debate, Mark," Casey said. She opened the passenger door of her car and pointed an imperious forefinger. "Now, get in and let's go."

Mark cocked his eyebrow at her tone and looked at Matt.

His brother smirked. "Don't look to me for help. I agree with her."

"All right, all right. You win," he said, easing into the car.

Officer Kaslowski waited until Casey took her place behind the wheel, then bent down and said, "We'll be right behind you, Detective."

"With my bum leg I'm going to have to drive slowly, so don't be alarmed."

"Gotcha."

Casey started the car, then paused and looked at Mark. "Your place or mine?"

He laughed. "Careful, sweetheart. I could take that for a proposition."

"That's how I meant it. That is…if you still want me."

"What?" Mark stared at her, stunned. "Are you serious?"

"I've never been more serious in my life."

"Of course I still want you. I love you. But—"

"Then it's settled." She reversed out of the parking place and headed for her house.

During the short ride neither spoke, but out of the corner of her eye Casey saw Mark look at her often.

She parked the car in the garage and led the way inside, still without uttering a word. Casey was afraid to speak, afraid she'd lose her nerve.

The first thing she noticed was the red light on her answering machine blinking. Ignoring the signal, she started up the stairs.

Someone had picked up Mark's duffel bag off the front lawn and left it in the foyer at the base of the stairs. He retrieved it and followed Casey up to her bedroom. In the middle of the room, she turned and saw him standing in the doorway, watching her.

Clasping her hands together to keep from wringing them, she licked her dry lips. "Is…is something wrong? Have you changed your mind?"

"No. I haven't changed my mind," he said quietly. "I am concerned about you, though. Are you sure you want to do this, Casey? It's been a day of emotional extremes. That can throw your whole world off-kilter, make you do things you wouldn't ordinarily do. I wouldn't want you to do anything you'd regret later."

Her nerves were strung so tight she was shaking inside, but she gathered her courage and walked toward him slowly. "You want to know what I regret? I regret that I didn't tell you before now that I love you."

Mark's eyes widened and he started to speak, but she didn't let him. She forged ahead, afraid that if she didn't get it all said now she'd lose her nerve.

"I regret that I didn't admit to myself how I felt until tonight. When I saw you get shot and fall face first on my lawn I thought I'd lost you, and all I could think about was that you would die, not knowing that I loved you."

She reached him and with trembling fingers began to unbutton his shirt. "I learned tonight that life is short, too short for regrets. Too short for holding back." She unfastened the last button, pulled the tail of his shirt free of his jeans and pushed it off his shoulders and down his arms, being careful of his injured back. The shirt dropped to the floor at his heels.

For a moment her gaze wandered over his bare shoulders and chest, then she buried her face in the mat of black hair. She inhaled deeply, her head spinning at the scent of him, overlaid with soap and good clean sweat and the out-of-doors.

"I'll never regret making love with you," she went on in a seductive whisper.

Her breath stirred the hair on Mark's chest and feathered, warm and moist, over his skin. He shivered, and Casey experienced a sweet sense of power. Emboldened, she stabbed her tongue through the short curls and tasted the salt on his skin. Matt groaned, his arms encircling her waist, clutching her to him as though he'd never let her go.

"I want to show you how much I care. Not just with words," she went on in loving torment, dragging her open mouth across his chest. "But with my heart and my body."

Mark ran his hands down over her hips and clutched her buttocks with both hands, and Casey's restraint gave way like water bursting through a dam.

"Oh, Mark, I love you so much," she cried, and began to strew hot, frantic kisses over his chest, punctuating each with a feverish declaration. "I love you. I love you. I love you."

Mark threw his head back and groaned. "Oh, baby. Baby. Aah…sweetheart, you're driving me crazy."

Paying no attention to his desperate cry, Casey grew more frantic by the second. She kissed his chest, went up on tiptoe and covered his collarbone and neck, the underside of his jaw with nipping little kisses, then she dropped lower again.

The tip of her tongue found a tiny nub buried in the thick mat of chest hair and flicked it. Mark sucked in his breath and shuddered. She followed the line of silky hairs down to his navel. Her tongue circled the tiny indentation, then stabbed inside.

Mark's control snapped.

Bending, he grabbed the hem of her sundress, and in one quick jerk, pulled the garment up and over her head and tossed it over his shoulder. The cotton dress hit the floor in the hallway behind him with a soft plop.

He grasped her shoulders and looked at her. Wearing only an ecru-colored strapless bra and matching bikini panties, she appeared almost nude. The hunger in his gaze turned his gray eyes a turbulent charcoal. He backed her up several steps until the backs of her legs bumped against the side of the bed.

Breathing hard, he cupped her upturned face between his hands and looked deep into her eyes. "I love you, Casey. More than life itself."

Her trembling legs seemed to turn to mush, and she gripped the sides of his waist for support. "I love you, too."

He angled his head and kissed her, lingeringly, lovingly, with all the emotion that filled his heart to overflowing.

Though the kiss was soft, almost reverent, he ended it abruptly and looked at her, need a desperate glow in his eyes. "I can't wait any longer."

In answer, Casey stripped out of her panties and bra and climbed into bed. Mark did the same. He gathered her to him and kissed her, this time with unrestrained hunger and demand. She responded eagerly, giving herself to him like a flower opening its petals to the sun.

There was no time for foreplay and none was needed. As the kiss went on he rolled her onto her back and opened her legs with his knee. Then, in one smooth stroke, he entered her.

They were one, Casey thought, and gave a sigh of deepest pleasure as she lifted her hips. It had been so long. So very long. And it felt so right.

At first their movements were slow and savoring, but as the pleasure grew more intense, so did their rhythm. Before long the ultimate delight beckoned, drawing them over the edge, flinging them into an abyss of joy so great that the universe seemed to shatter around them into billions of pieces.

A while later, when breathing grew normal and hearts had slowed, Mark shifted from her and onto his side. Only a dim light from the hall seeped into the room. Smiling, he traced her profile with his forefinger and murmured, "Are you all right?"

"Mmm. I'm wonderful," Casey replied, and raised her arms over her head and stretched like a contented cat. "How about you? How's your back?"

"A little sore and it burns a bit, but as long as I don't lie on it, it'll be okay."

He continued to explore her body, running his fingers over her collarbone, her shoulders, down over her breasts. "No regrets?"

She turned her head and her gaze met his in the semi-darkness. "No. None at all."

"Good. In that case, I think we should get married right away. Before your brothers find out that I seduced their sister and beat me to a bloody pulp."

"Hey, *I* seduced you, remember. And speaking of my brothers, I've been meaning to ask you, what did you say to them the other night that made them back off so quickly."

"I just told them the truth. That I was in love with you and intended to marry you as soon as I could get you to say yes. Of course, I also had to assure them that we weren't sleeping together, which at the time we weren't."

Casey narrowed her eyes at him. "So, you asked me to marry you just to keep my brothers from killing you, did you?"

"Hey, I'm no dummy."

Casey socked his shoulder lightly. "Just for that I ought to say no."

He took her hand in his and kissed her knuckles. "You wouldn't be that cruel, would you?"

Though he smiled, his eyes were serious, and all thought of teasing flew out of Casey's mind. Maybe they hadn't known each other long enough. Maybe it was too soon to make such a momentous decision, but she didn't care. She touched his cheek with her fingertips. "No, never. I love you, Mark. And I'll marry you anytime you say."

"Ah, Casey, my love." He leaned forward and kissed her with exquisite tenderness.

Just as the kiss threatened to escalate into something more, the bedside telephone rang. They broke apart like two guilty children. Casey glanced at the clock on her nightstand.

"Who in the world…?"

She picked up the receiver, and before she could say hello her boss's voice boomed, "Dammit, O'Toole, why haven't you called me back? I left a message on your answering machine."

"I, uh…I just got in," she lied. "What did you find out?"

"You were right. Ballistics show that the gun that was used to kill those three women was the same one used to shoot Dr. Adams."

Twenty

Casey pored over the files. She methodically reread every lab report and all the notes and interview transcripts, reexamined every photograph in minute detail.

It was getting late, she thought, checking her wristwatch. Dennis and most of the other guys had already gone home. Mark was probably waiting for her to pick him up.

He'd chafed all day under the constant police protection, but since she would be doing the guard duty after working hours, so far he'd gone along with the arrangement.

I should probably call it a day, Casey thought. She had already gone through the files so many times that she practically knew them by heart. Still, she couldn't give up. The answer had to be in here somewhere. It *had* to be.

Her father had always told her that whenever she was stumped on a case, to go back to the files. Nine times out of ten, the answer was there. You just had to keep going through them until it jumped out at you.

"Hi, Casey."

Stifling a groan, she looked up and gave Danny a wan smile. "Hi, sport. How's it going?"

"Good. I'm waiting for Keith. He told me to meet him here, but the sergeant said that he had to go somewhere. He left a message that he wouldn't be long and for me to wait here for him."

"I see."

"So I thought I'd come up here and see you. I really had a good time at the cookout yesterday," he said. "It was fun. And exciting. I told Keith all about how Dr. Adams delivered Mary Kate's babies and everything."

"Mmm. That was exciting, wasn't it," Casey replied absently.

"Yeah. It was. And you know what else? I just finished cleaning that huge fish tank over at the Ahoy restaurant. And I did it all by myself, too. Usually Keith helps me, but he said I could try it on my own today, and I did it."

Casey looked up and smiled vaguely, but gradually his words sank in, and one thing stood out in her mind. Of course! Why hadn't she thought of it before? Fish tank. Mark had a fish tank in his waiting room. Which meant someone had to clean it.

Tamping down on her growing excitement, she tried to keep her tone casual.

"Uh, Danny, how do you get to your jobs?"

"We have a van. It belongs to Keith, but I drive it most of the time."

"I see. I bet it's really nice, isn't it?"

"Uh-huh. It's white all over."

"Really. I'll bet it has pretty carpet inside, too, huh?"

"Oh, you should see it, Casey. It's a really pretty green. Kinda the color of a lime. Keith says it's ugly, but I like it."

"Really?" A chill rippled down Casey's spine. She looked at Danny and felt sick to her stomach. Could he have killed those women? Sweet, slow Danny? Had he tried to kill Mark?

God knew, he'd been angry enough yesterday to do Mark harm.

"You know, Danny, Dr. Adams has a beautiful fish tank. Is he one of your clients?"

"You mean Dr. Adams from yesterday?" At Casey's nod he shrugged. "I don't know. Maybe. I don't know all the clients by name. Keith has the directions to every client's place and the instructions for their job all typed up and sealed in plastic sheets. Every morning he gives me the sheets for the jobs I'm suppose to do that day. I just follow his instructions."

"I see. So Keith puts it all together for you? I'll bet his instructions are very detailed, huh?"

"Oh, yeah. Keith is real good at giving directions."

The sick feeling in the pit of Casey's stomach twisted into a hard knot. Keith. Of course. The murders had been well planned and executed. Even though Keith often took his brother hunting, Danny wasn't smart enough or organized enough to have committed the murders. But Keith was.

And Keith fit the profile. He was intelligent, his mother had died when he was young, his father was abusive, he was fanatically neat and organized. He was a Romeo who dated a lot of women, but wasn't that sometimes a sign of a man who couldn't relate to women?

If he had the contract to maintain Mark's fish tank, he had to have a key to the office—and access to Mark's files. But if that was the case, why wasn't Watson

Brothers on the list of people with a key that Martha Harvey had given her? Unless…

"Excuse me a minute, Danny." She snatched up the telephone while flipping through the files. When she located the number of the janitorial service she punched in the digits and checked her wristwatch, praying that someone would still be there.

The telephone was picked up on the third ring. "Triple A Janitorial Service," a bored voice said.

Casey identified herself and asked who cleaned fish tanks for their company.

"Oh, we subcontract those out to different companies."

"Who has the subcontract to clean Dr. Mark Adams's fish tank? He's in the Powers Building."

"I don't know. I'd have to look it up."

"Then do it," Casey snapped.

"Detective, it's late. I was walking out the door when you rang."

"I need that information. Now. Either you get it for me or I'll come to your home and haul you back down there. Got it?"

"Okay, okay. Hold on a sec."

Casey drummed her fingers on her desk. In the background she heard the clank of a file cabinet opening followed by the rustle of papers.

"Here it is. The company who has the Adams's contract is Watson Brothers."

The hairs on the back of Casey's neck stood on end. "Thanks," she said, and slammed down the receiver.

Grabbing her purse, she jumped up and headed for the door.

"Where you going, Casey?"

"Sorry, Danny, but I have an emergency. Gotta run."

She flew down the stairs, thumbing Mark's number into her cell phone as she went.

Other than a perp handcuffed to the bench, no one was around when she reached the lobby. She stopped by the sergeant's desk and rang the bell, but after five seconds when no one appeared she cursed under her breath and tore out the double doors. All of her senses were screaming there was no time to waste.

Outside she jumped into her patrol car and pulled out of the parking lot with a squeal of tires as Mark finally answered his phone.

"Hi, sweetheart."

"Mark, I'm on my way. Who's there with you?"

"Officer Watson just arrived and relieved Kaslowski. I was just shooting the breeze with the two of them. Why?"

"Oh, God," she groaned. "Where are you right now?"

"In my office."

"Listen to me, Mark, and listen carefully. I want you to lock yourself in your office. Don't let Keith Watson in. Don't let anyone in but me. Understand?"

"Not really, but if you say so I'll do it."

"Good. I think that Keith is the killer so, whatever you do, don't open the door to him."

"Holy— Okay, gotcha. I just locked the door."

"Good. I'll be there in two minutes."

She hung up and immediately dialed Dennis's cell phone. Siren blaring, she drove like a maniac, desperately swerving in and out of traffic.

"Yeah, Tiger? This had better be good," Dennis drawled when he picked up. "I'm almost home."

"Dennis, I think I've figured out who the killer is."

"No kidding. Who?"

"Keith Watson." As quickly as possible, she told him

what she'd learned. "I'm on my way to Mark's office now. I need you to meet me there."

"You got it. I'm turning around now."

Standing inside his office reception area, Mark watched the doorknob jiggle.

"Dr. Adams? Hey, Doc, do you know your door is locked?"

Mark moved silently and stood beside the door with his back against the wall.

"Hey, Doc, c'mon. Open up. This is Detective Watson. Kaslowski went home. I'm guarding you now."

Mark remained silent.

The doorknob jiggled again, harder this time.

"C'mon. Open the door, Doc." He waited a moment, then jiggled the knob again.

"I said open this door. Now," he ordered in a harsher voice. After a moment he cursed and rammed the door. It rattled on its hinges but held.

No longer making any pretense at friendliness, Keith snarled. "Dammit, open this door or I'll shoot the lock off."

Looking around for something to use as a weapon, Mark spied the bronze statuette of Hippocrates that Matt had given him. He grabbed the bronze casting and flattened his back against the wall again, just as the ear-shattering explosion of a gunshot blew the doorknob to smithereens.

Casey screeched her car to a stop in front of the Powers Building, bailed out and raced inside, her weapon drawn. She punched the elevator button and nearly cried with relief when the doors of one cubicle opened instantly.

The ride to the fourth floor seemed to take forever.

When the elevator stopped Casey squeezed out between the double doors before they'd opened all the way and stepped into the hall just in time to hear a gunshot from inside Mark's office.

Her heart nearly stopped. She rushed down the hall, sweeping her gun from one side to the other as she went. Before she reached the door to Mark's office, she saw that the lock had been shot off. "Oh, God," she murmured, and rushed to the doorway.

Inside Mark and Keith were locked in a struggle for Keith's gun. The strenuous fight had broken open Mark's wound and a bloodstain was spreading over the back of his white shirt.

Bracing her forearm against the door frame, Casey took aim. "Drop it, Keith," she barked. "It's all over."

The sound of her voice distracted Mark, and in that split second Keith had him in a choke hold, his gun pressed to Mark's temple.

"I don't think so. You drop your gun, Casey. Or I'll blow your boyfriend's brains out right here. I mean it."

"Keith, listen to me," Casey coaxed. "It's over. I'm not the only one who knows it was you who killed those women. Give it up."

"Uh-uh. It's not over until I'm behind bars, and that's not going to happen. Now, I'm going to give you to the count of three to put your gun down on the floor. If you don't, he's dead. One…"

"Keith, don't do this."

"Two…"

"Think about what you're doing?"

"Thr—"

"All right, all right. I'm putting my gun down."

"Casey, don't—"

"Shut up, pretty boy," Keith snarled, jamming the gun barrel tighter against Mark's temple.

"Now, kick the gun over here to me. That'a girl." Using one hand, Keith jerked Mark's hands behind his back and snapped his handcuffs on him. "Now, hand over your cuffs," he ordered Casey. "Nice and easy."

"Casey, don't—aaugh!" Mark cried out in agony when Keith struck his injured back with the barrel of his gun. Casey leaped forward to help him, but Keith brought his gun up and pointed it at her. "Back off! And you," he barked at Mark. "Shut up! Another word out of you and I'll kill you right here. Now, do as I told you, Casey, and gimme those cuffs."

"All right, all right. Just don't hurt him." Slowly, she reached under her blazer and unhooked the cuffs from the belt loop on her trousers, watching Keith all the while.

Just a one-second opening. That was all she needed, she thought. Her leg wasn't in any condition for a full-fledged fight, but if she could get in one strategically placed kick she could disable him long enough to get his gun.

"Don't even think about pulling one of your kick-boxing moves," Keith warned, as though he'd read her mind. "Put the cuffs on the desk, nice and easy, then turn around with your hands together behind you and back up to me."

Having no choice, Casey did as he ordered, and Keith snapped her cuffs around her wrists. She could have groaned when he squatted and removed her hideout gun from the ankle holster beneath her trouser leg. Although, as methodical and thorough as Keith was, she should have known he wouldn't forget that most cops had a backup weapon.

After disarming her, he then removed her pager and cell phone from her blazer pockets. "You won't be needing these. Calling for help isn't allowed in the game we're going to play."

When he was done he stepped back to admire his handiwork. "There, all trussed up like Christmas turkeys," he said with a nasty chuckle. "Just stay where you are, both of you."

Never taking his gaze off them, he fished his own cell phone out of the inside pocket of his suit jacket and dialed a number one-handed.

"Danny. It's me, Keith. Listen, sport, I want you to drive the van around to the back of the Powers Building and pick me up. Yes, you do know which one it is. You've been here many times. It's the tall green-granite-and-glass building on Bridger Boulevard. Yeah, that's the one. Pull up to the freight entrance and I'll meet you there." There was a longer pause, then Keith snapped, "Never mind why, just do as I say. Good boy. And, Danny. Hurry."

"Keith, I don't understand this. Why?" Casey asked. "Why did you kill those poor women? Why did you try to kill Mark?"

"You're talking about the last three women, right?"

Horror rounded her eyes. "There are more?"

"Sure. I've been hunting women for years. Literally," he added with a vile chuckle. "Until recently, I'd go to other counties and towns on my days off and pick up a redheaded woman. Sometimes by seduction, sometimes by force, depending on my mood. When I was through with them, I'd take them out to the woods for a game. Not one of those killings was ever connected to me, so I figured why go to so much trouble. Why not hunt in familiar territory.

"The first kill was an accident, but a funny thing happened. I found out that I enjoyed it. Tracking a human is the ultimate in big-game hunting."

Terror and revulsion made Casey's mouth so dry she could barely speak. "How...how many women have you killed?"

Keith shook his head. "Now, that would be telling, wouldn't it?"

"You'll never get away with killing us, Watson," Mark said.

"I warned you—"

"No! Please, don't shoot him," Casey cried, stepping in front of Mark.

Keith hesitated, then shrugged, smiling evilly. "All right. For now."

"How could you do such a horrible thing, Keith?" she asked. "You raped those women and then hunted them down like animals. Just for a thrill?"

"It was more than that. At least in the beginning it was. I was searching for the perfect woman. Actually, I was on an honorable quest. I had marriage in mind." He shrugged. "But as it turned out, none of the women I picked were good enough. They all shared one fatal flaw."

"Flaw?"

"Uh-huh. Don't you want to know what it was?" He paused, and when she nodded, he smiled. "They weren't you."

"*Me?* What do I have to do with your sick fantasy?"

"Don't call it that!" he snapped.

"Careful, Casey," Mark whispered in her ear. "Don't push him. He's not all there."

The look in Keith's eyes made Casey catch her breath

and take a step back. Oh, Lord. Mark was right, she thought. Keith was mad. Stark, raving mad.

Gradually Keith calmed, and his hateful smile returned. "For years I listened to Tim talk about you— how sweet you were, how loyal, how beautiful, what a wonderful wife you were, what a terrific family you had. What a great mother you were going to make someday. I came to realize that you were perfect for me.

"At first I tried to find someone like you, but as I said, that didn't work out. That's when I realized that you were meant for me, not Tim. So I killed him."

"What?" She jerked back a step, bumping into Mark's chest, so stunned she couldn't speak for a second. "You…*you* killed Tim? But…but you two were on a drug raid. You said that Juan Santos killed him. And the bullets that were taken from Tim's body were from Santos's gun."

Keith shrugged. "That was easy to set up. I killed Santos, then Tim covered me while I checked to make sure he was dead. I picked up Santos's gun, turned and pumped four shots into Tim, then I put the gun back into the dealer's hand. Ballistics showed that I killed Santos and Santos killed Tim."

"Oh, God. Oh, my poor Tim." Fury rose in her like a boiling geyser. "You bastard! You murderous, filthy bastard!" Casey lowered her head and ran at Keith, but he sidestepped her charge, then grabbed her, spun her around and slapped her hard across the face.

"Why you—" Mark took a step forward, but Keith barked, "Hold it right there," and put the barrel of his gun to Casey's forehead.

Gritting his teeth, Mark backed off.

"Now, get back over there with your lover, and let's get out of here," Keith snarled, giving her a shove.

Dennis was on the way, Casey thought. She had to stall somehow. "It's bad enough that you murdered all those innocent women, but how could you kill Tim?" she demanded. "Your own partner? How *could* you?"

"Actually, I felt kinda bad about Tim. I liked him. But I had no choice. I knew he would never give you up."

Casey made no effort to hide her repugnance. "You vile excuse for a human being."

"Easy, Casey," Mark whispered, but she was too enraged to heed his warning.

She looked Keith up and down and curled her lip. "Did you honestly believe that I would marry you just because Tim wasn't around anymore? Never. Not in a million years."

"Hey, don't talk to me like that. I did right by you. I gave you a year to grieve and get over Tim before I even asked you out. But every time I did you had some excuse."

"What? You never asked me out."

"Sure I did. Plenty of times I asked you to have a drink with me after work or to have dinner with me."

Casey stared at him, appalled, remembering the times lately when he'd tossed out a seemingly spur-of-the-moment invitation. Almost daily, after a shift, someone suggested stopping by Muldoon's for a drink or a bite. That was nothing unusual. She had assumed that's what Keith had been doing. Just being one of the guys.

A strange look came over Keith's face, his gaze went slightly out of focus, hatred twisting his features. "As for those women, don't waste your sympathy on them. They weren't innocent. None of them. I chose them precisely because they were all stupid, vain creatures. Worthless, really. I'm sure you read their files. Every one of them paid your lover to enhance her looks. They were all self-centered little bitches. All they cared about was their appearance and getting attention from men. The first time I went through the doc's files I felt as though I'd hit the mother lode of bitches to eliminate."

"Why does it matter so much to you if a woman enhances her appearance? That isn't a crime."

"It should be!" he snarled. "Especially when they're so obsessed with their looks that they abandon their husband and children! That's what my mother did."

"What? You told me she was dead."

"I lied. The slut had her boobs pumped up and walked out on us. She went to Hollywood to try her hand as an actress." Keith gave a bark of laughter, a bitter sound that had nothing to do with amusement. "You want to know how successful she was? The closest she came to being a movie star was performing in a string of porno flicks. My dad even bought a few of them. When he'd get really drunk he'd watch them. How sick is that?" Keith stopped abruptly and took several deep breaths, forcibly regaining control over himself. Gradually the glazed look faded from his eyes.

He turned to Mark with a look of seething hatred. "When you were turning down my invitations, I didn't realize that this guy had horned in and was trying to take what I worked so hard to get. I wasn't going to let that happen."

"So you shot Mark?"

"Yeah, I shot him. Would've killed him, too, if he hadn't turned when he did."

Keith turned his attention back to Casey. He stroked his fingertips down her cheek and his eyes held regret. "Too bad you had to figure out that it was me who killed those women. Now I'm gonna have to kill you, too. All my planning was for nothing.

"Oh, well. You win some, you lose some." He waved his gun toward the door. "Enough of this chitchat. It's time to go. Move it."

"Hold it, Watson. You're not going anywhere."

"Dennis! Thank God." Never in her life had Casey been so happy to see anyone. Her partner stood in the doorway with his gun aimed at Keith.

In a lightning-quick move, Keith grabbed her, held her in front of him as a shield and fired his gun. The explosion in the small room was deafening.

Casey screamed and Dennis let out an "Umph" and went down like a felled tree. His gun flew out of his hand and landed several feet away with a clatter.

"Dennis! Oh, God, Dennis!" Casey tried to go to him, but Keith held her tight and waved his gun at Mark. "You go first. And remember, one wrong move and Casey's dead."

"You're not going to get away with this, Watson," Mark warned.

"Oh, yeah? Watch me."

They had to step over Dennis to get out the door. Casey looked down at him with tears running down her face. "I'm sorry, partner. I'm so sorry."

"Shut up," Keith barked. "I say good riddance. I never did like that guy."

"Where are you taking us?"

Keith laughed. "We're going on a little hunt."

In the freight elevator on the way down Casey closed her eyes and thought of Mary Kate, and little Roger and the new babies. She felt as though an anvil were sitting on her heart.

Danny was waiting in the van. Keith hustled her and Mark into the back of the vehicle and slammed the doors.

"Why are Casey and Mark here?" Danny asked the instant Keith jumped into the passenger seat. "Why are they in handcuffs?"

"Never mind. Just drive where I tell you."

"But—"

"Dammit, Danny, I said drive."

"Okay. Don't get mad at me, Keith. I don't like it when you get mad at me."

"Just do as I say and I won't be mad. Okay, pal?"

"Okay," Danny agreed, eyeing his brother doubtfully.

The back of the van was stacked with long-handled fish nets and algae cleaners and various additives. A strong chemical smell permeated everything. Casey looked down at the puke-green carpet and thought of the other terrified women who had lain there, wondering what terrible fate awaited them. A violent shiver rippled through her. For a moment she was sure she was going to be ill.

"Where do you think he's taking us?" Mark whispered.

Casey had been listening to the directions that Keith gave his brother, and there was little doubt in her mind where they were going. "I think he's taking us to his favorite hunting ground. The forest service road above town. That's where his last three victims were found."

Mark gave her a sharp look, and she knew that he had only then realized what Keith had planned for them.

As Casey expected, the van turned left and started the steep climb up the gravel road. They went around three switchbacks before Keith ordered his brother to pull over. He bailed out and opened the rear doors and ordered her and Mark out of the van. He had exchanged his service revolver for a hunting rifle, she noticed.

The moment Casey's feet touched the ground, through the trees below, she caught a glimpse of the golden dome of the First National Bank Building and the spire of the Baptist church. She realized that they were at the exact spot where Keith had released Becky Belcamp. The spot where he had shown Casey the footprints and tire tracks less than an hour after he'd murdered the poor girl. The arrogance of that turned Casey's stomach.

Keith glanced around. "We've only got about an hour of daylight left, but that should be time enough. We're going to have ourselves a little hunt. Danny, unlock their cuffs."

"Okay. What're you gonna do, Keith?"

"Never mind. Just do what I told you, then get back in the van."

Danny removed Casey's cuffs first, then Mark's. "You're not gonna hurt Casey, are you?"

"Get in the van, Danny."

Bewildered and frightened, Danny looked from Casey to Mark, then back at his brother, but, reluctantly, he obeyed.

"Keith, don't do this," Casey said, rubbing her wrists where the cuffs had chafed them. "You're just going to make it harder on yourself if you kill us."

"Oh, I don't know. Maybe you'll be the ones who get away. You're both runners, aren't you? I'd say you've got a chance." He laughed. "Not much of one, seeing as how I can hit a target with this gun at four hundred yards. But a chance."

"You sick sonuva—"

Keith raised the rifle. "Careful, Doctor, or I'll be obliged to kill you right here. I'd advise you to save your breath for running. I'm going to give you two the same deal I gave the others. You'll have a one-minute head start." He looked at his wristwatch. "Beginning...now."

"C'mon!"

Mark was still glaring at Keith, but Casey grabbed his hand and tugged him along with her. Her gait was a combination of running, limping and skipping, but she covered ground as fast as she could.

"You shouldn't be getting that cut wet," Mark yelled as they splashed through the small stream running along the side of the road.

"Trust me. That's the least of our worries." They cleared the stream and started up the gradual slope on the other side. "We've gotta get into the trees where we'll be less visible," Casey yelled.

They plunged into the forest and tore through the underbrush, Mark in the lead, holding Casey's hand and towing her along with him. The bloodstain on the back of his shirt grew steadily larger, but they didn't dare stop to take a look.

Her own wound hurt like the very devil every time she put weight on her leg, but she gritted her teeth and kept going in her irregular skipping, hopping run.

They tore through the mountain forest full tilt, the coarse rasp of their breathing a desperate sound in the quiet woods. The only other sounds were the snap of twigs and branches underfoot and the rustle of leaves, the screech and chatter of disturbed birds overhead.

They burst through a line of waist-high scrub oak going full speed and only at the last second realized that on the other side of the brush was a ten-foot drop into a ravine. "Ah, sh—"

They both let out a yelp and tried to stop, but momentum carried them over the edge.

Instinctively, Mark twisted in midair to take the brunt of the fall and cushion Casey's landing. He hit the ground on his back with her on top of him and let out an "Oomph!"

She scrambled off of him and onto her hands and knees. "Are you all right?" Mark's chest heaved but his eyes were closed and he didn't answer. She patted his cheek. "Mark. Mark, talk to me. We have to get moving."

Still panting, he opened his eyes. "You…you'll have to go…on alone."

"What? No. Absolutely not."

"N-no choice. My…my leg is broken."

Casey looked down at his legs, and saw that one was twisted at an odd angle. "Oh, God."

She looked around. Think, Casey. *Think,* she admonished herself. There had to be a way out of this mess.

"All right, here's what we're going to do. There's a slight overhang at the top of the drop-off. I'm going to pull you over there under it. He'll have to walk right up to the edge of the ravine to see you. Once I get you hidden I'm going to run down the ravine about thirty yards or so and climb back up and work my way around behind him. I'll take him by surprise and attack from behind."

"No. It's too dangerous. He might see you. He's already on his way. The time is up. Anyway, you're in no condition to fight him."

"Mark, we don't have a choice. Now, stop arguing and help me get you over there under that overhang."

With her hands under his arms, Casey pulled with all her might. Gritting his teeth and grimacing, Mark pushed with his good leg. By the time they had him in place, beads of sweat had popped out all over his face, even though the temperature was beginning to drop.

Using a leafy broken branch, Casey quickly erased the drag marks from the dirt, then bent and planted a kiss on Mark's lips. "I love you," she said. "Sit tight. No matter what you hear. Okay?"

"Casey—"

"Okay?"

"All right," he finally agreed through clenched teeth.

She took off down the ravine in a crouch. After rounding a curve she went about fifteen feet farther, then climbed out of the trench, pulling herself up by grasping small bushes and saplings.

When she'd gained the top, she darted behind a thick spruce tree, hunkered down and tried to calm her breathing. She sat crouched, still as a wild doe, listening, only her eyes moving.

Then she heard him. Keith was an excellent hunter, she'd give him that. He made almost no sound. However, her father and brothers had taught her the ways of the woods, how to listen for what did not belong. Keith made only the faintest of rustling sounds, but they were too evenly spaced and slow, too rhythmic to be an animal.

Moving with agonizing care, Casey parted two branches of the spruce tree just enough to open up a slit. Through the narrow space she spotted Keith. He was no more than fifteen feet away, just beyond the tree where she was hiding, approaching the line of brush that bordered the ravine.

His head was down, his gaze fixed on the ground and the trail that she and Mark had left. He held the rifle in both hands, angled across his body.

Reaching the line of scrub oak, he reached out and parted the branches with the barrel of the rifle, and Casey's muscles bunched. She knew she'd never get a better chance.

Shooting out from behind the tree like a released spring, she tore across the short distance at top speed. Adrenaline pumped through her so hard she didn't feel the pulling pain that shot up her leg with every step.

She had hoped to catch Keith off guard and deliver a knockout blow to the back of his neck, but he heard her coming.

Everything seemed to happen in slow motion. As though slogging through molasses, Keith looked over his shoulder and began to turn at the same instant that she leaped into the air to deliver a flying kick. The look of surprise on his face would have been comical if the situation had not been so serious.

Both of her feet struck the side of his neck. The rifle went flying over the edge of the ravine, and with a cry of pain Keith fell back into the bushes.

Casey hit the ground tucked in a ball and instantly rolled to her feet.

With a furious growl that sounded more like an animal than a man, Keith fought his way out of the brush. Covered with bloody scratches, eyes wild, he let out a war whoop and charged her. Casey lashed out with her right leg, but Keith ducked.

She hit nothing but air and nearly lost her balance. He laughed and danced away like a prize fighter. "You're good, Casey. But you forget, I take martial arts, too."

In a flash, he launched an aggressive frontal attack, kicking and feinting and striking out with hands and feet. On the defensive, Casey was forced to back up. She managed to avoid the blows. Just barely.

She could feel her energy fading and could no longer

ignore the pain in her leg. She knew she had to deliver one decisive blow or she and Mark were dead.

Gathering her strength, she lashed out with her right leg, but the pain had slowed her kick. Keith ducked and grabbed her injured leg and squeezed it tight with both hands.

Casey screamed. Her back hit the ground, and she writhed and screamed over and over. Keith merely laughed and kept squeezing.

"Ca-sey!"

"Ah, your lover is calling you," Keith said. He let go of her leg and pulled his service revolver from his shoulder holster and aimed it at her heart. "Say goodbye, Casey. Last chance," he said in a nasty singsong.

Casey caught her breath and stilled. She stared at the obscene black hole at the end of the gun barrel, her heart pounding.

Keith had his back turned partway toward the ravine, but from the corner of her eye she saw the top of Mark's head and the barrel of a hunting rifle appear over the rim.

Bless him. Even with a broken leg, Mark had somehow managed to get the gun and was struggling to scale the drop-off and save her. He would never make it in time, but she loved him all the more for the effort.

Keith came a step closer, and Casey braced herself.

The crack of a rifle shot rent the air. She didn't move. She had expected to feel pain. Or shock. Instead she saw Keith stumble and drop his revolver. Crimson blossomed over the front of his shirt like a flower opening. He looked at her with wide-eyed bewilderment, then crumpled to the ground.

"What…?" Casey sat up and looked around and saw

Danny standing about fifty feet away, holding a rifle in his hands.

"Casey! *Casey!*" Mark screamed. "Damn you, Watson—"

"I'm okay, Mark," she called, but her gaze remained on Danny. His face crumpled and he threw down the rifle and ran to his brother. He fell to his knees beside Keith, tears streaming down his face.

"I'm sorry. I'm sorry," he cried. He cradled his brother in his arms and rocked him back and forth.

Keith's eyes flickered open. He gave Danny a weak smile. "It's…okay, sport," he mumbled. "It's…okay."

"I had to do it. I had to. I couldn't let you hurt Casey," Danny blubbered. "I just couldn't."

Casey picked up the revolver and climbed painfully to her feet. She hobbled over to the line of scrub oak that Keith had flattened and gave Mark a hand. When he looked up and saw her the heartfelt relief on his face, despite the agonizing pain he was in, tugged at her heart.

"Oh, God, sweetheart, I'm so glad to see you. I heard you scream and I thought—"

"I know. I know." Barely had Mark made it over the top of the drop-off when they heard the wail of a siren in the distance, coming steadily closer.

She and Mark exchanged a look and shook their heads. "*Now* they get here," she muttered, rolling her eyes.

"What happened? I heard a gunshot."

Casey nodded toward Danny, who was still rocking Keith and babbling and crying hysterically. "Danny shot Keith before he could shoot me."

"Caaa-sey!" someone called from lower down the mountain. "Caaa-sey! Dammit where are you, O'Toole?"

Casey turned to Mark with a dry look. "That's my boss."

Others took up the call, and Casey answered, "Up here! We're up here!"

A few minutes later Lieutenant Bradshaw and what looked like half the Mears Police Department came swarming up the mountainside through the trees.

"Are you okay, O'Toole?"

"I'm okay. Banged up and bruised, but alive. Mark's leg is broken, though, and his back has been reinjured. And Keith is shot." She paused, dreading what she had to tell him. "He's our killer."

"Yeah, I know. Dennis told us."

"Dennis?" Joy and hope exploded inside Casey. "He's alive?"

"Shoot, yeah. You can't kill that big Irishman with one bullet. We don't call him the Hulk for nothing. The guy's built like a bull."

"Thank God. Mary Kate would kill me if I let something happen to the big lug. How did you know where to find us, by the way?"

"Dennis," the boss replied with a rare grin. "After he dropped his gun, he figured he better play dead. Actually, he faded in and out of consciousness, but during one lucid moment he managed to call the station house on his cell phone and whisper "officer down" and his location. When we got there he was unconscious, but the paramedics managed to revive him. From what he heard Keith say, Dennis figured he was bringing the two of you out here."

"Keith is still alive, Lieutenant," one of the officers called. "But he's in bad shape."

The lieutenant tried to call for help on his cell phone,

but he couldn't get a signal in the thick woods. He cupped his hands around his mouth and called out, "Hey, Murphy, go back to the cars and radio for a couple of ambulances. We need to get these people to the hospital."

A short while later, after being carried down the mountainside on stretchers, Keith was loaded into one ambulance and Casey and Mark into the other. On the drive to the hospital, he reached across the space between them and took her hand. "I love you, Casey."

The paramedic cleared his throat and pretended to be busy checking the oxygen tubes and searching through the rack of supplies. Both Casey and Mark ignored him.

She smiled weakly and squeezed Mark's hand. "I love you, too."

"Sweetheart, I know that finding out how Tim really died has upset you. And that you're going to need time to come to grips with it all. I can wait. But I am going to hold you to the promise you made to me earlier this morning."

She frowned. "Promise?"

"You know...when you said that you would marry me."

Casey closed her eyes. "Lord. Was that only this morning? It seems like an eternity ago."

"I know." Mark rubbed his thumb back and forth over the silky skin and delicate bones on the back of her hand. "You, uh...you haven't changed your mind, have you?"

She smiled at him again. "No. I haven't changed my mind. I'll never change my mind about you." She looked at him with all she was feeling—all the sadness and pain, all the relief and weariness, all the love she felt for him—brimming in her eyes. "How does an autumn wedding in my parents' backyard sound to you?"

Mark squeezed her hand, his warm gaze holding hers. "That sounds perfect."

New York Times
Bestselling Author
SUZANNE BROCKMANN

Government agent Crash Hawken awakens in a hospital to
learn that he is the prime suspect in the assassination attempt
of a commanding officer. Charged with treason, conspiracy
and murder, he is alone—except for Nell Burns. Nell knows
that Crash could not have committed these crimes, and the
two are determined to find the truth—but first they have to
survive another day.

HAWKEN'S HEART

"Absolutely spellbinding..."
—*Romantic Times* on *Everyday, Average Jones*

GINNA GRAY

32032-4 PALE MOON RISING   ___ $6.50 U.S. ___ $7.99 CAN.
                    (limited quantities available)

TOTAL AMOUNT $ _____
POSTAGE & HANDLING $ _____
($1.00 FOR 1 BOOK, 50¢ for each additional)
APPLICABLE TAXES* $ _____
TOTAL PAYABLE $ _____
         (check or money order—please do not send cash)

To order, complete this form and send it, along with a check or money order for the total above, payable to MIRA Books, to: **In the U.S.:** 3010 Walden Avenue, P.O. Box 9077, Buffalo, NY 14269-9077; **In Canada:** P.O. Box 636, Fort Erie, Ontario, L2A 5X3.

Name: _____
Address: _____ City: _____
State/Prov.: _____ Zip/Postal Code: _____
Account Number (if applicable): _____

075 CSAS

*New York residents remit applicable sales taxes.
*Canadian residents remit applicable GST and provincial taxes.

MIRA®

www.MIRABooks.com   MGG0405BL